LOOK FOR GREG RUCKA'S NEXT NOVEL

FINDER

Available in hardcover from Bantam Books
in June 1997

Praise for Greg Rucka's *Keeper*

"A few top crime writers—Robert B. Parker in the
Spenser series, for instance—have wandered into
bodyguard territory. Rucka has the talent to make it
his own."
—*Publishers Weekly*

"A strong debut and a real contribution to the genre.
Keeper combines compelling plot with right-now
subtext. Greg Rucka is going to make his mark . . .
stay tuned!"
—Andrew Vachss

"Rucka tells a hell of a story . . . genuinely suspenseful
and attention-holding . . . I'll definitely be watching
for Rucka #2."
—*Deadly Pleasures*

"Both a thoughtful and thought-provoking debut . . .
Well written, with a prickly character you can get to
like. Try it, you'll like it."
—*Mystery Lovers Bookshop News*

"A fast-paced thriller . . . Kodiak is a man for the '90s.
He's young, he's sensitive, and he's politically astute.
I like him."
—*The Ottawa Citizen*

"Powerful."
—*Kirkus Reviews*

KEEPER

GREG RUCKA

BANTAM BOOKS
NEW YORK   TORONTO   LONDON   SYDNEY   AUCKLAND

This edition contains the complete text
of the original hardcover edition.
NOT ONE WORD HAS BEEN OMITTED.

KEEPER

A Bantam Book

PUBLISHING HISTORY
Bantam hardcover edition published July 1996
Bantam paperback edition / June 1997

ISBN 0-553-57428-0

Published simultaneously in the United States and Canada

Bantam Books are published by Bantam Books, a division of Bantam
Doubleday Dell Publishing Group, Inc. Its trademark, consisting of
the words "Bantam Books" and the portrayal of a rooster, is
Registered in U.S. Patent and Trademark Office and in other
countries. Marca Registrada. Bantam Books, 1540 Broadway, New
York, New York 10036.

PRINTED IN THE UNITED STATES OF AMERICA

OPM   10 9 8 7 6 5 4 3 2 1

For Art and Bernie

In the new code of laws which I suppose it will be necessary for you to make I desire you remember the ladies, and be more generous and favorable to them than your ancestors. Do not put such unlimited power into the hands of the husbands. Remember all men would be tyrants if they could. If particular care and attention is not paid to the ladies we are determined to foment a rebellion, and will not hold ourselves bound by any laws in which we have no voice, or representation.

Abigail Adams, letter to John Adams, March 31, 1776

Though this novel was inspired by actual incidents, it is a work of fiction and references to real people and organizations are included only to lend a sense of authenticity. All of the characters, whether central or peripheral, are wholly the product of the author's imagination, as are their actions, motivations, thoughts and conversations, and neither the characters nor the situations which were invented for them are intended to depict real people or real events. In particular, Sword of the Silent and its members are not meant to portray a real pro-life group and any resemblance to an actual group or individual is purely coincidental.

ACKNOWLEDGMENTS

I am indebted to a number of people for their assistance and guidance, not only in the areas touched upon by this novel, but in all that was required to reach this point.

At the Federal Bureau of Investigation: Special Agents John Weis, Bobbi Cotter, and Ernest J. Porter for their patient cooperation in assisting me with my research and keeping me informed as new information became available. Additional thanks to Special Agent Swanson D. Carter, Unit Chief, Office of Public and Congressional Affairs.

Gerard "Jerry" V. Hennelly, President of Executive Security Protection International, Inc. (ESPI, Inc.), who provided guidance and insight into the profession of the "true" bodyguard. My newest old friend.

Others who left their stamp on this work in a variety of ways: Officer William M. Conway, NYPD; N. Michael Rucka and Corrina Rucka; Elizabeth Rogers, NY EMS, Paramedic; Eric Lonergan, NY EMS, Paramedic; David Farschman; The Friday Mid-Day Coffee Klatch—Nic, Mike, and Mark; Daria "Or Should I Say Bridgett?" Penta; Casey Alenson Blaine; Kate Miciak; Peter Rubie; Sid, Frank, Peter, and Leslie.

Special thanks to Nunzio Andrew DeFilippis. Jillian loves Teah almost as much as I love you. May Walter Matusek live forever.

Finally, to Jennifer. She knows why.

KEEPER

CHAPTER ONE

Much as I wanted to, I didn't break the guy's nose.

Instead, I kept both hands on Alison's shoulders, using my body as a shield to get us through the crowd. At six feet and over one hundred and ninety pounds, I'm big enough to be intimidating, even wearing glasses. People normally get out of my way when I want them to.

But the guy stuck with us, even going so far as to lean his face closer to mine. His teeth were the product of either good genes or expensive orthodontia, and the fire was hot in his eyes. He yelled, "Don't let her murder your son!"

Another man pushed a camera at us and snapped a quick photograph, reflecting us in the lens. Over the prayers of several people who pleaded with Jesus to save the soul of our unborn child, I could hear the photographer say, "We won't forget you." Whether that was directed at us or the fetus wasn't clear.

Alison said nothing, her head low and near my chest, one hand around my back, one on my arm. I'd never felt her hold me like that. It almost hurt.

A young black man wearing a safety-orange vest over his T-shirt opened the glass door for us. As we went past he said, "Damn. We don't usually get this." He closed the door behind us, then turned and gave a nod to the uniformed security guard, who buzzed us through a second door, letting us into the ground-floor reception room.

For a disorienting moment we stood there, on the neat checkers of linoleum, still clinging to one another. New faces all around looked back, some embarrassed, some sad, some carefully blank. Eight women, waiting on chairs and couches, and only two of them looked obviously pregnant. One had a baby in her arms. Somehow the child could sleep through all the noise from outside.

A nurse behind the desk said, "Your name?"

Alison let go of me. "Alison Wallace."

The nurse checked a printout on the counter, then nodded. "You want the second floor. Through that door, down the hall, take the elevator or the stairs." She smiled at Alison. "Check in at the counter there." Then the nurse looked at me and asked, "You'll be going up with her?"

"Yes."

"Your name?"

"It's Atticus," Alison told her. "Atticus Kodiak."

I took Alison's hand. We went through the door and down a long hall, past a lounge and several examination rooms and offices. We passed a doctor in the hall and he gave us the same smile the nurse had.

Alison wanted to take the stairs. "I'll get to see the elevator after," she said. She let go of my hand when we reached the second floor, stepping into another waiting room, almost identical to the one on the ground floor but with nicer furnishings. More couches and chairs, magazine racks, coffee tables, a coffeemaker, a television. The walls were painted light blue, with white detailing at the trim.

At the opposite side of the room from the stairway was a glass partition where more nurses were controlling intake. There was a door beside the partition, and I figured it led to the procedure and recovery rooms. Another door on the wall to the right of that had a sign on it reading "Education and Services."

Alison told me to sit down, then went to the partition and checked in. We filled out her paperwork together, and I had to sign a waiver and a release form, not unlike the forms you fill out before getting your wisdom teeth pulled. Alison returned the completed paperwork, and we sat together for another forty-five minutes before the nurse called her name. I gave her a kiss on the cheek before she rose.

"This is the right thing," Alison said.

"I know."

She returned my kiss with dry lips, then went with the nurse. She didn't look back.

Three hours later, and I was still sitting on the same couch, skimming magazines and watching people. Five women were filling out forms, two with men beside them. One of the men was absolutely silent, barely aware of his companion. Another six people were waiting, pretending to read or watch television. Most were Latino or black, but one of the couples filling out forms was white and I suspected they had come from Columbia University. Occasionally a nurse would open the door beside the partition and announce a name, then escort the chosen through the door after checking her clipboard. Many more people had come and gone. They left with paper bags full of educational literature, dental dams, condoms, and tubes of Nonoxynal-9.

Turnaround with the sex-ed crowd was a lot faster, it seemed.

I stood and stretched, crossed to the window overlooking Amsterdam, trying to ease my nerves. This window had a grille over it, and I wondered why they didn't use them on the ground floor, too. It's harder to throw a brick through a grille, after all.

Nearly forty people milled around across the street, held behind a police barricade line by NYPD uniforms. The Federal Access to Clinic Entrances Act of 1994 had been designed to solve this problem, but so far it hadn't worked all that well. The law is considered by many to be unconstitutional, specifically in violation of the First Amendment, and challenges to it occur on a regular basis. As it was, protesters had positioned themselves at every approach to the clinic, and while they did not block access physically, they certainly created a daunting psychological gauntlet for a woman to run. There was no way to avoid them, as we had discovered the hard way. From the window, I saw placards and a couple of poles with dolls impaled on them. The dolls were naked and spattered with red paint. Several people held signs depicting a large cross draped in bloody barbed wire: "SOS" was painted in red in the upper right corner. Keeping well away from this group were other pro-lifers, more moderate contingents passing out pamphlets and singing hymns, their signs citing scripture, or stating, simply, "Stop Abortion Now."

Alison had chosen the clinic on recommendation from her OB/GYN. One of the deciding factors had been the assurance that the Women's LifeCare Clinic rarely had trouble with demonstrators. When we had called the clinic that morning, before coming in, the person we spoke to said that there was a "minor" protest in progress, but that shouldn't discourage us. It hadn't sounded too bad.

I had been willing to turn back when we saw the crowd, more concerned with Alison's peace of mind than anything else. But she had gotten angry.

"Hell with them," she had said. "I'm not going to be scared off by these assholes." Then she patted my arm and said, "Besides, I've got my bodyguard with me."

Her bodyguard, and the father of her child, I thought.

Getting out was going to be worse than going in, because now they knew we had been inside, and for how long. We would come out to more of the same, perhaps worse, and knowing that Alison would be on the far side of a particularly painful operation didn't help my mood. She had made her decision; she was the only person with the right to question it.

I saw a sign with "Abortion is Murder" on it, and swore under my breath.

"You're swearing and that's not nice. Don't swear."

The voice came out of a short, chubby woman, with light brown skin and a face shaped by Down's syndrome. She wore turquoise sweatpants stretched tight over her middle, tiny pink tennis shoes, and a hot-pink sweatshirt on which white cats chased each other around her body. She held a Walkman, but the headphones were off her head, and she was looking at me sternly.

"Don't swear."

"I apologize," I said.

She looked down at her pink tennis shoes and muttered something, then looked back to me and said, "It's all right, you're all right. My name is Katie."

"I'm Atticus."

"Atticus who?" She said it tentatively, pushing hard on the consonants.

"Kodiak."

Katie repeated my last name, tripping it over her tongue. She had a lot of trouble with it, and finally said, "Can't say it. Say it K, 'Cus K."

"That's right," I said. "Atticus K." Over her shoulder I tried to spot a parent or someone associated with her. No one was paying us any attention. Katie smiled and said carefully, "I'm very pleased to meet you, 'Cus." She stuck out her hand and I took it. Her hand was small, warm, and moist. Her fingers barely made it out of my palm, but

Katie shook my hand vigorously, then tugged me toward an empty couch.

"Got to sit down, got to sit down and stay out of the way," Katie said, but she didn't say it to me; she said it to herself. Then she dropped her voice further and said, "Yes, you do, Katie. You know that."

We sat on the couch and Katie fumbled with her Walkman for a moment, but the headphone wires were tangled and she couldn't straighten the cord.

"Can I help you?" I asked.

Katie thought about that, weighing the decision, then said, "Here, fix them." She thrust both the Walkman and the headphones into my lap. The Walkman was a cheap model, functional and without frills, as were the headphones. Both had been dinged about, and the pads on the headphones were ripped, exposing the speakers. I untangled the cabling and plugged the jack into the player. A Madonna tape rested inside.

I handed the player back to Katie and she put the headphones around her neck, then stared at me. Softly she said, "He has brown eyes," and then, louder, "Thanks, thank you."

"You're welcome. You like Madonna, Katie?"

"I like her a lot, 'Cus. She's sexy. Do you like Madonna?"

"Not particularly."

She laughed and pointed a finger at my chest and said, "You're silly. You like Madonna." She was smiling again, but this smile seemed more honest than the one she had used to introduce herself, broad and even. Her teeth were small and yellowed.

"All right. I like Madonna."

"I know! I know that. He's silly. You're silly."

"I think you're silly."

"I am not."

"Yes, you are."

"I am not. Stop it. I am not silly."

"Okay, I'm sorry, you're not silly."

"It's okay, it's okay, 'Cus." Katie played with the Walkman for a moment, opening and closing the cassette door, then said to herself, "Ask him. Ask him."

"Ask me what?"

She jerked her head around to look at me, surprised, and said, "Uh-oh, he heard us." She looked back down to her lap and poked the cassette player with her fingers for a few seconds. Then Katie said, " 'Cus, do you have a, uh, a girlfriend?"

I grinned. "Yes," I told her. "Her name is Alison."

"Oh." She toyed with the Walkman again, then said, "I have a boyfriend. His name is David and he's strong and protects me. But when he gets angry he loses his temper and he gets very mad. He turns into a monster and he doesn't like it, but he gets angry and can't con-con-control himself." She studied me and said, "David loves me a lot, though, he does. Is your girlfriend, is she here?"

"Yes, she is."

"I knew that, I know."

From the street came a roar, voices rising together with glee. I went back to the window. Most of the crowd had converged around a white Cadillac parked on the opposite side of the street, their SOS signs waving.

Katie peeked around my elbow, looking out the window. "Uh-oh," she said. "Uh-oh."

"Do you know who that is?" I asked her.

"Who is it? I don't know who it is."

The Caddy's front passenger door opened and a man got out, blond and short, though the angle made it hard to determine more than that. He began waving the crowd back. Then he opened one of the rear doors and another man emerged, this one a head taller, dressed in a neat summer suit. His hair was black, and he held a megaphone. Katie and I watched as the man in the suit climbed to the roof of his car.

For a moment, he stood there on the roof of the big

white Cadillac, surveying the crowd. Even from the window, I could see he was smiling.

"Oh, no! It's the Loud Man," Katie told me. "He's the Loud Man."

"Yeah?" I said.

"Very loud he's very very loud, 'Cus. Mommy doesn't like him."

I was about to ask where her mother was, when the Loud Man raised his megaphone and began to speak.

"I speak to you of murder," he said.

The crowd murmured.

"Murder again and bloody murder more," the man said. "Bodies upon bodies, broken and torn, filling their trash cans, their Dumpsters, their sinks. Cold metal, sharp metal, the coldest, sharpest things they have ever felt, their second feeling, pulling them from their mothers, from their safety, and warmth, and home."

He stopped, watching the mob soak up his words. In the summer heat, he only made them hotter. When he spoke, his pauses were perfectly placed for emphasis, the whole speech well rehearsed.

He pointed up at our window and bellowed, "Felice Romero, queen butcher of this abortuary, are you listening to me? Every murder is on your hands, every death is on your head, every soul is anchored to yours, and they weigh you, dragging you down to the Pit. Fire, Dr. Romero. Pain, the same pain you inflict on those helpless souls you tear screaming from their mothers' wombs every day!"

He stopped again, bowing his head and dropping the accusatory finger. Softly, nearly in tears, he added, "I give you Ezekiel 16:21, Dr. Romero: 'Is this of thy whoredoms a small matter, that thou hast slain my children, and delivered them to cause them to pass through the fire for them?' "

His head came up again and the crowd made more noise, apparently pleased with his scriptural choice.

"Your daughter, your own daughter. She is precisely the

kind of child you would destroy. You dare call yourself a mother? Dr. Romero, your hypocrisy knows no bounds.

"We remember," he said. "We are witness to your crimes, to every murder committed behind your walls. For the mothers are guilty, surely, that they let you kill in them what the Lord himself has placed. But you prey on that, and your bodies continue to mount.

"We remember each and every unborn child you murder, Dr. Romero. We remember each and every life you destroy. We are the Lord's eyes in this, and we know what you do. We will be the Lord's hands, and we will seek justice.

"We know what you do. And we will have justice!"

I turned away from the window, went back to the couch. Some of the others in the waiting room had gone to the window as well, and they continued to watch. Several looked shaken, and the nurses moved from person to person, speaking softly. If they were trying to reassure, it didn't look like they were doing a good job.

Katie sat back down beside me.

"He's very loud," she told me.

"Yes, he is," I agreed. "Is your mommy Dr. Romero?"

Katie smiled proudly. "My mommy is a doctor and she helps people. My mommy's smart." Then she put the headphones over her ears and pressed the "play" button, and it was as if nothing was happening outside of her at all. She sang along with whatever tune was being piped into her brain. She sang badly, toneless and inarticulate, but without self-consciousness, and when people in the room glanced at her, Katie ignored them, swaying on the couch. While singing, she took my hand and placed it between hers, patting it.

The door beside the partition opened and a young black woman called, "Mr. Kodiak?"

I stood up, slipping my hand out of Katie's. She didn't seem to notice, and continued to sing. I said, "Yes?"

"Dr. Romero would like to speak to you. Would you follow me?"

I started cataloging all the traumas that could have occurred, and in the seconds it took me to move from Katie to the door I compiled a pretty impressive list. The waiver and release forms were in my back pocket, and I found that my recall of all the potential complications was very clear. Alison was in trouble. Alison was in shock. Alison was being taken to the hospital. Alison's uterus had been punctured. Alison hadn't been completely evacuated. Alison was hemorrhaging. Alison had a heart attack. Alison had an aneurysm, a stroke, a seizure.

"This way," the woman said, and I followed her through the door, my heart seriously starting to knock about in my chest. The door swung shut behind us and the nurse led me down the corridor.

"What's happened?"

"Dr. Romero would like to speak with you," she repeated. She wore a cream-colored name tag over her left breast, "Delfleur, R.N." printed on it in blue letters.

The fact that my question had gone unanswered did nothing for my growing anxiety.

The hall ended with doors to my right and left. The right door was marked "Bathroom." The left door was marked "Dr. F. Romero, Administrator." The nurse knocked on the door then said, "Go on in." She turned and headed back to the waiting room.

I took a second, trying to stay calm. Then I opened the door.

CHAPTER TWO

It was a cramped office, with a window looking out at another building across the alley. A densely packed bookshelf ran along the opposite wall. A filing cabinet stood in a corner beside a trash can. Two chairs covered in pale orange fabric were placed in front of a metal desk; on the desk were papers, a typewriter, and a telephone. Framed degrees hung over the bookshelf, one from Columbia, another from Cornell. The room smelled of paper and stale cigarette smoke.

Behind the desk, speaking into the phone, sat a Hispanic woman in her late forties, her short black hair streaked silver. She had a narrow face and dark eyes behind black-framed glasses, and she was marking a paper on her desk with one hand, holding the phone with the other. She pointed her pen at me and made a horizontal swing, back and forth, and for a moment I had no idea what she wanted me to do. Then I turned and shut the door behind me. When I looked back she nodded and pointed the pen at one of the chairs in front of her desk. I sat.

"Yes, I think it's serious enough," she was saying. "No, more than that. . . . Yes . . . that's what I'm trying to do right now . . . the board should cover at least half. . . . I don't know. When I find out I'll call you back. . . . Yes."

She hung up the phone, then rose, extending her hand. "Mr. Kodiak? I'm Felice Romero."

I shook her hand and said, "Is Alison all right?"

She lit a cigarette and sat back down. "Alison's in recovery right now, completely evacuated. She should be ready to leave by the time we're finished."

I exhaled long, and tried to dry my palms on my jeans. "I thought something had gone wrong," I said.

Moving papers around on her desk, Dr. Romero uncovered an empty ashtray. She tipped it into the trash can anyway, saying, "I apologize. Lynn should have said something. No, she's fine. She'll be sore for a while and you two shouldn't engage in intercourse for at least sixty days, but you know that, you already filled out the release forms. I'd recommend reevaluating your method of birth control. Other than that, there were no complications. She was a model patient."

"I see."

Dr. Romero knocked ash into the tray and pushed her chair back, openly studying me. I adjusted my glasses. She took two drags on the cigarette, blowing smoke out of the side of her mouth.

"It's procedure here to ask the patient if they still want to have the abortion before we get started," she told me. "I wanted to know if Ms. Wallace might be having second thoughts, especially considering the crowd outside. She told me that you are a bodyguard and had kept the nuts outside away from her. Is that correct—you are a professional bodyguard?"

"What is this about?"

"I'm sorry, I'm on a schedule and there's been a lot of pressure here with Sword of the Silent out front."

"Sword of the Silent?" I remembered the signs bobbing in the street, their bloody crosses and barbed wire. "SOS?"

"Cute, isn't it?" Dr. Romero stuck the cigarette back in her mouth and began searching through the papers on her desk again. "They've been around for over a week now, ever since the conference was announced."

I was starting to feel exceptionally dim. "Conference?"

She stopped shuffling papers and stared at me. "You don't know? It's being called the Common Ground Conference, to be held downtown at the Manhattan Elysium Hotel in two weeks. Pro-choice and pro-life attendees, lectures, seminars, panels, all designed to stop the escalating violence. I'm one of the organizers." When I still looked blank she added, "Local media has been giving us fairly heavy coverage."

"I've been out of the country," I said.

"Really? Where?"

"I was on a job in England," I said. She seemed to expect me to elaborate, but I didn't. In my work, you don't talk about your clients.

After a second she asked, "How old are you, exactly?"

"Twenty-eight."

"Is that young for your profession?"

"Younger than many, older than some."

"What exactly does a bodyguard do?"

"Personal protection. I came out of the Army's Executive Protection program, served some time in the CID. I've been out about three years. I'm the real thing, doctor, not the kind that gets hired to break the kneecaps of Olympic hopefuls, in case you're wondering."

She laughed curtly and said, "You understand why I'm asking?"

"I understand how you could be confused," I told her.

"How much do you charge?"

"Depends on who I'm protecting and from what. It's rated against the kind of coverage and how many other people are needed. Solo, I charge one hundred and fifty an hour for fieldwork plus expenses, eighty an hour for consultation. But alone I can't do much. Real protection requires more bodyguards."

"If you were protecting two people, twenty-four hours a day?"

"I'd need to know what I was protecting them from before I could plan a detail," I said.

She nodded and handed me a sheet of paper, saying, "That came yesterday."

It was a photocopy of a letter, typed. It read:

To the Murdering Cunt Wetback Doctor—
  Hell is waiting for you, bitch. I'll send you there myself, my hands ripping the life out of your cumfilled fucking throat. I'll crack your spic skull, it'll look like the babies you break and pull screaming from their trapped mommas. I know what you do, you fucking bitch. Talk all you want, lie all you want, I know and you'll pay.
  I'm going to do it to you. Tie your fucking spic ass down and fucking rip your cunt in two, ram a Hoover all the way in you till you scream for me to stop.
  Open your mouth and I'll shut it for you, bitch. And it won't be murder, when I kill you, slut. It's going to be self-defense.
  Hell is waiting for you. I'm going to send you there.

It was signed with the same cross-and-barbed-wire crest that currently graced several of the placards outside.

"Who has the original?" I asked.

"The FBI. You're holding a federal offense." She said the last grimly, without mirth. "The NYPD has seen it, too. Detective Lozano at the Twenty-sixth Precinct."

"Is this the only one?"

In response she shoved a stack of paper in my direction. It was easily three hundred pages. "These have all come since the first of the year. We receive them every day. Some are short and to the point—the burn-in-hell variety—others are longer, more passionate and considered monologues urging us to stop our work here. Twenty-three letters in the last two weeks, and I haven't seen today's mail yet. It's gotten considerably worse since my involvement with Common Ground was announced."

"Are they all like this?" I looked back at the letter. It had been typed neatly, no blurs or smudges from correction fluid. Maybe off a computer.

"Content-wise? No. Some are better; some, believe it or not, are actually worse. Especially the more recent ones."

"You have any idea where they are coming from?"

"Sword of the Silent," she said. "Jonathan Crowell. If he isn't writing them, he knows who is."

"Jonathan Crowell? Tall white guy with a megaphone?"

"That's him. Very much of the Pensacola crowd. Following in the footsteps of John Burt, Randal Terry, Paul Hill, those people."

"I've heard of him. I tend to ignore radicals."

"Crowell's not a radical, Mr. Kodiak. He is a demagogue. He's an evil man who's trying to overcome a mediocre life by preaching hate and intolerance disguised with the name of Jesus Christ." Romero crushed out her cigarette. "That's the only reason to target this clinic. Rarely has a white man been so concerned about the reproductive rights available to blacks and Hispanics. But Crowell has targeted this clinic quite specifically. We serve the university, but mostly we serve the rest of Harlem. Single mothers are our stock-in-trade. We deal with reproductive services and education here. Abortions are a very small part of what we do. And for Crowell to target us is Crowell targeting nonwhites."

"He's that clearly a racist?" I asked.

"I'm certain he doesn't think of himself as one," Dr.

Romero said. "But I believe he is, yes." She gestured toward the letter in my hands. "Do you think that is a serious threat?"

"Frankly, no. This sounds more like terrorism than the precursor to an attempt on your life."

"I'm used to terrorism, Mr. Kodiak," Dr. Romero said flatly.

"Who's doing the conference security?" I asked.

"I really don't know. A friend of mine, Veronica Selby, is handling that end of things. Veronica's the primary organizer of the conference, and she's assured me that security will be good."

For Dr. Romero's sake, I hoped she was right. A lot of self-proclaimed security firms are nothing more than fly-by-nights that hand out badges for minimum wage.

She took the letter back from me and looked it over again. "I've lived with letters threatening me, degrading and demeaning me for a long time now," she said. "But this one frightens me."

"I can see why."

Dr. Romero leaned forward, resting her elbows on the desk. "I'd like to hire you. I want protection for myself and my daughter, here and at home."

"How old is Katie?"

She was surprised only for a moment. "Sixteen. You've met her?"

"In the waiting room."

"What do you think of her?"

"She's very sweet," I said. "She talks to herself a lot."

"Imaginary friends," Dr. Romero said. "It makes sense, when you think about it. Very few people actually talk to Katie rather than at her, and she finds communication with them quite difficult, too, I think. The people she speaks to understand her completely."

"I think you'd be better off with official protection," I said.

"I don't trust the police. I've known too many officers

who believe abortion is murder. Detective Lozano himself is antichoice."

"There's the FBI," I said. "Federal marshals, too."

She sighed, leaned back in her chair, and went for another cigarette. I wondered if she had always smoked, or if it was a habit she had adopted in response to her work.

"The agent who's been assigned to us, Special Agent Fowler, is only interested in pursuing the terrorism approach at this time," Dr. Romero said. "He is unconvinced that Crowell or Sword of the Silent is after me. Special Agent Fowler does not like conspiracies." She watched the flame from her lighter for a moment, then set it down on the desk without lighting the cigarette. "Our requests for federal marshals have been turned down, too. We're told they're needed more at clinics outside of New York." Felice Romero reached for the light again, used it, then said, "I want you to do it."

"The protection you want is expensive," I said.

"Give me a figure and I'll call our board of directors. They'll put up at least half. I'll cover the rest. I have money."

I thought about it, making rough calculations in my head. "If I were to do it," I said, "we'd be talking three thousand dollars a week. You can get security guards and rent-a-cops for less, but it won't be the protection you want."

"For that much money, what do I get?"

"Complete coverage, twenty-four hours a day, seven days a week."

She drew on the cigarette thoughtfully, then asked, "When can you start?"

I shook my head. "I recommend trying Sentinel Guards. Ask for Natalie Trent, tell her you talked to me. She can put everything together for you. They're a great firm. Her father runs it, and he's ex–Secret Service."

"Mr. Kodiak, you don't seem to be listening. I want you."

"I am listening, Doctor. But right now I've got other things on my plate."

She dropped ash on her desk, looked at it for a moment, then brushed it into the ashtray with her palm, smearing it across her desk. After she set the ashtray back down, she said:

"Many of the men who come in here with their girl-friends, when they do come, aren't exactly supportive. Most would have seen the mob out front and turned tail. Others would simply wait, bored. Others would wait, concerned. Many wait and grow angry. Sometimes they take that anger out on the women they came in with." She watched the smoke from her cigarette curling toward the ceiling vent.

I could hear the SOS protesters chanting outside. There was no question that Dr. Romero heard it, too.

She said, "Abortion is an emotional issue, not a cerebral one, Mr. Kodiak. It is a damned-if-you-do, damned-if-you-don't decision, and it's a decision impossible to make in this society without hurting someone. This is why no consensus has been reached on the subject and why people are now murdering doctors. It's why Common Ground is so important, because it's a chance for all the voices to be heard, and to be heard without threats or screaming. It doesn't matter to me whether you're pro-choice or anti-abortion, Mr. Kodiak. I don't want some apathetic ex-cop with a beer gut. I don't want lean SWAT team professionals. I want someone who understands that no matter what side of the line you're on, someone always gets hurt. What matters is that you know what it's like to cross that line." She ground out her cigarette and locked eyes on me.

"I'll consider it," I said. "Can I see Alison?"

"She'll meet you in the waiting room," Dr. Romero said, and reached for the phone. She was already arguing with someone on the line by the time I shut the door.

Katie wandered over after I'd been back in the waiting room for a few minutes, sitting down beside me on the couch. Without warning, she wrapped her arms around my middle and gave me a hug, saying, "Hello. I missed you."

I patted her back.

" 'Cus, 'Cus are you all—all right? You look sad, he looks sad."

"I'm fine, Katie."

She mumbled something into her chest, then slipped her hand in mine and sat quietly, her legs swinging just above the floor.

Twenty minutes later, Alison came through the admitting door in a wheelchair pushed by Lynn Delfleur. She saw me and smiled thinly, brushing brown hair out of her eyes, turning her head to Delfleur and murmuring something I couldn't catch. The nurse laughed. Sitting in the wheelchair she looked pale and tired, and still beautiful. I let go of Katie's hand and stood up. They came over to me and Delfleur said, "Take her home and treat her well."

"I always do."

"You want me to take you downstairs?" she asked Alison.

Alison shook her head.

"Leave the wheelchair at reception," Delfleur said.

I got behind the chair and took hold of the handles. Katie stood to the side, watching, still quiet, and I said, "It was nice meeting you, Katie."

"Nice to meet you, too, are you his girlfriend?"

Alison nodded.

"He's nice."

"Yes, he is," Alison said. Her voice was constricted and low.

We went to the elevator, and Katie watched us go. After the doors closed I leaned over and kissed the top of Alison's head. She said, "You don't waste any time."

"Well, you know me, I see a pretty girl and go to pieces."

"Can't let you out of my sight," she said.

The elevator stopped and I pushed her down the hall, passing a very young-looking Latina and a nurse as they entered one of the examination rooms. The girl looked at us with hollow eyes.

"How you doing?" I asked.

"I feel sick," Alison said. "I want to go home."

At reception another nurse took the wheelchair while I helped Alison up, and we worked out a way to walk, her on my left side, head on my shoulder, my left arm tightly around her waist. "Slowly," Alison cautioned me.

The security guard, a big black man in a clean white uniform, got to his feet and asked, "You want an escort?" His name tag identified him as "Sheldon Bullier."

"Absolutely," I said.

He picked up the phone and punched two numbers, then said, "Escort out at ground reception."

Less than a minute later the same thin man who had held the door for us on our way in entered the room. He introduced himself as Nate and said he'd lead, and we headed out the door.

The crowd was no bigger than before, but it certainly seemed more hostile, even at their legislated distance. Crowell and the Cadillac were gone. The moment we exited there was a response, people yelling and wailing. The roaming photographer snapped another shot of us as a chorus of "Mommy, mommy, you've murdered me" started. The protesters had the singsong down well, almost sounding like children. But not quite.

Seven men and women fell to their knees on the sidewalk across the street and began praying loudly for the soul of our baby, blocking a young, well-dressed couple, trying to reach us with pamphlets. The man who had harried us on the way in urged Jesus to strike us dead where we stood. We headed down the sidewalk to where I had parked. A voice shouted, "You've let her kill your son. He was your son!"

Under his breath, Nate said, "Freedom of speech."

Alison's hands dug into me, and I felt her tremble and try to pull me closer, and I squeezed her back, gently. We had cleared the safe perimeter, and were maybe another twenty feet from where I had parked her car.

Nate said, "Look out."

Four men and women were rushing toward us. All carried paper shopping bags, and as they reached into them I instinctively shifted my weight, pivoting left, and lifted Alison to put our backs to the clinic. Nate stopped one woman but the other three pushed right past him and came at us, yelling. A bushily bearded man reached into his bag, screaming, "Look what you've done!" but before he could withdraw his hand I'd turned again, loosening my grip on Alison so as to not pull her with me, and putting my shoulder into the man's chest. While I was at it I straight-armed the man beside him. They both reeled backward off the sidewalk, cursing. The bushy beard shouted, "He tried to kill me."

I felt Alison let go of me and turned to see the small black-haired woman who had slipped past screeching, "Murderer, murderer, murderer, murderer, murderer, murderer!" in Alison's face. She had dropped her bag and was shoving something into Alison's hands, and Alison was trying to push her away. Alison's hands were red and wet.

I grabbed the thumb of the woman's left hand in my right, pulling back and twisting hard, sweeping the back of her left knee with my right foot. She shrieked and went down on her rear; the mutilated doll she'd been pressing on Alison fell onto the sidewalk beside her. Red paint spilled out of the doll's cracked head, pooling beside the woman.

Alison was sagging against the wall. Tears streaked salt tracks on her cheeks, and I caught her, pulled her against me, and made it to her Honda. Without letting her go I unlocked the passenger door, opened it, and slid her inside. Then I slammed the door shut, locking it, making a quick scan. The protesters had lurched forward, their shouts shrill and coarse. Nate and I caught eyes and he thumbs-upped and I nodded, and he turned to begin forcing his way back to the clinic.

The black-haired woman still sat on the sidewalk, clutching her thumb, bushy beard trying to help her up. They both watched me, and I stared back hard, and they looked away. I got into the car, started the engine, and pulled out, seeing more people shouting at us in the rearview mirror.

Alison made no sound, her chin pressed to her chest, hair hiding her face, her hands palm-up in her lap, smeared with wet red paint. The front of her shirt had been spattered, too. After a moment she tried to wipe her hands off on her shirt, but then she gave up and sat motionless and silent.

We had been together for just under seven months. Seeing her sitting beside me on the passenger seat, bent and in retreat, burned me. This wasn't her, and I hated it and knew that she did, too.

At a light on Broadway I reached out, touching her shoulder. She shook her head and said, "Don't." The word rode on a single sob, and I withdrew my hand. We made it to her place on Eighty-fourth and I double-parked on the street. With her out of the car, I took the keys from her pocket and unlocked the town house's front door. She allowed me to guide her to the bathroom, then knelt at the toilet and vomited. I held her hair away from her face until she waved me away, then went to park the car.

When I returned, the bathroom door was shut and the shower was running. I went into the kitchen and hunted about for the teakettle. I wasn't overly familiar with the town house. Alison had been occupying it full-time only for the last six weeks, since starting work in the city, and although I'd visited it frequently, I hadn't done any significant exploring. The town house had been purchased by her parents and Alison had the run of it while she lived in Manhattan, on the sole condition that her mother could visit, unannounced, whenever she chose to. I liked her mother a lot. She had chosen to visit a few times and once caught us making love in the kitchen, which was no more embarrassing than being arrested streaking around the mayor's mansion, but no less than, well, than being walked in on by the mother of the woman you are making love with. Linda Wallace had taken it well, certainly better than I had. Currently, Linda was vacationing in France, bicycling around Provence. She would be calling soon, probably; the abortion was not a secret between her and her daughter.

I found the kettle in the cupboard over the oven, and a tin of Earl Grey hidden behind some macaroni in the pantry. I started the water heating and reread my instructions on how to care for Alison. Sleep seemed high on the list right now, and not a lot of movement. When I heard the shower stop I went back to the bedroom to turn down the covers and draw the blinds, then headed to the bathroom.

She called my name as I got there and I said, "I'm right here."

"Can you get my robe, please?"

I got her robe from her bedroom and came back, and Alison opened the door to the bathroom and took it from me without letting me see her. Then she opened the door wide and, clad in her robe, said, "I want to lie down."

"Sure," I said, and put an arm around her, guiding her to her room. There, she disrobed and got slowly under the covers, immediately closing her eyes. I pulled the blankets up around her and she shivered, sinking into the pillow. I kissed her cheek and said, "I'll check on you in a bit. Otherwise, I'll be in the kitchen if you need me."

She mumbled a response as I rose and made certain she was tucked in. At the door I added, "I'm sorry, Alison."

Her eyes opened, and she turned her head to look at me. But her gaze went through me and she stayed silent, and all I got was a small nod before she closed her eyes again.

I shut the door quietly, then went to the sitting room and turned down the air conditioner. In the bathroom I found some cleaning supplies under the sink and cleaned up the red paint smeared on the porcelain and tile. Finished, I found my way back to the kitchen, poured a mug of tea, and drank it sitting at the kitchen table. The air conditioner cycled, peacefully sucking me dry, the refrigerator humming with it. No noise other than appliances, no movement other than air and me, and I watched the steam curling out of my mug. The mug was black with a Star Trek insignia on it. Alison's late father had bought it, I had been informed.

I could cover Romero and her daughter. With additional help, with Rubin and Natalie, and, say, Dale, I could do it. I could possibly even keep them alive, but there are no guarantees in this business. Dale was at least as well trained as I; we had done the Army course together. Natalie had been trained by her father, and was probably better than I at this sort of work. Rubin had learned at my knee. He wasn't professional, but he was amateur in the way that Olympic athletes are amateurs, and we had been close friends forever. Rubin's learning was through osmosis, I supposed, and he had absorbed a lot.

Including me, that'd give us a four-person, twenty-four-hour-a-day, seven-day-a-week rotation. Two people to stay with Romero at the clinic when she worked; two people at her home while she slept; leave one person to stay with Katie during the day. Alternate that, have the remaining person cover Romero's clinic ingress and egress, and the protection would be fine, giving that person room to investigate and perform the advance work, what little would be needed.

I could do that, and thinking about it, I realized I

wanted to do it. If nothing else, I wanted to give back a little of what I'd had to take this morning.

After draining the cup I called Rubin. He took a few rings to answer, and I pictured him in our apartment, dropping his pad and pencils, swearing as he picked up the phone in his room. When he picked up I asked if he was busy.

"Nothing I can't put down; the art's on spec, anyway. How's Alison?"

"She's sleeping. I need you to call Natalie and Dale and have them meet me here, and I need you to bring me my gun. Can you do that?"

"I know Natalie's free, we were going to have dinner tonight. Dale's in your book?"

"Yeah."

"Okay, I'll be right over."

"Don't ring the bell. I'll be watching for you."

I cut the connection and pulled the sheet from the clinic across the counter, thinking. I wasn't committed yet; dialing the number on the page would change that.

"Women's LifeCare, may I help you?"

"My name is Kodiak. I'd like to speak with Dr. Romero."

"Hold, please." Classical music for forty seconds, then a click and, "I'll transfer you."

"Mr. Kodiak? Dr. Romero. Is Alison all right?"

"She's asleep. I think she's fine. Have you contacted Sentinel Guards yet?"

"Not yet."

"I'll take the job," I said.

I heard her light a cigarette before she said, "When can you start?"

"Tonight. We'll pick you up when you leave work and go from there. I'll need to hold a meeting at your place, and two of my people will stay behind and spend the night there. I'd do it but I don't want to leave Alison alone for too long."

"Commendable."

"Starting tonight you've got your twenty-four/seven."

"Who are these other people?"

"Colleagues. I can vouch for them."

"I'll have a check ready for you."

I told her what else I required and she asked a couple of questions and agreed to my terms, and I said I'd see her at six and bring a contract with me. She said thank you, and we got off the phone. As I hung up, I thought I heard Alison murmuring and went to look in on her. She was sleeping, her mouth slightly open, her head tilted and resting on her hair. I watched her from the doorway for a long time.

CHAPTER THREE

We didn't notice her when she came in. Late twenties, maybe, a little plain, looking like every other expectant mother who had entered the clinic in the last week of work. Sitting in the second-floor waiting room, her purse in her lap, her belly showing second trimester, she struck me as odd only because she was Caucasian and alone. Most of the white patients at the clinic came with someone else, a friend or lover to hold their hand. She had been nervous, but I had yet to see a patient who wasn't. Mostly, I put that down to the noise of the SOS protesters outside. So I didn't stop when she came in, but continued back to my office.

Romero had, not unreasonably, explained that she would not allow a guard on her when she was with a patient, and I didn't argue the point. Excuse me, ma'am, just put your legs in the stirrups and don't mind him, he's my bodyguard.

Not good for business, if nothing else.

So, while Romero did her job, I did mine. I had taken over an empty office on the second floor as our on-site command post and, while Natalie patrolled the second floor and Dale watched the first, I did as much advance work as possible over the phone. Truth to tell, there wasn't a whole lot of advance work to be done. Romero's schedule was simple. We had all our alternate routes memorized, our formations down, our communication clear. The only other thing for me to do was try to determine the source of the threats, and I could do only so much of that at the clinic. Mostly phone calls, either to Detective Lozano or Special Agent Fowler. My attempts to set up an interview with Jonathan Crowell at SOS had all failed. I got the feeling Crowell didn't want to talk to me.

So I called Rubin at Romero's apartment to check on Katie.

"How's it going?" I asked him.

"Fine," Rubin told me. "I'm bored senseless and Katie's having the time of her life. She's stolen my sketch pad and is working in charcoals now."

"Any problems?"

"Well, she's got charcoal dust all over herself, but I've managed to keep it off the furniture."

"You're a funny guy," I said. I could hear music in the background, and Katie was saying something.

"No, no problems," Rubin said. "No phone calls, no letters, and no protesters. I just finished checking the mail. It's clean. I really don't think they have her home address yet, Atticus."

"It's only a matter of time. Enough of her life is public record and it's there for them to find. All it takes is one SOS member who also works for the IRS or a bank. Let me know if you see anything suspicious."

"Of course," he said, sounding hurt. "Katie wants to speak to you."

"Put her on."

I listened as the phone changed hands, then Katie said, "Hello, who is this?"

"It's Atticus, Katie," I said, thinking it was a hell of a thing to ask after she had told Rubin she wanted to talk to me. "How you doing?"

"Oh, it's 'Cus, hello. When are you coming home?"

"Not for a while yet. Your mom hasn't finished work."

"Where's my mommy, can I talk to my mommy?" Katie asked.

"I'll see if she can call you later."

"Okay, she's working. We can't talk to her, but we can. Ask her, please, so I can talk to her."

"I will, I promise."

"Okay. David says hi, he says hi, and we'll see you, okay? I'll see you, okay?" she said, and then the phone was back to Rubin before I could answer.

"You'll be coming in at the same time?" he asked.

"Yeah. We'll radio our ETA once we're moving. You're not going too stir-crazy?"

He chuckled. "Hell, no. We've done finger-painting and *Sweatin' to the Oldies* and she's on charcoal now, like I said. After that, we're going to watch some episodes of *The Incredible Hulk*. Romero got them for her on video-tape. As far as I can figure, she can't really discern a difference between Bill Bixby and David Banner, but she sees the difference between Banner and the Hulk. It's sort of cool. Bixby's this consummate nice guy, but if you get him mad he becomes the incredible protector. Super strong, but only doing harm to evildoers."

"There's something to that."

"Would that we all could turn green and frighten our problems away."

"Don't get too many ideas. See you later," I said.

"Cool. Don't get shot," Rubin said.

At exactly two o'clock, I performed our hourly radio check. Both Dale and Natalie called in, told me that I was loud and clear. Rubin didn't respond because he was out of range. I went for a cup of coffee in the second-floor waiting room, and was headed back past the nurses' station when I heard sudden yelling and the sounds of metal hitting the floor.

Stupid Things You Think When The Adrenaline Pumps #87: Well, Jesus, Atticus, if you knew this was going to happen, why did you just pour yourself a cup of coffee?

I dropped the mug, running to the noise, and pulled my radio. Just before I keyed the transmitter, Natalie came over the air, saying, *"Room two twenty-three, principal's inside."*

I pressed the button and said, "En route." Came around the corner, bringing my gun out as I heard Dale call in that he was on his way.

It took maybe another five seconds to find the right door, and that was more than enough time to commit murder, but I couldn't move any faster. I found 223 as Natalie pushed inside, following her into the room.

The woman I'd seen in the waiting room earlier stood behind the examination table, a plastic pop bottle in her hand. The cap was off, and the bottle was half-filled with a red liquid that had been splashed over the equipment, walls, and Dr. Romero. The woman was shouting.

I went for Romero as Natalie went for the other woman. "She's pregnant," I shouted to Natalie. Felice Romero had her glasses off, and the skin that had been protected by them was untouched, although a thick strip of red ran from her dark hair down across her lab coat. I wrapped my arms around her, pivoted, and dropped her outside the room, just as Dale came around the corner.

"Principal's clear," I told him. "Get her secure and call the police." Then I turned back to see that Natalie had the pregnant woman pinned against the wall, one hand on the bottle, immobilizing it. Natalie's right forearm was pressed under the woman's chin.

"You've been marked!" the woman was screaming. "Anytime we want to, butcher! Anytime we want to!"

"Shut the fuck up," Natalie said, "or I will knee you so hard you'll miscarry right here."

The woman shut up. Whether because she believed the threat, or because Natalie had six inches on her and the ability to crush her larynx, I don't know.

I holstered my weapon and then took the bottle out of the woman's hand, setting it down on the counter.

"She got paint on my blouse," Natalie told me.

"You're overdressed anyway," I said.

"It's going on my expense report," she said.

I took the woman's purse and began looking through the contents. "Write it up," I told Natalie. "All expenses will be reviewed."

"Skinflint," she said.

"No free rides," I told her. The purse held a lipstick, a pocket Bible, a hairbrush, five subway tokens, a folded piece of paper, and a driver's license. The license was state of New York, and identified the pregnant woman as Mary Werthin. I showed the license to Natalie, who snorted, then I dropped it back in the purse and unfolded the sheet of paper.

It was a photocopied wanted poster, with a grainy picture of Dr. Romero centered on it. At the top of the sheet were the words WANTED FOR MURDER, and beneath the picture, DOCTOR FELICE ROMERO. At the bottom of the sheet was a list of her crimes. According to the paper, Dr. Romero had murdered over one thousand children.

I kept the wanted poster, putting it in a pocket, then set the purse on the counter beside the bottle.

"I want a lawyer," Mary Werthin said.

Natalie sighed heavily. "Would you cuff her, please?" she asked me.

"I don't know," I said. "You two look so nice together."

"You can't hold me, you're not the police," Mary Werthin said.

I got my cuffs and locked them around the hand that had held the bottle. Natalie backed up, releasing her grip, and I turned Werthin carefully toward the wall, and cuffed her other hand behind her back. Natalie dragged a chair away from the corner and I led Werthin to it. Once she was seated, Natalie went to the sink and ran some water over a paper towel, dabbing it at her blouse. The blouse was white, and the paint had pretty much ruined it. After a few more swipes at the paint, Natalie sighed and threw the towel in the trash can.

I said, "Whose idea was this, Mary?"

Mary didn't look at me. She found a paint blotch on the floor and examined that. After a while she said, "Anytime we want to, we can stop her. This was only a warning."

I looked around at the paint-spattered room. It wasn't as bad as I'd first thought coming in. "You stay with her," I told Natalie. "The police should be here in a couple of minutes. I'm going to check on the doctor."

Natalie nodded.

I picked up my coffee mug and stopped at the nurses' station. I asked Lynn Delfleur to check the appointment book for Mary Werthin. "When did she make her appointment?" I asked.

She flipped pages until she found the name, then said, "Two weeks ago. She came in for a counseling session last week, just before you guys started here."

"She was going to have an abortion?"

Lynn shook her head. "Prenatal checkup. Second trimester."

"You checked her ID when she showed up today?"

"I always check IDs," Lynn said.

"And she did nothing suspicious?"

She glared at me. "Not that I noticed."

I thanked her and continued down the hall.

Dr. Romero was in the bathroom opposite her office, the door shut, Dale standing outside. I'm tall, but Dale is big, with about two inches and thirty pounds on me, mostly muscle and bone. His face is broad and smooth, his Japanese features clear. As I approached he said, "She's unhurt. The glasses kept the paint out of her eyes."

"When that lady came in, you and Sheldon ran her through the metal detector, right?"

He nodded.

"Didn't check the purse?"

"We haven't been checking bags. I assume that's about to change?" He said it without sarcasm.

"Yeah. Go on downstairs, meet the cops when they get here," I told him. "We're holding the assailant in two twenty-three. Her name's Mary Werthin." I handed him my mug. "Dump that for me."

He took the mug with a nod and headed off down the hall. I could hear water running in the bathroom. After a moment, I knocked on the door.

"What?" Dr. Romero asked.

"It's me," I said. "Are you all right?"

"How the hell did that woman get in here?" she asked. "Why didn't you people stop her?"

"Ms. Werthin made her appointment two weeks ago. Lynn checked her ID. There's no way we could have known she was going to pull something like that."

"She could have had a gun," Dr. Romero said.

"No, she couldn't have. At least, not easily. She went through the metal detector downstairs. We haven't been checking bags. We'll start now."

"You're searching bags?"

"We will now," I repeated.

The door opened. The doctor was wearing a black T-shirt, and her hair was wet, but the paint had come off. She put her glasses on and said, "I'm not certain I want that."

"It's your choice, of course."

She stepped past me and across the hall, into her office, motioning for me to follow. I shut the door after me, and sat down in one of the chairs by her desk. Dr. Romero lit a cigarette, and remained standing.

"She could have killed me," she said after a moment.

"She could have."

"You're supposed to keep that from happening."

"Yes."

She turned and looked at me, waiting.

I hated this part of the job. This was the Cold Hard Truth part. I said, "I can't protect you completely. No one can. If somebody really wants you dead, if they've got the patience, half a brain, and a little money, they'll get the job done. It might take them ten years, but they'll do it. No depth of security will keep it from happening, no number of bodyguards, no amount of money. You could move to the Yukon Territory, and if somebody really wanted you dead, they would follow and find a way. There is no such thing as absolute protection.

"What you've hired me to do is to protect you to the best of my ability. My ability is substantial. I work with some of the best people around, and I'm very good at my job. But I can't guarantee you anything. From now on, we will search all bags that enter the building."

"Invasion of privacy," Dr. Romero said.

I nodded. "Yes, it is. But that's your choice. We can risk another Mary Werthin, or I can have every bag searched. No gun is going to find its way in here."

"But there are guns that can be smuggled past metal detectors."

"Knives, too," I admitted. "But both take a lot of money and some connections, and the odds of either of those items finding their way in here without whoever's carrying them attracting our attention are very low. And we're still not certain that the threat against you is lethal. What that woman did reeks of terrorism, not murder."

She struggled with it for almost a minute, finally sitting down in her chair. "All right, search the bags," she said.

I pulled my radio and keyed it, saying, "All units, SOP change: Search the bags."

Natalie radioed a confirmation, followed by Dale, followed by Sheldon.

"That woman . . . she didn't want to kill me," Felice said. "Even what she said, that was just a scare tactic, wasn't it?"

"I think so. She had a wanted poster for you." I took the sheet out of my pocket and unfolded it, placing it on her desk.

She smoked for a few seconds, looking at it. I waited. "Not a good picture," she said finally.

"No."

"You think this came from Sword of the Silent?"

"Possibly."

"I am used to being harassed, I've told you that. This won't work on me. Common Ground is in six days, and I won't be scared off." She said the last more to herself than to me. "I have done nothing wrong."

For nearly a minute Felice was quiet, thinking, and then she remembered I was there, and she ground out her cigarette. "Have the police officers stop by my office, please. I want to swear out a complaint."

"Natalie and I will do that, if you like. It'll keep your name out of it."

She thought about that, then nodded. "All right."

I stood up. "We'll leave at six-thirty," I said. "Call me if you need me."

"Of course."

Mary Werthin was taken away by two of New York's finest, who returned my cuffs to me before they left, having replaced them with a set of their own. After briefing Natalie and Dale on my conversation with Romero, I went to the Two-six to take care of the paperwork and to speak to Detective Lozano.

"You're not doing a very good job," he told me. His black hair was short and receding, and sweat shone on his forehead.

"She's still alive," I said.

"True enough." Lozano wiped his forehead with the back of his hand, then offered me a cup of horrible coffee, and I took it more out of courtesy than need. "She's made a statement," he said. "She says that you and Miss Trent assaulted her. She has no idea where the paint came from."

I laughed and handed him the letters that had arrived in the morning's mail. Four more, all offensive, which brought the grand total to seventeen since I'd begun the job a week ago. Today's batch was relatively tame. Only one threatened Romero's life. The author wrote that he or she would "butcher every doctor" who performed an abortion.

Lozano looked at the stack and made a face, then put them on his desk. "I'll get these to Fowler."

"Anything else on Ms. Werthin?" I asked.

"We put a call in to the SOS offices, and she is a dues-paying member. Doesn't prove jack-shit but it's a connection."

"They collect dues?"

"How do you think Crowell affords his suits?" Lozano shrugged. "Son of a bitch has more money than I do, that's for certain. That's not saying much, admittedly." He scratched his jaw with a chewed fingernail, wiped his forehead again. "Too fucking hot," he mumbled.

"The Feds have anything on her?"

"Fowler is running it, but I doubt they'll find anything. You could go talk to him."

"Where's he at?"

"How should I know? Goddamn feebies. I'll keep you informed," Lozano said.

I took that as my exit cue and headed back to the street, and ultimately back to the clinic.

Lozano had the unenviable assignment of watching the clinic and the protesters on both sides of the line. Special Agent Fowler had pretty much the same assignment, but on a federal level, and the LifeCare clinic was only one of several he was concerned with. Fowler and Lozano didn't get along for a number of reasons, but I supposed the major one was simply that Fowler was FBI and thirty-two, and Lozano was NYPD and late forties. There's a long and distinguished history spiced with plenty of animosity between the FBI and the NYPD. The NYPD looks upon the FBI as meddling, arrogant busybodies who can't use a toilet without executive authorization from Washington, D.C. Conversely, most of the special agents I've met think that NYPD detectives are arrogant, stuck-up bullies who believe an interrogation is simply Twenty Questions played with a baseball bat.

Every threat Dr. Romero or the clinic received got forwarded to Fowler as a matter of course, to be processed by the Bureau labs in D.C. Then the document would be copied and sent to the NYPD. Lozano had told me that this sometimes took a week or more. The FBI kept the originals. Today's letters would be no exception. Lozano didn't like being second, and since it was he who was most frequently on site, I had to grant him the point. Unlike Fowler, Lozano made a point of coming on scene when he heard that something was going down. He had been watching the day I first arrived at the clinic with Alison. Fowler worked out of the Bureau offices, and visited only when necessary.

Dale went for the car at five-thirty. I gave him the extra hour before we had to move Dr. Romero, so he could double-check the vehicle. Dale knows cars; he took the Crash Course when we were at SpecWar together. I went from the Executive Protection Squad to the CID, sort of a sideways transfer, but Dale stayed EPS from the ground up. We were renting a vehicle from Natalie's father, a souped-up Ford that Sentinel reserved for "high risk" clients.

I doubted we would need the bulletproof glass or the solid rubber tires. For that matter, I doubted that someone had wired a bomb to the ignition, but Romero was paying me to be certain.

Dale backed the gray Ford into the alley behind the clinic at six twenty-five, by which time Natalie and I had Romero ready to go. We walked her downstairs, waited while she said good night to the few staff members who were still around. While she did this, I went out to check the alley and talk to Dale.

"Clear," he told me.

I gave the surrounding rooftops one last survey, then unlocked the back car door nearest the clinic. "Two minutes," I told Dale, and went back inside. Dr. Romero had finished her good nights, and was now putting on her Kevlar vest with Natalie's assistance. For some reason, watching the two of them made me think of a bridal fitting, but I kept that observation to myself.

"I hate this thing," Dr. Romero told me as she slipped her coat back on over the vest. "As if it's not hot enough out there already."

"You'll love that thing when it stops a bullet." I handed her back her briefcase and the plastic bag she had put her paint-stained clothes in. "You ready?"

She nodded, and I looked at Natalie, and Natalie nodded. I used my radio and told Dale, "Pogo's coming out." The code name had been chosen by Felice herself, and she looked faintly embarrassed every time I said it.

To Natalie I said, "Go."

Natalie went out the door and headed straight to the Ford while I held Romero back in the hall. Natalie opened the car door, then came back into the building, turned around, and now, with Romero close behind her, went back out. I took up the rear, and then we were all in the car, Natalie, Dr. Romero, and myself, a cozy protective sandwich. I closed and locked our door, said, "Charlie," to Dale, and sat back as he pulled out onto 135th.

"We did Charlie day before yesterday," Natalie said, looking out the window.

Dr. Romero shifted uncomfortably between us.

"Everybody's a critic," I said, and looked out my own window. I'd worked out seven routes for our travel, and each had a call sign, A to G. All of us were absolutely familiar with them. All I had to do was give Dale a letter and he would know which route I wanted to take.

The routes mattered to me because, in my opinion, cars are death traps. If I'd had the people and the money, there would've been four more bodyguards on the road with us, two in a follow car and two in a lead car. All the security professionals I know have a particular paranoia—for some it's snipers; others, bombs. Mine is ambushes. When I'm not working, it doesn't bother me, but when I'm on, I'm very careful about avoiding anything that could be used to set up an ambush. And it's too damn easy to ambush someone in a car.

"I'm clear on my side," I said.

Dale grunted.

"Clear," Natalie said.

"So we're not being followed?" Dr. Romero asked.

"We are most definitely not being followed," Dale told her.

She sighed and wiped sweat from her forehead. "I don't suppose that means I can remove the vest?"

"No," Natalie said.

"Dale, you want to put the air conditioner on?" I said.

He shook his head. "Car's too heavy. We'll overheat."

I looked at the doctor sympathetically. The ride was hard for her, cramped between both Natalie and me. With the New York humidity, the vest, the tension of the ride, and the rotten day she'd had, she had every reason to get pissy. But she hadn't yet. She even managed to not smoke in the car, knowing that the windows couldn't be opened.

I radioed Rubin, told him we were fifteen minutes out. He said he'd be ready.

After a moment, Romero said, "I'm melting, I'm melting."

CHAPTER FOUR

"Mommy, my mommy's home," Katie said, taking the stairs as fast as she could. It wasn't very fast, honestly, but it was endearing as all get-out to watch. She jumped off the last step and flung her arms around Felice's waist. "I missed you, come sit with me, I missed you."

The Romero apartment was a halfhearted trilevel, and we entered at the bottom, the short flight of carpeted stairs Katie had descended from the main level off to our right, beyond the closet. To the left was a small bathroom, the door open and the light on. Rubin locked the front door behind us and headed back up the stairs with Dale and Natalie while I stood with Dr. Romero.

Felice kissed Katie on the forehead and said, "In a moment, sweetie. Your mother wants to change first." She gently stepped out of Katie's grasp and took off her coat, then the vest. She hung both on the coatrack.

Katie put her arms around my waist and said, " 'Cus! I

missed you, too, I did." It was a tight squeeze, and I wasn't ready for it.

"Thanks," I said hoarsely.

Just as abruptly, Katie released me and followed her mother up the stairs. I went up after them onto the main floor, basically a large open cube that served as mostly living room, with couch, table, chairs, and television, and a little bit of kitchen, defined by a counter that jutted out from the wall perpendicular to the stairs. The living room was carpeted the same as the stairs, a lush green, the kitchen tiled white.

Katie had finished hugging Natalie, and now moved to Dale, who looked damned silly with her clutching his thick waist. Dr. Romero thought so, too, and laughed, before saying to me, "I'm going to change. Give me ten minutes before you leave."

"Fine," I told her.

Rubin handed her the day's mail, saying, "All yours."

She nodded and took it with her into the bedroom.

Together, Katie and Dale moved to the couch in front of the television and sat down. Katie released him, quickly shifting her attention to the screen, then began talking, perhaps to Dale, about her day. I heard her mention David.

I checked that the curtains were drawn tight over the sliding glass door that led to the patio. The patio overlooked Fulton Street. Through the fabric, I could make out the sparks of light that shone from apartments in the building across the way.

Rubin was already packing up his art supplies, with Natalie's assistance.

"Where do you want to go?" he was asking her.

"I don't know, I was thinking seafood."

"Whoa, kids," I said. "He's off, you're not. You work tonight."

"I worked last night," Natalie said.

"I know. But it's you and Dale tonight, Natalie. You're off tomorrow."

Rubin gave me the I'm-not-going-to-get-laid-tonight-and-it's-your-fault look. I shrugged. He turned to look at Dale, making his ponytail whip around as he did so.

Dale said, "Not on your fucking life, Rubin."

Without looking away from the television, Katie said, "Don't swear it's not nice, Dale. David, he swore, that's bad."

Dale said, "Sorry, Katie." He looked back at Rubin and shook his head.

"It's okay, it's okay," Katie told Dale.

Rubin transferred his gaze to me.

"I've got plans," I said.

"I hate you," he said. "So I get the night off, and I don't get to spend it with my sweetie?"

"That's right."

"You're a cruel, cruel man, Mr. Kodiak," Natalie said. She gave Rubin a brief kiss and murmured, "Later."

Rubin savored the kiss, then groaned when Natalie moved away to the kitchen to get herself something to drink. After a moment he opened his eyes and looked at me again. "I adore that woman. And I hate you," he repeated.

"Yeah, but it's the good kind of hate, isn't it?" I took a seat beside Katie on the couch. They were watching the news, and I came in on the tail end of a story about a body and an alley. Another pointless death. The police were saying it looked like a mugging, maybe for drug money. Dale switched the channel to MTV.

"How was your day, Katie?" I asked.

"It—it was fun, we had fun and we did drawings. And David helped and Rubin helped and we made pictures, good pictures. And we watched the—the Hulk and had fun, and did you have a good day?"

"It was pretty good," I said.

"Melanie B died," she said, her eyes on the set. "Nobody knows what happened to her, but she died and that's sad."

Dr. Romero emerged from her bedroom, wearing denim shorts and a T-shirt and looking better for the change of clothes and the brief shower she'd grabbed. She lit a cigarette and went into the kitchenette, motioning me after her.

"Who do I get tonight?"

"Dale and Natalie. Rubin and I will be by tomorrow around seven, same as before."

Dr. Romero nodded, then began searching the freezer for something to defrost for dinner. "I'll see you then," she said. "Katie? You want enchiladas for dinner?"

"Enchiladas!" Katie shouted. "I adore enchiladas!"

Felice smiled the way only a mother can smile at her child, then said to Natalie and Dale, "Is that all right with you two?"

They both said that enchiladas sounded grand.

Rubin and I said good night to everyone, then caught the number six train back up to Bleecker. We stopped at the Grand Union a block from our place for some soda, then walked to our apartment on Thompson.

We had a railroad apartment that we paid far too much for. My room was immediately right off the hall as you entered. The kitchen was beyond it, then the bathroom, and then finally the hall opened into one large living room. Rubin's room was at the far end of the apartment, in what was still technically the living room. We had installed a folding wall partition a year or so back to provide the illusion of privacy, but it didn't really work. If he had company for the night, and I ventured further than the kitchen, I heard far more than I needed to.

I put the soda in the fridge while Rubin continued to his room. We had a few bottles of Anchor Steam left, so I opened one for each of us and brought his to him. He had dumped his bag and was already pulling on a pair of cut-offs. I sat on the chair, looking out across the courtyard, and he took up position on the futon with a hairbrush and a couple of comic books. He put the beer on the little table by the television, out of the way of the comics, and began to brush his hair. Rubin is Puerto Rican, and his hair is almost the same light brown as his skin and eyes. We've known each other since we were kids, we went through Basic Training together, and he hasn't had a haircut since we left the service. He's been collecting his comics twice that long.

"You're a hippie artist freak," I said.

"I'm not the one who's got holes in his ear."

"Earrings are cool."

"On pirates," Rubin said. "Not on bodyguards. Makes you look like a . . . wimp."

"I'd rather look like a wimp than a . . . girl."

He laughed, setting the hairbrush down and taking up his beer. "You know, you talk like that, and I know you want me."

"Is it that obvious?"

"This is the nineties. Homoeroticism is hip."

"Except in certain states."

"And those don't count," he said. "You're going to see Alison tonight, aren't you?"

"Uh-huh," I said.

"You're going to see Alison and I am going to stay home alone."

"Uh-huh."

"Is that fair?"

"Nope."

"So you admit it?"

"Uh-huh."

He drank from his bottle, then opened his first comic book. "Have a nice time, you bastard."

"I will," I said, and left hoping that I was telling the truth.

———

We went for Chinese at a small restaurant off Broadway near her place. We'd eaten there a couple times before and it was beginning to feel familiar. The manager gave us a wave before we were led to a table.

Alison looked good, her color back in her skin and her eyes clear. She was wearing her hair untied, and kept having to brush it back out of her face each time she bent to the plate with her chopsticks. I told her about my day, and she told me about hers. She was working at Oxford University Press that summer, but she didn't think of that as her job. Her job was her band.

"We got a gig," Alison said. "Brownie's, Wednesday after this one."

"Is that good?"

"You don't remember going to Brownie's?"

"Come on, you know me. I don't know from clubs," I said.

"We went last month, saw C Is For Coyote."

"Okay, yeah. They were good."

She poured herself some more tea. "It's a good gig. You going to be able to make it?"

"It'll depend on the job. I'll try, but I can't promise anything."

"How's that going?"

"All things being equal, well. Today was a little out of the ordinary, but I think we're doing all right."

"Good."

I looked at her, realized that she was watching me closely.

"What is it?" I asked.

"What?"

"What's wrong? You feeling okay?"

"I'm fine with the abortion," Alison said.

"That's not what I was asking."

"Oh," she said. She drank her tea, then leaned back in

her chair as the waiter dropped our bill and two fortune cookies on the table. We divided the check, then she took one cookie and I took the other.

" 'Long life and happiness will be yours,' " she read.

"Mine's 'The strongest mind does not dissemble.' More an aphorism than a fortune, I think."

She laughed and said, "At Vassar I had a friend who always tacked on the phrase 'in bed' at the end of her fortunes. The strongest mind does not dissemble in bed."

"Cute."

"Long life and happiness will be yours—"

"In bed," I said.

"Exactly."

We went out onto Broadway, enjoying the night. It was still warm, but the humidity had fallen, and it was good weather for walking. I took her hand and we went like that for a while.

"My mother called," Alison told me. "Sends her best."

"I do the same."

"She wanted to know how we're doing."

"What'd you tell her?"

"I told her that we were fine. Not great, not bad."

I nodded, then said, "I'm sorry I haven't been able to spend more time with you."

She didn't say anything.

"It's not avoidance."

"I know," Alison said. "You're busy. I am, too." We were quiet for nearly another block. Then she said, "Atticus? Do you wonder?"

I knew exactly what she meant. "Once in a while."

"Me, too. More than I thought I would." She squeezed my hand. "Not second thoughts, exactly. But it sort of puts things in perspective. Makes me wonder what exactly I'm doing with my life, that sort of thing."

"And what are you doing with your life, Alison?"

"Right now? Taking a walk."

I dropped her off with a good-night kiss and headed back downtown, getting home a little before midnight. Rubin was in his room, and I could hear his voice, low, and knew he was talking to Natalie on the phone.

I went to sleep after thinking about Katie and Felice, and then Alison, and wondering what sort of father I'd have made.

CHAPTER FIVE

"Katie and I are going to the movies," Felice informed me the following evening.

I was sitting on the couch in their apartment, Katie beside me with her head on my arm more than my shoulder, totally focused on the early-evening MTV lineup. Natalie and Rubin had been granted their much-coveted night off together, leaving Dale and me to provide coverage. Currently, Dale was showering in the downstairs bathroom. It had been a quiet day, and I had been expecting a quiet night.

"You are going to what?" I asked.

"I promised her we'd go to the movies tonight."

"Absolutely not," I said.

Felice adjusted her glasses and frowned at me. "I told her I would take her to the movies," she said.

Katie lifted her head to look at her mother. "Is it the movie? Are we going to see the movie?"

"That's right, honey. Go get your coat."

Katie slid off the couch, cast a last glance at the video in progress, then headed toward the stairs up to her room. She pumped her arms as if jogging, moving as fast as she could.

Wonderful, I thought. Now I get to be the bad guy. "When did you decide you were going to do this?" I asked Felice.

"Last night."

"But you didn't tell me until now."

She lit a cigarette, then crossed out of the kitchen to pick up her windbreaker draped over the back of a chair. The windbreaker was light blue with navy blue piping. She checked her purse before saying, "You would have forbidden it."

"I don't have the power to forbid anything, Doctor. But you're right, I would have advised against it."

"She wants to see a movie, Atticus. It's summer, she's out of school, and she's bored."

I sighed. This wasn't the first time my principal had decided to exert some passive/aggressive resistance to my presence. Nobody likes being told what to do, even if they are paying someone to do so. The situation would be different if we were going directly from the clinic. The apartment still seemed secure, and so far nobody had been following us.

"I'm going to have to call Rubin and Natalie," I said.

Relief washed her features like a breeze lifting a kite. "Thank you."

"If nothing happens, then you can thank me," I said, and headed for the phone.

Natalie and Rubin were at the movie theater in Murray Hill, around Thirty-second Street, when we arrived. Rubin had grumbled when he answered the phone, but both he and Natalie had smiles on as we walked up, and Katie let go of her mother's and my hands to run and give them both hugs, saying, "We're at a movie, we're seeing a movie."

They led her back to us, and then Natalie extended a hand, showing six tickets. "They're seating already," she told me. "We should go on in."

Katie put her hand back in mine, and we stepped up to the line, Natalie leading, and the usher took our tickets and directed us to the appropriate theater. The appropriate theater was down a flight of stairs, and Katie had trouble with the steps. She refused all assistance, saying, "I can do it, I can."

Felice stayed right beside her on the way down, and I could see her resisting the urge to reach out and steady her daughter when she faltered. When Katie made it to the bottom, both of them looked proud enough to burst.

"See? I did it, by myself, I did it," Katie said loudly.

Felice gave her a hug.

The film was an animated Disney feature, one of the new releases, full of color and music, and fairly distracting. Felice was really the only person who paid full attention to it; Katie fell asleep halfway into the movie, snoring gently, her chin pressed to her chest. A subway tunnel had been burrowed through the ground close by, and every ten minutes or so the theater would fill with the rumbling of a train, loud enough to defeat the soundtrack. Katie didn't wake up.

Dale, Natalie, Rubin, and I devoted our time to watching the house, keeping a bead on the audience. There weren't a lot of people at the show, but we did our jobs, and consequently I don't have the first idea what the movie was about.

When the film ended, Felice woke Katie, saying, "Honey? We're going home now. Time to get up."

Katie opened and closed her mouth a couple of times,

tasting sleep, then rubbed her eyes and opened them. "It was a good movie," she announced.

"It was a wonderful movie," her mother confirmed.

Katie nodded, then reached for my hand, and I helped her out of the seat. We started back up the aisle.

"Did you like your movie, 'Cus?" Katie asked.

"I liked it a lot."

"Does your girl-girlfriend, does she like movies?"

"Yes," I said. "Alison likes movies."

"Did she like this movie?"

"I don't think she's seen this movie, Katie."

We had to stop at the stairs again, Katie once more refusing any help, and it took five minutes to get to the top, with plenty of people casting sidelong glances or just plain old-fashioned stares our way. At the top of the stairs, behind the railing, three pack-boys watched our progress. They looked to be in their late teens at most, decked out to look tough. We were three-quarters up when I heard the Alpha of the pack mutter, "God, what's that retard doing?"

He hadn't said it loudly, but the pack snickered. Katie froze on the stairs. Her shoulders rounded in as if to shield her chest, and she lowered her eyes to her feet. Then she held out a hand to her mother, saying, "I need help, Mommy. Help me."

Dale was leading up, and he swiveled his head to catch the Alpha, then turned and started to offer Katie his hand, but Felice stopped him by shaking her head. "You can do it, sweetie," she told Katie.

"Fucking retard," the Alpha said louder.

Katie rocked from her right foot to her left and back, one hand gripping the railing. Over her, Dale made eye contact with me, and I gave him a slight nod. He climbed the rest of the way and positioned himself at the top, maybe ten feet from the pack. His presence was enough to silence them, but the Alpha was now in trouble, looking from Dale to his two pals, then back at us; if he backed down, he lost face, and in front of his pack, it wasn't something he could afford to do.

Katie restarted, one foot carefully placed before the next, and we climbed steadily to the top without stopping. At the landing Felice gave Katie a hug, but she didn't respond, still staring at her sneakers, too aware of the ignorant, mocking eyes on her.

"That was great, sweetheart," Felice told her. She gave Katie another squeeze, then looked at me. "Let's go."

We fell in and moved out to the sidewalk. I told Dale to get the car and bring it around.

"I would prefer to take care of the problem inside," he said.

"I'd like that, too," Rubin added.

"Go get the car," I said.

Dale looked back to the lobby, then headed off. Rubin and I kept scanning the street, while Natalie started talking to Katie about the movie. Katie had begun responding when the pack came out of the theater. The Alpha stopped, looking over at us. He pulled cigarettes from inside his Chicago Bulls team jacket, and I caught a piece of molded plastic, Day-Glo green. He lit his cigarette, thumbed the match.

I met his eyes and made the look hard, hoping that he wouldn't be stupid.

He decided to be stupid.

"You know why retards make good bitches?" he asked his friends. "It's 'cause they're real easy to train, you know?"

Rubin looked for a cue off me. I didn't give him anything, just kept my look on the Alpha.

Katie had gone silent again.

"That one's too fucking fat, though," the Alpha added, inspired.

"You don't want to start anything," I told him. "You really don't want to start anything. Walk away."

"Fuck you, bud. You think I'm scared of you, of some fucking retards?"

Felice spun, said, "Young man, don't you have a store to rob somewhere?"

He looked indignant, bobbing his head back like an ostrich. He took a couple of steps forward, saying, "You talking to me?"

"Stupid and deaf," Felice said, and then she turned her back to him.

Here we go, I thought.

The Alpha looked at his crew and saw that they were watching him, looked back at us, and gauged the situation. He took another two steps forward, saying, "I'll fucking show you, stupid bitch." Then he started to reach into his jacket with his right, and that's when I went.

It took one long stride to get in his face, my right going to his, locking his arm against his body. I put my left hand behind his head, took a handful of hair, and then spun him so he was facing his crew. I yanked back hard with my left, pulling his arm out of his jacket with my right, and then I hopped up, right knee in his back, and drove him to the sidewalk. He hit it hard, his right arm immobilized and his left too busy reaching for me. He smelled like a Laundromat, and I knew why. In his right hand, still held tightly, was a squirt gun, one of the nice, new, pneumatic kinds with a big reservoir. The kind that can squirt twenty feet or so on a good day.

He had loaded it with bleach. One shot to the eyes, and you'd be blind.

The pack started to back up, and then they broke and ran and I looked over my shoulder to see that Rubin had opened his coat to show them his gun.

Alpha was swearing a blue streak, so I pulled back harder on his hair and put more of my weight on my knee and said, "Quiet."

Rubin came around and took the squirt gun from his hand, sniffing at it. "Nasty toy," he said.

"I know," I said.

"Fucker, let me up you motherfucker."

Rubin pointed the barrel of the squirt gun at his face. He said, "Excuse me?"

Alpha shut up.

I leaned my head next to his right ear and whispered, "Okay, asshole, here's the deal. I'm going to let you go. But don't try this shit again on anyone, or you'll end up with a bleach enema, got it?"

He didn't say anything.

"Got it?" I asked again, twisting his hair.

"Got it," he said.

"Good. Now we're going to stand up, and if you try anything, I'll break your neck."

We stood and he didn't try anything.

"Felice, will you and Katie come over here?" I called.

Rubin raised an eyebrow at me. I grinned.

Felice came around, holding Katie's hand, stopping next to Rubin. Natalie was right with them, grinning.

"Apologize," I told Alpha.

"What?"

"Stupid *and* deaf," I said. "Apologize."

He wavered, then took a deep breath and said, to Felice, "Lady, I'm sorry."

"I accept your apology," she said.

I turned his head to Katie. "Again," I said.

"I'm sorry," he muttered.

"No, once more with feeling," I said.

"I'm really sorry, I'm really sorry, please accept my apology."

Katie just looked up at him, and it was impossible to see what she was thinking, what she felt. Then she smiled, and said, "Okay, you're mean. I don't like you, you're mean. Go away."

I let him go, and we watched him run down the street.

Dale returned with the car, and we all went for ice cream before going back to the apartment.

CHAPTER SIX

The bottle flew on a frozen rope, a hell of a throw, shattering against the brick clinic wall two inches from where Dr. Romero's head had been, sending green Heineken slivers dancing to the sidewalk. The glass broke clear and loud, and all the noise, all the people on both sides of the line fell quiet.

Dale had caught the arm movement before the release and shouted, "Bottle——left," and I had taken Dr. Romero down, butting the back of her right knee with mine, collapsing her like an aluminum can. She went down to her knees, her hands coming around to shield her head, with me wrapped about her body for extra protection. Coming back up, I caught sight of the thrower, a squat white man, yelling in victory, his hand raised in triumph.

Natalie spun to cover us, all red hair and motion, and together we half dragged, half carried Dr. Romero to the clinic door where Sheldon thrust out his hand and helped pull her inside. He propelled her efficiently past the security gate, and Natalie followed before he blocked the entrance with his body. I was off the steps and already running across the street past Dale, shouting for him to follow me.

The lines seemed still stunned, little movement and little noise, snagged in the tar of the action. Some of the prolifers were backing away, disgusted with their radical cousins. A cluster of people holding NARAL signs were starting to move, but the uniformed police held them back, trying desperately to keep the two groups separate. Throwing the bottle had changed the tenor of the crowd, starting a countdown to contact, and everyone was wearing their anger and indignation like clothes soaked in gasoline. All it would take was a match.

Then I saw the thrower being congratulated by a big blond man in a Columbia University sweatshirt, property of the athletics department, saw the thrower basking in the attention, and I threw the match myself, leaping over the line and into the crowd.

I took the thrower in the side and rode him into the pavement. I heard his skull hit the street, felt the shock of impact rush through him. University was stunned, involuntarily half-stepping back with a gasp. Coming up, I twisted the thrower's arm around his back, heard him cry out, then used that as a handle to pull him upright. University reached in to bear-hug me, and I pivoted the thrower between us and began backing up, shouting at him to keep his distance. University took two steps toward me but the thrower shouted, "Do it!" and that stopped the other man. Dale had a hand on my back, clearing the path behind us.

The police were wading into the crowd, trying to get to us and not gaining much ground. Behind them a news crew circled for position. The mounted spot on the cameraman's unit flashed on, and he pressed in to get a good shot, the reporter with him on point, but both were repelled by a gray-haired woman who thrust a NARAL sign at the camera. An Asian cop took a punch on his shoulder and responded by putting the teenage offender in a head lock. Someone was screaming that she had been assaulted.

"You're in the shit," I shouted in the thrower's ear.

"Fuck my ass, cockbreath," he snarled back.

I twisted his arm until he made a noise, still backing toward the sidewalk. "Fucking coward. You been pregnant?" Someone grabbed my shoulder and I heard Dale grunt and then the touch was gone. "Self-righteous bastard," I said to the thrower. "Who gave you the right? Who gave you the fucking right?"

I felt the curb against my left heel and stepped up smoothly, yanking the man after me. "You're under citizen's arrest," I told the thrower.

"Natalie got a cop," Dale shouted in my ear. "Get him inside."

The news crew made us, then, the cameraman just behind the reporter, and they forced their way to the steps as Dale and I tried to manhandle the thrower through the door. The thrower chose this moment to start resisting again, as the reporter, a white woman with blond hair and pale brown lipstick, leaned forward and started to shout a question at us. The thrower lashed his right foot out before we could react, and Dale almost lost him. The reporter recoiled and dropped her microphone, then swore and tried to take a swing at him but I beat her to it, taking a handful of the thrower's hair and yanking hard back. He yelped like a dog whose tail has been stepped on. Dale fixed his grip on the thrower and we managed him through the door.

The cop was waiting, and without any preamble he spun the thrower back around, pressed him to a wall, and slapped the cuffs on him. I got a good look at his face while the cop patted him down, and then placed him.

"You're Crowell's driver," I said.

The thrower jerked his head toward me, alarmed, then went back to staring at the wall.

"You're shorter in person," I said.

That must have hit a nerve, because he let loose with a torrent of profanity that nearly drowned out the noise from the street.

"Big words for such a little guy," I said.

He tried to go for me; the cop slammed him hard back against the wall and read him his rights. While the officer called for a sector car, the thrower said, "I'll get you, cocksucker."

"Taller men have tried," I told him. Then I turned to Dale and asked, "Where's the principal?"

"Secured. She's okay, no scrapes, not a thing."

"Good."

Through the barred window I could see the police restraining and separating the protesters, running a gauntlet of SOS signs and NARAL banners. Another naked baby doll fell in the street, red paint on its too-pink skin. Feet quickly broke the doll off the coat hanger it had been impaled on.

There were sirens now, but in Manhattan there are always sirens. Placards were falling into the street, forgotten in the melee. Any trace of civility had gone the way of the dodo, and the police were starting to get angry, shouting as incoherently as everyone else.

"What are you charging him with?" I asked the cop, gesturing at the thrower.

"Inciting, felonious assault."

"Tack on attempted murder. He's a member of SOS, and they've been threatening the doctor's life."

The cop blinked at me.

"I'll follow you to the precinct," I told him. "Two-six, right?"

"Yes, sir."

I shook my head and told Dale to stay put, then went to find Romero. The thrower never took his eyes off me.

———

Felice slumped in a chair in the lounge on the first floor, drinking a cup of tea with both hands around the mug. Natalie stood by the door as I entered.

"Dr. Romero?"

"Two times," she said. "How long have you been working for me, now? Ten days?"

"Ten days," Natalie confirmed.

"And this is the second time someone has attacked me." She looked up from the mug at Natalie and me. "Did you get him?"

"He's under arrest now. I'm going to follow him to the Two-six and talk to Lozano."

"If that had hit my head," Felice said, then stopped. "If it had hit my head and broken, I could be blind."

We didn't say anything.

"My hands won't stop shaking," Felice said.

I looked at Natalie, who said, softly, "I put a lot of honey in the tea."

"I'll be back in a few hours," I told her. "I should be in radio range, if there's an emergency. Otherwise I'll be at the Two-six."

I closed the door quietly when I left.

CHAPTER SEVEN

As far as interrogation rooms went, the one they put the thrower in was pretty run-of-the-mill. One table, bolted down. Two chairs, bolted down. One one-way glass window, dirty. One detective, frustrated.

Lozano worked on him for over an hour, with me watching from behind the smudged glass, and we learned next to nothing except the man's name, and that had come from the computer, not from the suspect.

Clarence Jesse Barry, thirty-three years old, and sporting a yellow-sheet that detailed crimes from criminal possession to attempted rape. It made me wonder if all Sword of the Silent members had such checkered pasts.

The only honest thing Mr. Barry said was, "Get me my lawyer." He said that after Lozano showed him the three photocopied wanted posters for Romero that had been taken from Barry's person before he went into holding. Lozano went after him hard on the posters, and after he'd tried being smart for a while Lozano must have gotten to him, because Clarence played his lawyer card.

At which point Lozano rose and left the interrogation room, circling back to where I stood. He arrived with two paper cups of that awful coffee. We looked through the glass together at Barry. Barry looked at the window and smiled. He didn't look at the wanted posters arrayed on the table before him.

"I am disappointed," Lozano said. He had removed his suit coat, and his white button-up shirt was wrinkled but clean. There was an orange plastic lighter in his breast pocket that showed through the fabric.

"Maybe he wants you to earn your pay," I said.

"Public-spirited asshole, isn't he?"

"You should have said something about his height. He loves that."

Lozano looked at me and grinned. "I'll keep that in mind." He finished his coffee in two gulps, then crumpled the cup and viciously shot it overhand to the trash can in the corner. The cup hit the inside lip of the can with a low ring and dropped inside, and the trash can rocked slightly on the impact.

He said, *"El café es una porquería.* Means, this coffee is for shit. Roughly."

"The gesture communicated the sentiment."

"Good to know a little Spanish," he said. "Say it with me. *El café es una porquería.*"

I said it with him.

"You learn fast."

"I'm a gifted linguist."

"Sure you are."

The door opened into our viewing room and Special Agent Fowler came in, shaking his head and saying, "Dude, sorry I'm late."

"Why break a pattern?" Lozano said.

"Scott," I said.

"Atticus. Detective." Fowler looked at Lozano for a moment, who didn't turn away from the window, then shifted his eyes to Barry. "What'd I miss?"

"He confessed," Lozano said. "Came completely clean. He's writing it up now."

"Uh-huh," Fowler said. He ran a hand through his hair. His hair was straw blond, and he was wearing a subdued blue suit with a white shirt and a navy tie. He had a good tan on, too, and it looked darker than I suppose it actually was against his collar and in this light. He was wearing his glasses, thin-lensed, and he had his diamond stud stuck in his left ear. All in all, he looked just out of high school.

I thought, no wonder Lozano hates him.

"He have the wanted posters on him?" Fowler asked.

"Yeah," I said.

"Brilliant detective work," Lozano muttered.

"Where'd he get them?" Fowler asked.

"He wouldn't say. He lawyered up before you got here," Lozano said.

"What'd you do?" Fowler asked.

"I interrogated the suspect, Special Agent Fowler."

Scott made a face.

"You know what?" I said. "I'm going to go back to the clinic, I think. Check on Dr. Romero. You guys get in touch if anything happens, okay?"

"Of course," Fowler said.

Lozano just grunted in my direction.

Felice was in with her last patient of the day when I got back, so I checked up with Natalie and Dale, told them about the grade-school performances at the precinct.

"No wonder she hired us," Dale said before he went for the car.

"Barry was with Crowell the first day I was here," I told Natalie. "He was in the car with Crowell. Did he show?"

"No. Did you think he would?"

"I don't know. I get the impression Crowell only descends from his heaven every once in a while to stir the pot."

"You talked to him yet?" Natalie asked.

"Can't get through to him," I said. "His office keeps giving me the runaround. He was supposed to call me this morning to set up an appointment to talk."

She frowned. "Some advance work."

"I'm doing the best I can with what I've got. I can't take the time to chase him down, you know that. We need another guard."

"I know a PI we could use for the strictly investigational stuff," Natalie said. "We could ask Felice to put her on the payroll."

I shook my head. "I don't want to do that to her. She's footing half the bill as it is, and despite what she told me, I think it's a hardship. And Felice's been feeding us when we're at her place. I don't want her to have to pay for another body."

Natalie sighed and ran her hand through her red hair. "It's probably best," she said. "You and Bridie would never get along. But you're going to feel really stupid if something happens because we're undermanned."

"I'll feel really stupid whether we're undermanned or not," I said. "Believe me, I'll find a way."

The egress was handled with the same precision as all the previous times. No one shot at us, no one got in our way, and no one followed us, as far as we could tell. We took the Baker route home that evening, which put us on the FDR for ten minutes of the ride. I brought Romero up to speed while Dale drove.

"Barry," she said, frowning. "I've never heard of him."

"He's definitely one of Crowell's."

"Crowell has a lot of people," she said flatly.

"I need to talk to him," I said.

Romero raised her eyebrows at me.

"Procedure."

She tugged at the collar of her Kevlar vest and exhaled down into her shirt. Then she looked back to me and said, "Lucky you."

Katie greeted us exactly as always, hugging the stuffing out of her mother, then me, then Natalie, and finally Dale. Rubin handed the doctor her mail and she disappeared into her bedroom, as had become her custom, while Katie dragged me to the television with her. On the way there I dismissed Dale and wished him a good night.

"Elaine is very sick," Katie told me when we were seated. "She's very sick and she's dying and David can't save her." Then she looked at me and said, solemnly, "It's very sad."

"I'm sorry," I said.

"People die," Katie told me. "Bixby Bill died and Melanie B died and maybe Elaine, too." Then she put both her arms around me and snuggled close, watching the television screen.

Rubin said, "You ought to tell her that you're taken."

I stuck my tongue out at him.

"You staying tonight?" he asked me.

"Just to talk to the doctor after she gets changed. You and Natalie tonight."

He gave me an evil grin.

"Not while you're working, you don't," I said.

Rubin looked hurt. "Do you think I take my duties so lightly that I would risk our principal and her daughter for one night of sordid pleasure?"

I nodded.

"You know me too well," he said.

From the bedroom, Dr. Romero said, "Atticus? Could you come here, please?"

Natalie, Rubin, and I exchanged looks. "Sure," I said,

and extricated myself from Katie's grasp. She didn't seem to mind.

Felice was sitting on her bed, now wearing jeans and a faded Amnesty International T-shirt. Her feet were bare, and she held a sheet of paper in her hand. She looked small and frightened.

"I thought it was a charity solicitation," she said.

I took the paper. It read:

> BUTCHER BITCH—
> ONE BULLET,
> TWO BULLET,
> EACH IN YOUR HEAD.
> BANG BANG.
> YOU'RE DEAD.
> BOOM BOOM.
> DEAD DEAD.
> THERE IS NO SUCH THING AS
> COMMON GROUND.
> JUST KILLING GROUND.
> YOUR KILLING GROUND.
> I WILL HAVE JUSTICE.
> YOU'RE NOT MY FIRST.
> I WILL HAVE JUSTICE.

No signature.

I set the letter carefully on the bed, went back to the bedroom door, and said softly to Natalie, "Call Fowler. We got a letter."

Then I went back to Felice.

"They just won't stop," she said. Her voice was very low.

"I don't want you going to the conference," I said.

She looked at me.

"Hotels are almost impossible to secure, and with only four people I absolutely cannot do it."

"You think that's what—of course. He doesn't want me to speak, whoever wrote it. A man wrote that."

After a second, I said, "I can't protect you at the conference, not as it stands. It's too easy for someone to get a gun or a bomb into a place like the Elysium. And it's already been publicized that you'll be there."

Felice inhaled deeply, then reached for her pack of cigarettes. "I'm going," she said. "I won't be frightened off."

"I can't provide adequate protection there," I said.

"Can't or won't?"

"Can't."

She stared at the pack of cigarettes for a few seconds, then lit one and smoked, watching my face. "You're serious, I've never seen you look this serious," she said.

"The stakes have changed," I told her. "You could have been seriously injured this morning. And it was a stupid thing for someone to do and that worries me. So far, there's been a terror-campaign logic to this. The bottle . . ." I left it unfinished.

But she was right with me. "That was an attack, wasn't it? Testing the defenses, maybe?"

"Yes."

"I'm going."

"Felice, listen to me. It's a hotel, do you understand? Suppose a man wants you dead. He knows you will be there in three days, giving a lecture, sitting on a panel. He checks into the hotel tomorrow, all he has to do is wait, polishing his gun. Do you see the scale? Everybody in the hotel—all the guests, the staff, the temps—everybody must be checked and cleared before you can go. It's impossible for me to do that and to protect you at the same time with just four people."

Felice got up and took the ashtray off her nightstand, tapping her cigarette on the rim. After a moment she said, "I am going to speak at Common Ground. I helped organize the damn thing, and I will be heard there."

I started to open my mouth but she held up a warning

finger. "Let me finish. I agree with you. I don't want to die, Atticus. I won't go to the conference if you tell me it can't be made safe. But I want you to talk to Veronica, Veronica Selby. She's the one who got the hotel in the first place, and she told me that she'd take care of security. Talk to Veronica, and if she can't make you reasonably happy, I won't go." She sat back down on the bed. "Fair enough?"

"I won't take chances here, Felice," I said.

"I know," she said. "And I appreciate that."

Fowler arrived shortly after we finished talking. I got Selby's phone number from Felice and gave the woman a call while Scott talked to Dr. Romero.

The phone was answered on the second ring.

"Hello?" The soft voice held just the slightest southern accent.

"This is Atticus Kodiak calling for Veronica Selby," I said.

"Speaking."

"I'm in charge of security for Dr. Felice Romero, Ms. Selby. I was wondering if I could come and speak with you?"

"Is Felice all right?"

"She's doing well enough."

"When did you have in mind, Mr. Kodiak?"

"I was thinking in about half an hour," I said.

"Oh," Selby said. "Well . . . yes, that would be fine. I'll expect you shortly, then." She told me her address and I copied it down on a sheet of paper. "Please give Felice and Katie my regards," she said.

"I'll do that."

Fowler had bagged the letter and the envelope, though we all knew there wouldn't be any prints. The serious threats always came back from the lab clean. I asked him if he could give me a ride up to Selby's place on Park Avenue, and he said he'd be glad to.

"She told me to send her regards," I said to Dr. Romero.

Romero managed a crooked smile.

"I'll get back to you later tonight," I told her. "You can reach me by pager or at home. Don't hesitate to call."

"I won't," she said.

Katie gave me another hug before I left, saying, "Come back, okay, 'Cus? Come back soon."

Fowler drove well, very legally. Once we were rolling he said, "You're going to hate this but Barry is out. The charges were dismissed."

"What?" I asked. "How the fuck did that happen?"

"Dude, I know. Looks like NYPD blew the paperwork. Barry claims that he didn't understand his Miranda. I think maybe one of the cops on the desk is sympathetic to the cause."

"He's been arrested enough, he fucking knows his Miranda by heart," I said.

"He didn't even say anything in interview to take to trial. But he's out, and I'm sorry, man. I thought you should know."

"I can't believe this," I said.

"It gets worse. He's running with another guy, too, Sean Rich, who came to pick him up. Both are apparently tight with Crowell."

"How is that worse?"

"Rich has a record," Fowler said. "In Florida. Pensacola."

Pensacola, the town with two dead doctors who performed abortions to its name. "Jesus."

"Yeah."

I didn't speak for a few moments, fuming. It had been a righteous collar, and Barry was out anyway. And now it sounded like there was a ringer up from the land of the faux-Christian Nazis. All of that plus the throwing of the bottle; it hadn't been thrown at Romero, it had been thrown at us, to see how we would react.

"Do you think they're really going to go after her?" Fowler asked.

"She's high profile, she's a woman, she's a minority. She's the perfect target. They'll go for her at that conference. Wouldn't you? They know exactly where she'll be, when she'll be, and if she goes down in front of the crowd—you can't buy that kind of publicity. Barry is SOS, we both know that. Crowell's up to something."

"Don't let her attend, man," Fowler said.

"If I don't like the security, I won't, believe me, Scott," I said.

He made a careful turn onto Park. "I don't think Crowell will do it. I don't like conspiracies." He pulled up outside Selby's apartment building. "Don't like conspiracies, and I don't like conspiracy theories at all, man. They're too easy. You're looking for a nut with a gun, not the Illuminati."

"I'll take a conspiracy over a nut with a gun any day," I told him, unbuckling my seat belt. "At least, with a conspiracy, you know where you stand."

He was still laughing when I got out of the car.

CHAPTER EIGHT

Selby's apartment building had the feel of New York when it was still the classiest, most cultured city on earth. Whether or not it is now is subject to debate, but then again, whether it ever was is probably subject to the same debate. The lobby was marble, the fixtures were brass, and the plants were very green. To top it all off, the doorman was dapper, his uniform neatly pressed. He looked like a Royal Guard. He greeted me by name, saying that Ms. Selby was expecting me. I felt horribly underdressed, and acutely aware that I had a gun on my hip.

Selby's apartment was on the second floor, and I knocked on her door and waited. The door was opened almost immediately by a woman roughly my height who allowed me in, shut the door behind me, and offered to take my jacket, saying her name was Madeline. I declined, and she bade me follow her down a short hallway. She motioned me into the room, then turned and left.

The curtains were drawn, and even with the last of dusk giving way to night the sitting room appeared bright and airy. The fixtures were predominantly white, with some green and some blue thrown in. There was an overstuffed couch and a low coffee table, bare, several bookshelves, and a desk by one of the windows, with a PC on top of it. The computer was running, and a screen saver of rain falling over a city skyline played on the monitor. Every so often lightning would flash across the skyline.

On the walls hung two framed posters, both Monets with beautiful fields and delicate sunlight. A wood carving hung over the computer, PEACE in polished mahogany letters, spelled in Greek, Hebrew, and English. There were other pictures of a vague religious nature, but nothing garish. As I stepped into the room I heard the sound of paws scrabbling on a hardwood floor, then saw a golden retriever corner hard from another room and run toward me. The dog passed me and stopped at Selby's feet, turning twice to look at both of us, then lowering itself to the ground.

Veronica Selby sat in a wheelchair, opposite the couch, wearing white pants and a dark blue blouse that looked like silk and comfortable. She was utterly stunning, certainly one of the most beautiful women I had ever seen. The blouse clung to her upper body, revealing the shape of strong shoulders and a proud back. She was on the near side of forty. Her hair was golden—literally—drawn around the right side of her neck and tied with a blue ribbon. She wore a small gold cross on a necklace, and the slightest application of makeup to highlight her blue eyes and her cheeks. With her left hand she stroked the dog behind its long, floppy ears.

She extended her right hand and said, "Mr. Kodiak, I'm pleased to meet you." I heard the soft southern thread of accent in her voice again.

"The pleasure is mine," I said, and shook her hand. Her grip was good, not too strong. She had nothing to prove.

"Please, have a seat."

The couch didn't give much when I sat on it. I said, "I realize that this was short notice."

"I assume this concerns Common Ground?"

"That's right."

"It has my absolute attention." Time was only beginning to work on her. At her eyes were the slightest lines, and her mouth exhibited barely a wrinkle. She would keep her beauty for the rest of her life. "What can I do for you, Mr. Kodiak?"

"Dr. Romero told me that you are taking care of security at the Elysium."

"Yes, I am," Selby said.

"I'd like to know what's being done."

"Felice is still receiving threats?"

I nodded.

Veronica Selby shook her head. "That anyone would do so in the name of God is abhorrent."

"Frankly, I think it's abhorrent, period."

She smiled. "Yes. May I ask—are you pro-abortion?"

I should have realized it when I first saw the apartment, I thought. I had assumed that Felice and Selby were on the same side. But it was being called Common Ground for a reason.

"Yes, I am," I said.

"I see. Yet your job is to protect the lives of the innocent, isn't it?"

"That's one way of looking at it." I shifted on the couch, wishing it would give just a little bit.

"I'm curious, you understand," Veronica Selby said. "I've spent twenty years now, off and on, trying to know the minds on both sides of the issue. You're uncomfortable talking about this."

"The issue's not the reason I'm here."

"No, you want to know about the security at the hotel. Fair enough," she said. "I've hired two firms, Vigilant Security and another called Aware, and officers of Midtown North will be present, too."

"And?"

She looked embarrassed. "I'm afraid that's all I've done."

Three days, I thought, and must have made a face, because she said, "I'm open to suggestions."

"Ms. Selby, I've advised Dr. Romero not to attend the conference because I believe there is a substantial chance that someone will try to kill her if she goes. My team and I cannot secure both the hotel and her person at the same time. Felice has agreed not to attend unless I approve the security."

Selby's expression slid, turning to disappointment. "No, please. Felice must be there. She's vital to making this work; it's essential that she attend and speak. Her commitment . . . she's got to be there . . . this may be the last chance any of us gets to talk instead of scream. If she doesn't come, easily half of the pro-abortion groups won't attend either." She moved her chair forward, closer to me, intent. The dog rose and looked at her.

"Please, Mr. Kodiak. You don't know how important this conference is, how desperately I want it to succeed," Veronica Selby said. "You must tell me what I need to do. The conference must be safe, not just for Felice but for all of us."

I was floored, not so much by her words, but by her passion. It had been a long time since I'd heard somebody speak with her sincerity, and, in a way, it was immediately intimate, as if I'd glimpsed something in her others would take years to see.

Selby kept her eyes on me, then suddenly seemed to become self-conscious. The dog put his head in her lap, rolling his eyes at me. Her hands went immediately to his glossy head.

"I can be somewhat . . . intense, I suppose," she said softly. "Forgive me."

"There's no need to apologize," I said.

"Will you tell me, please? What do I need to do?" she asked again.

I took off my glasses and rubbed my eyes. So much needed to be done, so much that I had assumed would already have been taken care of, to make the conference safe. The smart thing to do would be to tell Selby that I was sorry, but Romero wasn't going to show.

That would have been the smart thing to do, instead of being swayed by passion and courage.

I put my glasses back on. "First, you've got the wrong people," I said. "The police are a nice touch, and their help will be appreciated, but they're not in the business of protection. They apprehend for a living, if you see the distinction. Same thing with most security guard firms; you tend to get a lot of ex-cops, or cop wannabes. If they see someone with a gun, their instinct is to go after that person first, rather than to protect the target.

"There's really only one way to do this, and the problem is that to do it right, you need a lot of money—"

"I'm rich." Selby said it simply. "Money isn't a problem."

I absorbed that, then said, "Call Sentinel Guards tomorrow morning. Make an appointment to meet with Elliot Trent, and mention my name. His daughter works with me. He can come to see you, if you like. Tell him exactly what Common Ground is, everything you have planned for the conference, and tell him you've got 72 hours before it happens. You want complete protection. Those are the words to use: complete protection."

"What does that mean, exactly?"

"Sentinel will do as complete a background check on as many attendees to the conference, and as many employees of the hotel as possible, in the time remaining. They'll try to check on all the guests, too, and make certain that none of them is a potential troublemaker. They'll place guards in uniforms and plainclothes, they'll have metal detectors, a command post, even dogs for sniffing out explosives."

I looked at her and then said, "It's got to be done like that, and they've got to do it. Otherwise, I'll advise Dr. Romero not to attend. We're in the hole as it is. This should have been done weeks ago."

"I didn't realize . . ."

"Talk to Trent tomorrow. Tell him to call me after you speak with him."

"I will," Selby said, wheeling over to the computer. She nudged the mouse and the screen saver went off. She opened an appointment book on the screen and began to type. "Will you look this over, please?" she asked.

I got off the couch and looked over her shoulder at the monitor. She'd gotten all the important points of what I'd said, and I told her as much.

"One other thing," I said. "I need a list of all attendees, if you have one. Trent will, too."

"I've got it right here." She opened a document, set it up to print. There was a whine as her laser printer charged and began spitting out paper, and Selby said, "I updated it today. We're at twenty-two speakers, over two thousand registered attendees, but frankly I'm expecting more."

"How many more?"

"Perhaps twice or even three times that number."

"Christ," I said.

She looked at me sharply.

"I apologize," I said. "No offense was intended."

Selby made a small smile. "Taking the Lord's name in vain . . . I'm used to hearing it outside. Just not in my own home."

She gathered the paper from the printer and handed it to me. As I flipped through the sheets, Selby said, "I'll let you know as more names are added."

I was about to thank her when I saw Crowell's name. "Why's Jonathan Crowell on the list?"

"He'll be speaking," she said.

"Are you kidding? That man doesn't believe in common anything."

She wheeled back to where the dog now lay, saying, "Jordan, come here." The dog immediately rose and returned his head to her lap, wagging his tail.

Selby said, "Mr. Crowell's point of view deserves to be heard."

"No."

She frowned. "Everyone who wishes to speak must be heard, Mr. Kodiak. We all have that right. I don't agree with what he does, or what he says. But if Dr. Romero can speak, then he must be given the opportunity as well. That's the whole purpose of this conference."

"That means that SOS will be there," I said.

She nodded. "And they will behave or be expelled. Those are the ground rules for the conference. There will be no screaming tantrums, no accusations."

I wondered how the hell she was going to manage that, but didn't say anything. Barry threw a bottle, and now SOS would be attending Common Ground. Suddenly, my day seemed to be in a serious nosedive.

"He's not that bad," she said. "Crowell, I mean. His rhetoric is that of an angry man, but . . . he sincerely believes that abortion is murder, and I cannot fault him for that."

"You speak as if you know him," I said.

"We've had an acquaintance over the years. He's strained it recently." She looked at her hands, then at me again, the small smile back in place. "I've been lobbying against abortion for nearly twenty years now, Mr. Kodiak. I've lectured all over the country, I've published everywhere I could get accepted. I've even managed two or three books. Through all of this, I've met many people on both sides. I have enemies on my own side and friends, like Felice Romero, on the other."

It struck me that she had more to say about Crowell, but I didn't want to press her. I folded the papers, put them in my jacket pocket. "When you see Trent, make certain you tell him that Crowell and his troops will be there."

"I will," she said. "You're leaving?"

"I've got some other things to take care of tonight."

"Let me show you out, then," Selby said.

"That's not necessary," I said. "Have a good night."

"You as well. Thank you again for coming."

I started for the door and she said, "Mr. Kodiak? Do you think that SOS will really be a problem?"

I stopped and looked back at her, gorgeous in her wheelchair, just as passionate, just as concerned as before.

"Yes," I said. "They really will."

CHAPTER NINE

I went straight home, opened a beer, and dialed Romero's number. Natalie answered.

"It's Atticus. I need you to call your father. Tell him that Veronica Selby will be calling tomorrow, and she'll want the works."

"How bad is it?" she asked.

"Oh, it's about as bad as it can be. We're a good three weeks behind."

"No way we can do this, Atticus," Natalie said.

"I know."

She was quiet for a moment. I heard Romero ask her how my meeting with Selby had gone. Natalie said fine, then said, to me, "I'm going to change phones. Hold on." I heard her set the receiver down, then ask Romero if she could use the phone in the bedroom. Felice said yes.

I drank some beer. I knew what was coming, and couldn't fault her. Of all my colleagues, frankly, Natalie's the best. At least as good as I am, and certainly better looking.

She picked up the extension and someone hung up the other phone, and as soon as she felt the line was secure, she said, "You absolutely cannot let her attend. There's no way that Sentinel can catch up, no way they can clear everybody by the day after tomorrow."

"I know."

"Goddamn you, Atticus. I know you and I know what you're thinking. You can't let her do it."

I didn't say anything.

"She's got a daughter, for God's sake."

"I know."

She was quiet again. "Is it worth her life?" Natalie asked, finally.

"It's her life, Natalie. I'll give her the options and let her make the decision."

"You know what she'll say."

"Yes, I do," I said. I finished my beer. I was paying for a lot of NYNEX silence. I took the beer to the sink and washed out the bottle. After I put it in the recycling, I asked, "Do you want out?"

"Of course not," Natalie said immediately. "Don't be an ass. I'm in for the whole op. But it's a mistake, and I would be remiss in my job if I didn't tell you that."

"Will you be able to sell your father on it?"

She sighed. "He won't like it at all. It'll put the firm's reputation at risk. He'll give me the 'She's our responsibility, too' lecture, and he won't be wrong."

"Tell him it's my reputation, not his."

"I will."

"If we can't get Sentinel, we're fucked," I said.

"We're fucked anyway, Atticus. All right, I'll call him, do my best Daddy's-little-girl act. But don't expect him to give Selby a discount. I'll call you back."

"Okay. Don't tell Romero anything yet."

"Talk to you in a bit."

I hung up and stared out the kitchen window for a few minutes, looking across the alley. Then I took off my gun and pager and sat at the table. My gun is an HK P7, hammerless, and its cocking mechanism is in the grip, making it ideal for one-handed use. It's a good body-guard's weapon, and looking at it, I wondered if I wasn't creating a situation where I'd be forced to use it. I didn't much care for that thought, and looked out the window instead.

There wasn't much happening in the apartments across the alley, just occasional silhouettes against drawn blinds.

Twenty minutes passed before the phone rang. I answered it immediately.

"He said he'll do it," Natalie told me. "He'll cancel his morning appointments and meet with her right after she contacts him. But he told me to tell you that you're an idiot, and you'll be washed up if this goes wrong."

"Have I mentioned how much I like your father?"

"No, and I wouldn't start now. See you in the morning."

"Night."

"Good night."

After making dinner for myself, I called Alison, hoping that I could see her, or at least get her on the phone long enough to talk. She wasn't in; probably rehearsing. I left a short message, told her it was nothing urgent, and that I'd try to reach her tomorrow.

Then I went to bed.

Sleep came fast, and I dropped into my dream cycle like a sinker through the surface of a lake. Veronica Selby was explaining to me that plastic coat hangers were invented by her, actually, to keep women from using them to muti-late themselves. Dr. Romero told her she was way out of line, but she said it in a friendly enough way, and Selby took it well, asking the doctor in return why she hadn't aborted Katie.

"I couldn't," Dr. Romero told her. "I wouldn't have even if I had known."

They talked, and I sat on a black leather couch next to Katie, watching television. Bill Bixby turned into Lou Ferrigno, and together the two of them trashed a clinic held by fat men wearing ski masks. On the screen I saw a child's doll, naked and anatomically incorrect, with its crotch split open. Its crotch had been detailed to look like a vagina, but someone had bored a hole through it, and from within spilled festering, bloody matter, burned and broken chunks of skin that could have been anything from fetal remains to chicken entrails. "She's dead," Katie told me.

Then Felice was being chased by men who all looked like Barry. The many Barrys held paper knives, which they had managed to smuggle past the metal detectors without a problem. Felice stopped running, turning to face them down. She said, "You're all such little men, why are you here?"

Before I could reach her, they descended, the knives rising and falling, until they cut out her womb. The chief Barry held it aloft, presenting it to Crowell as he floated down from heaven on wires. Crowell took it, and said to Felice, "No more children for you."

CHAPTER TEN

The phone was ringing. I heard it in the dream and made for it, climbing desperately, until finally my eyes opened and I jerked up. It was still dark, and I stumbled out of my room and into the kitchen, stubbing my toe on the utility cart while trying to reach the table.

"Atticus, it's Rubin. Dr. Romero and Natalie just left here. The burglar alarm at the clinic went off."

"Damn," I said. "All right, I'll get right over there."

"Okay," Rubin said softly.

It took half a second, and then I recognized the tone in his voice. Doubt.

"What is it?" I asked.

"I don't know," he said. "The phone rang right after they left, and I thought it was the police again, or the alarm company. But nobody was there, they just hung up after I answered. It feels like somebody's probing."

"You want me to come over there?"

"Yes," Rubin said.

"All right, I'll send Dale to the clinic. Give me twenty minutes. Katie's all right?"

"She's in her room, sleeping."

"You checked?"

"Yes. Called the doorman, too. He says nobody he hasn't recognized has come in."

"Twenty minutes," I said and hung up.

I turned on the kitchen light and winced, then called Dale. He got it on the second ring, and was remarkably lucid. I briefed him and he said he'd get there ASAP.

I dressed fast, grabbed my gun and pager, and ran down all six flights of stairs onto Thompson, pulling my jacket on as I went. I flagged a passing cab on Houston and told the driver to get to Gold Street as fast as he could. It was four in the morning and the sky was still dark, the streets still bare, and everything shining in the false moisture of night. The dream still had its claws in me, and I tried to shake them out as the cab popped and swerved its way south.

The driver stopped in front of Romero's building, and I scanned the street before getting out, looking for anything out of the ordinary. There was nothing to see. The driver took his money and the doorman let me through. Rubin was waiting at Romero's door and stepped out of my way to let me inside. I heard him lock the door after me.

The main floor looked fine, and I took the steps up to the third level quickly, found Katie's door, and looked inside. She was asleep in the bed, snoring. The room smelled of perfume and soap.

Rubin handed me a mug of coffee when I got back downstairs. His eyes were puffy, with heavy bags underneath. I took the mug and checked the other rooms, not expecting to find anything and not being disappointed. Then I moved the curtain back from the window and unlocked the sliding door, stepping out onto the concrete patio. Rubin followed me.

The air was cool outside, and helped push the last of my cobwebs away. The coffee was hot and too sweet.

"False alarm?" Rubin asked.

"Maybe." There was movement across the street, a man in a dark windbreaker walking down toward the Seaport. Several lights shone in the opposite building, and movement fluttered the curtains in a couple of windows, people rising for the day or maybe preparing for bed. A homeless person slept on a grate at the corner of the building, unmoving. But mostly the city was still wrapped in night, and mostly there was nothing to see.

"God, I'm tired," he said, rubbing his eyes.

"What exactly happened?"

"Felice got the call about a half hour ago, and she tore out of here. Natalie wanted to call you first, but Felice wouldn't wait.

"I hung up the phone and it rang and I picked it up, and then nothing. Just the click, like I said. Disconnect."

"Anything else?"

Rubin rubbed his eyes again. "I don't know. I got twigged, you know, so I decided I'd take a peek out here . . . and I swear to God I saw someone in one of the windows." He looked at me, and his expression was almost apologetic. "Just standing there, not doing a goddamn thing but staring out, right at me."

"Could you see who it was?"

"Shit, Atticus, I could only see a silhouette. The person could've had their goddamn *back* to me, I wouldn't have been able to tell. Looked like a guy, looked about your size, but I don't know. It doesn't mean anything."

"Which window?"

He extended an ink-stained index finger. "Seventh in from the left on the third floor."

The window was lit, but barely, as if there was only one source of light inside, and I could dimly make out the railing on the fire escape. Curtains or some kind of blind obscured the view, and if anyone was moving inside, they weren't visible. On either side of the window there were no lights, and no way to tell if it was one apartment or several. From where we stood, it looked like someone could establish line of sight into the Romero living room, but their field of fire would have been tight, maybe only five degrees at the most. Move to the right a couple of windows and that field would open up to almost twenty degrees, maybe more.

"This is probably nothing, right?" Rubin asked. "Somebody just got the number and was making a run-of-the-mill terror call? Coincidence?"

The light in the window went out, and I stared hard for a few moments at the darkened square, thinking, then let my eyes lock on the building entrance. After a minute or so a woman left, walking a dog past the dozing doorman under the awning. The woman was using a walking stick, and the dog was on a retractable leash. Both looked old. Nobody else entered or left. "Maybe."

"Maybe what?"

"Maybe it's nothing. We should find out who's in that apartment, though."

"I don't want to start jumping at ghosts."

"We'll verify that it's occupied, that's all. Find out if the name on the rental agreement matches any name that Fowler or Lozano have."

We surveyed the street for a while without speaking. Early office suits were beginning to appear, heading toward Wall Street with briefcases laden with trade secrets and stock reports. The thought, unbidden and unexpected, came into my mind that each person moving now, every light across the way, represented a life or multiple lives.

"It's been going on for so long now," Rubin said. "It seems like we've been doing this job forever."

"Eleven days isn't long," I said.

"For you, maybe. I feel like every day is the same. Not that they are, of course, I know that, and if I try really hard, I can remember that, too. But the fact that I have to try really hard to begin with is what bothers me."

"Have you gotten any sleep?"

"What, tonight? About two hours."

"Go to bed. I'll cover until Natalie gets back with the doctor." I put a hand on his shoulder. "You can only do so much. Get some rest."

"You don't think I'm paranoid, do you?"

"Paranoia is our game, Rubin."

He smiled and said, "See you in a few hours." He started back into the apartment, then stopped. "Katie shouldn't be a problem when she gets up. She's having her period, now, though, so make sure she changes her pads. She forgets sometimes."

I gave Rubin five minutes to settle in before I turned back inside myself, going straight to the house phone and ringing the lobby. Philippe the doorman answered immediately, and I told him what I wanted him to do.

"I shouldn't leave my post," he told me.

"This is a favor for Dr. Romero."

He listened again, then agreed, and I went back out on the patio to watch.

It took him four minutes to lock up, get the coffees, and cross the street. Philippe offered one cup to the other doorman, and they stood side by side for a moment, drinking and talking. Philippe told a joke, with broad hand gestures, and the other doorman laughed. They talked some more, and then the other doorman nodded and went inside, leaving Philippe alone on the sidewalk. His uniform looked pink in the light under the awning.

The other doorman came back, told Philippe what he wanted to know. They shook hands, and though I couldn't see it, I was sure Philippe slipped the other man some money.

I went back to the house phone, and picked it up as it rang.

"The apartment is owned by Mrs. Batina Friendly," Philippe told me. "She shares it with her dog. She's out taking a walk right now."

Which was what I had thought, but it pays to be certain. "How much do I owe you?" I asked him.

"Twenty bucks," Philippe said.

"Thanks."

"No problem."

Dr. Romero had set out two deck chairs on the patio, white enamel paint with orange rubber slats, and after Rubin left I sat in one of them, waiting for the sunrise.

While I watched the street, I wondered what Katie's dreams were like. She wasn't as affected by her Down's as some people I had met, but she was more impaired than others. Talking to her, it always seemed as if we understood intention without sharing language. The only reason anyone assumed her thoughts to be simple and childish was because she had difficulty in communicating. Did she dream about Bill Bixby and the Incredible Hulk? Rubin's frankness about Katie's menstrual cycle had surprised me; it was stupid, but I hadn't realized she would ovulate. At sixteen, Katie Romero was growing into the body of a woman and certainly had the growing desires of one, as well. If her fantasy life was active, who could blame her? Ultimately, she was alone, with no one to share herself with completely, because words would always get in the way.

The sky continued to color, and it was just before six when the phone rang inside. It hadn't been ringing for long, I know, but for a moment my memory had a gap I couldn't fill, and I answered it with the fear and guilt of someone who may have nodded off to sleep.

"Atticus?"

"How's it look, Natalie?"

"Someone tried to crowbar the back door, mangled the locking plate, but didn't get inside. I'm trying to get Felice out of here, but she won't leave until she's positive that nothing is missing. Dale's with her, now. Fowler's coming down, so we're waiting on him right now. How's things there?"

"Quiet. Rubin got a call after you two left, no voice, just a disconnect. He thought it might be a probe, so he asked me to come down here."

"Anything to it?"

"He went to the window and took the glance, says that there was somebody in one of the windows of the opposite building, looking out. He said he thinks it was a male, perhaps my height, but it was all in silhouette."

"What do you want to do about it?"

"I've already identified the apartment, and it seems safe. When Rubin's up I'll head to the clinic. You guys aren't going to be coming back down, I assume?"

"At this rate, no, we'll be staying," Natalie said. "All right, I'll see you when you get here. Any other orders?"

"Keep her safe," I said.

"I am my sister's keeper," Natalie said, and hung up.

Katie started moving a little before seven, coming down the stairs to where I was reading on the couch, yawning. Her heavily lidded eyes looked even smaller, and she rubbed them several times before they appeared of use to her. Her nightgown was yellow with small blue prancing horses printed on it, and it made her look fat. At the bottom of the stairs she stopped and looked at me.

"Where's my mommy?"

"She had to go out."

"The phone, who was on the phone, calling here?"

"That was Natalie. Your mommy's all right."

"I know that, I know she is," she said. She pointed to

the drawn curtains, where daylight was showing. "Breakfast time, what's for breakfast, 'Cus?"

"What do you want?"

"I want waffles, want waffles and syrup."

"Go get dressed and I'll make you waffles with syrup."

"Okay. I'll do it. 'Cus, where's my mommy? Where is she?"

"She had to go to the clinic. She'll be back before too long."

"My mommy works, that's right," she said, turning back up the stairs. "Mommy works so people don't like her because she does a job."

She disappeared into the bathroom above and I stepped around the counter into the kitchen, looking for a skillet or waffle maker. The light in the kitchen wasn't strong enough to cast shadows on the curtains. After some rummaging, I eventually discovered a waffle iron at the back of a cabinet, hidden behind an automatic juicer. It took another few minutes to get everything together for the batter, and I started to worry that the waffles wouldn't be ready by the time Katie was dressed. But the water in the bathroom continued to run, and I had finished a first batch and was working on the second before she came down, wearing baggy jeans and a T-shirt with the cover of Madonna's "True Blue" album printed on it. When she turned I could see concert dates on the back.

"Did you change pads?" I asked.

She looked angrily down at her bare feet, saying, "He shouldn't talk about that. He shouldn't be talking about that, to me. I did. I did it." She looked at me again and said, "I did."

"Why don't you sit down and I'll bring you breakfast."

She headed for the television, in a line across the glass doors, and I said, "Katie, sit at the table, please."

She changed her course without protest, settling into a wicker chair that creaked, then looked to me expectantly. I brought her a plate of three waffles, stacked, and a glass of orange juice. She went for the orange juice first, and when she drank she placed her tongue inside the glass. It seemed a slow and difficult way to drink, but pointing that out seemed petty. If it made her happy, why criticize? I returned to the table with a bottle of Log Cabin and a cup of coffee for me.

"How did you sleep?" I asked.

"Fine. I slept fine." She opened the bottle of syrup and held it in both hands, pouring the contents onto her waffles. She poured a lot of syrup.

"Katie, don't you think that's enough?"

She looked at me, honestly surprised, then said, "Oops, oh no! That's too much!" She turned the bottle quickly right side up and the syrup line suspended between bottle and table turned, too, getting all over the side of the bottle and her hands. "Yuck," she said. "Yuck, oh, oops, yuck."

I started to take the bottle from her but she clung to it. "No, I can do it. I can do it. Get a towel, go get a towel to clean it up."

So I got a paper towel from the roll over the sink, wetted it, and returned to her. The bottle was upright and capped in the middle of the table, still drooling a strand of syrup. Katie was licking her fingers, but she stopped to use the wet towel. She cleaned her hands vigorously. "Elaine died," she told me. "She died all sick and David couldn't help her." She looked down and rubbed the towel over the table, concentrating on the spot where the syrup had fallen. "It's very sad."

"I'm sorry," I said.

She dropped the paper towel and took up her fork and knife. As she cut the first waffle to pieces she said, "It's only a television show."

I used the mug to hide my smile, drinking coffee and nodding at her. "Yes, it is."

"It's only a television show," she repeated. "Elaine didn't really die and Bixby Bill and she can get married now. That's not sad, it isn't."

"No."

She went through the waffles quickly, barely stopping to breathe between bites. When the last scraps were gone, she coated her fork with the remaining syrup and took care of that, too. Finished, she put the utensils back on the plate, saying, "Is there more?"

"Are you sure you want more? It's awfully fattening."

"No, don't get fat. I'm not fat, I'm pretty. Don't get fat," she said. " 'Cus, I don't want anymore syrup."

"How about waffles?"

"No, I don't want waffles. I'm finished. I've got to exercise, after breakfast, I've got to exercise. Can I do my tape?"

"Sure, where is it?"

The tape was a workout video, and I rewound it and started it on the VCR. Katie took her position in front of the television, hands on her hips, grim determination in her eyes. Waffle crumbs stuck to the corners of her mouth, and I pointed them out to her. She thanked me, licking them off, and began her workout while I removed the dishes from the table and started cleaning up. From where I stood behind the kitchen counter, I had line of sight straight to the window. Katie stayed clear of the doors as she exercised. Hers wasn't an efficient workout, but she took it seriously, following the movements as best she could, never once slacking off or taking an unauthorized break.

When the videotape ended she went to the television and switched to MTV, staying on her feet for a few more minutes, dancing to the forced beat. Eventually she sat on the couch, wiping imaginary sweat from her brow.

"Where is he?" she asked.

"Who?"

"Where is he? Where is Rubin, 'Cus? Where is he?"

"He's getting some sleep."

"No, he's not," Rubin said. He was wearing boxer shorts and looked marginally better than last night, a towel in his hand. "He's taking a shower." He went down the stairs to the entry bathroom.

Katie laughed, and announced that Rubin was silly.

We sat together, watching MTV. Katie seemed to have absolutely no musical preference, although the one Madonna video we saw captured her attention completely, and she sang along with it heartily. The video was an older one, I think, but I'm not a real fan of the medium, so I could be mistaken. Madonna paraded in front of incredibly handsome, incredibly well-defined men and women, coaxing them to sexual frenzy. Not only was Katie attentive, she was beatific in her awe.

The phone rang and I went to answer it. It was Lozano.

"Natalie said you were there," he told me.

"What? Hold on," I said and set down the phone, going back to the television and turning it down.

"Use the remote," Katie said.

"Where is it?"

"I don't know, no. Turn it down, he's turning it down. There, who is it? Is it my mommy?"

"No, it's the police."

"It's the police, looking for Melanie B. Is it my mother?"

"Is Dr. Romero all right?" I asked Lozano.

"She's fine. I want—"

"Hold on," I said. "Your mother's all right, Katie."

"Good, that's good that she's all right. The police call when people are dead," she said. She rose and began hunting around the couch. "I'll get the control, the control for the television for you."

"Sorry, Detective," I told Lozano. "What can I do for you?"

"Just wanted to let you know what we've got, which is practically nothing. A unit found a crowbar in the alley, but there were no prints on it. Fowler's sending it to D.C."

"A crowbar?"

"Don't ask me, Kodiak. I just work for the city, not the

Mighty Federal Machine," he said. "You going to the clinic?"

"When my guard here is ready, yeah, I'll be going up-town. He got a call last night that might have been some-thing, but it's looking okay now."

Rubin came up the stairs at that point, freshly scrubbed and wearing clean clothes, and the change had affected his personality. He was smiling, and flicked the end of his towel at me. I failed a halfhearted dodge, turning toward the far wall. He'd have to attack me from behind, and Rubin wouldn't do that.

"Conference is tomorrow?"

"Day after," I said.

"It's going to get worse before it gets better, bud," Lozano said.

"Well, that's just what I wanted to hear," I said, turning back around. Rubin was in the kitchen, drinking orange juice out of the container. He caught my eye and I shook my head and he set down the carton on the counter, hunt-ing for a glass. I heard him ask Katie if she wanted one. She said yes, and continued searching the cushions on the couch.

"It should never have been made legal," Lozano said.

"But it is," I said. Katie turned on the standing lamp in the corner to get more light.

"Yes, it is. And until the law changes—"

The glass door, the sliding portion, shattered and fell, a translucent wall that tore the curtain as it collapsed into the room, pulling the fabric off its runners. Glass hit the carpet intact but burst on impact, singing as it broke. Out of my hand fell the phone and to my left Rubin was drop-ping the orange juice. The carton hit the kitchen floor bot-tom first, then pitched to a side. Juice splashed on the tile floor and Rubin's pant leg. The report was next, full and ugly, large caliber. Katie jerked where she was standing in front of the light, beside the couch, just inside what was now the kill zone, and she fell, her chest leading, hitting the side of the couch and then bouncing off it, soft and buoyant, hitting the carpet on her side, and I was diving to her, shouting for cover and police and an ambulance and thinking quite clearly that it was a very good thing, a very good thing, that Lozano was on the phone, because all he had to do was turn around and shout and there would be an ambulance and the police and it would be all right, everything would be all right.

Another report, the second or maybe the third, just after I got to her, and I slipped my hands underneath her shoulders, pulling Katie back to the kitchen, around the counter, and Rubin was helping me, grabbing her shirt, his head low, and I had the awful sensation that none of this was real; it was a practical, a live fire exercise; certainly not real. When we dragged her we smeared a red stain on the carpet, a bloody snail's trail that became wet and shiny on the tile floor. Rubin was crawling out to the phone already, grabbing the hanging receiver and barking into it, scurrying back to our cover as he did so.

Another shot and I heard it punch hard against the counter as I knelt over Katie, her eyes open and filling with tears. She was speaking and I strained to listen while running my hands over her, trying to find the wound. The blood kept coming with a mind of its own.

"My mommy," Katie Romero said, and it was hard to understand her, and it hurt her to make the words, but she kept repeating, "Mommy, I want my mommy, where is she? I want my mommy."

The hole had been punched in her side three inches below her armpit, just inside her right breast, and the blood coming out was candy-red arterial issue, and I covered the wound with my hand, pushing down hard trying to get a seal to stop the bleeding and Rubin was shouting to get an ambulance fucking now, we were taking fire.

And Katie stopped calling for her mother, no air available to do it, and I was still looking for an exit wound, not finding one, wondering where it had gone, if it was still inside. I tilted her head back, my palm on her forehead, and put my cheek beside her mouth and two fingers on her carotid, waiting for air to come out, for blood to move, for a breath. Fifteen slow seconds, certain I counted too fast, and there was nothing coming out, her chest wasn't moving.

With one hand I sealed her nostrils and then covered her mouth with mine. My lips surrounded hers, she had a small mouth, and my seal was absolute. Two full breaths, Katie's chest rising. The air rustled out past my cheek.

"No pulse, no breathing," I said.

Rubin was landmarking, his hands already sliding up Katie's rib cage to find the xiphoid. I gave another two breaths and he starting compressing and I started breathing and that was it, with Rubin quietly saying "One-and-two-and-three-and-four-and-five and—" breath breath, "one-and-two-and-three-and-four-and-five and—" breath breath. Compressions, breaths, and the air wasn't going down, I was tasting waffles and syrup and orange juice and jerked my head back, spitting, turning Katie's head. I opened her mouth and swept the inside with an index finger, scooping out chewed breakfast and clearing her airway, then repositioning her head. Two breaths.

"Continue."

Compress, relax, compress, relax, compress, relax, compress, relax, compress, relax, and two breaths, and again, we weren't perfect, we were going too fast, I knew that, the air was going in and coming out, and again compress, relax, compress, relax, compress, relax, compress, relax. Stop. Check for pulse. One one-thousand two one-thousand three one-thousand four one-thousand five one-thousand no pulse *where the fuck is the ambulance* "No pulse, continue," breath, exhale, breath, exhale, compress, relax, compress, relax *where the fuck is the ambulance* compress, relax, compress, relax, compress, relax, breath, exhale, breath, exhale, and again compress, relax, compress, relax *if she took the shot in the lung where's the exit wound* compress, relax, compress, relax *two shots or was it three shots or was it four shots only one shot hit her the second shot rifle* compress, relax, breath, exhale, breath, exhale *where am I in the count should I check pulse God don't let her die* compress, relax, compress, relax, compress, relax, more breaths compress, relax, breath, compress relax breath *ten minutes irreversible brain damage where the fuck where the fuck where the fuck the door's locked oh fuck me the door's still locked. . . .*

Check pulse. Nothing, "Rubin, unlock the door, go unlock the door." My free hand took the gun from my hip and handed it to him. He took the gun so fast I wasn't sure he had taken it at all, and he got up and went for the door as I landmarked, above the xiphoid notch, yes and one hand, seal, breath, compress, over and over and over and over and over and he was back.

"Door's open. Coming in on breathing," and he moved to her mouth and I moved over her chest and she was so small and my hands were so big on that fucking Madonna T-shirt, a beatific smile and a bloody halo that's not true blue.

We weren't even checking for pulse anymore.

The paramedics came, a man and a woman, both intent and aggressive, and the man ordered Rubin away from Katie's head and immediately set about administering oxygen with a bag-valve mask. They didn't say anything to me, so I kept compressing while Rubin explained as best he could what had happened. Over their radios I heard others and looked up through sweat-stung lashes to see two uniforms standing just above the stairs, looking confused. One of the cops said something to the woman in front of me, who was busily setting up a line.

"Shut up," she told him. "Ringers running," she told her partner.

He nodded and said, "Stop compressing."

I sat back on my haunches, feeling hot and light-headed, watching as he intubated Katie, sliding the tube down her throat like a professional magician; now you see it, now you don't.

The woman had set up the monitor, was now looking at Katie's absence of rhythm on the LED screen. To hook the system up she had sliced Katie's shirt open down the middle, and the bloodstained fabric pulled back to reveal her body, and even with her natural skin color she seemed pale, dying. The monitor confirmed that, and as the woman busied herself with the IV line, pushing first one drug, then another, I bent to resume compressions.

Another ambulance crew arrived, and then they were loading Katie onto a stretcher, and I was being roughly pushed out of the way, into the arms of a cop who started to ask me something I never gave him a chance to finish. I followed the stretcher down the stairs and into the hall, Rubin right behind me. The elevator was locked open and they moved everything inside. Rubin and I took the stairs down to the lobby. One of the uniforms came after us, and Rubin was explaining the situation in broken phrases that sounded ungainly and unknowable.

From the lobby, Katie was rolled to the back of one ambulance, where both paramedics climbed inside. One of the late arrivals, an EMT, slammed the double doors shut and went around to the front of the rig, and Rubin and I followed the other to the remaining ambulance. The driver was medium-sized and white, with black curly hair and black-framed glasses, and he just nodded to us when we started to climb inside.

"Where're they taking her?" the cop asked him.

"Bellevue."

Buckled up, and then the rig was off with a lurch, lights and sirens down the street and swaying onto the FDR Drive, following the other rig as it sped to the hospital.

"Somebody needs to call her mother," I said.

"Lozano said he'd do it," Rubin said.

We arrived at Bellevue only thirty seconds or so after the ALS rig, in time to jump out and follow the stretcher through the double doors on the loading dock down the hall. Katie was on her back, the monitor still running. They had put a second line in her, but both bags now rested above her head on the stretcher, shut down for transport. We followed them down a hall, made a sharp right, and ended up in a crammed narrow route with stretchers stacked to one side. The paramedics barely had room to move, and we stayed well behind, keeping out of their way, but not wanting to lose them. Left and now an open space, still more stretchers, and through electric double doors into the ER, and more stretchers, now with people in them, their feet sticking out from under covers or uncovered. The room had a smell that rammed its way up my nose and made me gag, twisted with the cloying memory of maple syrup, and my stomach heaved, for a second, then retreated.

The medics turned Katie's gurney to the left, in front of a new set of double doors, and a doctor was standing there, wearing sea-blue scrubs and gloves and goggles and barely audible, saying, "This the Romero kid?"

We never heard the answer; they were already inside and it was clear we had come as far as we could. The doors snapped shut on hydraulic coils, locked with hard clicks, and Rubin and I stood side by side, looking through the small glass windows at the eight people suddenly surrounding Katie's body. They moved her off the gurney and onto another table, the medics backing away, and a phalanx of doctors, men and women, some in scrubs, others not, all goggled, gloved, and masked, bent to work. Instruments flashed off trays in gloved milky hands and the sound of machinery, hard and strong, started up. The doctors bent to the task, and it was clear to me, right then, that Katie was dead.

Rubin was covered in blood, all over his shirt and pants, up both arms, a vampire's ice cream sundae. I probably didn't look any better.

Then a nurse told us to move, to get out of the way and go register the patient.

"She's Catholic," I told her.

"We take all kinds."

"No," I said. "She's Catholic."

"I'll get a priest. Go register the patient."

She gave us directions to registration, but they didn't stick. Rubin and I started down a hallway, passing an alcove containing a bald-headed man on a bench, and dodged an orderly who glared at us, then continued on.

"Where are we going?" Rubin asked.

I shook my head, and we turned around, heading back to the nurses' station. Another door through admitting opened as we returned, and Felice Romero rushed in, Natalie and Dale right behind her, and another doctor from the clinic, Marion Faisall. Lozano followed a second later. Dr. Romero didn't see us, going straight to the station and exchanging quick words with the nurse there. The nurse gestured and Felice turned, moving to the Trauma Room doors, but the nurse shouted after her and Natalie moved, grabbing her arm at the elbow. The grip stopped her, and Felice turned back to Natalie, eyes wild and mouth in a silent scream.

Felice saw us, and saw it in our faces. It was as if someone had thrown a solid punch into her stomach, and she began to bend, shaking her head, as if trying to fold into herself and disappear. Natalie and Dale helped her to the alcove, setting her on one of the benches. Dale stayed by her, an arm around her shoulders, head beside hers but looking out, always looking. Natalie made straight for us. Dr. Faisall just stood beside the alcove.

"How?" Natalie asked. Her eyes were terribly cold.

"Sniper," I said. "We did everything we could." My words sounded whispered, and for a moment I doubted that I had indeed spoken at all. But Natalie nodded, looking us both over, then reached for Rubin.

Lozano was looking at me. I left Rubin and Natalie and walked to him. Behind the counter a phone rang, and one of the staff moved to answer it. Fowler had entered, leading another two police officers, and they all stood idly by the ER doors. We were filling the place up. Beyond the doors, somewhere outside the room, people were shouting, and Lozano turned his head to listen, then said, "Press."

"Fast."

"They were at the clinic, saw Romero and company leave with us. How's the kid?"

"She's not going to make it," I told him.

"Don't talk like that, you don't know that."

Lozano didn't know what he was talking about, but there was no fire in me to argue the point.

"You see anything?" he asked me.

"No."

"I'm not handling it; it's not my precinct."

"Fine."

"Maybe your friend did?" Lozano asked. "See something?"

"Maybe."

He pushed off the counter, saying, "I'll ask," and headed for Rubin. He walked carefully, as if disturbing the air in the ER meant the difference between life and death. Rubin and Natalie were against a wall, heads bent toward each other, and Rubin was speaking to her, softly. Dr. Faisall said something to Natalie, and after a moment Natalie nodded, said something in return. The doctor headed toward one of the pay phones on the wall.

The shouting outside died, and an orderly stuck her head around the door. "Can you give me a hand, here?"

she asked one of the uniforms. "They won't take no for an answer."

Fowler snapped, "Keep them out of here." The uniforms clutched, but Lozano nodded and they went out the door. As it shut a rumble of voices started, then snapped off as the latch clicked. Lozano resumed questioning Rubin, but he cast a sidelong glance at Fowler as the officers left the room. An Asian priest arrived, entered the Trauma Room without ceremony.

After a while, someone told me to take a seat.

I didn't.

Thirty-two minutes after we arrived at Bellevue the Trauma Room doors opened and from where I was standing I could see inside, and I knew what the doctor was going to say. He was a black man, well over six feet tall and very skinny, with his scrubs hanging off his shoulders and hips, barely held on by his bones. His hair was covered in a surgical cap, but his goggles, gloves, and mask were off, and as he came out he ran his hand across his forehead, smearing the beaded sweat there. He looked around and then said, "Felice?"

She came out of the alcove, Dale beside her. "Say it, Remy," Dr. Romero said.

"I'm sorry. We pronounced her at eight forty-eight. We did everything we could."

"I want to see her."

He nodded.

I went into the room after them.

She had been covered on the table, and the overhead lights cast harsh shadows in the folds of the sheet, shaped to Katie's body underneath. The floor under the table was littered with discarded wrappings, papers, gauze, tape, some bloody, some not. The rolling carts of shiny instruments weren't shiny, and the dishes the tools had sat in were dark at the bottom, surgical steel coated with body fluids. Clamps, forceps, scalpels, catheters, needles, saws, equipment now dirty with blood and bone stacked on other instruments in more carts. The room had become suddenly empty, and as the doctor and Felice looked at Katie's body, two people came in the other side of the room and began cleaning up. There was a second table, just like this one, but gleaming clean, with instruments ready to go.

Katie's hand jutted from under the sheet on my side. Not really her hand, just her fingers. She had been wearing pink nail polish, the color of bubble gum. A tube disappeared under the sheet by her hand.

Dr. Romero pulled the sheet back to look at her daughter's face. Someone had closed Katie's eyes. Felice put her hand on Katie's forehead, brushing hair back from where it had fallen across the girl's cheek. For a moment her fingers traced the bones in her daughter's face, touching the chubby cheeks and chin. She made a small noise, the sound of a caught animal, shook her head once as if to clear it, and now, stroking Katie's hair, kissed her forehead.

"I love you, sweetheart," she said. "I love you very much."

Then she replaced the sheet over Katie and turned to look at the doctor, who had remained silent and immobile during all of this. She started to say thank you, but couldn't. She took one step, then another.

We caught her before she hit the deck, and the doctor shouted for someone to bring in a stretcher. Together we lifted Dr. Romero onto it, sliding the gurney out into the hallway. As we came out another orderly was coming in, preparing to move Katie to the morgue. The ER speakers blared an impending arrival, traumatic arrest, ETA sixty seconds, and Remy let me go, turning back into the room, heading for the clean table, the next victim.

The doors shut behind him as he entered, and before they closed completely, I caught a glimpse of Katie being

wheeled out of the room. Her hand had been tucked back
under the sheet and with it the last evidence of her was
gone, and all that remained was a cover for the dead and a
stack of bloody surgical instruments needing to be steril-
ized.

CHAPTER ELEVEN

Dr. Romero was out for only three or four minutes, and for her sake, I was sorry it didn't last longer. She was regaining consciousness within a minute of the stretcher being placed against a wall.

Her glasses were off, safe in my hand, and without them to protect her eyes I could read everything in them when she began looking around. Confusion transforming into comprehension and then despair, all as she sat up, Dale helping her, and carefully swung her legs off the side of the stretcher.

"Don't get up yet," I said.

But I needn't have said anything. The sobs tore at her fiercely, muscle spasms that rocked the stretcher and made me fear she'd fall. The casters on the stretcher clicked with her tremors. She reached a hand toward me and for some reason I thought she wanted her glasses, but as I extended them to her she grabbed my wrist and pulled me in, using me as a support to pull herself to her feet, and then she was crying against me. Her shudders shifted into me, her wailing sobs and the pain in my chest getting stronger and stronger, fighting to be let out. No tears for me; I fought that back with everything I had left. No tears yet. Not now and not here, and not when Felice needed to hold on to something, when the something was me.

I couldn't think of anything else to do.

Amidst this and the noise of the ER came another sound, a mob of cameras and flashbulbs, and the sounds of the press being restrained. A door had opened, then closed again.

Natalie spoke in my ear. "We need to move her."

I nodded, not wanting to say anything.

Natalie spoke softly to Dale, telling him to find a route out and get a cab, have it waiting by the loading dock. He moved out of my periphery, and as he did so more movement caught my eye, Rubin coming in closer and something more.

"Sir, I want you to leave," I heard Fowler say. "Leave, now, or I'll have you brought in for harassment."

"I came to express my condolences," said Crowell.

My first instinct was to go for my gun, and my hand was halfway back before I remembered Rubin had it. Felice was turning, looking up at the sound of the voice, and I let her go to see him, standing inside the doors from the Walk-In Clinic, the eyes of the media pressed against the glass staring in. Crowell was wearing a light suit similar to the one I'd first seen him in, drab linen pants and a white shirt with a tan tie, holding his jacket over his arm like a butler waiting to dress his master. Fowler was approaching, Lozano and another officer with him, and as they did so the blond man beside Crowell took two steps forward. He did it with the air and posture of a bully.

It felt like I moved forward easily, as if I stepped on the air and not the ground, and as I moved I told Crowell what I was going to do to him, and why I was going to do it, but to recall the exact words is more than I can honestly do now. I wanted his blood and was going to get it, until Fowler grabbed me and Rubin grabbed me and Lozano grabbed me and everyone told me to calm down, to calm the fuck down.

Not that I didn't feel calm. I didn't feel anything but an almost arousing thrill at the terror in Jonathan Crowell's face as he backed up, slipping behind the other man.

"Atticus, stop it," said Rubin. "Stop it." He slipped in front of me, put both hands on my chest, and pushed back hard, and I stopped resisting but he didn't move me back.

"Scared?" I asked Crowell. "Terrified?"

"Stop it."

"Fucking coward," I said. "Your goon there can't protect you, Jonathan," I said. "You're a marked man. Your time is running out. You're going to die, and nothing you can do will stop that. You happy? You like what you've created? You took a life today, a young woman who could never hurt anyone. Are you proud? How can you fucking sleep at night?"

"Atticus, that's enough." Rubin pushed harder, once, sending me back off his hands until we separated, and I caught my balance, straightened.

"Yeah, that's enough," I said.

Crowell was behind his man, looking out from around the other's blond hair. The blond looked like a beaten pit bull, ready to put the bite on someone, and although I knew it wouldn't happen here, I desperately wanted it to be me. Crowell wasn't saying anything, and Lozano was approaching him, speaking softly, saying that he had some questions that Crowell and Mr. Rich should answer.

"This is not what I have ever been about," Crowell told Lozano. "I am for life and have always been opposed to murder. This is a tragedy.

"I wanted to express my condolences," he said again.

Dr. Romero said: "You wanted to do nothing of the sort. You're here for the reporters, trying to make yourself look big." She walked toward him, Natalie right on her, and for a moment the division seemed perfect, everybody else incidental. Crowell and Rich on one side, Romero and Natalie on the other.

"You're not big. You're nothing," Felice said softly. "You killed my daughter, and you claim to work in the name of God. You did all of this to be big, and all you are is small and narrow and scared. So don't pretend you care what happened to me today, and don't pretend to care about my daughter. Because I hold you responsible. Kodiak is right, you're a murderer and you're scared. Hide behind your speeches, lie as best you can, but you know the truth, and you know this is your work.

"Tiny little man, nothing little man. You call me a butcher and you took a true life today. How can you even compare the two? Go away, little man. Go away and try to make yourself big again."

She stopped in his face, looking up at him, tear tracks shimmering on her and power roaring in her, and nobody could say anything. Crowell's mouth was open as he looked at her, but he didn't even seem to be breathing. Then Natalie took Dr. Romero's arm and turned her, coming eye to eye with Rich, brushing him with an elbow, and the two women walked out of the room.

Rubin and I followed, heading out the door and back to the loading dock.

CHAPTER TWELVE

She was standing in the hall, just beyond the door, facing us. She had raven black hair about her shoulders, almost blue where the light caught it, accentuating the paleness of her skin. She was at least as tall as I, and slim, with strength in her shoulders and a beautiful oval face, strong-jawed with a narrow chin and a small mouth with full lips, and very blue eyes. Both her ears were pierced several times, small hoops and studs, with one hoop high in the cartilage on her left ear. Another hoop, thinner than the rest, was through her left nostril.

Not a reporter, I thought.

Her leather biker jacket was open, and she had a white tank top on beneath it, tucked into faded blue jeans. Her feet were in a pair of well-worn Doc Martens.

Definitely not a reporter, I thought.

The blue eyes flicked over each of us, then settled on me, and she said, "Kodiak?"

"Not now," I said, and continued down the hall.

"Natalie, tell him who I am," she said.

Natalie said, "This is a bad time, Bridgett."

Bridgett said, "This won't sit."

"Later."

"I'll come with you," Bridgett said.

"Like hell," I said.

She fell into step with us, on my right. "I'm a PI," Bridgett said to me. "I've been hired to help you, to investigate the threats."

"By who?" I asked.

Natalie answered that one. "Dr. Faisall wanted an investigator, asked me for a recommendation."

"And I appreciate it," Bridgett said, moving up in front of me and neatly cutting my peripheral vision. "I need to talk to you about Crowell."

"If you don't stop blocking my vision, I'll break your arm," I said.

"Forgive me," she said. "I assume somebody was blocking your vision this morning, too?"

On my left, Natalie visibly flinched.

"Who the fuck do you think you are?" I said.

"Bridgett Logan," she said, pulling her wallet and holding it out in front of me. "I'm with Agra and Donnovan Investigations. My PI license, see? Want to know what's on my driver's license, too? It says I'm twenty-eight, six feet one, my birthday's November ninth, and my eyes are blue."

I said to Natalie, "Keep going, I'll catch up. Keep your radio on." Then I stopped and put a bloodstained arm out to block Logan's progress, and we faced each other for a few seconds while I stood her against the wall. I got a whiff of shampoo and mint off her.

"I need to talk to you about Crowell," she said.

"Not now."

"Then I'll come with you," she said. "I'm working for the clinic."

"No, you won't," I said. "And I don't care if you were hired by the whole governing board of NARAL. I've got a grieving principal to secure and people to debrief, and I can't do it if I'm playing Q and A with private eyes."

"Then I'll come with you and we can do it after," Logan said.

The frustration and rage I felt at that moment were almost unbearable. Here was this woman showing up and implying it was negligence on my part that Katie was dead, having the gall to do it in front of Felice. And she just stood in front of me, eyes met to mine, no sign of backing off. The light caught on the niobium ring through her nostril, reflecting blue.

"They'll leave without us," she said.

"Uh-huh."

She shook her head, then reached in a pocket for a roll of Life Savers. She pulled one into her mouth with her teeth, never taking her eyes from mine, then offered me the roll. Pep-O-Mint. "Have a sweet, stud," Logan said. "Lighten up."

I ignored the roll. "Why don't you just scurry on home, or something, and I'll contact you when I'm ready."

She straightened her back a little more, drawing up to her full height. "Scurry?" she said softly.

I figured that the cab had left by then, so I moved my arm and turned my back to her, started walking to the loading dock. She fell in on my right and asked, "Where'd they take the doctor?"

"I don't know."

"Some bodyguard," Logan said. "At this rate, you'll lose both of them."

I stopped again, and went face-to-face with her, angry enough that it showed. Her jaw tightened.

"This is the wrong time to be pushing me," I said quietly. "The absolute wrong time. My client just lost her daughter, and if you think that means business as usual to me, you're walking with the wrong crowd." I pointed back to the ER. "Crowell's that way, maybe you'd be happier working for him. Otherwise, go away, now. I'll contact you when I am ready. Not a moment before."

I turned from Bridgett Logan and headed down the hall.

The rest of the morning was a confusion after I rendezvoused with the others—a ragged collage of statements given to the police and the Feds, of movement and more movement, trying to find Felice a safe place to grieve. Rubin finally suggested using his studio, and by one that afternoon we had settled Dr. Romero in.

The studio Rubin used was a joint venture with some other artists he knew, an attempt to find work space without having to pay Manhattan's ridiculous prices for privacy. Each artist paid a quarter of the rent, they all had open access, and they all respected each other's space. It was nothing more than a large loft in Chelsea, broken into four roughly equal quadrants. On the north side of the room were four large windows that looked out over the street, and Dale immediately went to those to double-check our security.

The room had an adjoining bathroom and kitchenette, but that was the extent of the space. Dr. Romero moved to Rubin's corner, spiritless and disinterested in what we were doing. After our departure from the hospital she had crumbled again, ignoring us, returning to the pain inside.

I helped her settle, spreading the army blanket that Rubin kept with his equipment. If she wanted to lie down, at least she could be almost comfortable.

"I want to go home," Felice said.

"We can't," I told her. "It isn't secure." Her apartment would have to be cleaned up, I knew, and she shouldn't have to be the one to do it. The bloodstains would probably never come out of the carpet.

"It's my home," she said.

"I know, Felice. I'm sorry."

She turned, looked at me for the first time since we left the hospital. "What did you say?" she asked.

"We can't take you home. I'm sorry."

The blow came up so fast I didn't even think about moving, and then my head was ringing and she was drawing her right hand back again. Her voice was as smooth and cold as a sheet of arctic ice.

"You bastard," Felice said, slapping me again. "You bastard, you're sorry?" Her hand flew again, and I didn't flinch, just felt the blow echo inside my head, and then she was timing her slaps to the words, each one hitting for punctuation, emphasis, and a terrible anger. "You liar, you bastard liar, you said you'd keep us safe, you said—"

Natalie was between us suddenly, and I stepped back, feeling my left cheek burn and blood leak into my mouth. Felice tried to push past Natalie, explaining deliberately that I was a liar, that I had lied, that I had killed her baby. Natalie took her by the shoulders and told Felice to stop.

"Bastard," Felice said, and then pulled away from Natalie. She sat on a stool, looking at the wall Rubin had painted with spray-painted scenes, cops and Latin Kings and life on the mean streets.

Natalie turned to me. She said, "Sentinel has a safe apartment. We can send Dale to get the car and then move her. You want me to call my father?"

Felice was smoking, and that was the only way I could tell she was breathing.

"Atticus? You want me to call my father?"

I nodded, starting to move toward Felice. Natalie put up an arm and shook her head and I stopped. When she was sure I wouldn't move, she went to the phone and started dialing, drawing her red hair back to place the receiver against her ear.

My cheek still burned, and I touched it again, looking at each of my people. Ostensibly, we seemed to be holding up all right, keeping our grief separate from the work at hand.

But Dale was checking the window over and over again, and he's not the nervous type. And Rubin was now sitting on a stool, staring at his bloody hands. And Natalie was trying hard to keep her voice under control while she spoke to her father.

Little things.

"Rubin," I said. "Go get cleaned up."

He kept looking at his hands. Then he nodded, slowly found some spare clothes under one of his palettes, and went into the bathroom. I heard the shower start.

Natalie hung up the phone. "Somebody's already using it," she said. "Some damn brat from Saudi Arabia, and my father won't move him. We can get it sometime tomorrow."

"Did he see Selby?"

"He was at her place when the news broke the story about Katie. Says that Selby took it hard, that she wanted to go to the hospital to see—"

From the window, Dale said, "We've got a watcher."

Both Natalie and I immediately went to him.

"Green Porsche parked on the corner right after we got here," Dale said, indicating it. "A guy got out, wearing a baseball cap, headed around the corner." He looked at me. "Took him five minutes, but he doubled back, just came into the building."

"Carrying?" I said.

"Hands were clear."

"Pistol, probably," Natalie said.

I nodded, drew my weapon. "Dale, keep watching, use the radio." Then I went to the bathroom door and knocked on it, saying, "Get dressed and get out here. Dale needs backup."

Natalie was waiting for me by the door, her Glock out. I looked back at where Romero was still seated. She hadn't moved.

I turned the bolt on the door soundlessly, and Natalie grabbed one of the handles, prepared to slide it back on its runners. The door was metal and covered in flaking gray paint. I backed to the other side of the door and went down to a crouch, then gave her a nod.

She ran the door back with one quick motion and I rolled out as soon as there was room, seeing motion at the end of the hall and coming up with my weapon. I had sighted the dot on the end of my barrel to Bridgett Logan's throat before I recognized her.

Both her hands came up immediately. "Friendly, friendly!" she said.

She had put on a Yankee cap, piled her hair under it, and was sitting on the floor beside the stairs. I kept my gun on her, hearing Natalie move behind me.

"Are you fucking insane?" Natalie asked. "You could've gotten yourself shot."

Logan didn't answer her, keeping her hands up and her eyes on me.

After a moment, Natalie said, "It's all right, Atticus."

I released the handle on my gun, uncocking it, letting air leak out of my nose. Then I got up and holstered my weapon, saying, "Go away." I went back inside.

She followed me in, Natalie behind her. "Kodiak," Bridgett Logan said. "We need to talk."

"I told you, when I'm ready."

Natalie slid the door shut and locked it, saying, "Did you follow us?"

"Him," Bridgett said, gesturing at me. She turned to me and said, "You made it damn hard to do, too."

Dale and Rubin were around Romero, and I gave them a short nod. They backed off the doctor, but not a lot, still wary of Logan.

She said, "Nobody was following me."

"You're certain?" I asked.

"Yes," Bridgett said.

"Good." I pointed at the door.

She shook her head. "You've got me whether you like it or not. I've been hired to assist and to lead an independent investigation, and I need your help." Lowering her voice, she said, "I'm not leaving until we've got things squared, Kodiak. You'll have to throw me out, and I guarantee you, I won't make that easy."

I watched Dr. Romero. She smoked, staring at the floor.

"Are we all right here?" I asked Natalie.

"We're fine for now," she said. "Just go with Bridgett, Atticus. Get home, clean up, answer her questions. Three of us here will be fine."

Logan didn't say anything.

"Okay," I said. "Fine, let's go."

It was Logan's Porsche, a forest-green turbocharged 911 Carrera with a sunroof and whale tail. She disarmed the alarm and unlocked my door, ushering me into the vehicle with definite pride.

"Where am I taking you?" she said, turning the stereo on. Sisters of Mercy blared, and she adjusted the volume to a low roar.

"Thompson, off Bleecker," I said.

She nodded. We hit a light and she pulled her roll of Life Savers again, dropped three in her mouth one after the other, crunching each. Then she killed the roll, popping the last one, sucking this time. She tossed the empty wrapper over her shoulder into the tiny backseat. "Oral fixation," she said.

I nodded and continued to look out the window.

The light changed and we started rolling again. She drove quickly, but with absolute control, using the Porsche perfectly. She used its speed, too, edging eighty at one point on Broadway.

"Have you talked to Fowler or Lozano?" she asked.

"Not since making statements."

"The CSU's report of both the apartment and the shooter's position came back," she told me. "The FBI's leading on the case. They triangulated back to a point of origin for the shots.''

"And?"

"Second-floor fire escape landing. Looks like someone came down from the roof and took the shot from the landing on the second floor. Witnesses have given a description of the shooter: white male, blond or light brown hair, approximately six feet tall. No eye color, strong, broad-shouldered. They're continuing the canvass.''

"Sounds like Barry," I said.

"He's a little short for it," Bridgett said. "I'm thinking it's the guy who was with Crowell at the hospital."

"Rich."

"NYPD is checking their alibis," she said.

"Good for them," I said and was silent for the rest of the drive.

I picked up the mail in the lobby, then led Bridgett Logan up the six flights of stairs to the apartment I shared with Rubin. I put her in the kitchen and told her I was going to shower and change.

"Mind if I use your phone?" she asked, removing her jacket and hanging it on the back of the chair.

"Why not?" I said and went into my room where I stripped, threw my clothes in a corner, then grabbed my robe. As I went down the hall to the bathroom Bridgett stopped dialing long enough to turn and watch me.

"Can I make coffee or anything?"

"Whatever you want," I said and went to take my shower.

The blood on my hands had dried and flaked off, and the two chances I'd had previously to use a bathroom had gotten me only so clean. I stayed under the water for twenty minutes, scrubbing hard, then soaking up the steam. The hot shower felt good. It was midafternoon

now, and the day was only getting longer, and I only
wanted it to end.

After I had dressed in some clean jeans and a decent
shirt, food became a sudden priority. Bridgett was still
seated at the table where I had left her.

"Talked to NYPD," she said. "They've got a make on
the weapon."

"You want a sandwich?"

She shook her head. "Remington M-seven hundred,
thirty-ought-six," she said.

I got two bottles of beer from the fridge and held one
out to her. She looked at it and at me, then nodded. I
opened both of them, handed one to her, then started to
make myself a sandwich.

"They found two intact slugs at Romero's apartment,"
Bridgett said. "If they find the weapon they'll be able to
make the match."

I nodded, and layered mustard on one of my slices of
bread. I put the sandwich together, tore a paper towel to
use as a place mat, and set my meal on the table. The
indicator light on the answering machine was blinking, so
I pressed "play" and then cleaned up the kitchen as the
messages ran.

Eight messages from reporters, one from Alison, who
said, "Atticus? Oh, God, I just heard. Are you okay? I
don't know where to reach you and I don't want to use
your pager, so if you get this, give me a call, okay? I'm at
work until five, and then I'll be in all night. I'm so sorry."

I sat back at the table and picked up my sandwich.

"Significant other?" Bridgett asked.

I nodded.

"You going to call her?"

"I'm going to eat first," I said. The sandwich was good,
lean pastrami and thin slices of provolone. I'd found some
crisp lettuce on a back shelf and added that to it. I was
almost finished when I tasted it.

Syrup.

Maple syrup.

Bridgett asked, "Are you okay?"

I shook my head, gagging, rose to the sink and I spat. The beer didn't kill the taste, even when I rinsed my mouth out with it twice. She had risen, now standing beside me at the sink, and as I hunched over, Bridgett put a hand on my back as I coughed and my eyes clouded with tears. I was certain I was going to vomit; then I was fine and standing up, catching my breath.

"Are you okay?" she asked again.

I shook my head. "Syrup," I said.

"I'm sorry?"

"Katie had waffles for breakfast." I blew a long breath out. "We did CPR on her, Rubin and me. I should warn him."

She hesitated, then put her hand on my back again. I stiffened and she withdrew it, going back to her seat at the table.

For a while I just stood at the sink, thinking about it. Finally I said, "What do you want?"

"I want to see Crowell and I want you to come with me," Bridgett said.

"Why?"

"Two reasons. First, I understand you scared the crap out of him at the hospital. Lozano says that Crowell was in fear for his life. Second, you were there when Katie died, and if he's got an ounce of conscience and he is responsible, he'll be hard-pressed to lie to your face."

"He's the last man I want to see right now."

She seemed to relax a bit, stretching her legs out in front of her with a sigh. She had long legs. "I know. If it's one of Crowell's people that did this, going to see him is a hell of a good way to shake things up."

I gave it a little more thought, then nodded. "Let me make a phone call first," I said. "I'll meet you at your car."

She rose and started for the door. Then she stopped and

looked back at me. "That crack I made at the hospital," she said. "That was cruel. I owe you an apology."

I didn't say anything and she shook her head slightly, then said, "I'll be downstairs."

After she shut the door, I called Alison at work. A co-worker picked up her phone and told me that she was at lunch. I didn't leave a message.

Before leaving I put my weapon back on, feeling the weight of the gun in my hand before saddling it to my hip. On my desk was a manila folder, swollen with copies of all the threats Felice and the clinic had received since Common Ground had been announced. I took that as well, wondering how Crowell would react to them.

Going down the stairs I realized that if Bridgett Logan was right about how Crowell reacted to me, perhaps there was more Common Ground between him and Felice than I had realized.

Both knew fear.

CHAPTER THIRTEEN

"How much do you know about Sword of the Silent?" Bridgett Logan asked me as she guided her Porsche uptown. I had a private address for Crowell on Central Park West in the low nineties, and we had a ways to go before we got there.

"Enough," I said. "They formed in late '88, shortly after Randal Terry and Operation: Rescue made it big in Atlanta. Crowell has boasted that their national membership is over one hundred thousand, but that's probably ten times higher than it really is. They target a clinic in a given city and then use terror tactics to intimidate both patients and personnel. Since the Federal Access to Clinic Entrances legislation was passed in '94 they've had to cool off a bit and get smarter about it, but they're still doing it."

"What kind of tactics?"

"Special Agent Fowler gave me copies of almost fifty

arrest reports from the last six months or so, all of them for suspected SOS members," I said. "They range from illegal possession of a weapon, menacing, stalking, to two members in California who are awaiting trial for attempted murder. Another member in North Dakota is being sought for questioning in the death of a doctor there."

"And none of that has ever been tied back to Crowell?"

"Not as far as I know."

"So he's either very smart or very lucky."

"It would make me a lot happier if he was lucky," I said.

"I'll bet."

I cringed as she shot the Porsche through a collapsing vise made by two cabs on either side of us. Somehow, we made it through the gap unscathed. Bridgett chuckled. "Car like this," she said, "you've got to drive aggressively or it gets mad at you."

"It's very nice," I said.

"Nice?" Bridgett said, her eyes going wide. "Nice? This is a Twin Turbo Porsche Carrera nine-eleven, over four hundred horses of power, all-wheel drive, the works. This animal tops out at over one hundred and eighty miles per hour, zero to sixty in three point seven seconds, and stops on a dime leaving you wanting a cigarette.

"This car is pure sex, stud. It is not 'nice.' "

I let that sink in, looking around at the leather interior, listening to the engine growl underneath the music from the tape deck. It was an amazing car.

"You're a PI?" I asked.

"That's what the license says."

"How the hell can you afford a car like this? Are you crooked?"

Bridgett grinned, flashed white teeth at me. "It's my inheritance from my ma," she said.

"Your mother left you a Porsche."

"My mother was in coach class on a seven-thirty-seven

that crashed and burned in Cincinnati," she said. "She was well insured."

"I'm sorry," I said.

"Yeah, it sucks. Two years now." She found a new roll of Life Savers in a pocket, tore off the top with her teeth, and pulled one into her mouth. These were Wint-O-Green. "What do you know about Crowell?"

"He's in his early fifties, says he went to Harvard Divinity," I said. "I doubt that but haven't checked. Fowler says he's got a record, an arrest in '75 in Wichita for A and B against a woman who worked at the local CBS affiliate. Charges were dismissed. Arrested again three years later in Indiana for firebombing a clinic there. Spent three years inside. He's written two books, both about abortion and the collapse of the American morality."

"A Renaissance man," Bridgett said.

"I suppose."

She didn't say anything else until we had parked across from Crowell's apartment building. Then she killed the engine, and looked at the folder I'd taken from the apartment. "What's that?"

"Copies of the threats sent to the clinic," I said, and handed it to her. She began leafing through them as I said, "They're in chronological order, back to when the conference was announced."

She nodded without looking up. "You going to let Romero go?"

"I have to," I said.

Bridgett looked at me. "They didn't get her this morning, they'll try again, right? They'll try for her there."

"Probably."

"Then don't let her go."

"I can't forbid her from doing anything. I can only advise her against it."

"Hell of a job you've got," she said, and looked back at the letters. I looked across the street, watching the traffic in front of the building.

Bridgett made small noises to herself while reading, whether of amusement or disgust, I wasn't sure. Finally, she said, "There's no sexist like a holy sexist. How do you think these are done?" She gestured at the letters.

"Somebody, perhaps several somebodys, sits around a keyboard and types them up. I think they're done in committee, but I don't know why I think that. They print it out and copy it, destroy the original, then drop the copy in the mail."

"They probably delete the file from the computer, too," she said.

I started to agree, then stopped, and looked carefully at the man entering the apartment building.

"That's Barry," I said.

Bridgett turned to look. "No shit? I wonder where he's been."

"In for questioning?"

She shook her head. "They were done with them hours ago." She took the keys out of the ignition and opened her door. "Coming?"

I nodded and took the file, then got out of the Porsche and followed her across the street. She led without looking for traffic, forcing a Mazda to swerve out of her way. She waited for me on the sidewalk, set the alarm on the Porsche from her remote, then slipped her arm around my waist, and said, "Let's go, stud."

We walked right past the doorman, Bridgett giggling at me and saying, "You're so nasty!" She slipped one hand under my shirt and then licked my ear. The doorman politely averted his gaze, and she clung to me while we waited for the elevator. Inside the car, she punched 14 and, when the doors closed, released me, taking the file with her. "Mind if I hold this?"

I shrugged. "You lick well," I told her.

"And not only ears," she said. "But don't get any ideas."

Crowell was in 14J, and Bridgett Logan knocked on the door twice, hard. We waited patiently, side by side, as we were examined through the eyehole. Then the door opened and Clarence Barry was standing there, a film of sweat on his forehead. He still had on his windbreaker, and for a moment I thought he looked alarmed.

Barry barely acknowledged Bridgett, working hard to intimidate me through posture and eye contact. We locked each other up and his hand drifted a fraction toward the gun on his hip, then returned to neutral at his waist.

"Hello, cocksucker," he said to me. "You're a dead man."

"Just back from hiding the rifle?" I asked him.

Bridgett said, "Boys, boys, not in the hall."

Barry ignored her. "I'm going to fucking do your ass, then I'll waste this bitch," he said.

He was making a serious threat, he meant what he was saying, and the viciousness of his words surprised me. It's frightening to be told by a man carrying a gun that he's going to kill you. But that fear went quickly as our stares lengthened, and suddenly I couldn't take him seriously at all, this childish petulance, the bruises on his face where he had hit the pavement with me on his back, his nose broken from that impact. He was only an ape in a suit, and it wasn't a particularly nice suit, at that. He'd have had better luck trying to intimidate me while sitting on the toilet.

Bridgett said, "My name's Bridgett Logan. I was wondering if I could speak to Mr. Crowell."

"He's busy." He had an accent, hard Appalachian, and when he spoke he moved his right hand over his mouth, maybe reassuring himself that it had indeed worked. A small tattoo of a dagger, green with age, folded between his thumb and forefinger.

"He'll see us. We're here from the LifeCare clinic. We want to ask him a few questions."

"He's not here, bitch."

"Thought you said he was busy?" I said.

"He's busy not being here," he said to me. Then he smiled, pleased with the inventiveness of his answer.

"Mr. Crowell," Bridgett called. "Can I talk to you?"

For a moment we all stood in silence, waiting, then, as Barry started to close the door, a voice said, "Who else is out there?"

"The bodyguard," Barry said.

"Show them in, Clarence."

Clarence would have preferred to show us out, preferably through the window. Somehow he restrained his baser urge and opened the door again. Bridgett went right past him into an open living room, but I waited a moment, simply smiling at Barry. The hate in his eyes was delicious; the resentment foamed inside him. He wanted so badly to hurt me and his master wouldn't let him. I followed Bridgett.

Jonathan Crowell stood in front of a big black leather recliner, and he motioned Bridgett and me to the big black leather sofa that sat opposite it. He gave Bridgett a good look-over before doing anything else, and she gave him one of her own.

"I trust you're not here to beat me up?" Crowell finally asked me.

"Depends on what happens next, I suppose," I said.

He smiled at me, and I thought that I was wrong, that he and Felice had nothing in common at all. He sank back into his recliner and asked, "Then what can I do for you?"

"Where's Rich?" I sat down beside Bridgett.

Crowell raised his eyebrows at me. "I have no idea."

"I got the impression at the hospital that he was your bodyguard."

"No, Mr. Kodiak. I have no need for anyone like you."

"Really? Then what does Rich do?"

His forced gentility slipped. "He's our Personnel Director. And before you ask, I'll tell you exactly what I told the NYPD and the FBI. Mr. Rich, Mr. Barry, and myself were having breakfast with an SOS chapter in Yonkers this morning. None of us murdered little Katie Romero."

"Well, none of you pulled the trigger, at least," I said.

Bridgett shot me a look designed to drop charging elephants. I gave her my best turns-knees-into-water smile. It didn't work. She said easily to Crowell, "We have some questions we're hoping you can answer."

Barry came around from behind me, sliding around the room like an oil spill, shutting the doors and checking for traps. He moved to stand behind Crowell's chair, trying to stare at both Bridgett and me at the same time. After a while he gave up on Bridgett and concentrated solely on me.

"I've already spoken to the authorities," Crowell said. He smoothed his tie carefully down along his chest, assuring himself that it was entirely centered. The tie was silk, striped blue and white on a green background. His shirt was ivory-white and heavily starched, with French cuffs, and tucked neatly into tan pleated pants. On crossed feet hung black leather shoes with pristine soles, as if he had never touched the ground in them. According to his manner, that was precisely what he wanted you to think.

"This is independent," Bridgett told him. "We've got some questions about the letters Dr. Romero and the clinic have received."

Crowell took a sip of mineral water from a bottle on the table beside his chair and said, to me, "I don't imagine I'll be of any more help to you than I was to that Mexican."

"Detective Lozano, you mean?" I asked.

Crowell nodded and turned his head to look out the window at the view across Central Park.

"He's Cuban," I said.

He waved a hand in dismissal. The hand was clean and sported a class ring from Harvard on one finger. I wondered how much it had cost him. "I don't know anything about the letters," Crowell said.

Bridgett opened the folder and set each letter out, chronologically, on the coffee table before Crowell. It took a minute and all the space on the table, and Crowell made a sour face to pass the time. Barry never moved; I'm not certain he even blinked. When Bridgett was finished Crowell looked at them briefly, then out the window. "I've never seen these before."

"Didn't Detective Lozano show them to you?" Bridgett asked.

He considered that, then looked at me again. "Yes, yes he did. And the FBI men, too. I meant, I've never seen the originals."

"So you have seen these before?" Bridgett pressed, the glint of a very sharp edge in her voice.

Crowell stood and walked to the window and stood there, admiring the expensive view. At least, I thought he was admiring the view. He pointed. "The Jewish Museum is over there." He lowered his arm and waited. When he got no response from us he waited some more, then said, "It's all just decay down there. You do know that, don't you? This city is only a small part of this country, but it embodies everything in this nation. Everything here can be found between Maine and Alaska. And it's all falling apart."

"So you have seen these before, Mr. Crowell?" Bridgett repeated. The edge in her voice was clearer now, and the muscles in her jaw tightened after she spoke.

Without turning Crowell said, "And it is falling apart from the heart, from the center. As this city is the center of this nation, this nation is falling apart. As the family is falling apart, so is this city, corrupted, diminished by parasites who refuse God's law. The true values of the American family have been distorted by all those people who now live here, groups with their perverted special interests and their selfish, hedonistic concerns. They are slowly tugging the thread that built this city, unraveling it, and thus the country, leaving us a ruin that may never be repaired."

It was as if he spoke to a huge audience beyond the pane of glass and had forgotten we were in the room. Barry was staring at his back, probably expecting Crowell to sprout wings and a halo.

"I'm right, you know that," Crowell continued. "You never hear about a Christian being arrested for dealing crack. Godless is what we have become, forsaking the Word for our own petty delights. And unless we find God again, we shall be destroyed." He turned and his eyes rested on Bridgett. "Unless our women understand their duty, we shall be destroyed." He looked at me. "Unless our men lead the way, we shall be destroyed."

He turned back to the window and raised both his arms so he looked, in silhouette, like Christ on the Cross. He rolled his head back and said, nearly sobbing, "Unless each and every baby killer is stopped, each and every factory of death is dismantled, we shall all be destroyed. Unless we stop the holocaust of the unborn innocents, we shall all be destroyed. There can be no rest, no hope, no salvation for any of us, until we stop this mad butchery of our own children."

It was grand theater. He didn't move, rigid in his own imagined crucifixion. Bridgett shifted on the couch, making the leather sigh, the tension coiled in her, looking for an out.

Considering the scene Crowell was playing, his apartment was remarkably secular. Only one religious artifact, a large stainless-steel cross wrapped in barbed wire, hung on the wall over the television cabinet. He had two shelves loaded with books, a large easy chair for reading beside them. A well-shined brass lamp stood beside the chair. On the floor beside the coffee table, where Bridgett had moved them to lay out the letters, were hardcover copies of his two books, *Abortuaries and the Death of America* and *Innocence Slaughtered*. Neither copy looked to have ever been opened. I picked up one and looked at the photograph on the back. Crowell looked out sternly at the camera. I put the book back on the floor. The carpet was slate gray, as empty of feeling as the apartment.

Clarence Barry beamed at Crowell's back. Still no wings.

The only emotion worth speaking of was Crowell's, whose arms must have been aching something fierce.

Bridgett Logan said, "So . . . your answer is no?"

Crowell lowered his arms gracefully and spun slowly on the Italian-shod ball of his right foot to face us. "You see," he said, "it is not that I want the blight purged from us with fire and wrath. It is simply that the blight must be purged, and if fire and wrath are the only instruments for the task, then they, of course, must be used.

"Our Lord does not act alone. He acts through us."

Bridgett found her roll of Life Savers and began chewing on one.

"No compromise?" I asked.

He smiled thinly. "One does not bargain with God, Mr. Kodiak. If we are moved to act, then act we must and by any means at our disposal."

"Even if those means are murder?" Bridgett asked, looking at the roll of candy in her hand.

"Man's law is nothing. God's law is supreme. Man can only mock God. Man mocks God's laws all the time. Man means nothing if Man does not live according to God's law," Crowell said. He said it to me. Not once since we had started speaking had he looked at Bridgett. When he chose to answer her, he relayed the answer through me as if I were her interpreter.

"Correct me if I'm way off base here, but isn't murder against God's law?" she asked.

"That is precisely the point," he said to me.

Bridgett's shoulders shifted, and I expected her to throw her roll of candy at Crowell, but she didn't. Instead, she ate another Life Saver.

I asked, "You plan to attend the Common Ground summit, don't you?"

He hesitated for a moment, then nodded.

"The entire purpose of the summit is to find compromise," I said. "By attending, won't you be participating in the mockery you've just so eloquently denounced?"

"We all have a right to speak," Crowell said to me. I think he liked it that I had called him eloquent. "I would be more than a fool if I let such an opportunity to spread my message pass me by without seizing it."

"And that Katie Romero's death has made you all the more visible has nothing to do with it?" Bridgett asked.

"I am not an opportunist," he told me. "I am a servant of Our Lord."

"Your rhetoric's lovely," I said. "Really, it is. And the theological aspects of the debate are fascinating, too, but really immaterial, and neither answers our questions. We're asking you if you know who is threatening Dr. Romero."

He returned to his seat and picked up his mineral water. "I have answered your questions, Mr. Kodiak. But, as God's law obviously means nothing to you, I'll explain it to you clearly. You are not a Christian, and I should know better than to try to appeal to you as one."

"Or to me," Bridgett said. Crowell ignored her. She pulled a new pack of Life Savers from her pocket and began unwrapping them, dropping the foil on the carpet. Barry started at the offense, but remained in place, looking as if he'd love to snap her neck.

"I do not know who is sending those letters," Crowell said. "And if I did, I do not think I would tell you. I do not know who murdered Dr. Romero's poor daughter, but if I did know that, I certainly would not tell you; I would tell the police. And as for the conference, yes, I believe Common Ground is a mockery, and it will surely fail. And that, to completely answer your previous question, is my entire reason for going. I will bring down the house by speaking the truth."

"Did you tell this to the police and FBI?" Bridgett asked.

"I told them something similar," he said to me.

"He told them something similar," I said to Bridgett. "But he didn't tell them the same thing. Because knowledge that a crime is going to be committed, and not telling the police about it, that's called being an accessory."

"It's called being an accessory," Bridgett told Crowell. She offered him a red Life Saver.

"*If* I did know, I said. But I do not." Crowell smiled.

"You wouldn't tell me if someone was planning to murder Dr. Romero?" I asked.

"We're talking about letters, not murder."

"No," I said. "We're talking about murder. Is that what happened? Somebody thought they were shooting Felice and murdered Katie by mistake?"

"Your implication is that I know who shot the girl," Crowell said.

"Very good. That's exactly my implication," I said, leaning forward.

Barry tensed to move, but Crowell kept his eyes on me, and if he was intimidated, he didn't show it. "This interrogation is over," he said evenly. "I have business to attend to."

"The letters come from your group," Bridgett said. "Someone in Sword of the Silent is mailing these letters, possibly several people. That means that someone you are responsible for wants to stop abortion, and thinks that killing Dr. Romero is the way to do it. And maybe that someone murdered Katie Romero by accident this morning. Doesn't that bother you at all?"

For the first time since we'd walked into the room, Crowell's eyes rested on her. Very carefully he said, "If I were to subscribe to your theory, young lady, then my only possible answer would be, yes, it does. Just as it should bother you and Mr. Kodiak that Felice Romero has murdered thousands of preborn children this year. If I am culpable in this thing, then you are equally culpable in that."

He looked at his watch. It had a gold band and looked exceptionally expensive. "You can show yourselves out," Crowell said. "And I expect I'll see you on Saturday, Mr. Kodiak. At the conference."

I helped Bridgett gather up the letters and then we stood and Crowell stood, and nobody offered anybody a hand. We walked to the door and Clarence Barry cut in front of us to open it.

As I went out the door after Bridgett, Barry leaned in to my ear and hissed, "You're dead and you're mine."

The sky had filled with clouds the color of fresh bruises. Bridgett strode right across the street, again ignoring the traffic, and I thought she was going to her car, but instead she went for the stone wall separating the rest of Manhattan on the west from Central Park. She perched on the wall and searched her pockets with one hand, waving me toward her with the other. She started in on another candy, offering me one from the roll. I took it and felt my mouth suddenly cool.

"Tasty, huh?"

"Why don't you smoke?"

"Can't stand cigarettes," she said. "Don't mind the occasional cigar, though, if it's from Cuba."

I looked up at Crowell's windows.

"Well?"

"They're up to something. You didn't catch it, but your boyfriend in there looked more than a little worried when his boss said they had business to do." She looked up at the sky and squinted. "Looks like rain."

"What now?" I asked.

"Crowell's going out, you heard him say it. I want to follow him."

"Good luck. He'll make you the second he leaves. You're not exactly inconspicuous."

She tapped her nose ring. "You'd be surprised."

"If he starts on foot, you're in trouble."

"This is Manhattan. There's always a cab when you need one. It's the law."

"You trying to get rid of me?"

"*You* didn't want anything to do with *me*, remember? You head back to your people, check on Romero." She fished another pocket and came out with a business card and a pen. She scribbled something on the back, then handed it to me. "My home number's on there. Give me a call tonight." The card had Agra and Donnovan on it, her name below, and Investigator beneath that. The agency's address was listed on Fifth, and there were two phone numbers, office and car. She'd written her home number on the back.

"You really should have a backup," I said.

"I'll be fine."

"You're that good?"

"I'm better," Bridgett Logan said, and she wasn't joking.

The discussion became academic because at that moment Crowell and Barry appeared in the doorway, stopping to chastise the doorman. It looked like Crowell was doing most of the chastising, and they didn't seem to have noticed us across the street. Some of the angry notes Crowell hit made it through the traffic to us.

Bridgett saw them when I did and spun on her backside, dropping over the wall and into the park. I felt like an idiot as I followed her. We sat for a moment with our backs to the stone. An empty bottle of malt liquor dug into my leg. At least it wasn't broken glass. I hoped I wasn't sitting in dog shit.

"Should I call you Rockford or Spenser, maybe?" I asked.

"Eat me." She turned and stuck her nose over the wall,

dropping the folder with the letters in it on my lap. An elderly black woman in a pretty summer dress stopped and stared at us as she walked an Airedale along the path. I smiled at her. She smiled at me. The Airedale licked its nose.

"Nice day," I said to her.

She nodded and said, "Looks like rain, though." They continued on.

"Well?" I asked Bridgett.

"They're done with the doorman and now they're talking to each other out front. They didn't see us."

"Oh, goody."

"Wait—wait—a Cadillac just pulled up."

I peeked over the wall beside her. The driver's window was down and Rich was at the wheel. "The third man," I said.

"Looks like Rich," she said.

"Looks like Rich," I agreed.

Crowell opened the front passenger's door and got in. Barry shut the door for him.

I ducked back down as Bridgett lowered her nose and backed up on all fours a few feet until she could stand without being too obvious. "I'm going to go for my car," she said. "Follow Crowell."

"Better hurry."

"Call me, stud," she said, and took off up the path parallel to where she had parked the car. I watched her vault the wall and disappear.

I sat with the folder on my lap feeling stupid. Then I decided what the hell and took another peep over the wall. A bus had pulled up across the street, and I couldn't see either Crowell or Barry, and Bridgett's Porsche was disappearing to the south, so I stood up and brushed the seat of my pants off. They were damp, hopefully with nothing more offensive than water. The bus roared as it pulled away, and revealed no one recognizable in front of Crowell's building. Enough with this, I decided. She's the PI, let her do the tailing.

As I went over the wall and started up to the subway stop at Ninety-sixth Street, the sky opened. By the time I crossed at Ninety-fourth to catch the downtown track none of me was dry, and the folder had transformed into a limp cardboard sandwich. My glasses started to fog, my sneakers squished, and my pants clung to my legs, the seams chafing as I walked. The steps down to the train were cracked tile, slippery and treacherous. I pushed my token in and stepped up to the platform, listening to the water falling down the stairs. My hair stuck against my neck, dripping water down my back, and I shook my head to move things around, but it didn't do much good.

One corner of my shirt was not absolutely drenched, having been tucked in, and with it my glasses became functional again. After putting them back on I shot a look down the tunnel, trying to spot the advancing train. The tunnel was empty.

Waiting behind the yellow line, I looked across at the uptown platform and saw Barry leaning against a pylon, smoking. He was looking at his feet and as he shifted his glance around I turned, trying to conceal myself.

Uptown was the clinic. There was a stop on 135th, I knew; I'd been using it. My gut went tight, apprehensive. Bridgett was supposed to follow Crowell, and according to her, Barry hadn't been pleased about their going out for "business." The odds were he wasn't going to another prayer meeting. On top of that, Barry was a hard case, a son of a bitch, and I wasn't going to give him the chance to throw another bottle, to be party to the murder of another girl. I wasn't going to be scared off by his threats. That wasn't going to happen.

By the time I had concluded all of this, I was vaulting the exit turnstile, charging across the street to the uptown track. Vaulting was stupid, and I slipped when I landed, losing my balance and nearly cracking my head on the tile.

Overcompensating, I used the hand holding the folder to stop me from tipping into the wall, nearly kicking a vagrant as I did so. The folder crumpled with my weight but nothing fell out. The vagrant cursed and then fell back asleep. Water splashed up my pants as I ran up the stairs, looked both ways, and sprinted across the street. The rain was coming down so hard and so fast it seemed to be jumping skyward from the pavement.

From the uptown entrance came the sound of the subway train crushing air out of its way as it entered the station. Down the stairs two, three at a time, I jumped the entrance turnstile, enraging the girl working the change booth. Whatever she screamed was lost in the bulletproof glass protecting her from the rest of the world, and I caught the doors on the train just as they started to close.

The doors met on my left arm, sighed, jerked open again, and let me through.

Thing with New York, most people don't pay attention to anything out of the ordinary. It's not that they don't see it, they just don't want to confront it. So it was with me, standing inside the door, wet and clutching a sodden and torn manila folder, trickling a puddle at my feet. The only person in the car who paid me any mind was a toddler in her father's lap. She pointed at me and giggled. Her father stared straight ahead. The train lurched forward, and the driver announced our next stop as something that might have been Saskatoon, but which I translated as 103rd Street. Using one of the handgrips to steady myself, I looked for Barry. He wasn't in the car.

I'd come in at the south end of the train, and checked that end first. Looking through the connecting door into the other car brought me a pretty full view, but left the near corners vacant. Halfway to the north end of the car it struck me that I was being exceptionally dim. If I was so certain Barry was headed for the clinic, all I had to do was get out at 135th, so I sat down and tried to get my glasses dried again. I succeeded in making the big drops turn into smaller streaks, but that was it.

It was my luck to get an air-conditioned car, too, and by the time we hit 135th Street I was shivering in my wet clothes. Getting back onto the humid platform was small relief turned great when I glimpsed Barry as he started up the stairs. I followed a group of Latino kids out of the station and into the downpour. A bolt of lightning lanced the sky, thunder flowing over it. The kids shrieked, then laughed, joking in a babble of Spanish.

Barry wasn't worried about being followed. He headed straight as a lame bull on a charge to the corner, then surprised me by turning right and heading to Eighth Avenue. Halfway down the block he turned into a diner, and I crossed to the opposite side of the street. He gave no sign of having made me, but from across the street I could barely read the lettering on the diner's window through the rain, let alone see anything inside. After waiting five minutes I crossed over, coming at the restaurant from the right corner of the awning. A steady stream of runoff from the rain gutter doused me as I looked in the window. It had begun to steam up, but it was possible to make out faces inside.

Barry sat at a full booth, his profile to the window, making points to the rest of the group with a meat-tenderizer of a hand. I recognized one other person in the booth, then another when a woman joined them. The woman was the same small, bitter one who had accosted Alison on our way out after her abortion, the one who performed elective surgeries on toy babies. It took a few seconds to be certain about the other one. None other than the bushily bearded man I had straight-armed into the street. He was the hardest to recognize; he had shaved off the beard. Without it, his chin looked naked and soft. I realized as I hadn't when we'd tussled that he was overweight, perhaps by as much as thirty or forty pounds.

Barry produced a small walkie-talkie from his drenched

suit jacket and showed it to everyone at the table. They nodded in complete understanding or agreement, and he keyed it and spoke briefly to the grille.

A much-abused pay phone hung against a building three doors east, but I didn't want to be that close in case anyone came out. Back on the other side of the street was another phone, between a video rental closet and a liquor store, and I dodged cars and cabs and people with umbrellas to get to it. I didn't have any coins other than subway tokens and rushed into the liquor store for change.

The counterman was surly and demanded I buy something. I grabbed a tin of Altoids and gave him a five. He took all the time in the world to make change, and didn't seem to understand that I wanted quarters. While he played with his register, I looked out the door and saw people leaving the diner. As far as I could see, Barry wasn't among them.

"I thought you wanted change, man," the counterman snarled. I went back to him and he gave me my bills first, the change after, coin by coin. I almost asked him if he was on Crowell's payroll.

Barry stood in the doorway of the diner talking to one of his cronies when I stepped out of the store. I put my back to them at the phone. The quarters were clumsy between my fingers. I dialed the clinic and turned around, waiting for somebody to pick up while keeping my eyes on the front of the diner. Barry was heading back inside, and down 135th I could see the troop of Crowell's Christian foot soldiers, doggedly putting one foot in front of the other, heads down in the rain.

But Barry hadn't left yet; he was waiting for something. The diner could have a back door, in which case I was screwed, but I didn't think that was the planned exit. They had done their tricks and thought they were clean. They wouldn't be pulling anything more out of their hats.

"Women's LifeCare, may I help you?"

"Lynn, this is Atticus. Put Sheldon on."

Delfleur put me on hold fast, and I was afraid she'd thought it was a prank call and cut me off. As I waited, Barry emerged from the diner once more, starting a cigarette, using the building to shield his lighter from the rain. Then he went to the pay phone, and with the smoke dangling from his lips, brought out his walkie-talkie again. What I would have done for one now I didn't think about; it was lying on my futon at home.

Barry spoke into the radio, then brought it to his ear to listen to the reply. At that point Sheldon came on the phone. "What's up?"

"What's it look like there?"

He didn't waste any time. "We've got a small group of the moderates, here, you know, offering post-abortion counseling, but they're well outnumbered by SOSers. About one hundred of them out front, maybe more. The back alley's had people moving in and out of it all day; we've got maybe twenty-five there, now. Some are carrying backpacks, sacks, looks like they've got equipment. Building's secure, not a whole lot of patients today, seeing as how the doctor isn't in. We've had people shouting at us all day, since the news broke, you believe it? Feminist Majority is here, too, preparing to counter if anything should happen. There are a few 'We loved Katie' signs."

"Anything else?"

"That FBI guy is here, says they've got intelligence that something's going down. Neither he or I like the Ryder truck that's been parked across the street for the last two hours. Nobody's opened it up yet. We've got some cops here with hats and bats, and there's a VW van unloading more people as I speak."

"I'm looking at one of Crowell's lapdogs right now," I told him, watching Barry pick up the pay phone and dial. "He's just met with a group of protesters and sent them back to the clinic. I don't know—"

"Hold on," Sheldon said. Over the receiver I heard him say, "Keep him on the line—keep him on the line, and use the checklist, and find the FBI dude." He came back to me. "Got to evacuate. Bomb threat."

I dropped the receiver and the folder and sprinted across the street to where Barry was still speaking on the phone.

"—in the abortuary room," he was saying. "It'll blow every fucking one of you into pieces."

Well, maybe Crowell wouldn't be polite enough to roll over when faced with my and Bridgett's double-teaming interrogation, but this wasn't bad, and it was all I needed. Barry caught me reflected in the window as I moved, but too late. Taking his left shoulder with my right hand, I spun him back around, then drove my left forearm up under his chin, pinioning him against the wall. His face flushed, and he started to bring his fist around to punch, but I put my right knee into his stomach. He would have doubled over if I'd let him, but instead my forearm kept him upright and the air came out of him like foul exhaust, bitter smoke and bitter thoughts. His nose was broken from our first dance, when he had kissed asphalt, so it couldn't be easy for him to breathe.

The phone swung on its cable, and I could hear a tinny voice asking if he was still there.

"Bomb threat, Clarence?" I asked Barry, patting him down with my right hand. He was carrying his radio on his hip and I pulled it off his belt and dropped it on the pavement. His eyes darted to it, then back to me. They were opened wide, the small blood vessels revealed above and below his corneas, and his eyes repeated what they'd said earlier: He hated me. "Moving up from just one murder, huh, shithead? Going for double digits, now? Bomb threat? Is it real? Is it real, Clarence?"

He didn't say anything. I kept moving my hand, finding his wallet and dropping that, too. I found his gun, exactly where I'd seen it earlier. It was a semiautomatic pistol, a Smith & Wesson, and it slipped easily from its holster. I brought it around to his stomach, shielding the weapon with my body. We locked eyes and listened to the rain for a second or two before I said, "Nice gun."

My thumb found the safety and I moved back just enough for him to see me flick it off. He did, his eyes going down and then coming back to my face. Hatred turned to terror fed by hatred, and in that moment it could have gone either way—resistance or compliance.

"You wanted a piece of me, that right? How about I take a piece from you, Clarence? You chamber your first round? It's double action, I pull the trigger, you roll the dice." I pushed the barrel hard into his stomach, keeping it pressed there, waiting for his answer.

When he didn't speak I pulled the trigger.

He screamed and his muscles went slack and suddenly I was holding him up in the rain with my forearm and the gun and no help from him.

"Take that as a no," I said.

He couldn't speak, shaking, trying to stand, scrabbling at the wet wall. The scent of urine rose off him, suddenly. I took my grip off him long enough to work the slide on the pistol. The round clicked into place loudly, assured, and there was no question this time. I put my forearm back under his throat and he began to sob as I jabbed him again with the gun.

"Now, don't start crying on me, Clarence," I said.

"It's a fake," he whimpered.

"If you're lying I'll kill you."

"You'll kill me anyway. It's a fake, man."

With the gun as a prod we moved sideways to the phone. I took my left arm off Barry and felt for the phone cord, finding it and bringing the receiver to my ear.

"Hello?"

"Lynn, it's Atticus. Clarence wants to tell you something." I pressed the phone against Barry's face.

"It's a fake," Barry whispered.

"Thank God," I heard Lynn say as I brought the phone back to my ear.

"Call the cops," I said. "We're at a diner on a Hundred Thirty-fifth at Eighth."

When the cops found us we were inside, Barry sitting at the counter, me beside him, his gun off to a side. The manager and waitress, the only people in the place, were concerned until I explained that Barry was a terrorist. Then the waitress spat on him. Barry took it, not moving, sitting in his wet pants, his hands flat on the counter. The manager went outside and came back with Barry's wallet and the radio. Miraculously, neither had been stolen.

Two uniforms led by Lozano showed up and I rose when they came in, backing away from the counter. Lozano came in angry, harried, and said without preamble, "Mirandize him."

The uniforms paused for a moment, unsure which of us he meant, then the younger cop went to Barry, and when Lozano made no protest, his partner followed. The pat down was thorough and slow, and the officer who did it made a lot of noise about Clarence's loose bladder. Lozano glared at me while they cuffed him, read him his rights, and led him out. They read him his rights slowly, taking no chances this time. It was almost satisfying to watch.

At the door, Barry turned, gave me a hard stare, and said, "I'm going to fucking do you."

I blew him a kiss.

"Shut him the fuck up," Lozano told the cops. After the door swung closed with a little tinkle of bells Lozano pointed to the Smith & Wesson on the counter and gave me the evil eye and I shook my head.

Lozano said, "How's the coffee here?"

"Ground fresh daily."

The manager poured two mugs and we sat at one of the booths. Lozano sipped his coffee silently, and I didn't feel the need to say anything, so I followed suit. I took the mug carefully when I drank, fighting my shaking hands, hoping Lozano wouldn't notice. He did, I'm certain, but didn't say anything. After a minute or two, the manager said, "Hey, you, uh, want this gun, here?"

Lozano turned his head and nodded and the manager started to pick it up. "Stop," Lozano said. It was a bark. The manager stopped, then shrugged and went to the pie case, scrubbing at the glass with a rag and not looking at us. The waitress sat down, saying, "Fucking city." When the manager was finished with the pie case he went to clean the stool Barry had used.

"You touch the weapon?" Lozano asked me.

"I took it off him."

"You got a witness?"

"No. But he's got the empty holster, not me," I said.

Lozano looked at the ceiling and shut his eyes, saying, "This is turning into one bitch of a day. They kill the girl, then they pull this." He looked back to the counter, then finished his coffee. "You're sure the call was a fake?"

"Absolutely."

Lozano turned to look full at me, and I tried hard not to look guilty. He raised the mug in his left hand, sticking his arm out as if signaling a turn.

"Fucking city," the waitress repeated, and she walked to the coffeemaker and took the pot from the burner, then refilled our cups. Her uniform was powder blue and she wore white nylons with a run on the inside of her left leg.

"What'd you do to him?" Lozano asked, looking again at the counter.

"Nothing," I said.

"Nothing made him piss on himself?"

"I caught him on the phone making the threat. I took his gun when he tried to fight me. He lost bladder control when he lost the piece."

"You threaten him?"

"No."

He didn't believe me, and his body language made no

bones about that. "Why're you lying to me, Atticus? I thought we were friends, here."

"We are, Detective. I didn't do anything to him."

He sipped some more of his coffee. "How'd you know he's the one that phoned the threat?"

"I heard him. He told me it was a fake."

"Did he? Anybody else hear that?"

"Just me."

"So, you were following this guy? Eight hours after Katie Romero is murdered, you just happen to be following one of our prime suspects, a guy who threw a bottle at Katie's mother? You just happen to be following a guy you already mixed it up with once? Tell me this isn't what it looks like, Atticus."

I explained what had happened, including the meeting with Crowell, to set the stage. I did not tell him about pulling the trigger on Barry. Lozano drank his coffee in silence while I spoke, measuring my words with his eyes on mine.

"Where's the dick?"

"Jeez, Detective. Don't you have a better slang term for a private investigator?"

"You prefer peeper? Where is she?"

"I don't know. She went after Crowell."

"We've spoken to Crowell twice already. You two shouldn't have gone to see him. And following Barry, that's loco. What the hell were you thinking? Why aren't you watching Romero?"

"She's well covered," I said.

"Yeah, but not by you, and that's your job." Lozano finished his second cup of coffee, putting the mug down hard. "You worry me, Kodiak. If Barry says you used excessive force, if I find one single witness, I'll rein you in and I'll rein you in hard." He stood up, pulling his wallet out of his back pocket. He put a five carefully on the table and said, "The girl is dead, and that is rotten, sad action. Don't make it worse."

"Don't forget the gun," I said. Outside, the rain had slowed and the streets were dark and slick.

He stared down at the weapon, snapping on a surgical glove without looking at his hands. Then he took the pistol and dropped it into a paper bag provided by the manager.

"This better not be your way of dealing with grief," Lozano said. "You tell that peeper of yours to come talk to me, get this all straightened out. She doesn't, I'm going to go looking for her."

"I'll tell her," I said.

"You keep your head straight," he said to me, and left.

CHAPTER FOURTEEN

I used the diner bathroom after Lozano left. I stood in front of the mirror, leaning on the sink, for what seemed like a long time. My blood was roaring in my ears.

If Barry had chambered his first round, he would have been dying from a gut wound even as I was staring at my reflection. If Barry had chambered his first round, I would have been on my way to prison, and I wouldn't be coming back for a very long time. If Barry had chambered his first round, I would have murdered him in cold blood while looking in his eyes, and I would have been happy doing it.

The trigger had gone back before I had realized I was pulling it. The hammer had fallen before I knew what I had done. And when the pistol had dry-fired, all I had thought of was racking the slide and trying again.

What I wanted to do was be sick, to vomit in the dirty, cramped bathroom at the back of this tacky diner. I wanted to throw up and get whatever was inside me out. I gagged over the sink, spitting sticky strands of saliva, but succeeded only in getting stomach cramps that pinched me from diaphragm to groin. Nothing came up; it wouldn't let go.

After a while I ran some cold water and splashed my face, melting the tears away. Then I cleaned my glasses and left.

The walk to the clinic was short, the rain tapering from downpour to downtrickle, and I came to the corner of 135th and Amsterdam in time to see protest become pandemonium.

The rain had done nothing to the crowd of protesters. A few had tried to cover up, pulling windbreakers over their heads to shield themselves, but that was all the consideration the weather warranted, except to an elderly woman on the east side of Amsterdam. Holding a sheaf of sodden photocopies in one hand, she tilted her head back and called out something about the cleansing power of God. Her and Robert De Niro.

People were screaming at each other. A chorus of anti-abortionists had started a chant of "Two, four, eight, ten, All you women want to be men." NARAL and the Feminist Majority had trained countertroops, mostly women, from their teens to their forties, arms locked, an immobile line. They countered with, "Two, four, eight, ten, Why are your leaders always men?"

A corps of police officers in riot gear were pushing people back across their perimeter line, their face shields still up, waiting for the order. The actual court-designated property line for the clinic was somewhere in the middle of the street, as arbitrary now as it had ever been. Both groups ignored it freely. The antis had rushed hard and strong, and now were being driven back. Both factions had crossed the line, where the officers held it, looking grim.

Watching the bodies twist and press against each other, I realized how angry I was, and I felt the weight of the holster on my hip.

And I knew I couldn't trust myself.

Parked up on the sidewalk was a large yellow Ryder truck, and I stepped around it, trying to get a look in the back. It was open and empty but for a young man sitting with his legs dangling over the edge. He had a compact two-way radio on his belt. He gestured to the sky and said, "Out of nowhere, huh?"

"Yeah."

"You fall back?"

I nodded.

"You should get back in there. Crowell's coming."

"Really?"

"You bet."

I didn't move for a moment, and the young man continued to watch me. His face was small and soft, and his posture vaguely confrontational. He pulled the radio off his belt and held it against his thigh.

"You're not with us, are you?" he asked.

"Depends. Who are you?"

"Sword of the Silent."

"Ah, no, I'm not with you, then."

"You condone the murder of babies?" He asked it evenly enough.

"There's some debate about that. Calling them babies, I mean."

"All life is sacred. Only God has the right to take life. Baby murderers are no better than common criminals, protected by a godless president who promotes godless laws."

I was tempted to ask him if he was a vegetarian, but instead said, "Crowell teach you that?"

"Our Lord taught me that. He died teaching us all that."

I said, "Actually, I'm Jewish."

He didn't even blink. "Of course. I should have known. And you complain about the Holocaust, while another happens under your nose."

"Been nice talking to you," I said.

"I'll pray for your soul," he told me as I walked away.

A car horn started barking, coming closer, and several people lowered their "Stop the Murder" signs and headed toward the source, the white Cadillac that Rich had driven up outside Crowell's building. It parked illegally just long enough to let Crowell out. The rain had picked up again, and I tried to wipe my glasses off again but gave up and looked past the water drops. I couldn't see either Bridgett or her car anywhere on the street.

The arrival had an obvious effect. Both sides got louder. A lot louder. Crowell emerged from the Caddy, waving nonchalantly, like a movie star at a premiere. Other than a raincoat, he was dressed just as before. The moderates began backing to the opposite side of the street, trying to distance themselves from SOS. Crowell leaned back inside the car and brought out a bullhorn, then slammed the door. As the Cadillac pulled away, he began to speak.

"Dr. Romero," he said, his voice low and crackling. "Dr. Romero, can you hear me? What would you do if you had only five minutes left to live?"

The crowd went nuts.

Son of a bitch, I thought. He knows she isn't here and he pulls this. Her daughter dead hardly eight hours, and he pulls this.

Son of a bitch.

The noise dulled to a low roar, then Crowell said, "Listen to me, now," and the SOS crowd went silent. "Listen to me, now," he said again. "Please, in the name of God and all that Jesus holds holy, please, do not murder any more babies. Stop your slaughter of those silent innocents who die beyond your doors. Your own child today joined the ranks of the fallen, and yet you continue. Oh, dear God, please stop, please do not let her kill any more babies, do not let her murder any more women or their children. Please . . . oh, please."

Everyone was listening and everyone was still. Along the pro-choice line I caught a rustle of movement, some bowed heads speaking to one another, but that was all. The moderates had regrouped at the corner, and were watching the proceedings sadly.

"Beloved, my Christian friends, we are now at a time where our resolve will be most surely tested.

"We all have heard what has happened today. We all know the events visited upon Dr. Romero this morning."

Some people actually cheered. But then Crowell raised his left hand and they again fell silent. Raindrops beaded and dripped from the end of his bullhorn.

"We do not rejoice in this," he said. "As the Lord said to the Israelites on the shores of the Red Sea, these too are my children, and you will find no glory in their deaths.

"We find no glory in the Lord's punishments. Yet we must remain strong, our resolve must not falter. We have all heard of Common Ground. We have heard of the promise of peace through compromise. The events of this day surely speak to such a reconciliation, seductively draw us to more mainstream protests.

"But it is a lie! There can be no common ground, there can be no rest, no peace, no reconciliation. This is a war of absolutes. We cannot just save half a baby, rescue only some of the preborn. It is all or nothing, all or nothing, and what has been visited upon Dr. Felice Romero this day, that is her punishment, and not ours!"

This earned him more cheers and, finally, some aggressive booing and heckling. Crowell didn't seem to mind either reaction. I could see movement at the second floor windows of the clinic, several scared and bewildered faces looking out of the waiting room above.

"This is a house of sin, of horror and torture, of women trapped and bound, held helpless where their children are torn from them. Bloody and broken, these infants come from their screaming mothers. We must never forget this.

"This 'surgery,'" Crowell shouted, and he made the word drip with scorn, "this, 'elective and ambulatory procedure' is murder, bloody, calculated, state-sanctioned murder! It is barbarism, and it is, most of all, a crime against God! And we must never, ever, stop our fight! In the name of God and Our Lord Jesus Christ, we must fight on!"

Crowell's declaration echoed. A counterchant started, not quite on time, and instead of clear words it sounded like garbled tape, chewed and torn.

This was just what his people wanted to hear. They were soaking up every word, assenting, nodding. Crowell wiped rain out of his eyes and said, at first softly, then louder and louder, "No common ground. No common ground. No common ground," until the crowd picked up the cadence of the words, and began chanting them with him. The volume swelled, thunderously loud suddenly, swallowing up the counterchant of *"Choice, choice, choice."* Then Crowell waved his hand once and silenced them again.

"The Lord is vengeful," he shouted. "The Lord is strong. The Lord will destroy that which offends Him. With fire and cleansing wrath, will the Lord purify this place."

Cries from everyone, Amens and Praise Gods and Go to Hells. Men and women exhorted Jesus to right now descend from heaven and smite everyone inside the building. And the crowd was moving suddenly, a great surge toward the clinic doors. I took a step forward.

A window on the ground floor broke and inside the building, someone screamed. Another window shattered, then several, simultaneously. A woman shrieked and fell back, dropping her NARAL sign, blood on her forehead.

During a portion of the Gulf War I had been assigned to

coordinate the protection of a general, and we had been in Tel Aviv when Hussein started dropping SCUDs on Israel. They came at night, the few times they came at all, and they came out of a stillness and silence suddenly pierced by air-raid sirens and people desperate for their lives. There would be nothing, then the sirens, and then immediate movement, people frantically trying to bring loved ones to safety, to save themselves. It was a crowd mentality I had never seen before, people moving ferociously for one reason.

This was worse. This wasn't for survival. These people wanted blood.

Everything I was wanted to move, everything I had ever learned told me to act, to do something. But I stood in the rainfall, on the sidewalk, inadequate, fighting the cold irrational rage of the mob. Lists of options presented themselves to me, courses of action and protection and security, and instead of doing what I was meant to do, what I was trained to do, I dropped anchor and just let myself be beaten upon by the rain.

Crowell was climbing back into the Cadillac, his head low. Police tried to reach him, failing, pinned in by the rushing crowd.

It was as if Crowell's troops had spurs driving them. They threw themselves against the opposing line, the cops, and the clinic building like amphetamine-keyed lemmings. Young kids, just children, were pushed forward into the crowd by their parents, urged to rush the clinic, and some were crying, clinging to their mothers or fathers. Another first-floor window broke.

The doors were holding, nobody was getting inside. The pro-choice line had regrouped and reformed, and was now forging a reinforced cordon, pressing the antis away from the building. With their success, the police seemed to get the upper hand, too, and the massive push turned into fractured fits and starts, kamikaze missions flown by apathetic pilots.

The Cadillac had pulled away, now replaced by emergency vehicles, police cars, an EMS rig. The initial threat was gone, already, but it had been replaced by the death rattle of the assault. Some still resisted passively, and some seemed not to have been involved at all, serenely holding their signs and repeating their rain-soaked litany of hope and salvation.

Entering the clinic was out of the question. Thirty or forty people were still crushed against the door or on the stairs leading to the entrance. I tried to spot faces, again seeing the bushy beard, now ex–bushy beard, as he was dragged by two uniformed officers to the first paddy wagon.

"Hey, stud, can I offer you a cup of coffee?"

Bridgett Logan was beside me. Her hair had been flattened by the rain, and it clung to her face, making her skin seem almost alabaster pale, and her eyes vividly blue. She smiled at my reaction to her, holding the cup out.

The heat from the cup warmed my hands. My fingers looked like flesh-colored raisins, and they began to hurt as I popped the tab on the cover, sipping. The coffee was hot and sweet, a lot of sugar, no cream.

"You like it?"

"It's awful sweet."

"You're a sweetie." She was drinking hers black, the top off the cup, and side by side we surveyed the street together. After a while she said, "How long you been here?"

"Little before Crowell arrived. You?"

"Little after him. Lost him, figured that meant he'd be coming here, booked back. I'm parked at the back of the clinic. Missed Crowell's speech, though. Made it just in time for the floor show."

"You should have heard the monologue. He managed to remove any guilt the SOS crowd might have had about protesting the same day that Katie Romero died."

"Oooh," she moaned, wiping raindrops from her face. "That man just makes my knees go to water."

She drained her cup and crumpled it, and we walked back on the sidewalk, getting against a doorway for shelter. Looking over at the stairs, I saw what the problem was with the entrance. Six people had chained themselves together, wrapping links about their necks, then looping the ends around the banisters on either side and locking them with the standard Kryptonite locks. Bolt cutters just don't work on those things. A couple of uniforms were talking to the group, trying to persuade them to surrender the keys. Then one of the officers went to get the bolt cutters anyway, probably to use on the chains.

"How'd you get here?" Bridgett asked. I told her. I even told her about Barry. When I was finished she asked, "You knew that he hadn't chambered that round, right?"

"No."

She bit her lower lip, eyes narrowing. She shook her head, once, then said, "Where are the letters?"

"Stuck to the sidewalk by that diner. They were a write-off anyway."

"With the rain, yeah. I'll call Lozano, straighten him out," she said. She dropped her crumpled cup in the trash can on the corner. "So, you figure that Crowell's friend Clarence was going to call somebody with that radio of his after he made his bomb threat and tell them exactly when to rush?"

"Yeah, that's what I figure. The attempted break-in last night was probably to make the threat more serious."

"They would have gotten inside while everyone was trying to get out. Nice job, fighting the good fight."

"It's not good," I said. "It's just a fight."

She began searching her pockets and I remembered I'd bought the tin of Altoids with her in mind. I fished it out of my pocket and handed it to her. She took it, saying, "Cool. These things are great."

"Don't let it be said I don't think of you."

After sucking on an Altoid for a few seconds she crunched it between her teeth and said, "You're pro-abortion, right?"

"I'm more pro a woman's right to choose."

"One of those," she said.

"One of those what?"

She sighed. The mint was gone and she took out another one. "Sensitive-fucking-men. Whatever you want, honey. Whatever works for you. It's your choice. Of course it is. Has been all along."

"I'm not following you."

"Men have been behind this thing from the start. It's always been a woman's right to choose. That's obvious, and that's not the problem. That's not what it's about for men."

"So what is it about?"

"Look at Crowell. Look at John Burt, and his boot camp for pregnant mothers in Pensacola. He takes half their welfare checks to cover expenses, you know that? What do *you* think it's about, stud? It's all about power over women. It's all about the fact that men believe they have the right to give women the choice in the first place. That's all it's ever been fucking about." She tossed the mint into her mouth, then said, "Hey! Look at that, the door's clear." She started across the street, her head high in the rain.

CHAPTER FIFTEEN

"That wasn't a rush," Sheldon said. "That was a god-damn riot."

We looked out the broken reception window onto Amsterdam where the rain was falling in waves. Now and then the crackle of police radios carried inside, over the voices and traffic from the street. At our feet glass shards peppered the black-and-white linoleum, and when any of us moved the pieces cracked and popped. Paint, red, tacky and bright, streaked and puddled on the walls, furniture, and floor.

Scott Fowler was speaking in low tones on one of the phones at reception, talking to his supervisor. He had nodded at me once when I came in, but that was it.

Two paddy wagons were outside, prisoners being transferred from one to the other. After the second was filled, a uniform slammed the doors shut and locked it up, thumping the side of the vehicle. It started down the street. I watched the officer walk to the other wagon, now empty, kneeling down near the driver's door to say something to the man who had locked himself to the drive shaft. The gag was getting old; Randal Terry's people had perfected the inventive application of Kryptonite bicycle locks and drive shafts in the late '80s. Someone would have to drill the lock off the man, a dangerous job, considering he had locked himself around the neck. If the drill slipped, the man was dead. Hard to tell if the protester was brave or just stupid.

Lynn Delfleur hung up her phone and said to Sheldon, "Someone should be out to fix the windows in a half hour."

"Fine. I don't think anyone else will try to come inside," he said. To me, he added, "You told us this would happen, that we needed screens instead of bars."

"It would have been too expensive to remove the bars and install grilles," I said.

He shook his head. "It's cheaper to just replace the windows."

I shrugged.

Fowler hung up the phone and said, "Atticus? Let's talk." Then he headed through the door into the staff lounge. I followed him, and Bridgett followed me.

When we got inside he shut the door and looked at Bridgett. When he tore his eyes away from her, he looked at me expectantly.

"Special Agent Scott Fowler, this is Bridgett Logan," I said, feeling very Emily Post. "She's with Agra and Donovan Investigations, and is being retained by the clinic to pursue an independent investigation."

"Pleasure," Fowler said, offering her his hand.

"Charmed," she said, then crunched her latest Altoid at him.

He lingered on the grip, I thought, but then let go and said to me, "Romero's safe?"

"Yes."

"How's she holding up?"

"Not well."

He frowned sympathetically, then pulled a folded sheet from his jacket pocket. "Came this morning. The original should be in D.C. by now."

I took the paper, unfolded it, then set it on the table so both Bridgett and I could read it.

Another letter.

DOCTOR OF PAIN—
WILL YOU CRY LIKE THEY CRY?
WEEP LIKE THEY WEEP?
BLEED AS THEY BLEED?
WAIL AS THEY WAIL?
DO YOU KNOW THEIR PAIN?
YOU WILL KNOW THEIR PAIN.
YOU WILL KNOW THEIR PAIN.
I WILL HAVE JUSTICE.

And again, no signature.

"And nothing on the envelope or letter, I assume?" Bridgett was scowling.

"Not so far," Fowler told her.

"This would've been sent when?" I asked.

"Local postmark," he said. "Stamped day before yesterday. I know what you're thinking, and I agree. It looks like it's by the same author that wrote the one Romero got at her home last night."

"Still wants justice," I said.

"This was probably sent the day after that other one. I'm sure they're sequential."

"There was another one like this?" Bridgett asked.

"It wasn't in the file," I said. "Never had a chance to copy it. It came last night to Romero's apartment, and Scott here took it straight to the Bureau. But the same phrase was used, that bit about having justice."

"Probably from the shooter," Fowler said. "Nothing

from the lab on that one, either, unless you want to hear about the paper type, so on."

"No, thank you," I said.

Bridgett ran her fingers through her wet hair, ruffling it back behind her ears. "You think that the fellow who shot Katie just did it on the spur of the moment?"

"Huh?" Fowler said.

She sighed and rolled her eyes my way, then back to Scott. "If the guy who wrote this is the shooter, then he took the shot on Katie as opportunity, maybe thinking that she was her mother. Because if he had planned to shoot Dr. Romero this morning, Dr. Romero never would have received this letter, right? Because she would be dead."

"She's right," I said.

Scott's brow creased slightly. "I suppose. Or Katie was the intended target all along."

"That makes no sense," Bridgett said.

Fowler's eyes never left her face. He might as well have been holding a sign asking Bridgett to have her way with him. "Well, perhaps the author knows the shooter," he said.

"Or he may be entirely independent, another nut entirely," I said. "We've got nothing to connect Katie's murder with the guy who wrote this."

"So, no clue as to the identity of the writer," Bridgett said.

"I'm working on it," Fowler said.

I folded the letter again and handed it back to him. "Anything else?"

"Federal marshals are on the way here," he said. "And they'll want to take over the security on Romero, as well."

I shook my head. "After the conference."

Both of them looked at me like I had just fallen out of the sky, complete with halo and harp. "You're joking, right?" Fowler asked.

"No. She's devastated right now, and I won't rotate new personnel in on her while she's grieving and disoriented. I assume the marshals will be at the conference, and I'll be happy to liaison with them, but they're not taking over my principal until Felice is ready for the change."

Fowler threw up his hands. "Jeez, Atticus, you've been riding me for marshals since this damn thing started."

"I know, and I'm glad they're coming in, but I want them kept away from her until I say otherwise. I'll let you know when she's ready for new people."

He didn't like it and didn't bother to hide it. "I'll see what I can do."

"Thanks," I said. "If that's it, then I'm going to head back to Romero and spell some of my people for a bit."

"Fine," he said. "I'll expect to hear from you later."

"You will." I went for the door.

"I'll walk you out," I heard Bridgett say.

Outside, she said, "You want a lift?"

I hesitated, looked at the rain, nodded. "Just make sure we're not followed," I said.

"I can do that."

We got into her Porsche and she pulled out, the wipers sighing against the windshield. By my watch it was a little after six, and the traffic was starting to get thick. I realized that just by the very nature of how Bridgett drove, tailing us would be difficult. She ran lights for sport. With the rain, it was almost a contact sport.

"What do you think?" she asked.

"About?"

"Those letters. You think there's more than one person after her?"

"I expect so. I have no idea how many people want her dead. Looking at that SOS crowd earlier, figure that all of them would love a shot at her."

"Not nice people," she said.

"Well, the SOSers, yeah, I agree. The problem is, they make all the other Right-to-Lifers look bad. They don't deserve that. There are plenty of antiabortion folks who would like nothing more than for Crowell and SOS to dry up and blow away. He's destroying their legitimacy."

"I don't have a hell of a lot of sympathy for their plight." Bridgett said it curtly.

"They have a right to be heard, like anybody else. Crowell's making that impossible."

"Well, there's the conference to give everybody their say."

"Yes, there is."

She didn't reply, and we drove for another twenty minutes or so with both of us checking mirrors. Neither of us thought we were being followed. Still, she parked three blocks south of the studio, just to be safe.

"I'll call Lozano when I get home," she said, flipping off the windshield wipers.

"Find out what Barry said when you do."

"Planning on it." Bridgett pulled a pad from her jacket pocket and a pen, and said, "Lemme have your number, stud." I told her my home and pager numbers, and she said, "I'll call tonight."

"I won't be in until after midnight," I said. "I've got to give my people some time off."

She nodded. "Tomorrow, then."

I got out of the car. The rain had finally stopped. Bridgett pulled my door closed, raised a hand in farewell, and pulled away.

CHAPTER SIXTEEN

I picked up three cups of coffee, some sandwiches, and two packs of cigarettes at the bodega on the corner, then went up to the studio and knocked loudly on the door. After a second I heard Dale shout, "Who is it?"

"Kodiak."

The bolt turned and I heard the bar slide back and then he said, "Go ahead, it's open."

When I ran the door back on its track, his gun was out, held in both hands, barrel pointing about maybe three or four inches from my feet. Dale nodded, released the hammer on his revolver slowly, and holstered while I shut the door again and looked around. It was dark in the studio, the only illumination from the street and the fixture in the bathroom. The light spilled out past the open door onto the floor. Natalie stood against the far wall, and her angle of fire would have cut me to flank steak if she had decided I was a threat. Rubin was standing in front of where Dr.

Romero was lying on a blanket on the floor. She looked asleep.

"Took you long enough," Natalie said. "I was afraid Bridie might've hurt you."

"Bridgett, you mean? She frightens me," I said.

Natalie laughed.

Dale sat on an unfinished stool in the near corner, and I handed the paper bag of groceries to him. "Coffee and sandwiches."

"You always did take good care of your crew," he said softly.

"Lord knows I try," I whispered. "I want you both to go home, get some rest," I told Rubin and Natalie. "Come back at midnight and relieve Dale and me."

Natalie nodded, and holstered her Glock. "She's been sleeping for the last two hours or so," she said, her voice low. "Hasn't said much of anything, hasn't eaten, hasn't used the bathroom. Been smoking too much."

"All right. You might want to call Bridgett when you get home. She can fill you in on what all happened today," I said.

"I will." She went to get her coat.

I told Rubin, "Be careful when you eat. I ended up tasting the memory of Katie's waffles."

He said, "I can't get the taste of orange juice out of my mouth."

"It'll pass," I said.

Rubin shook his head. "I've never seen death like that."

"No." I was trying to think of something more to say, something that would make it better, when Natalie came back, smoothing her blouse and skirt.

"I spoke to Felice about it," Natalie said. "I don't know if it took."

"She's right," I said. "It was my fault. You two get some rest."

Rubin nodded and Natalie shook her head. "You know that's a lie."

"Not to Felice."

She just shook her head again, then went to open the door. Dale set down the bag and drew his weapon once again and I drew mine, squeezing the grip and feeling the gun cock. Nobody was outside, and Natalie and Rubin went through and I approached and slid the door back, locking it.

Dale handed me a cup of coffee, saying, "You want one of the sandwiches?"

"I'm not hungry. Just leave one for Felice."

"No problem," Dale said. He resumed his seat on the stool, putting his feet up on a cardboard box and his back against the wall, his revolver off to his side.

I took my coffee and went over to the window. A police car was going down the block, but didn't seem to be doing anything more than a normal cruise. To my left, Felice Romero slept, curled on the blanket by the radiator, wrapped like a refugee. Someone had put a jacket over her shoulders, and her face was cut in half by streetlight and shadow, stark and angular in repose. I walked around the room once, slowly, looking in nooks and crannies and knowing that if anything had needed to be secured, Natalie or Dale or Rubin had already done it. When that was finished I went back to the window and took a seat on a folding chair, my feet up on the sill.

My coffee lasted almost an hour, and when the cup was empty I crushed it, folded it, unfolded it, tore it, and then, its entertainment value entirely exhausted, threw it out. Sitting post, as Dale and I were, is boring. It takes a lot of concentration and a lot of energy to remain aware and focused when there is really nothing to be aware of or focused on. Thank God the rain had stopped. The only thing worse than standing post in the dark is standing post in the dark in the rain. It's hard to stay awake anyway, but when water is beating a lullaby, it becomes next to impossible.

Around ten Dale got off his stool and headed to the

bathroom. I listened to him urinate and flush and then he opened the door and went back to his seat quietly. Down on the street three men staggered off the opposite sidewalk and into the gutter. After a bit they realized their mistake and mounted the curb again with the effort of the first expedition to conquer Everest. When they disappeared around the corner I sighed, loudly, not meaning to, just trying to oxygenate my body enough to keep from sleeping.

In Rubin's corner Felice stirred. I heard Dale shift on the stool, and I raised my hand to him, waved him back. She sat up, the jacket falling to the floor. She coughed, rich smoker's hacks, then rose, coming over to me. Her lighter flamed in the darkness.

"How long will I have to remain here?" she asked.

"Until tomorrow. We've got a safe apartment, but we may not have access to it until late in the day," I said.

"I don't know where to go." She didn't say it as much to me as to herself. I remembered the blood on the carpet. I knew then that she would sell the place, and I knew she would move somewhere else, maybe outside of the city, maybe outside of the state. It seemed to me that I should share this with her, let her know that I knew and that I understood, but I didn't.

She dragged a chair over the wooden floor and sat in it beside me. A cinder on the edge of her cigarette jumped as she knocked ash into an empty bottle. She put the bottle on the floor between her feet and remained hunched, able to reach it.

"Federal marshals are coming in," I said softly. "They'll want to take over your security."

"Are you quitting?" Felice asked.

"No," I said. "Absolutely not. I'm just saying you have a choice. You can have them protecting you."

"I want you protecting me."

"All right," I said.

"No marshals. You. Natalie. Dale. Rubin."

"I'll tell Fowler."

She drew on the cigarette, then exhaled, blowing the smoke over the cinder and making it flare brighter. When she spoke her voice was low and even.

"I tell you about my husband?"

"After you hired me, yes."

"He's an architect in Albany. We separated four years ago, just about, because my work was hurting his life. People were sending hate mail to his office, accosting his clients. They were parking outside of our house and scaring the neighbors, and he got to where he couldn't take it anymore." She smoked for a few seconds, silently, thinking. At the back of the room, I heard Dale shift again on the stool.

"Not to say that was all that did it," Felice continued. "Marriages have survived worse, but they were better marriages. I used to wonder if Katie hadn't been Down's if we would have stayed together. Maybe without her we could have taken the strain. Probably not. It's not so bad, now, but at first I used to miss him horribly. I'd come home to our apartment and Katie would always ask where Daddy was. She understood divorce, the concept of married people not wanting to be married anymore, but only inasmuch as the television explained it to her. She spent a few months expecting Marcus to return. But she seemed to forget about him pretty quickly. No visits, out of sight, out of mind."

She dropped the cigarette into the bottle, and there must have been some soda or water or something left in it, because there was a sharp hiss and then the cinder went out. She picked up the bottle by its neck and swung it in a small circle, making certain the cigarette was dead. "Do you think he's heard?" she asked.

"I'd think it's likely."

"I should call him."

"Tomorrow."

"Of course, tomorrow. How do you make funeral arrangements, do you know? I've never had to. I suppose you just call some funeral home and tell them where the body is and when you'd like it ready by. Give them your credit card number. Well, I've got time, don't I?" Her voice wobbled. "They won, didn't they? They've made my clinic a war zone and they've murdered my daughter and I don't have anything left to fight with. Tomorrow. Tomorrow and then the day after, and then, after the conference, I will no longer require your services, Mr. Kodiak."

She turned her head to look at me, meeting my eyes, and then she looked back out the window. "I am to be added to the growing list of defeated doctors," she said. "But at least I'm still out alive. I at least have that, don't I?" She said the last with an edge that could have cut a diamond.

"Abortion. Abortion. Abortion." She lit another cigarette. "It's the only word I know that doesn't turn into nothing when you say it over and over. Oh, my God, they killed my daughter because of what I do . . . because I believe . . . oh, God . . . oh, my dear dear God. . . ."

The cigarette dropped from between her fingers, bouncing on the floor, showering red flares into the darkness that flashed and disappeared, extinguished as if they had never been.

Natalie and Rubin returned a little before midnight. Felice was asleep, and Dale and I moved quietly to let the others in, unwilling to disturb her rest. For a while it had seemed she would never sleep again, but when she had calmed I'd led her back to the blanket, saying, "Tomorrow will be better."

"No," she had said. "Tomorrow will be the same."

After everyone was inside we gathered at the far end of the room, away from where the doctor slept, and huddled like a football team planning defensive strategy. Rubin looked better for the rest he had received, as did Natalie, and frankly I was overjoyed to see them. From thirty blocks away I could hear my bed calling.

"I really want to move her," I said to Natalie. "So if the safe apartment Sentinel has frees up early, let me know."

"If we can't get it until late, you want to take her back to Gold Street, return her to familiar surroundings?"

I nodded. "I'll be back by eight. One of you can go down to her apartment and check it out then."

"We can get police protection, can't we?" Dale asked.

"Cops," Natalie said. "No damn good."

"But better than nothing," he said.

"Felice doesn't want us being replaced," I told them. "So we're going to have to work with the marshals when they show, because they certainly won't go away. That may be for the best, getting them to do some extra coverage."

Everybody nodded, and we got ready to leave. Before Dale and I left, I walked over to where Felice was sleeping and spent a minute or two watching her.

She slept with grief as her lover.

CHAPTER SEVENTEEN

My futon was waiting like an escort service's best bet, comfortable and almost comforting. I was pulling back the sheets when the phone in the kitchen rang.

I didn't swear too much.

It was Alison. She said, "Hey, you. How you doing?"

"I'm all right," I said. It was a lie, but I didn't think it mattered.

"I'm so sorry, Atticus. I am so sorry for you and for the doctor. I called around eight and Rubin said you'd be back before one, so . . . well, I wanted to talk to you."

I sat on the windowsill. The apartment was pleasantly cool. I liked the darkness. "I'm glad," I said. "I tried to return your call this afternoon but you were at lunch."

"Yeah," she said.

It seemed like she wanted me to say something more, but I was too tired to come up with anything. I let the silence grow for a while, then said, "How are you doing?"

Alison made a clicking noise, then said, "I'm okay, I'm . . . no, I'm lying. I really need to talk to you, but this isn't . . . well, this doesn't seem like the best time."

"No, it's all right," I said, looking down at the alley. "What's up?"

She sighed, and that's when I realized exactly what was happening on her end of the phone. A squadron of stunt butterflies started aerial maneuvers in my stomach.

"I've been thinking about us," Alison said. "Jesus, this is . . . this isn't how I wanted to do this. I've been thinking about us, Atticus, and I don't think . . . I mean, I don't want us to see each other anymore. Not like we have been."

The pause sat there like roadkill for almost a minute before I said, "I'm sorry if I haven't been there for you, Alison. If that's—"

"That's not it," she said. "I mean, it's not just the abortion, it's that . . . I like you a lot, you know that. I even love you, you know, but after the abortion I started thinking about us, I mean, really about us. I couldn't see a future together, you know? Us as parents? You and me? And I realized that . . . that you're not the man I'm going to spend the rest of my life with."

"Oh," I said.

"I'm really sorry," Alison said. "This isn't how I wanted to do this."

"Yeah, your timing leaves a lot to be desired."

"You said you were doing fine."

"I lied," I said.

We shared the silence for a few more seconds. Then Alison said, "I had to tell you this, you understand, don't you? You wouldn't want me to lie to you, not about this."

"No, I wouldn't."

"I'm sorry."

"Me, too, Alison."

More silence.

"You can give me a call, you know? Whenever you want. We're still friends."

"You bet," I said.

She caught the tone, and hers changed, too. She said, "Well, good night, then. You take care."

"You, too."

I listened to the dial tone. Then I rose and replaced the receiver in its cradle. I looked at where the phone sat on the table, next to the answering machine, next to where I had dropped my pager and my gun. The phone was matte black, nothing more than a shadow in the darkened room.

I picked up the unit and threw it against the wall as hard as I could. The cord snapped, the cable whipping back and clattering on the table. The unit itself hit the wall at an angle, first the base, then the receiver. Then it fell to the floor.

From the next apartment, somebody shouted at me to knock it the fuck off.

"I own a gun," I said loudly.

Then I went to bed.

Sleep was elusive. I spent a long time staring at my ceiling and listening to the city. The caffeine I'd ingested had run its course hours before, but still my pulse bucked and, try as I could, it seemed I would never sleep.

Then I was dreaming.

I come through the door of Crowell's apartment with the HK in my hand, low, careful, knowing that I am going to shoot somebody. But it's also Romero's apartment, the way locations can be only in dreams, and as I start up the stairs to the main floor I hear a step. Crowell turns onto the landing above me, raising his right hand. There's a book in his other hand. I sight and fire three shots, a simple line from his stomach to his throat, and he dies with the book falling from his hand, bouncing each step to my feet, where it lies open. It's a Bible, but it's a story about the Incredible Hulk. Katie's voice calls, " 'Cus? 'Cus?" There's another sound I can't identify, a thin curl of sound like music.

I continue up, and at the main floor hear movement from the landing above and swing my gun without looking, firing another shot. I keep going, I don't care. Out of the kitchen comes Barry and I shoot him before he can throw anything at me. He dies gracefully, without bleeding, without pain.

The plate-glass door has been replaced, and the curtains are drawn. I see movement on the patio, a silhouette, and fire another two shots, feeling the gun kick pleasantly in my hand, hearing the spent shells eject cleanly and bounce off the wall and table. Special Agent Fowler falls through the door, shocked that he's suddenly dead. I didn't want to kill him, I realize, I thought that would be Rich.

But I'll get over it.

But something nags at me. Who did I shoot in the living room, then? Turning around to check, Dr. Romero is right behind me. She's entirely unafraid of the gun or me, she doesn't flinch when I bring the barrel up to her.

Dr. Romero says, "Look what you've done." She points to the landing above her.

I go up the stairs with her watching me, but she doesn't move. As I'm climbing, I hear the door open downstairs, and watch Natalie and Dale and Rubin all come to surround the doctor. Good, I think. They're doing their job.

Bridgett Logan is sitting at the top of the stairs. She doesn't look at me as I go past, but offers me a Wint-O-Green Life Saver from the roll in her hand saying, "Nice shot, stud."

Katie Romero is sitting on the floor, the Walkman headphones on her ears, pieces of paper with crippled drawings in bright crayon surrounding her. She looks fine, except that there's a perfect entrance wound in her left eye from my shot, and a chunk of her face is gone.

Madonna squeals from the headphones that hang on what's left of her head.

Then the alarm was beeping and I was trying to turn it off. Neurons finally began hitting their receptors, and I realized the alarm didn't beep, it buzzed, it was my pager that beeped, so the way to make the noise stop was to answer the page. I lurched to the kitchen, dragging my sweaty sheets after me, tripping over them. I shut off the pager and looked at the number that had been sent, but didn't recognize it. I reached for the phone and then remembered where I had put it.

There was a black mark on the wall from the impact.

I shuffled down the hall to Rubin's room and used his phone.

"Yeah?" Bridgett said.

"Morning," I said. The clock over Rubin's bed said that it was five after seven.

"Did I wake you? You weren't answering your phone."

I thought about explaining that the phone nearest my room was broken, and that Rubin's was too far away to hear, but decided against it. I rubbed my eyes and said, "No, you didn't wake me. What's up?"

"I'm reading letters. A real education in anatomy, let me tell you."

"Where'd you get the copies?"

"I talked to Lozano in person, got replacements. He was very accommodating."

"How'd that go?" I asked, sitting on Rubin's bed. One of Natalie's shirts was draped over the bedpost.

"He wanted to know if I thought you were doing all right."

"What'd you tell him?"

"I told him you were off your twig. No, I said you were fine."

"So he doesn't think I was stalking Barry?"

"If he does, he didn't share his suspicion with me. Anyway, I'm looking over all the threats again, and I'm wondering if you can give me a hand. There's a lot to go through."

"I've got to go cover Romero, see if we can move her. If we get settled into a new location and secured I'll give you a call."

"Do that. One more thing—Barry is being arraigned this morning. As far as I could tell, he didn't tell Lozano that you skipped a groove yesterday."

"Decent of him," I said.

"Yeah, he's the salt of the earth. Talk to you later, stud."

I hung up the phone. For some reason there was no hot water in the building, which led to me taking a very short shower. I dressed, affixed holster and pager to my belt, grabbed a jacket, and hit the street. I stopped long enough for a cup of coffee and a bagel at a bodega on the way to the subway station, finished them both on the platform, and made it to the studio by eight on the dot, certain that I hadn't been followed.

Nothing much had changed. Dale arrived a few minutes after I did, at which point Natalie called her father and determined that we wouldn't be able to access the safe apartment until late that afternoon. I relayed that information to Felice.

"I'd like to go home," she said softly. "I'd like a chance to clean up and get my papers and things for the conference."

"You're certain? I can send someone to get your things."

Her eyes were puffy behind her glasses this morning. She put a hand on my forearm. "I want to go home," she said. "Just for a little bit."

I didn't have the heart to argue.

I dispatched Dale to get the car and sent Natalie to the Gold Street apartment to secure it, then called Fowler to tell him that we would be taking Romero back to her place for a little while.

"I'll let NYPD know," he said. "You planning on staying there long?"

"Not if we can help it."

"Good," he said. "She's still going to Common Ground?"

"We haven't talked about it. But the answer is probably yes."

He sighed. "Not good," he said. "Katie's death has pushed the news national, Atticus. We've got people from D.C. down here now. That conference is going to be a five-ring media circus."

"I haven't seen the papers."

"It's everywhere," Scott said. "And it's only going to lure more nutcases out of the woodwork."

"We'll deal with it," I told him. "Marshals on scene yet?"

"They're already covering the clinic, waiting to hear from Romero. I explained that they weren't going to be needed for close coverage, but that didn't sit too well with the deputy who's running the show."

"I talked to Felice about it," I said. "She wants us to remain on duty."

"I'll pass that along. They won't like it."

"I can deal with bruising a few egos."

"Let's hope that's the only bruising that'll happen."

Natalie was waiting when we arrived at the Romero apartment, and as I closed the door she helped the doctor out of the bulletproof vest. We walked up the short flight of stairs to the main floor, Natalie and Dale in front of Felice, Rubin and me behind her.

When she reached the top of the stairs, Dr. Romero stopped, wavered. I put a hand on her shoulder to support her if she fainted, but she didn't.

"Oh, my God," she said. "Oh, Atticus, look at what they've done to my home."

There were toner stains on the kitchen counter and around the remains of the sliding door from where the CSU technicians had tried to lift fingerprints. On the floor were torn wrappers from all sorts of equipment, both forensic and medical. The spilled orange juice had dried to a sticky stain on the linoleum, and the whole room stank of juice and blood and chemicals, and just the memory of perfume. The bloodstain on the sofa where Katie had fallen had dried dark, and the smear from where I'd pulled her into the kitchen looked like a drunk had dragged a giant paintbrush across the floor.

"This . . . this was a bad idea," Felice said.

I put an arm around her and led her to her bedroom. At least that room was untouched. Once beyond that door, Dr. Romero went straight to the bed and sat down.

"We can take you back to the studio," I said.

She shook her head, and her mouth was clamped shut so tightly the blood left her lips, draining them white.

"You want me to leave you alone for a couple of minutes?" That earned a nod, and I said, "You just call my name, okay, Felice?"

Another nod.

I closed the door as I went out.

Dale, Natalie, and Rubin were all looking at me.

"She's right," Dale told me. "This was a bad idea."

I nodded.

"What were you thinking?"

"She wanted to come home," I said.

They all kept watching me, until finally Natalie turned her head and looked the apartment over again. She sighed, said, "Let's get this place cleaned up."

We got to work, and it wasn't until I was moving furniture back in place by the bedroom door that I heard her crying. It was a soft and lonely sound, and it wanted no company.

After we finished, Natalie got on the phone to her father again, spoke quietly to him, and then hung up. She simply shook her head at me and went back to her seat on the sofa beside Rubin, who had started reading a magazine. Dale sat at the table, idly sliding the salt and pepper shakers back and forth. I tried not to pace.

Then Felice screamed, high and terrified, and I ran into the bedroom and saw only her clothes, folded neatly on the bed. Pivoting to my left as Dale came in after me, I went to her bathroom door and tried the handle; it was locked. Felice screamed again. I kicked the door just below the knob, and it flew open, rebounding back off the wall so I had to stop it from shutting again with my right hand.

She was standing in her bathrobe with a pool of bloody water spreading around her feet from where it was flowing out of the toilet. The water looked pink as it spilled past the white porcelain, then went to red on the darker floor. Dale said something as I reached for Romero, pulling her to me. Felice turned to me as I drew her in, shutting her mouth, cutting off her scream, and her eyes were wide and uncomprehending. I lifted her up in my arms and Dale moved aside as I carried her out of the bathroom, past Natalie and Rubin at the doorway, back to her bed.

Felice wouldn't let go of me, and I had to pry one hand free to reach into my pocket. I held out the business card Bridgett had given me and said, "Natalie, call her, ask her if we can use her place, bring Dr. Romero over there *now*. Then call Fowler and Lozano."

Natalie took the card and I turned my head to look back into the bathroom. Dale had removed the top of the toilet tank and was reaching inside, trying to stop the flow of bloody water. I looked to Rubin and said, "Get a bag together for the doctor—clothes, stuff like that."

"Right," he said, and headed for her closet.

I knelt down beside the bed, pulling a corner of her bathrobe back over Felice's legs.

"It's okay," I told her. "It's just water, somebody just backed up the pipes. It's okay."

Her mouth was still open, her lower jaw shaking, her whole body trembling. But her eyes came back to me from wherever she had been looking. I stroked her hair and repeated, "It's okay, Felice, it's just water, it's just water."

She put her other hand back around me and pulled her face to my chest, hiding and crying.

Natalie came back. She said, "Bridgett'll be waiting for us."

I nodded and told her to keep an eye on the door until the police came.

I heard Dale say to Rubin, "Cruel motherfuckers who did this, very cruel."

After the police arrived, I left Natalie alone with Dr. Romero and gave Dale and Rubin their brief. Natalie had copied Bridgett's home address onto a piece of paper, and I handed it to Dale, saying, "You'll take Felice to Logan's place, and you'll lock it down. Take the car. Natalie and I'll catch up after we're done here. Call if anything happens, if anything turns up. Make sure Felice gets whatever she needs, but do not let her out of your sight."

Normally, one of the two of them would have given me a smart-ass answer—"What do you think we are, stupid?"—or along those lines. But this time neither of them did. Dale collared one of the cops, and the two of them went down to the car. Scott Fowler came in as they were leaving, and he took the stairs up slowly, looking around.

"You didn't clean the apartment, did you?" he asked.

"Yeah."

"Shit," he said.

"Yeah," I said. By being conscientious, we had effectively destroyed any forensic evidence.

Fowler went to talk to the officer in charge of the scene, and a few minutes after that Dale came back without the cop. He grabbed the vest off the coatrack before he came up the stairs, handing it to me as he said, "I've got the cop watching the car."

Then the bedroom door opened and Felice came out, Natalie with her. Fowler and the cops stopped speaking when the door opened, turning to look, then politely turning back away. Dr. Romero was dressed now, a pair of blue jeans and a white T-shirt, holding a leather briefcase with both hands.

"Ready?" I asked her.

"Yes," she said.

I held up the vest, and Felice handed her briefcase to Natalie. She slipped into the Kevlar and I made certain it was securely fastened. After she had her briefcase back, Felice said to me, "Thank you."

Fowler and two other cops helped us with the egress, and we got her in the car without trouble. Rubin and a cop sat on either side of the doctor in the backseat, with another uniform in the front next to Dale.

"Call me when you get secure," I told him.

"Understood," Dale said. I shut his door and backed away. Felice was looking at me as the car pulled out.

I stopped to get her mail on the way back upstairs, and amongst the bills and mailers, saw an envelope that looked all too familiar. I showed it to Fowler and he took it and bagged it without bothering to open the envelope.

"We'll read it at the lab," he said. "Maybe get a better chance of working some useful information off it."

"Have you pulled DNA off any of them?" Natalie asked.

"Not off these latest ones. Whoever's doing it is using a sponge or washcloth to wet the glue, not their tongue." Scott pulled his cellular and made a quick call, asking for a courier. "Who knows?" he told us after he hung up. "Maybe this one'll be different."

"Only if our luck changes," I said.

———

The police didn't find anything significant. The toilet had been backed up with butcher's cuttings and blood, and forensics determined the blood wasn't human, and surmised that the cuttings were from pigs. Other than that, there was nothing. Best guess was that whoever had clogged the pipes had come in through the broken terrace door.

Two hours after Dale called to tell us they were in, Natalie and I left to join them at Bridgett's. Fowler said he'd call us when he had details on the latest letter. We said thank you, and then took the stairs down to the street. It was nearly eleven in the morning, Friday.

On the subway, Natalie said, "Conference is tomorrow."

"Yeah."

"You been to the Elysium yet?"

"I'll go over there this afternoon, do a walk-through," I said.

She took her notepad from her jacket pocket, pulled out a folded sheet, and handed it to me. "You'll need this. It's the convention schedule."

I glanced over the sheet. It listed panels and talks by title, but didn't tell where the events were going to be held in the hotel. "When'd you pick this up?"

"Couple days ago," she said. "Romero had a stack of them at the clinic. When you're done with the walk-through, give me a list of the changes you'll want and I'll make sure my father gets them done."

"It'd be easier if you came along."

"Maybe," Natalie said. "But one of us should stay on the principal from now until the conference is over, and it'd be better if that's me."

"Yeah?"

"Felice is starting to rely a little too heavily on you," she said. "And you know how that can affect the op. She can't forget that there are other guards around her."

It took me a second to recognize how correct she was. "I wasn't seeing it," I said. "But you're right."

"Transference is normal, Atticus, you know that. It's one of the by-products of our job. Yesterday she hated you, today you're her salvation."

"I thought it was because I'm so roguishly handsome," I said.

"And witty," Natalie said. "It's not too bad yet, but we might want to head it off."

"Sort of flattering, really."

"I wouldn't rely on it as a method of meeting women," she said.

CHAPTER EIGHTEEN

Bridgett's apartment was in a small brownstone in Chelsea on the fifth floor. The building was recently renovated, clean, and the stairs didn't creak. Natalie knocked on the door, saying, "It's us."

Several locks turned and Rubin pulled the door back, letting us through. The door opened into a hall that ran to the left to a tiny living room. After Rubin locked up he led us down the hall.

It was a comfortable, if cramped, apartment, with photographs framed on the walls and a lot of old, perhaps antique, wooden furniture. There was a lumpy easy chair and a faded sofa arranged facing one wall in the living room, a small television and VCR unit that sat on an oak bureau. The television was tuned to CNN.

Dr. Romero was on the couch, her briefcase open beside her, a legal pad on her lap. She said, "Atticus," when I came in, and tried a smile that almost worked, but never reached her eyes. Dale rose from where he was filling the easy chair.

"You're feeling better?" I asked Dr. Romero.

"Showered and had some food," she said. "Working on the funeral preparations. It'll be Monday, the day after the conference. It's keeping my mind busy, you see."

"Good."

"I'm . . . I'm sorry about the apartment."

"That's nothing you should apologize for," I told her.

"If you say so."

"I do," I said. I looked around at everyone. "Let's have a powwow."

Natalie and Rubin joined Felice on the couch, and I motioned Dale back to the easy chair. Bridgett came in from another hall, past the kitchen. She was wearing a black T-shirt and torn black jeans today, flashing skin at thighs and knees, and she said, "Hey, stud. This private?"

"No, stay. You should hear this, too."

"Bitchin'," she said, and leaned against the door frame.

"The conference is tomorrow," I said. "And the threat is still active. It may come from SOS, it may come from another quarter entirely, but I think everyone can agree that an attempt will probably be made. Security for the conference will be good, but that is no guarantee; it never is.

"Do you still plan to attend?" I asked Felice.

She capped her pen and set it on her legal pad. "I've got to go," she said. "They killed my little girl trying to keep me quiet, trying to keep me still. They've won enough off me; I won't give them another victory."

Bridgett shook her head. "Excuse me, but if they kill you, isn't that their final victory? At least in this battle?"

"If they kill me," Felice said.

Bridgett pulled the tin of Altoids from her hip pocket and popped a mint, offering the container around. Natalie and Rubin each took one.

"I'm going to attend," Felice said. "Damn them."

"All right," I said. "Then you will do the following, to the letter, until after the conference. From now until tomorrow night, you go nowhere, do nothing, without at least one other guard with you at all times. This means everything, from sleeping to showering to eating." I looked at my crew. "This means one of you is on her at all times, no excuses."

"When are we going hot?" Rubin asked.

"The conference starts at ten-hundred tomorrow morning," Natalie said. She pulled her notepad out of her jacket pocket and flipped a couple of pages, then found the entry she wanted. "It's scheduled to run until twenty-hundred." She asked Dr. Romero, "When do you plan to arrive?"

"I'm speaking at the opening with Veronica," Felice said. "Then I'm scheduled for a panel at noon and a talk at three. The talk should finish by five."

"Do you know the locations of those talks?" I asked her.

"The panel will be in the Imperial Ballroom, and my talk is to be held in the New York Room," she said. As she spoke, Natalie wrote this new information down. "I believe that Veronica and I are to speak in the Imperial, as well."

Natalie tore the sheet from her pad and handed it to me. I folded it and put it in my pocket next to the schedule. "We're going to need a general briefing with all the agencies involved," I said. "And the only time I see when we'll have a chance to do that is before the conference itself starts. Figure we'll go hot at oh-seven-hundred. Transport at oh-seven-thirty, and we place Dr. Romero in the command post by oh-eight-hundred. We'll hold the general briefing there at oh-eight-thirty. Egress at seventeen-hundred if possible. We return to normal coverage only after Dr. Romero is secured at the safe apartment tomorrow night." While I was speaking, my pager went off, and I silenced it, then checked the number.

"How are we covering in the hot zone?" Dale asked.

"When Dr. Romero is speaking or in any group, all of us. Otherwise I'll be on the principal unless needed elsewhere, in which case one of you will sub in. Dale, you'll be responsible for evac and exits," I said. "Rubin will cover entrances, and Natalie will be the floater. As always, the chain of command will run from me to Natalie to Dale to Rubin."

"Joy," Rubin said.

"Understood?" I asked.

Everyone gave me a nod, even Bridgett.

"Good," I said, and checked my watch. It was almost twelve-thirty. "I'm going to head over to the Elysium now, do the walk-through, and plan the routes."

Bridgett pushed off the door frame and said, "You need a phone? Use the one in my office."

I followed her down the hall. The floor was hardwood, highly polished. She guided me through a door on her right into a small office with an oak desk in a corner. The desk was huge, and I wondered how she had fit it into the room. Its surface was covered with papers, a Macintosh computer stuck in one corner, cables running from it to the printer on the floor. She pointed me to the chair in front of it, pulling a seat for herself from the corner. Both of the chairs were backless, the kind where you rested your knees on pads below the seat. I picked up the phone and dialed.

"Who you calling?" she asked.

"Fowler," I said.

She made a face, then said, "I've got a friend, a reporter. Did some digging for me. You know that Veronica Selby has published four books about abortion and how to protest it?"

"She'd mentioned as much to me."

"Lectures, articles—she's very busy."

"And?"

"She and Crowell were at one point engaged."

Fowler answered his phone before I could respond further, and Bridgett just grinned at my shock.

"Got a preliminary report on the letter," Scott told me. "It reads: 'Dear Butcher Bitch, two down, one to go. Not twins, not triplets. Murdered babies, punished mothers. I will have justice.' That's it."

"Read it again," I said, and grabbed a pen and one of the scraps of paper on Bridgett's desk. Fowler read the letter again and I copied it down, then handed it to her to read, saying to Scott, "Did you find anything on the letter?"

"That's the good news," he said. "The lab pulled fiber traces from the envelope, blue. Could have been carried inside a coat pocket or something. It's not a lot, but it's progress. I'm still waiting for the lab to finish."

"Not a mail carrier's jacket?" I asked.

"No, definitely not. That was the first check we ran. What do you make of the letter, that 'two down' business?"

"No idea."

"Sounds like the writer is Katie's murderer," Fowler said.

"Then who's the second victim?"

"That's a good question. Felice have any other children, anything like that?"

"No."

"Maybe Katie was pregnant?"

"Are you kidding? Absolutely not," I said. "Besides, she was having her period when she was shot."

Bridgett's eyebrows rose. I shrugged at her.

"I'm just theorizing," Fowler said.

"Well, trash that particular theory. Is that it?"

"No, there's one other thing. Barry is out on bail."

Twice the bastard had been caught dead to rights, and twice he had been set free. "How?" I fought to keep my voice level.

"He made bail, Atticus. All he was charged with was

aggravated harassment for the phone call and criminal possession of a weapon for the gun. The call itself is only a misdemeanor, it's the CPW charge that's a felony. He walked on fifty thousand, cash or bond.''

"Where'd the money come from?"

"Crowell.''

"Barry needs to be in custody," I said. "He's our prime suspect, Scott, and the conference is tomorrow.''

"I know. NYPD has been following him since he got out. They'll pull him back in if he gives them cause.''

"They better not lose him.''

"I know.''

"I mean it, Scott.''

"Watch your tone, Atticus," he said. "Everybody's doing the best they can.''

"Bullshit," I said, and hung up.

Bridgett was looking at me, expectant.

"Barry got out," I told her. "That motherfucker is walking the streets again.''

"Tough break, stud," she said.

"Would you stop with that?"

"You don't like being called stud?"

"Not particularly, no.''

"Too bad . . . stud," she said, and popped another Altoid.

I got up and headed back into the hall, mostly hoping to find a safe outlet for my anger. And I was angry now, could feel it rumbling. I was having a hard enough time trying to protect Romero as it was without legal loopholes, incompetents, and liars getting in my way.

"Where you going?" Bridgett asked, coming after me.

"Out. I've got to do the walk-through.''

"I'll come with you.''

"Can I stop you?"

"Maybe with your gun, but I don't think you're that kind of boy," she said.

"You have no idea what kind of boy I am," I said.

"But I'm learning."

We entered the living room. "Bridgett and I are going out. We'll be back about four for the transport," I told Natalie.

"We'll be ready."

Bridgett grabbed her leather jacket from the counter between the living room and the kitchen, slipping into it. Felice stopped what she was doing with her papers to watch us go, and when her eyes found me I discovered that I couldn't look at her. I went to the front door, out of sight, to wait.

No, Felice didn't hate me today. Maybe she didn't even blame me. Natalie was probably correct; I had gone from failure to savior in under twenty-four hours, and as I watched Bridgett Logan come down the hall, her car keys in her hand, I wasn't certain which position I liked better.

CHAPTER NINETEEN

We got into Bridgett's Porsche, and I told her we were going to Park Avenue first.

"The Elysium's on Fifty-third, isn't it? Between Sixth and Seventh?"

"We're making a stop. Unless you're unwilling, in which case I'll just take a cab," I said.

"Whoa, easy, stud. We can make a stop first, sure. So, where am I headed?" I told her to drive uptown and she nodded and ran the Porsche like a demon. "So, whose place are we going to?"

"Veronica Selby's."

The doorman who looked like a royal guard stopped us from entering, and gave us the evil eye while he called Selby on the house phone. He said my last name like it was a disease. It didn't help my mood.

"You can go ahead," the doorman told Bridgett.

I led the way, knocked on the door twice, and was about to rap it again when it was opened by the same woman who had let me in before.

"Veronica is in the living room," she said, and then led us down the hall, then retreated and disappeared as she had before.

Selby was wearing khakis and a white T-shirt today. Her wheelchair was positioned in front of her computer. As we entered she turned and smiled, saying, "This is a surprise, Mr. Kodiak. . . ." Then her smile faded as she read my face.

"Time to confess," I said.

"Excuse me?"

"You held back last time I was here, and I didn't push, because it didn't seem necessary. But now it's out of control, and I want to know everything you know about Crowell, SOS, and his plans."

She drew herself up in the wheelchair. "Are you implying—"

"Goddamnit, stop it," I said. "I know that you were engaged to the man."

That put the brakes on. She looked away from me to a point on the wall. "I was," Veronica Selby said. "But that doesn't mean that I know anything—"

I interrupted again. "No, don't try playing that hand. Katie Romero is in the morgue with holes where her heart should be. Her mother is attending Common Ground tomorrow knowing that she may die, too. Now, you stop with this innocent bullshit now, and you tell me the truth, or I swear to God that Felice won't show tomorrow, and you'll be going it alone."

She turned her head, showing me that lovely neck again, and still not showing me her eyes. "It was a long time ago."

"How long?"

"Five years, no—six. I met him in Albany and I

was . . . I was discouraged, do you understand?" Selby finally looked up at me. "He was charming, and he got things done, or so I thought. And I was tired, so tired of fighting and losing all the time."

"And Crowell is your idea of a winner?"

"He was . . . I thought he was getting things done." She touched the gold cross at her throat. "But he wasn't. He was making things worse."

"You should have told me, you should have told me when I first talked to you. I only found out because Ms. Logan here did a check on Crowell's past."

Selby looked at Bridgett, tilting her chin in a greeting. "Pleased to meet you," she said softly. Her accent was stronger now, southern grace rising to the occasion.

"The pleasure is mine," Bridgett said.

"Why didn't you tell me?" I asked.

Selby went back to worrying the cross, her fingers tracing its shape over and over. "I was ashamed. I was seduced by him, and I was terribly ashamed. Won't you both sit down? Please?"

Bridgett sat on the couch and slid over, making room for me beside her. I positioned myself on the edge of the cushion. Selby rolled closer to us, stopping at the end of the coffee table, folding her hands in her lap.

"It wasn't seduction of the flesh, exactly," she said. "What Jonathan Crowell seduced was my spirit and faith. I've . . . Mr. Kodiak, I think I am a weak person, and I don't know if you can understand that. I conceived when I was only fifteen, and I had an abortion. I aborted my daughter with a coat hanger after drinking a bottle of gin.

"The difficult thing, the right thing, would have been to carry my baby to term, to let her live. But I was a coward and I was weak, and so I murdered her. I nearly died myself as a result, both inside and out. When I left the hospital, my legs were . . ." Her hands strayed to the wheels of the chair, then back to her lap.

"This is my life, Mr. Kodiak. I believe from the bottom

of my soul and with all my heart that abortion is murder, and that murder is wrong. But I believe more that Jesus Christ is my salvation." She stopped speaking for a moment, looking past me. I turned, and the woman who had let us in was standing in the archway.

"It's all right, Madeline," Selby said. "Perhaps you could bring us some tea?"

"Certainly, Ronnie," Madeline said. She hesitated, watching me, then went back down the hall.

Selby continued, "What Jonathan Crowell said to me, fundamentally, absolutely, I agree with to this day. To abort a child is to murder a child. And I heard him say what I felt, except say it more eloquently, and I heard him say it at a time when I was succumbing to weakness again. I had lost my faith, and I thought that through Jonathan I could find it again."

"You didn't," I said.

She almost smiled. "It took me a while. It took me long enough to have accepted one ring from him, and to want a second. But then I realized exactly what he was doing."

"Which is?"

" 'He that sayeth I know Him, and keepeth not His commandments, is a liar, and the truth is not in him,' " she said. "Jonathan Crowell claims to act in the name of Our Lord, to do His bidding. Jonathan has claimed His authority, but refuses to submit to the same. And that is a sin, Mr. Kodiak. That is a terrible, almost unforgivable sin."

Madeline returned with a silver tray. There were three glasses and a pitcher of iced tea on it. She set the tray on the coffee table and then put a hand on Selby's shoulder, eyeing Bridgett and me. Selby said, "Thank you."

Madeline nodded, then left, and I poured three glasses.

"I should have told you," Selby said after accepting her glass. "But you reacted so strongly when you saw his name on the list, and I was terrified that Felice wouldn't come, that you wouldn't let her attend Common Ground."

"Do you think Crowell is behind Katie's murder?" Bridgett asked.

"I hope not, I hope . . . he's certainly responsible for some of the letters," Selby said. "Indirectly, at least. Jonathan would never write them himself; instead, he would encourage others to do that work for him."

"And what about Dr. Romero?" I asked. "Do you think he is trying to kill her?"

"I don't know if Jonathan is trying to kill Felice," she said. "But I think he is capable of justifying such a murder. He has assumed that authority. Whether he would actually try to do it, I don't know."

"Do you know Clarence Barry?"

She frowned. "Clarence Barry? I knew him through Jonathan."

"Would he murder a sixteen-year-old retarded girl?"

Selby said, "Clarence Barry is so full of hate he could do anything. He used to make jokes about . . . Let's just say he speculated about what Jonathan and I would do in bed, had we gotten married. His speculation wasn't kind, and centered on the fact that I have very little movement in my legs." She emptied her glass, turning it in her hand and watching the ice slide before setting it on the tray with a gentle click. "I'll make certain that Jonathan isn't admitted to the conference," she said.

"Is he a martyr?" I asked.

"Jonathan? It's one of the parts he plays, but it isn't anything more than an act."

"Then don't bar him from attending," I said. "If we keep him from coming, we create a martyr. If he comes, we'll be able to keep tabs on him. And if he's not willing to sacrifice himself to his cause, then Felice may actually be safer if he is there."

"I see," Selby said.

I stood. "We've got to go."

Bridgett set her glass down. "Thanks for the tea," she said, rising.

"Certainly." Selby turned her chair slightly toward me, so we were facing, and offered her hand. I took it. "Will you allow Felice to attend?" she asked.

"She'll attend," I said. "We'll see you tomorrow morning."

"Tomorrow will be a good day," she said.

Madeline showed us out.

We parked in the garage provided by the Elysium, and before we went up into the hotel, I asked the attendant what the security was like around the cars.

"Cameras," he said. "We check for new plates every evening."

"Is that all?"

He shrugged.

I thanked him and then Bridgett and I went up to the lobby. "Let's hope nobody wants to take out the whole building," I said.

"You think they'd use a car bomb?" Bridgett asked.

"They're in vogue," I said.

"That would be totally sprung."

"And murdering doctors isn't?"

We came in from the garage, near the center of the lobby. It was beautifully appointed, broad, heavily carpeted, decorated in browns and golds. Quite stylish. The front entrance was actually on the west side of the building, allowing one to enter near a variety of services, from a sports bar and café to the south and a bar and lounge to the north. After a moment to look around and count the cameras, I took Bridgett to the bar. We each bought a Coke and had a seat.

"What are you doing?" she asked.

"Just looking. How many guards do you see?"

She downed a handful of complimentary mixed nuts, chewing thoughtfully. After a minute of watching the lobby, Bridgett said, "I count three. They're the ones in the blazer-and-slack combos, right?"

I nodded. "There are five," I said, and pointed them out. "Then there are those two, house detectives, probably." Both were in plainclothes, and one was actually lurking near us. I smiled at him and he looked hard at Bridgett and me, then moved on.

"Thinks I'm tricking," Bridgett said. "Guess I should've worn my nice clothes, huh?"

"Or one less nose ring," I said.

We finished our sodas and then walked over to the reader board. The board was electronic, with announcements scrolling past in bright red LED. A pediatrics convention was in town; so was a technical writers' symposium. The board listed "Common Ground: Abortion in the United States" near the end of its cycle, noting that registration began at eight the next morning. I looked over the schedule Natalie had given me, then handed it to Bridgett.

"Let's check the rooms," I said.

The Imperial Ballroom was almost large enough to earn its name, but apart from that, didn't look as if it would pose a problem. There were three sets of doors off the hallway that led into the room, but two of those could easily be sealed to control the access. On the south side of the west wall was another door, and when I opened that I was in a service hallway.

"Are we allowed back here?" Bridgett asked me.

"That's half the point," I told her.

We followed the hall along and passed several storerooms, two kitchens, and twelve staff people. Not one person stopped us or asked what we were doing. The hall ended on a loading dock, and a camera was positioned there to watch whoever came in or out. I gave it the finger. Hopefully, somebody was awake in the control room, and flipped me off in return.

"This isn't good, is it?" Bridgett asked.

"It's not too bad, actually," I said. "This is all single access. Sentinel will put one person here, in a uniform. As long as the instructions are simple and clear, there shouldn't be a problem." I pushed the door back open and we headed back the way we had come.

Two men were waiting for us at the end of the hall. About ten feet away from them, the elder of the two said, "You're still wearing those damn earrings, Kodiak."

I grinned and tugged on the two hoops in my left earlobe. "So I don't lose my head," I said. "Makes it easy to hold."

"Hate to have those yanked in a fight," the other one said. I didn't know him, but his voice was wonderfully distinctive, rich and with an accent.

"Bridgett Logan," I said, indicating the first man, "this is Elliot Trent, Natalie's father."

"We've met," Bridgett said.

"Yes, we have," Trent said. "I assume you've since replaced your camera?"

Bridgett grinned. "Oh, yeah. The agency's still waiting to be reimbursed."

"An oversight," Trent said. "I'll have a check cut to you today." He went so far as to make note of it in the leather portfolio he was carrying. Then he closed the portfolio and said, "Why don't we go upstairs, so I can give you an operations brief?"

We followed Trent and the other man up to the third floor, where the New York Room was. This was the room where Romero would give her talk, and it was already laid out for the event. According to the sign on the wall, the room could seat five hundred people. Elliot Trent took us up to the front of the room, and sat on the edge of the stage, in front of the table. Bridgett and I took seats, and the other man stood for a moment longer, then sat on the opposite side of the aisle. Like Trent, he was dressed conservatively, in that style of dress that seems to linger long after the wearer has left government employ. His skin was very tan, and his hair and eyes were very brown.

"You haven't met Yossi, have you?" Trent asked me.

"No," I said, and extended my hand.

He took it and gave me a firm shake, saying, "Yossi Sella."

"Yossi is fresh from the Shin Bet," Trent said. "Their Executive Protection Squad. We've stolen him away. Much as you've done with my daughter, I might add."

"You mean he's dating your best friend?" I said.

Trent looked appalled, but Sella laughed.

"Let's get to work, shall we?" Trent said.

He had maps of each floor of the conference, showing the rooms that were going to be used, the rooms that were scheduled to be empty, and all the service routes that led to the conference areas. Marked on the maps were security checkpoints, guard posts, and camera emplacements.

"I want restricted access here," I told him. "The elevator should be the only way up, and I want to control the flow into the room."

"There's an escalator onto this floor," Sella said. "And two stairwells."

"The escalator will have to be locked off."

Trent nodded. "We'll put a guard in uniform at the top, just in case. There'll also be one uniform at each stairway."

"What are the cameras like?" I asked.

"They've got good people in their security room," Sella answered. "Not the best, but they pay attention. That's how we saw you in the hallway, on the cameras." He smiled and raised his middle finger at me. Bridgett laughed.

"Can we have a Sentinel uniform in there?" I asked Trent.

Trent shook his head. "But that'll be covered by the marshals."

"How's the communication?"

His frown deepened. "Not great. Because of the publicity, every agency wants to be seen as responding to the best of their ability."

"We're being crowded," Sella said. "But we'll manage."

"I want a general briefing for eight-thirty in the morning," I told Trent. "Where we can make introductions, set up the pecking order, so on. Can you arrange that?"

He nodded and made another note on his pad. "I already discussed the importance of a briefing with Ms. Selby, so she's prepared for the eventuality."

I got up and started walking around the room. "This is the only place Dr. Romero will speak solo," I said. "If there's a try, my instinct is it'll be here."

Trent pointed to a door in the corner. "That leads to the kitchen. No refreshments are being served, so we'll lock it down before her talk begins."

About five feet from the doors into the room were a series of switches mounted on the wall, sliders and buttons. One of the buttons was square and red, and I pressed it.

All the lights went out, and the room was completely dark.

"Well, that's definitely not good," I heard Bridgett say.

I pressed it again.

"We need to cover this up," I said, when the lights came back on.

Trent made another note. "Anything else you can think of, Atticus?" he asked.

"Couple more things. First of all, I want a designated watcher outside each event Dr. Romero attends. Make sure that person has photographs of Barry, Rich, and Crowell, and make sure the only job they have is to look for those faces. I want to know if they show.

"Second, at each event Romero attends, nobody carries anything in. They check their bags, purses, whatever. Additionally, I want all attendees run through a metal detector."

"We'll be doing spot searches at the registration desk," Trent said. "That's where the metal detector will be set up."

"Then get somebody with a hand-held," I said. "No way I want anything snuck into a room where Romero is speaking."

"We can't demand that people check their bags," he objected. "Too much flack."

"I don't give a shit about flack, Elliot."

"No, you wouldn't. But how we look does matter. My agency is the marquee name here."

"Listen. I don't give a shit," I said again. "It's my principal."

"We should be certain," Sella told Trent.

"We can search bags," Trent said. "But we cannot check them. Logistically, that's more than we can handle."

"Thorough searches," I said.

"Of course," he said. He checked his watch and then looked at me. "Is that all?"

"One last thing. I want a room for Romero to stay in while she's not speaking. Nothing fancy, just someplace she can be comfortable until she's on."

Sella smiled. "We've already taken care of that. The command post is in a large suite, and one of the adjoining rooms has already been designated for Dr. Romero."

"Then that's it," I said to Trent. "I'll have Natalie phone you tonight with any additions and details on Romero's transport."

Trent closed his leather portfolio and rose, rebuttoning his jacket. "We'll see you tomorrow, then. The apartment should be clear by now, so if you want to move the doctor, go right ahead."

"We will. Thanks for the loan."

Trent nodded. He knew he was doing me a favor; we both knew eventually I'd be asked to pay it back.

Sella got up and we shook once more, then he took

Bridgett's hand and crooned, "I hope we'll be seeing each other again."

"I'm sure I'll see you tomorrow," Bridgett said.

He released her hand, saying, "Until then."

We watched them go. She was paying, it seemed to me, particular attention to Sella as he departed.

"Cute ass on that one," she said to me after the door shut.

"Tomorrow you can ask for a close-up."

"Tomorrow maybe I will."

We headed out of the room, taking the stairs down to the lobby. "What's the deal with the camera?" I asked.

"Sentinel was hired to protect an oil exec," Bridgett told me. "Agra and Donnovan was hired by said exec's wife shortly thereafter to prove the gentleman was engaging in extramarital recreation. This was at the end of my apprenticeship, before I got licensed, about a year ago. Anyway, I got pictures of this fellow romping with a brunette at a hotel in Boston."

"You beat Sentinel security?" I asked.

"It took time and money and me dressing up in a maid's uniform, but yes. Rigged a couple of distractions and managed to get in and click away. And on my way out I ran into Natalie and another guard."

"And she took the camera?"

"No, the other one did. Stomped it to pieces. Took the whole thing very personally, unlike Natalie, who thought it was funny. I don't think she liked the client." We were at the garage and she handed the attendant our parking stub. He disappeared to find the car.

"How much money were you out?"

Bridgett laughed. "We weren't. It was all expenses, and we got a bonus for completion."

"You lost the pictures."

She popped a Life Saver into her mouth. "Who said there was only one camera, stud?"

CHAPTER TWENTY

Dale drove us to the safe apartment, with Rubin in the front seat and Felice sandwiched in her Kevlar between Natalie and myself. The drive took thirty minutes, with Dale winding his way along the streets. The apartment was in the Upper West Side, only two blocks from where Alison lived. When I thought about that, I felt the emptiness again, and felt too the rage that had possessed me to smash a phone against a wall.

Bridgett and I had returned to her place shortly after five. We'd found Dr. Romero ready to go.

"You're coming along, aren't you?" Felice asked me.

"I'll be riding with you."

Romero gathered her stuff together and Natalie gave me an I-told-you-so look. I shrugged, then arranged to meet Bridgett back at her place before eight.

The apartment was on the ground floor on a quiet street, and we were met by a Sentinel employee who handed Natalie the keys and showed her how to disarm the alarm. It was nicely furnished inside, classic styling that oozed money and power, designed to make Sentinel's clients feel as if they were at their new home-away-from-home. The air had a slightly antiseptic tang from the rushed cleaning it had gotten before being turned over to us.

All five of us made a quick walk-through. The kitchen was fully outfitted, all the cupboards crammed with canned goods and other foodstuffs. The two bedrooms were small, each decorated with classic prints of English country foxhunts. We ended our tour in the living room. It wasn't particularly spacious, but it was certainly comfortable, and there were no bloodstains on the carpet. Dr. Romero sat at the desk there and went back to her papers.

Dale asked, "We're all sleeping here?"

"You three and Felice will," I said. "I'll be back here early tomorrow before the transport."

"I'll need to go home before then," he told me. "Get a change of clothes and some stuff."

Rubin said, "I'd like some clean underwear myself."

I looked at Natalie and said, "You willing to go down to just two for a while tonight?"

"That's our minimum," she said. "We're good here. The glass is bulletproof, the doors are almost unbreachable, and we've got everything we could want."

"Dale, you go home, get what you need, and get back here by ten tonight," I said. "Rubin'll go after you get back." I asked Natalie what she wanted to do about herself.

"What time are you planning on getting here tomorrow morning?" she asked.

"I was thinking seven or so."

"Make it six and I'll run home, then meet you back here."

"Deal," I said. "One other thing before I go. Give your

father a call, see if we can get Dr. Romero a Kevlar dress shirt for tomorrow."

Felice looked up from where she was writing. "I don't want to wear the vest at the conference."

"This'll look and feel mostly like an ordinary shirt," I told her.

"Mostly?"

"Well, it's not silk, let's put it that way."

She stared at me, unsmiling, and said, "If you think that's best."

"Will white be okay?" Natalie asked her.

"I have a choice?"

"A rainbow of colors to choose from," she said.

"White will be fine, thank you."

Natalie looked at me and said, "They actually do a nice blouse, believe it or not. I'll have some options brought by for her to look at."

"Fashion show," Rubin snorted.

I noted the phone number of the apartment, told everyone I'd see them tomorrow, and left.

Bridgett said, "The thing is, I can't find anything to tie these directly to Crowell."

I looked at her over the coffee table in her living room, then looked back at the pile of letters she had set there. Yellow tabs of Post-Its stuck out from various letters, and she had filled several pages of a college rule notebook with her notes on what she had found. The apartment was dark now, and the only light came from a lamp in the corner.

"Then we're just not seeing it," I said.

She fussed with her nose ring, then sat back in the easy chair. "Well, stud, I'm open to suggestions."

I looked at the piles. "How are these arranged?"

"The big pile, those are from organizations other than SOS. Anything that claimed affiliation with some right-to-life group. Not necessarily threats in the SOS sense, but possibly dangerous. The second one, medium there, that's SOS."

I looked at the pile she meant. It was easily three hundred pages. "All of it?"

"If it had the emblem, you know, that cross and barbed-wire thing, or the letterhead, or mention of either Crowell or the organization, it went into that pile." She arched her hips in the chair, pulling the tin of Altoids from her back pocket and then relaxing again. She dropped three of them in her mouth, one after the other. "Last pile, that's just the letters that didn't have any clear association."

"And the latest ones, those are in that pile?"

"Bingo."

I picked up that pile, found the handwritten transcript of the letter Fowler had read to me, then the two others of the same style and read them again, in the order received. *'Dear Butcher Bitch, two down, one to go. Not twins, not triplets. Murdered babies, punished mothers. I will have Justice.'* The only SOS connection was in the letter writer's desire for justice, a sentiment Crowell had shared with the crowd outside of the clinic.

And in that crowd, anybody could have written these letters, I thought.

The answer clicked fast and solid and I knew, intuitively knew, the answer was correct. At the same time, I realized exactly how much trouble we were in, all of us, me, the squad, and most of all, Felice Romero.

"What? What are you thinking?" Bridgett asked.

"It's not Crowell," I said. "We've been blind, we've been focusing on him because he's big and he's using the conference, and we haven't even considered that the threats could be coming from somebody who doesn't care about Common Ground at all."

"Then why try to kill Felice?"

"You're assuming that Katie's murder was an accident. What if it wasn't, what if somebody was gunning for her specifically?"

"But killing Katie serves only one purpose, stud; it keeps Romero from attending Common Ground."

"But it doesn't," I said. "I mean, look, Katie's dead and Felice is still going."

"Then what's the motive?"

"Revenge." I handed her the letters. "We're looking for a man who knows a woman who had an abortion. This is all about revenge. Why else kill Katie?"

Bridgett read the letters, marking them with her black felt-tip pen. For five minutes we didn't speak, me thinking of the possibilities, and Bridgett trying to find a hole in my logic. She set down the pen finally, took a handful of her hair, and tugged, saying, "Fuck a duck."

"No Crowell," I said.

"This doesn't rule him out," Bridgett objected. "He could still be connected to this."

"I don't think so," I said. "It's got to be some guy who's wife or girlfriend or mother or whoever had an abortion."

"That doesn't absolve SOS or Crowell," Bridgett said, and her voice climbed slightly, pressing her point.

"Look at the letters," I said. "There's no reference to the organization. On these other ones," and I pointed at the medium-sized pile, "you said there was the SOS emblem, some sort of signifier. But on these new ones, nothing."

She pushed her hair back into place, then began gnawing on her bottom lip. "It explains the letter at the clinic yesterday," she conceded. "The writer was shooting at Katie, not Romero, so he knew Romero would get the letter."

"Makes the writer and the shooter one and the same," I said. "And that goes to revenge. He's telling Felice what he's doing, because if she doesn't know why he killed Katie, why he's going to kill her, there's no point. He writes these letters to let her know."

"But they're obtuse, stud. I mean, if that's what this guy wants, why not just say, 'Dr. Romero, you killed my wife's baby, and I'm going to kill you'?"

"He wants her to suffer. Why else kill Katie?"

"You murdered my child, I'll murder yours?" she said.

"Yes."

Once again, she reread the letters. "So you're saying that we've been looking in the wrong place."

"That's what I'm saying." I pulled my glasses off and rubbed my eyes.

"So you've been trying to protect Dr. Romero from a threat that's coming from a different direction entirely?"

I nodded.

"You're fucked," she said softly.

I nodded again.

"Okay," Bridgett said. "Let's work the problem, right? If it's revenge, then the abortion in question had to be through the clinic. The author has claimed two bodies, and we know one of them is Katie, so the other is who?"

"Not Romero," I said.

"No, not Romero. Not if your theory is correct, anyway. He won't claim her until she's dead. It's got to be the mother, then, right? The woman who had the abortion. He's killed the mother for having the abortion, and he's killed Katie because Romero performed the abortion, to let her know what it felt like."

"So it's a question of finding the man who impregnated a woman who went to the Women's LifeCare Clinic in the last year or so and who had an abortion," I said. "That can't be too hard, right? Only one, maybe two thousand candidates?"

"No, we're looking for a dead woman," Bridgett said. "And these letters started only a couple of weeks ago, so it's got to be a patient that died fairly recently." She got up and went to the phone on the kitchen counter. "I'll call Dr. Faisall, see if I can get access to the patient files."

"It may not be worth it," I said. "Common Ground is tomorrow, Bridgett."

Without stopping her dialing, she said, "You're being awfully defeatist." Then she was talking to Dr. Faisall, explaining our theory and asking if she could please look at the patient records of the last few months. The inactive records, Bridgett specified, people who were no longer coming in for one reason or another.

I put my glasses back on and then my pager went off. I silenced it and held it up for Bridgett to see. She nodded, told Dr. Faisall she would be by the clinic in the morning, then hung up and stepped out of the way for me at the phone.

It was Fowler. There was significant background noise over the phone, multiple voices and what sounded like radios crackling.

"Atticus, is Romero secure?"

"Very," I said.

"Barry lost his tail," Fowler said. "He went to see Crowell, left there, and headed to Grand Central. Took the shuttle to Times Square. NYPD lost him near Port Authority. We think he's left the city."

"But you don't know?"

"No, we don't. A bench warrant's been issued, and there's an APB out on him. I interviewed Crowell after we heard Barry had bugged, and he was convincingly surprised. Crowell told me that he had fired Barry."

"Hold on," I said, and relayed the information to Bridgett.

"Ask Fowler if he knows about Barry's personal life," she said.

I ran that one at him and Scott said, "What? Why?"

"He ever been married? Have a girlfriend, siblings, anything?"

"No girlfriend," Fowler said. "No known acquaintances except Crowell. He's got two sisters in Tennessee. We think that may be where he's headed. Look, I've got to go, coordinate this thing with NYPD. It's a monkey-show over here."

"Sounds like it was from the beginning. You never should have lost him."

"Fuck you," he said cheerfully, and banged the phone down.

Bridgett had gone down the hall, and now came back, fastening a shoulder holster into place, a Sig Sauer P220 now riding under her right arm. She reached for her jacket, saying, "Let's go."

"You think we're going to find Barry?" I said.

Bridgett shook her head. "But I can think of a good place to start looking."

She parked off Fulton, about a block from Romero's apartment. The streetlights shone on all the people out for a Friday night walk to the South Street Seaport, holding hands or clustered in groups that we had to step around.

"I want to see the apartment," Bridgett had said once we were in the Porsche.

"The police have—"

"I know," she said. "But I haven't."

"We don't know if Barry is the shooter," I said.

"I doubt he is. But the shooter backed up the pipes, under our current theory. I want to see if he left anything behind."

"Anything that the police and FBI might have missed, you mean," I said.

"Do you have a better idea?" she shot back.

"We could go to Crowell's and beat him within an inch of his life," I said.

"No, we couldn't. You'd end up in jail, and what would Romero do without you?"

"What's that supposed to mean?"

"Nothing. Here, have a mint, stud."

I took the mint and crunched on it, and neither of us spoke for the rest of the drive.

Philippe was at the door and I remembered I owed him twenty bucks, so I gave him the money before we went past. Bridgett watched the exchange of currency without comment. We took the stairs to the second floor, passing a young man I didn't recognize as we started down Romero's hall. Bridgett stayed ahead of me and didn't stop. When we'd instituted security for Romero, I had made a point of getting to know each face on the doctor's floor.

This guy wasn't one of them.

Could be anybody, I thought.

But I stopped and turned around and said, "Hey, excuse me?"

He had opened the door to the stairwell, and he turned his head. His hair was buzz-cut short, dirty blond, and his arms were thick and powerful. A pair of brown leather gloves were thrust into the back pocket of his jeans. His face was that of a boy. His eyes were hazel, and they met mine.

Gloves, I thought. In summer.

Then he ran.

"Bridgett!" I shouted and started after him, yanking the door to the stairwell back in time to see him exiting into the lobby. I swung over the railing, and felt my left ankle twist and then give as I came down on the last step. I sprawled forward through the door before it swung shut completely.

"Stop that man!" I shouted to Philippe.

He took a second to react, then pivoted, putting his body between the other man and the door, but the other man didn't stop, just bent low and then blasted forward like a linebacker after a quarterback when the blitz is on. Philippe went through the glass door backward, hitting the cement sidewalk hard, the glass showering about them both. The other man regained his footing almost immediately and kept going.

Bridgett ran past me as I got up, and I was ten feet behind her when we hit the street. Philippe was coughing as I went past, struggling to his feet, and I assumed he was fine.

Bridgett had pulled up, looking frantically both ways, growling, "Where's that pest-bastard?"

There was a ripple in the Friday-night crowd, heading south toward the Seaport. I started that way, Bridgett following me. I'm not much for running, only when chased, I suppose, but I am quick.

This guy was, too, and he had the lead on us.

We hit the open promenade of the Seaport in time to see him push through a crowd that had surrounded a fire-eater. My left ankle was killing me, protesting with sincere pain every time I came down on it. Bridgett cut left around the crowd, and I went right, and we met up again on the other side, each scanning. The crowd was bubbly, liquid, shifting easily now, and with a lot of noise, conversation, patter, laughter.

He was nowhere to be seen.

"Fuck!" Bridgett shouted. "Fuck fuck fuck!"

A young couple pulled their son away from us, and the crowd thinned near where we stood.

"Son of a bitch," Bridgett said breathlessly. "Mother of . . . oh, I'm so mad I could just—what the fuck are you looking at?" The last was directed at a young woman wearing a Fordham T-shirt.

"Whoa," the woman said, and backed away with her friends.

"Preppy bitch," Bridgett said.

"I know who he is," I said.

"What?"

"That guy, I know where I've seen him before. Outside the clinic, the day the bottle was thrown. He was with Barry, he was wearing a Columbia University sweatshirt."

"You're sure it's the same guy?"

"It's the same guy."

"Good, okay, good, that means we can find his name," she said. "That means we can find out who he is."

"No."

"What do you mean, no?"

"He wasn't arrested."

She squeezed her eyes closed, putting both her hands to her head and sliding them up into her dark hair. Her hair fell back and she exhaled sharply, then opened her eyes and said, "He was in her apartment, wasn't he?"

"Maybe," I said. "Probably."

"We'll get prints off her door. I've got a kit in the Porsche."

I shook my head. "No, he had gloves. He must have worn them in the apartment."

"The stairwell!" Bridgett said.

We gave the crowd one last look-over, but it was futile. Then we turned and started back up the street.

"Quit limping," she told me.

"Fuck you," I said sweetly.

Philippe was on the phone when we got back to the building. Bridgett continued on to her car for her print kit. I waited until he hung up. "Just ordered a new door," he said. "Who the hell was that guy?"

"An athlete," I said.

"No shit?" He brushed specks of glass from his uniform, muttering.

"You're okay?"

"Didn't get cut, if that's what you mean. Don't know how."

"Lucky."

"You get him?"

I shook my head.

He went to get a broom, saying, "Should I call the police?"

"We'll handle it," I told him.

Bridgett dusted the doors to the stairwell, both front and back, and then worked the railing. She pulled numerous useless prints, but got a portion of a palm off the inside of the first-floor door where we figured University had pushed it open.

"It's a nice partial," she said, blowing gently on the toner.

She prepared the cards and I used the doorman's phone to call Fowler's cellular. I told him what happened, that I recognized the man from outside the clinic, and that Bridgett had pulled a possible print. Fowler said he'd get there as soon as he could, and told us not to disturb anything more.

"Let us do our job," he said. "You protect Romero: That's what you do. I find clues and bad guys: That's what I do. Got it?"

"We'll be in the apartment," I said.

"No, you won't," he said. "Don't even go near it. You'll destroy evidence."

"We'll wait in the lobby," I said.

"That's a good boy. Keep it up and you'll get a puppy treat."

I barked at him before he hung up.

Bridgett didn't want to wait in the lobby. "I just want to look around," she said.

"We wait."

She grumbled and checked her pockets for more candy, coming up empty and heading to a deli next door to re-stock. The first patrol car pulled up as she returned, starting in on the first roll. The CSU arrived a few minutes later. Bridgett was starting on a new roll, Spear-O-Mint, when Fowler showed up and told us to wait in the lobby. We followed him up to Romero's apartment.

It would have been funny, I think, if the situation was different. But walking into the apartment again, taking the flight of stairs onto the main floor, and seeing, again, the whole living room in forensic disarray, a pressure built behind my eyes. While Bridgett dogged Fowler through the apartment, I stood by the stairs, and watched the technicians work. This wasn't the same as when Katie died, I knew that, but it was hard to get past it, and my dream from the night before came back sharply.

Cops and techs coming up the stairs kept brushing past me. The third time the same officer bumped me I snapped, "Watch what the hell you're doing."

The patrolman turned and said, "You got a problem?"

"You can stop fucking pushing me every time you come up the stairs, that's my problem."

He shoved his face to mine, leaving half an inch of hostile air separating us. "You can wait outside, or you can shut up, but you're at a crime scene and you've got no rights, asshole."

I almost put my fist in his stomach, but Bridgett got to me first, saying, "Come here, would you?" and pulling me by the arm. The cop and I kept eye contact until Bridgett nudged me into the bedroom.

"What the fuck's your problem?" she asked.

"No problem," I said. "I just don't like being pushed."

"You don't like . . ." She shook her head. "Try the decaf, stud, calm down."

"Don't call me stud."

"Sit down, stud," Bridgett told me.

I glared at her and she pushed my chest with her index finger firmly. "Sit." I took a seat on the bed, watching while the CSU analyzed the stained footprints on the carpet by the bathroom. One of the techs asked me to take off my sneakers so she could run a comparison, and I complied without comment. My ankle was starting to swell, and it hurt to remove my shoe.

"Five sets," I heard her tell Fowler. "I can tell you that already. One of them's his," and she pointed the toe of my Reebok at me. "I assume we've got matches for the others at the lab. But we do have a fresh one."

"You didn't come in here before we arrived?" Fowler asked me.

"No."

The CSU tech gave me my sneakers back, and after that, feeling claustrophobic, I limped back down to the lobby. I thought about calling the safe apartment to check on everything, decided against it. There was a bench out front of the building, so I sat on that and waited. The doorman was fussing at the workmen who were replacing the broken door.

Bridgett came out ten minutes later and said, "Mint?"

I took one, looked at it, then threw it across the street.

"That was a waste of a perfectly good mint," she said. "You hungry?"

"I suppose," I said.

"I know a great place. Come on."

Bridgett parked against the curb on Third Avenue and we walked back to the Abbey Tavern. It was dim inside and fairly busy, the bar full. Bridgett turned a sharp right and was greeted by a gray-haired man wearing a subdued suit.

"Bridie, it's been how long?"

She said, "Two months, I think, Chris."

"And those holes, dear Lord, look! Your parents would scream if they saw what you've done to that beautiful face. And how many have you added since I saw you last?"

"Two more," Bridgett said.

"You're mad."

It might have been me, but I could have sworn I heard an accent creeping into her speech.

Chris grabbed two menus and walked us to a booth. After we were seated he said, "I'll send Shannon right over." He gave me a smile, then left the table.

Bridgett shook hair out of her eyes. "You're not Irish, are you?"

"Not unless it's a well-kept family secret," I said.

Our waitress Shannon was short and slender, and gave Bridgett a hug when she reached our table. I was introduced, and Shannon gave Bridgett an approving look, then told us the specials. I picked the lamb stew; Bridgett ordered a large salad. We both ordered pints of Guinness.

"Come here a lot, do you?" I asked.

She nodded and grinned. "My people. And yours?"

"I'm a mutt. Some Czech, some Russian, some Polish."

Our food arrived and we bent to the task. The stew was substantial, and it came with a basket of soda bread that made for perfect company. I cleaned out my bowl and sat back, finishing my stout. "Good choice," I said.

"You want some of this?"

"No, thanks."

She pushed her greens around some more, then set down her fork and knife and pulled out another mint. "So?" she asked. "You want to talk about it?"

"I don't know, actually."

"Fair enough."

Shannon returned and shook her head at Bridgett's bowl. "You'll waste into nothing," she said as she cleared the table. Then she returned and gave us each a cup of coffee.

"Were you going to belt that cop?" Bridgett asked me.

"I might've."

"Dumb."

"I know."

She tapped the side of her cup with a fingernail. Her nails were short, but clean and unpainted. I wondered if she went for manicures.

"Have you ever had an abortion?" I asked her.

"No," Bridgett said. "No, never an abortion."

"The woman I was seeing, she had one. That's how I met Romero."

"Alison?"

"That's her," I said. "We've been seeing each other for about seven months, and she called me when I got in last night, told me that I wasn't the man she wanted to grow old with."

Bridgett raised her eyebrows.

"Not in those words," I amended. "Close, but not those words."

"Her timing is for shit."

"I told her that."

Shannon returned and refilled our coffee cups. Bridgett waited until she was gone, then said, "This because of her abortion?"

"I think in part. If nothing else, it made her take another look at me. And I hadn't been around—I wasn't super supportive after the fact. I was working for Romero."

"You don't sound too certain about the decision."

"No, it was the right thing to do, I really believe that. I can't be a father yet, and Alison sure as hell didn't want to be a mother. It's just that working for Romero, in a way it was an easy excuse. Made the abortion something I didn't have to deal with."

"Not anymore."

"No," I said. "And Katie's dead, and that is so wrong and it makes me so angry . . . shouldn't our child mean the same thing?" I toyed with my coffee cup, watching the way the liquid sloshed along the sides. It made me think of the bloody water pouring from the toilet in Romero's bathroom. "I look at people like Veronica Selby, even Crowell, for God's sake, and I wonder."

"Don't give Crowell that much credit. He doesn't see sanctity of life, he sees a road to attention."

"I think he's a son of a bitch, don't worry. I can't imagine what would be left of him if I got him alone in an alley for a few minutes."

"Him or Barry?"

"Both," I said.

"Romero's still alive."

"Tell me that tomorrow night," I said.

"It's a date," she said as Shannon slipped the check onto the table. Bridgett picked it up before I could, saying, "It's on me."

"Next one's mine," I told her.

"Then I'll pick somewhere extremely expensive tomorrow night," she said. "I don't know what to tell you, Atticus. You're not necessarily talking to the right person, here. I respect Selby, everything I know about her. But I disagree with her fundamental argument. This sounds harsh, but that fetus Alison aborted wasn't anything more than a parasite. It could never have survived without a host, and it was giving nothing in return. Equating that to the murder of Katie Romero, that's only going to fuck with your head, because they are absolutely two different things. Katie Romero, even if she suffered from Down's syndrome, was never a parasite. Her potential was realized, and continued to grow.

"A bastard with a rifle cut that short."

She put some bills on the table and we stood up, stopping to say good night to Chris on the way out. "Don't be gone so long next time," he said to Bridgett. "We've been missing you."

"Promise," she said.

We walked back to her car.

"Get in, stud," Bridgett said. "I'll take you home."

CHAPTER TWENTY-ONE

We drove in silence, each of us thinking, I'm sure, about what exactly she and I were doing, and, perhaps, were going to do back at my apartment. She was very attractive to me that night, we both knew it. But if Bridgett came upstairs, I wouldn't want her to stay, and part of me was preparing what I wanted to say to her if it came to that.

When we reached Thompson, Bridgett couldn't find a place to park. Even the illegal spaces were taken, including the red zone right in front of the hydrant by my building.

"You can just drop me off."

"Let me walk you home."

"You're a perfect gentleman," I told her.

"A foxy chick like yourself shouldn't be walking the streets alone this time of night."

She parked on MacDougal, and together we walked back toward Thompson. It was well after one: Bleecker had few people on it and Thompson was empty. We went into the little entrance cubicle to my lobby, and I unlocked the interior door, and held it open so Bridgett could slide past. I shut the door and she waited for me to get back in front of her, since the hallway was too tight to walk comfortably side by side.

He was waiting on the stairs, and I guess he was expecting only me. As I put my foot on the first step he came around the landing above, and then I was forced back off the steps and into the wall, a baseball bat pressed horizontally against my throat. It was a good hard press, and I couldn't breathe. Barry finished the move by bringing his face close to mine, saying, "Motherfucker, this time I'll make you piss your pants, motherfucker."

Which was a mistake, because Bridgett put her pistol to his temple and said, "Drop it, shithead." She cocked the Sig for emphasis.

He debated the decision for a moment; it was clearly in his eyes as they moved from me to his left, trying to see her. His pressure didn't let up, and my vision began to cloud with dots moving in from the periphery.

"Now," Bridgett said. "Or I'll paint the wall in Early Neanderthal Brain. That means you, Clarence."

Barry looked back in my eyes, the same mad-hatred look he had pointed at me when Lozano led him away, and then took a step back. Bridgett let the barrel leave his temple, but kept the gun trained on him. As the bat cleared my chin, I brought my head down and began coughing, trying to find my breath.

"Drop the bat," Bridgett said.

Barry was still looking at me, the bat now at waist level, held lengthwise with both hands. "Fucker lost me my job," he said. "Fucker ruining my life, thinks he can make me some faggot pussy, making people laugh at me."

"Drop the fucking bat now, Clarence," Bridgett said.

"Yeah, I'll drop it, cunt," he said, and then he jabbed the bat sharply to his left, catching her hard in the chest with the end. Bridgett staggered, losing her aim, and went down on one knee. Barry brought the bat up again and around, zeroing once more on me. This time I was ready for it, and blocked his arm with my left forearm, shunting his swing off to the side. As the blow came down I snapped my forehead into his nose, felt it give, and pulled back to grab the bat. He brought his free hand up to my face, clawing my glasses off, and we both went back against the wall again. I got a second hand on the bat, twisted, and slammed his wrist against the banister. He dropped the bat, and caught me with a backhand that made my head ring. I lost my grip on him entirely, and staggered back into Bridgett.

Barry took a look at Bridgett where she was coming back up with her gun, then turned and went out the side door into the alley.

"Bastards never finish what they start," Bridgett said as she pushed me after him. Her voice was breathy and strained from the blow. I took the short stairs out to the alley in one jump, landing in time to hear garbage cans ahead of us clang and fall. Bridgett came out right behind me, her gun in her right hand, and we turned in time to see Barry start over the fence.

"Stop or I'll shoot," Bridgett shouted at him, bringing her weapon up.

Barry didn't stop and he didn't look back and she brought the gun back down as I tried to make it to the fence. I jumped at the last moment, and my ankle wailed in pain. Barry pulled his foot clear, and I got a handful of nothing, scrabbling at the blurred chain links on the fence. Barry dropped and sprinted through the common courtyard between buildings, then out the alley onto MacDougal.

"This has not been a good night for chases," Bridgett said.

I went back to get my glasses.

————

Barry hadn't bothered with my apartment. Rubin had reconnected the phone in the kitchen while he had been home, so, while Bridgett dumped her coat and holster on the floor, then headed to the bathroom, I called Fowler's cellular and told him the good news.

"So he didn't leave town," Fowler said.

"Very astute of you," I told him, sitting on the windowsill and trying to work my sneaker off without causing my ankle any more damage.

"You want somebody to come by?"

"And do what?" I said. My ankle stabbed a pain up my leg and I decided trying to remove the shoe was probably a bad idea for now. "Bridgett and I both saw him. You pick him up, we'll identify him. There's no point. He's not coming back tonight."

"How can you be so sure?"

"He's not that dumb," I said. "He's crazy, but not dumb. I'm here, Bridgett's here, we've both got guns. He'd have to be absolutely insane to want to risk it."

"Logan's spending the night?"

"Shut up," I told him.

"You could be receiving other visitors," Fowler said. "If Barry found you, it can't be that hard for anyone else. You've been seen around the clinic."

"If somebody else was planning on coming by, they would have done it a while ago, Scott," I said. "My ex-girlfriend and I were photographed going into and out of the clinic on our first visit. I'm sure there's a file on each of us somewhere."

"With your names, addresses, so on."

"Exactly," I said.

"Why's Barry after you?" Fowler asked. "Romero I understand, you don't make much sense."

"I embarrassed him," I said.

"You embarrass a lot of people."

"Thank you, Scott. I know you mean that in the nicest possible way."

"What did you do to him, particularly?"

"I scared him," I said as Bridgett came out of the hall-way from the bathroom. She was pulling on her shirt, and I saw another ring, this one through the top of her navel. The ring reflected with the same deep emerald green of her bra, making her skin seem delicate and radiant. I looked out onto the alley before I could see anything else.

"You scared him enough to make him come after you?" Fowler asked.

"The impression I get is that he's blaming me for losing his job."

Fowler was quiet for a moment, and I risked looking back at Bridgett. She had finished with her shirt and was opening the refrigerator. "Beer?" she asked.

I nodded.

Fowler said, "Hate to say this, but if he's after you, maybe that's a good thing. That means he's got less time for Romero."

"That still leaves the gentleman from earlier this evening."

"We're running the prints. We should have something by tomorrow."

We said our good-byes, and Bridgett handed me a bottle of Anchor Steam, taking one for herself. I had some of the beer, then put the bottle on the table and tried again to get my sneaker off. It was easier to do with two hands and no phone. Then I limped to the sink and grabbed a dish towel. With ice from the freezer I made a pack, then went back to the table.

"Elevate your foot," Bridgett told me.

I grunted and swung my leg onto the table, and she took the ice pack and set it around my ankle. I put the beer bottle against my left cheek, where Barry had connected below my eye.

Bridgett slid her chair back against the wall, stretching her legs out in front of her.

"Are you okay?" I asked.

"The bat caught me smack in the middle of the breast-bone," Bridgett said, and indicated the spot between her breasts. "Missed my tits, which is good, but it's going to be a lovely bruise. Nicer than the one you're going to have."

"This will be a mighty fine bruise," I told her, pulling the bottle back to give her a look.

"Amateur stuff."

We finished our beers, and Bridgett said, "I should go. We've both got an early day tomorrow."

"You going to come by the conference?"

"I'm going to the clinic first, look at those inactive files. I'll try to come by in the early afternoon. Will you have any time if I find something out?"

"Probably not, but we'll see."

She rose and put her holster back on, not bothering to stabilize it to her belt. As she slipped into her leather jacket I got my leg off the table and stood up, then went with her to the door.

"Be careful on your way home," I told her.

She gave me a look and then it softened, and she said, "Don't worry about me, stud."

We looked at each other a moment longer, and I got that rush in my stomach, a mixture of anxiety and anticipation.

"Good night," Bridgett said, and she remained in the doorway.

"Night," I said. My pulse was racing faster than it had when Barry attacked in the lobby.

Her mouth turned into a small smile, and for a moment she looked all of fifteen. Then she stepped into the hall, and I watched her go to the stairs, start down them.

I shut the door and set all the locks and got ready for bed. Before I turned off the lights, I put my gun beside my futon. It wouldn't do anything to my dreams, but it would sure as hell slow Barry down.

———

In my dream, we're escorting Romero to the conference, Natalie on point, Rubin and Dale at each flanking position, and me on Romero. We're taking her downstairs, to a panel, and as we get to the floor where she is to speak, the crowd surges in our direction. We try to fall back and keep our zone intact, but it fractures, and I pull Romero back behind me, pushing her up the stairs. I'm keying my palm button, shouting for assistance into the mike on my lapel, but there's nothing; my radio's dead.

Romero is clear behind me, and I start to turn to cover the rest of her retreat, and I see a man with a gun.

I've never seen this man before. He looks like Barry, but not quite. He looks like Crowell, but not quite. He looks mostly like the man in the hall, the one from Columbia.

But not quite.

The gun is a semiautomatic, a Browning, and I do the one thing left for me to do, the one thing it's always been about.

I put myself between the gun and Romero, and the pistol fires, and I feel the slug hit me dead in the middle of the sternum, feel the shock of impact rattle through my body. As I go down, Natalie, Dale, and Rubin all fall on the shooter, swarming and crushing him to the floor. He's out of the picture.

His threat, as they say, has been eliminated.

I put my right hand on my chest, where I've been shot, and I'm afraid to look, but I do anyway.

My hand is clean.

Looking around, behind me, I see Dr. Romero. She's fallen, sprawled over the steps, and there is a hole in her chest where there should be one in mine, there is blood spilling from her mouth where there should be some in mine.

I was up again before dawn.

CHAPTER TWENTY-TWO

We took Dr. Romero in through the service entrance at a quarter past eight in the morning, Natalie leading on point, Dale on the left flank, Rubin on the right, and me in the rear a half-step behind Romero to the right. We had been cleared all the way in, a marshal radioing me before we left the car that an escort would meet us at the end of the hall.

Uniformed NYPD officers, holding paper cups of coffee and looking almost awake, had covered the entrance. Dale stayed behind the wheel while we got out, pulling out when we were clear of the car and then quickly backing into place. It would save us time if we had to leave in a hurry. But if things got that bad, it probably wouldn't matter.

I keyed the small button on my left palm and said, "Pogo is in." All of us were wearing radios with roughly the same setup. The unit sat on my belt, black metal and plastic about the size of a pack of cigarettes, with three wires running off it. The first went down my left sleeve, my off hand, and ended in the transmit button. The second ran up the back of my shirt to my right ear, ending in the receiver. The third ran along the inside of my coat to the lapel, where the mike rested. The mike was small, and very sensitive, easily picking up conversation when the button was keyed.

In my ear I heard the dispatcher announce our arrival to all units. *"Confirmed, Pogo is on scene."*

Dale was back in the fourth position by the time we entered the hallway. The cops moved only to let us pass, and as we walked down the concrete corridor, more like a bunker's than a hotel's, we passed two other guards in the black and gold of Sentinel's security uniforms. The hall ended with doors on the right, where two men in blue marshal's jackets waited for us. One of them went to the door on the right, preparing to open it.

The dispatcher said, *"Pogo is clear through the Imperial Room."*

"That's a negative," I said. "Pogo will not, repeat not, enter through the Imperial Room. Pogo will proceed to the CP by an alternate route."

Natalie put her hand over the marshal's, pushing the door shut again and saying, "What the fuck are you doing?"

He looked confused. The second marshal pulled his radio and began speaking into it.

The dispatcher came back at me saying, *"South stairwell clear to third floor."*

"Ten-four," I said. "Natalie, proceed."

She dropped her arm and looked at the man in front of her, and he looked at the other marshal, who was listening to his radio. The marshal on the radio nodded to his partner, and they opened the door ahead of us. We collapsed a little closer about Felice as we started up. The radio traffic as we moved was mostly minor. Our frequency was secured for just the protection detail, limited to my crew, the dispatcher in the command post, and myself. If there was news happening on another channel, it was up to the dispatcher to inform us.

As we got to the third floor, the dispatcher came back on, saying, *"Pogo is clear all the way in."*

The marshals opened the door onto the hall, each stepping out on either side of us, and we went through, from the concrete to the carpet. The command post was two doors down on the left, and we passed two more guards in Sentinel uniforms on our way, and another NYPD uniform.

One of the marshals opened the door for us, and we stepped inside. The large suite was quiet: that would change once the conference got going. The curtains had been drawn over the windows, and all the lights in the room were on. A large table at one end of the suite was covered with papers and maps, and copies of the Common Ground schedule were taped to the wall in four separate places.

Fowler, Trent, and Lozano were all there, as well as two other men I didn't recognize. A woman wearing a black headset over her short blond hair was seated at a desk, scribbling notes onto a pad. She was hooked to one radio via the headset, and had another at hand. She turned to look at us as we entered, then keyed her headset and said, *"Dispatch to all units, Pogo is secure."* A man in NYPD uniform and sergeant's stripes looked at us when she did, then spoke into his radio, too.

Elliot Trent turned from where he was standing behind the dispatcher and said, "This way," then led us into a bedroom on the side.

"Five minutes until the briefing," he said. "I've ordered coffee and Danish."

"Fine," I said.

Trent nodded and went back out, shutting the door behind him.

Felice dropped her briefcase on the bed, then went after the buttons on her overcoat. The overcoat looked like a Burberry, but was layered Kevlar, much like the blouse she was wearing, but stronger. With the coat and blouse, she would survive just about any shot, if the blunt trauma didn't kill her.

No guarantees.

Felice put the overcoat on the bed, then sat down, smoothing her skirt and looking at me. The skirt was light brown, and fell to just above her ankles. She was wearing flats, and the blouse that Natalie had found was pearl white and looked quite nice on her.

"Now what?" she asked. Her face was drawn, and her makeup did nothing to hide her fatigue.

"Now you wait," I said. "We'll have a general briefing that you'll want to attend, just so everyone can identify you. Otherwise, there's nothing for you to do but try and relax."

Dr. Romero nodded, then reached for her briefcase and opened it, returning to her papers.

People began arriving for the briefing about five minutes later, Veronica Selby and Madeline among them. Selby and Romero spoke quietly to each other for a few moments before we actually began, Selby holding both of Felice's hands in her lap while the two women talked.

By the time we were ready to start, the main room of the command post was crammed with people, among them several federal marshals, FBI agents, NYPD brass, and Sentinel personnel. Elliot Trent made a brief welcome, then introduced Selby. She didn't speak for long, mostly thanking everyone for their assistance and participation thus far, and emphasizing the need for the conference to be peaceful. Then we went around the room, introducing ourselves and stating our agency.

There wasn't a whole lot more to say. Everyone present

knew that the threat against Romero was legitimate. Everyone present knew that Barry, Rich, and Crowell were all to be considered possible trouble. Fowler circulated a description of the man Bridgett and I had encountered the night before, saying that if anyone matching the description was seen doing anything suspicious, he and I were to be notified ASAP.

By the time we were finished, the coffeepots were empty, and there wasn't a Danish to be seen.

I took Romero back to her room, accompanied by Selby and Madeline, then told Rubin to stay with them while I went back out to finish speaking with the others.

Fowler was speaking to his supervisor, who shook my hand and then, after looking around, nodded once and said, "Looks like things are well in hand." Then he headed for the door, stopping to chat with the two NYPD captains who had attended the briefing. Lozano was with them, and he backed off when the new arrival came.

"Christopher 'Big Man' Carter," Fowler told me. "Special Agent in Charge, Manhattan. Wouldn't know it to look at him."

"As long as he stays out of the way."

"Come on," Fowler said. "You should meet Pascal."

He led me to a substantial tower of a man who hadn't spoken during the briefing. His hair was gray and cut neatly and close, and his eyes were brown, and very hard. He had his marshal's badge hanging from a chain around his neck.

"Burt Pascal, this is Atticus Kodiak," Fowler said.

"When do we take over?" Pascal asked me, gripping my hand.

"When Dr. Romero says so," I said.

He shook his head, saying, "Poor woman." He gave a polite smile to both Natalie and Dale, then moved on to talk to more of his people.

As Pascal left, one of the two captains detached from

where he had been cornered by the SAIC, and came over to us. Lozano came with him.

"Captain Harner," he introduced himself. "Donald Harner, Midtown North." He wore glasses, and was almost entirely bald, with worry lines etched from his mouth to his forehead. "SOS sent us a copy of a press release they're going to deliver when this thing starts. They're boycotting, claiming that the whole conference is a sham."

"What a shock," Natalie said.

"I'm going to have my people stay outside mostly, deal with the protesters. They're already gathering out in front of the hotel," Captain Harner said.

"Keep an eye on them," I said.

"Peaceful protest," Harner told me. "We won't be able to move them if they follow the rules and behave." Then his radio went off and he excused himself.

"I'm going to do a walk," Natalie told me, adjusting the wire that ran to her palm. "See how it looks down there."

I grabbed Dale and told him to double-check our egress routes. "Make sure the guards know what's what," I told him. "Anybody comes running down those routes not shouting the password, they're to stop and detain them."

"And the password of the day is?" Dale asked.

"Wolf," I said.

He repeated it. "You sure that's not too hard for them?" Dale asked. "I mean, if they're given the chance they'll totally fuck it up."

Trent, who was listening, said, "My people know their job."

"Take Rubin with you," I told Dale.

I waited in the bedroom with Dr. Romero. Selby and Madeline had left shortly after Dale. Selby said she wanted to make certain things were proceeding well at the registration desk.

"I'll see you in about two hours," she told Felice before she left. "We're really going to do this."

"We really are," Dr. Romero said, and the two women hugged.

They left, and Felice went back to her briefcase, and I sat on the couch, because there was only so much securing of the command post I could do. After a while, she gave up on her papers and went to the television, turning it on and then sitting beside me on the couch. We still had an hour before she and Selby were to speak, and the difficulty of the wait showed in her posture and manner. I had left the door open to the other room, and occasionally the noise filtered in suddenly louder, and Felice would turn first in the direction of the noise, then to me.

"I'm nervous," she said softly, as if making confession. "I don't know what worries me more. Speaking in front of all these people, or . . . I mean it's silly, isn't it? I should be more terrified of dying than of having to talk in front of a crowd, but I'm not."

"You'll be fine," I said.

CNN carried a story on Katie's death. Various political figures were seen decrying the violence, and two sound bites were played, one of the president, who broadly condemned the action, and another of a southern senator who admitted it was a tragedy, but then went on to say that abortion was the issue that needed to be addressed, and implied that the horror in Katie's murder lay there rather than with the person who had fired the rifle. Footage followed of a protest outside the Women's LifeCare Clinic. The reporter closed by mentioning Common Ground, and said there would be more information later in the hour.

We watched the report in silence, and then Felice said, "We'll be burying her in Westchester, have a small service at the graveside. There's a plot there, my husband's family. She will love a green place, I think."

"A lot of people will want to attend," I said.

"I don't want that. Just the people that knew her. That's

the most important thing," she said. "I'd like you and the others to be there."

"We'll be there, Felice. You've got us until you say otherwise. Certainly through tomorrow."

"And after that?"

I shifted on the couch, trying to keep the base of my radio from digging into my hip. "The purpose of the threats was to keep you from coming here today," I said. "To keep Common Ground from happening."

"So tomorrow, I'm no longer worth killing?"

"Perhaps."

"I hope so," Felice said, softly. "I really do hope so." She smoothed her skirt with both hands, playing with one of the pleats. "You know what frightens me more than anything? That I won't say the right things. That nothing will change after all this, that it will all just continue as before . . . that my daughter will have died for nothing."

Fowler came in with Lozano, and we talked briefly. Neither had any good news.

"Still waiting on the prints," Fowler told me. "We should have them by the end of the day."

"After the conference," I said.

"Well, you heard the briefing. The description's been given out to everyone here. It's the best we can do until we have a name on this guy."

"Let's hope it's enough."

Lozano said, "Nobody's seen Barry, Rich, or Crowell. Not outside, not inside."

"Crowell's supposed to speak," I said.

"One o'clock panel. About the limits of legal protest," Fowler said. "I can't wait."

"He hasn't canceled?" I asked.

"Not as far as I know," Lozano said. "I'll check again with Selby."

From the couch, Dr. Romero said, "He won't cancel.

It's a performance like any other for that man. He'll arrive at the last minute, as if he's doing us all a favor. The boycott is just to emphasize his contempt for all of us here. Just wait. He'll show."

Roughly a half hour before Romero and Selby were to deliver the opening address, Natalie radioed me. *"I'm sending Rubin up to cover you. I need you down at registration."*

"Got it."

Rubin came into the CP about three minutes after that, saying, "It's a clusterfuck down there."

Dr. Romero looked over at me as I got up and put my suit coat back on. "I'll be right back," I told her, then went out and took the stairs down to the lobby, straightening my tie as I went.

Natalie was arguing with SAIC Carter by the metal detector. Her father stood beside her, clearly wishing he was somewhere else.

The detector had been set up in the open area outside the Imperial Ballroom, with ropes running from either side of it to the walls to keep people from bypassing the checkpoint. The registration desk was beyond the detector, and several people were already entering the ballroom, wearing red, white, and blue convention tags on their jackets or shirts.

On the other side of the detector, leading into the lobby, people were crammed wall-to-wall, and getting impatient.

"Change the goddamn setting," the Special Agent in Charge was saying.

"It wasn't me who only brought in one metal detector," Natalie responded, and cast a pointed look at her father.

"It's broken," Trent said. "We're bringing people over with hand-helds."

"What's the problem?" I asked Natalie.

"The problem is that the head Fed here wants us to change the setting," she told me. Her eyes were blazing.

"It's going off at everything," Carter said. "Take it down a quarter turn, you'll still catch anything coming through."

I checked the dial on the side of the metal detector. It was cranked all the way to the right.

"It doesn't take a whole hell of a lot of metal to make a bomb," Natalie insisted. "Guns aren't the only things we're worried about."

"It's going off on goddamn bobby pins," Carter said. "And right now we're filling the lobby with people who can't get where they are going. You listen to me, there's as great a risk in the fucking lobby as in the fucking ballroom at this point. A bomb will do as much damage in both places. All of these people are potential victims, and the longer they wait the more at risk they become."

"How long until the hand-helds get here?" I asked Trent.

"Fifteen minutes at the most," he said. "We've got two here already, we can hand-scan some of these people."

"That's not good enough," Natalie said.

"Jesus H. Christ," Carter said. "What do you want, to cavity-search them, too?"

"If it'll catch a weapon," Natalie said. "You bet your ass."

"It'll catch a weapon, damnit," Carter said. "It's catching on fillings." He appealed to me. "Turn it down."

"Wait a minute," I said.

"Turn the fucking thing down," he said. He reached around the side of the detector and turned the knob down a notch. "There. That wasn't so hard, was it, honey?" he said to Natalie.

"Pompous son of a—" Natalie started.

I grabbed her, turning to Trent and saying, "We'll work with it. Make sure that everyone gets at least one pass with either the detector or the hand-helds."

Natalie pulled herself away from me, and I pointed her over to a corner, away from Carter. As we did that, I heard Trent call two Sentinel uniforms down to give him a hand at the detector. They began processing people through again.

"They're fucking our security," she said to me.

"I know," I told her.

She brushed her hair back over her right ear with an angry hand, nearly yanking her earpiece free. She turned her head to look back at the SAIC, who was now clearly king of his domain, then looked at me again. "I hate that guy," she said. "Asshole feeb."

"Yeah," I said.

"It makes our job harder, Atticus." She took a couple more deep breaths, then said, "I'm fine. Really, I'm fine."

"You sure?"

"Oh, yeah. I've dealt with sexist assholes before, why should he be any different?"

"No reason."

"Exactly," Natalie said. "No reason." She looked at where the crowd was now flowing toward registration. "Son of a bitch."

"Give me twenty minutes or so," I said. "Radio when it's clear to bring her down."

"Understood." She turned back to me and said, "It's just tension, I know. You know and I know, just tension. I'm fine now. Just had to blow off some steam."

"Made your father's day."

"Think I embarrassed him enough?"

"Close, maybe."

"See you soon," she said, and with a bitter little smile headed back to the metal detector.

I sat beside Romero on the raised platform at the south end of the Imperial Ballroom, trying to look inconspicuous. Also on the platform were Veronica Selby, a city councilman, a pastor from a church in Buffalo, a doctor from Mount Zion, and a nun.

The room was packed for the opening, faces and faces and faces, each with a pair of hands, always moving. Dale was on the door to the west, scanning the crowd and ready to secure our escape if it came to that, while Rubin stood by the entrance, watching everyone as they came in. Between Rubin and myself, we had a full view of the room. Natalie was outside, floating, and I could hear her commentary in my ear.

"No sign SOS . . . no sign Crowell . . . Rubin, black jacket, baseball cap, watch him . . . nothing at registration . . . crowd's stable out front. . . ."

When Selby went to speak, she parked her wheelchair just in front of the podium, and the nun handed her the microphone. She was greeted with applause, and began by thanking people for coming.

That was the last clear thing I heard her say before her voice turned into a background noise against Natalie's commentary. I kept my eyes moving over the crowd, listening to Natalie's hot wash of information, and wished I could stand up, roam, move, instead of needing to pretend I was a panelist.

In my ear, I heard Rubin say, *"Baseball cap, hands clear."*

Dale said, *"Third row, fifth from center, bouquet of flowers."*

"A lot of people carrying flowers," Rubin said.

A man with light brown hair moved a red backpack onto his lap in the second row.

"Second row, third from left, backpack on lap," I said softly.

Rubin took six steps, saying, *"Looking . . . looks like a program."*

The backpack returned to the floor.

A lot of applause filled my ears, and Selby was rolling back to her place on the podium.

"Pogo's up," I said.

Dr. Romero rose and her right hand brushed my shoulder as she went to the podium.

"Confirmed," Natalie said.

"Movement on the aisle, eighth row," Dale said.

"Camera," Rubin said.

"Fucking reporters."

"Another one," Rubin said.

"News crew in the lobby," Natalie said. *"I'll hold them."*

There were several flashes as pictures were taken.

". . . compelled to be doctors, lawyers, police officers, or bodyguards," Romero was saying. "We make a choice, and we make it with the same joy, trepidation, and fear as we make all the other choices in our lives. . . ."

"Eleventh row, red skirt getting up," Dale said.

"Moving . . . heading your way," Rubin said.

I heard a woman ask Dale directions to the bathroom. He directed her out past Rubin, then said, *"I'm clear."*

"Clear," Rubin agreed.

". . . disagree? Witness Drs. Britton and Gunn," Romero said. "Witness the women shot while working in a clinic in Boston, or the individual who is confined to a wheelchair for simply managing a clinic in Springfield. Witness my daughter, whose only crime was that I was her mother. . . ."

"All units, we have an altercation at the west entrance," the dispatcher said in my ear. *"NYPD responding, all other posts hold steady."*

"Confirmed," I said softly.

"I've got a visual on that," Natalie said. *"Three women, NYPD on scene. They're breaking it up."*

"Bald man, last row, west side aisle, reaching for something," Rubin said. *"Wrapped in cloth, whatever it is. . . ."*

I tried to figure the fastest way to take Romero down to the floor. I couldn't see the person Rubin was referring to,

and tried to shift in my seat without making too much of a
distraction.

"I see him," Dale said. *"Can't get a make on what's in
his hands, moving."*

". . . result of cooperation, of two very different ideol-
ogies finding a common ground for discussion, and
through that, for hope. . . ."

"What is it?" I asked.

". . . *can't see,"* Rubin said. *". , , unwrapping . . . ,
well, fuck. It's a sweater."*

"Confirmed. He's putting on a sweater," Dale said.

I started breathing again.

"Air conditioner's on too high," Rubin said.

". . . if one of us can, then we all will profit. No one
need change sides. . . ."

"She's wrapping up," I said.

"Understood," Rubin said.

"Coming back," Natalie said.

". . . instead, agree on how we will fight one another,
if fighting is what we must do. But let us remember the
white flag of truce. Let us remember that flag is flying
here, now. Thank you very much for coming," Dr. Romero said. She took a step back as the crowd began to
applaud, then stopped as the ovation turned standing.

"They're going to their feet," Dale said.

I rose as the crowd did, and they continued to applaud.
Felice Romero looked around some more, stunned more
than anything else, and I moved forward to her. The
crowd rising was nice for her, but it made my job hell.

"Natalie, get in here," I said. "All others, stay on post."

"Confirmed," Natalie said.

"Confirmed," Rubin said, then Dale.

From the front row four women came to the platform,
offering Romero a bouquet of flowers. Felice started to
reach for them, then looked over at me. I nodded and she
took them. In her ear I said, "Hand them to me."

She nodded and handed me the bouquet, and I set it on my chair.

"The flowers are for Pogo," I said to my lapel.

"Understood."

Natalie emerged from the surging crowd, below the platform and in front of Felice. Dr. Romero handed me another bouquet, this one with an attached card. More people were coming forward, offering flowers or envelopes, though one held up a box covered in wrapping paper. I stepped forward for that and took it.

"I'll make sure she gets this," I told the man. He was old and gray and smelled of patchouli. The box felt light for its size, and nothing shifted as I put it on the chair. The man smiled and nodded at me, then backed into the crowd.

The flowers kept coming.

CHAPTER TWENTY-THREE

Felice sat on the couch in the command post. The lunch room service had brought sat untouched on the cart in front of her, as she read yet another card and tried to stop crying. Dozens of flowers were in the room, standing in glasses of water and lying on the table and bed. Roses, daisies, carnations, and even some lilies. Most were white, though some of the flowers were pale pink or yellow.

We had screened all the sealed envelopes and the one box for explosives and metal and had come up negative. Felice had held the first envelope without opening it, and I knew she was afraid of what they might call her this time.

But she had opened the envelope anyway and found not a threat or condemnation, but a condolence card.

Dear Doctor Romero:
Please accept our sincerest sympathies for the loss of your daughter. Our prayers are with you at this

*time, and although we know your pain will never go
away entirely, we wish you memories of joy.*
                        Sincerely,
                        Christian Mothers for Life

Over twenty-five signatures were on the card in different color inks.

Every card was a variation on the first, some longer,
some shorter, but all offering support for Dr. Romero's
loss from both the pro-life and pro-choice sides. Additionally, some praised her courage with words of admiration
that made her blush when she read them. She opened the
box to find a white scarf that had been hand-knitted, em-
broidered with the words "Common Ground." His card
had said, simply, "May this warm you when you are cold."
The scarf smelled of patchouli, too.

Felice read the last card and set it carefully with the
others, saying, "I'd forgotten, you know?" She wiped her
eyes with a napkin from the cart, removing her glasses
first. Then she blew her nose. "I absolutely did not expect
this."

"This'll probably happen again at your panel and at
your talk," I said. "When they bring you gifts, hand them
directly to me. If it isn't wrapped, if it's anything they want
you to open then and there, let me handle it."

"I will," she said.

Natalie said in my ear, *"We're ready in the Imperial."*

"Crowell shown up?"

"That's a negative," she said. *"No sign of him. Don't
think he's coming."*

"We're going to take a few minutes to get down there,"
I said.

"All right. Then I'll check three."

I grinned. It was our code for using the bathroom. That
way if anyone was listening, they wouldn't know we were
suddenly short one person on our detail. "Confirmed," I
said.

"The panel?" Felice asked me.

"It's time."

She wiped her eyes again, then put her glasses back on. I helped her into her blazer, and she took my hand when she slipped into it, turning to face me. She said, "Thank you, Atticus."

"It's not over yet," I said.

"I know. But I haven't ever thanked you, I don't think. And I want you to know."

"You're welcome," I said. "You're doing fine."

"Am I?"

"Yes. Katie would be proud."

Natalie came back on, saying, *"I'm check four."*

"Confirmed. Pogo is on the move."

The panel was titled, "Abortion and Reproductive Rights: Means of Family Planning." Six people were on the panel, and it was moderated by none other than Madeline, whose last name turned out to be Schramm. It also turned out that she was a full professor of Ethics at NYU. The table on the dais was long, set five feet back from the edge of the platform, with the panelists all seated facing the room. Each person had a microphone, a pad of paper, a pencil, and a glass of water. A full pitcher was placed on either side of the moderator for refills. Dr. Romero sat second in from the left, beside the director of Planned Parenthood for Manhattan on one side, and a man from Social Services on the other. On the other side of Madeline sat Veronica Selby, a professor of religion from some seminary upstate, and an author from Vermont.

I stood about four feet behind Romero, a little to the left. This time, my view of the room was unobstructed, and I could see just about everything. Again Dale and Rubin were covering the exit and entrance, and again, Natalie was floating outside.

The room was packed. People stood at the back and sat

on the floor in front of the platform. Before we had started, two Sentinel uniforms had walked through at our request and made certain all the aisles were clear. So far, they had remained that way, and the crowd was remarkably still, paying careful attention.

The dispatcher came over my radio shortly after Romero was seated, saying, *"Mr. Kodiak, be advised we have confirmation of one Sean Rich at the west entrance."*

"What's he doing?" I said.

There was a pause, then the dispatcher came back on. *"Working with the protesters. NYPD is watching him. Detective Lozano is here with me. He says Rich appears to be alone."*

"Keep me informed," I said.

"Ten-four."

"All guards," I said. "Confirm receipt of last conversation."

Natalie, Rubin, and Dale called in order, each saying they had heard.

"Be on the lookout," I said.

"Like we're not already?" Rubin said. He said it softly enough that the mike almost didn't pick it up.

"Rubin, repeat please?"

There was a pause. *"Uh, negative, Atticus. Was just giving some guy directions. I'm clear."*

Forty minutes into the panel, when Madeline was taking questions from the audience, a man in the sixth row suddenly struck the person in the seat next to him.

"Fight," I said to my mike, and moved directly behind Romero's seat.

"Got it," said Rubin.

The dispatcher came on, *"Units responding."*

Natalie appeared in the doorway, then started working her way down the aisle. Two Sentinel units followed her in about three seconds later, converging on where the two men were grappling. The people on either side of them had risen and recoiled. No one left the room.

"Gentlemen!" Madeline said. "Gentlemen, stop it!"

Not surprisingly, the two men continued to pummel and tear at each other and then they were being pulled apart by the guards, Natalie supervising. I heard her tell the uniforms to eject the men from the conference.

"NYPD responding," the dispatcher said in my ear.

From my left I saw the door behind Dale open and I brought my hands down onto Felice's shoulders, preparing to sweep the chair out from under her with my foot. Rich with a gun, I thought. Perfect.

"Dale, door," I said.

He turned and his right hand started back for his gun before he realized he was looking at a cop.

"What the fuck are you doing?" I heard him say.

The police officer said he was responding to the fight.

"Not through this door you don't," Dale told him. He jerked the cop into the room, then slammed the door. *"Nothing,"* he told me.

"I see," I said.

"Going to have to chat with the guards in the hallway," he said.

"After Pogo's secure."

"Of course."

I watched the policeman meet up with the two Sentinel uniforms and their angry charges. Spontaneous applause broke out in the audience when they were evicted from the room.

"It's unfortunate," Madeline told the crowd. "I think we were all hoping we could make it through this day without any violence. Let's hope that's all we'll have to worry about."

I let my hands slide off Felice and took two steps back, resuming my position.

Rubin, Dale, and I were walking Felice back to the command post when Natalie came over my radio.

"Atticus, be advised that I've been informed by NYPD that Rich left the premises over an hour ago."

"Why the hell wasn't I notified?"

"Lozano just found out," Natalie said. *"Apparently some sergeant on the ground thought that his arrival was the only important thing."*

"Wonderful."

We entered the CP, and I walked Felice to the bedroom, where she poured herself a cup of coffee and lit a cigarette. Fowler followed us in from the main room.

Dale said, "I'm going to go yell at the guards."

"You do that."

Rubin said, "I'm going to watch him yell at the guards."

"You do that, too."

They both left, and I sat on the sofa and removed my glasses. I got myself a glass of water from the room service cart, pulled four ibuprofen from my coat, and swallowed them. Shortly after the two pugilists had been dragged from the room, I'd felt the beginnings of a headache start at each of my temples. The ache had slid its way to my forehead by the time we were ready to remove Dr. Romero, and now it was enough to distract me from my sore ankle.

"How you holding up?" Fowler asked me.

I made a face.

He took his notepad out of a pocket and flipped it open, then waited for me to put my glasses back on. He said, "The prints on the stairwell came back. I've got an identification for you. Name is Paul Grant. No record, found his prints through the California DMV. Twenty years old, six feet three, two hundred and fourteen pounds. Blue eyes, blond hair. They're faxing a picture."

"I don't know the name," I said. "Sounds like the right guy, though."

"There's no record of a Grant with SOS. We're looking

for other information, and the Bureau office in Los Angeles is sending someone out to his home in Irvine to talk to his parents. Should have more information by the end of the day."

I nodded and rubbed my temples, thinking. Then I said, "Can you make sure that description gets passed to all the guards, everybody, along with the previous one?"

Fowler nodded. "I'll do that now."

"Crowell never showed?" I asked him.

"Not as far as I know. Guess he backed down."

I didn't like that. Crowell not showing worried me. Felice's analysis of his personality had seemed correct. If he was missing as great an opportunity as this, there had to be a good reason. And for Crowell, it seemed to me, a good reason and self-preservation would be identical.

Something was going to come down, I was certain. Grant or no, Bridgett's theories about SOS aside, Crowell wasn't going to let this convention end without leaving his mark on it somehow.

Fowler asked, "That all?"

"For now. Thanks."

He stopped at the door. "You're almost through this thing," he said. "Try to relax."

I didn't bother to respond.

". . . simply, a woman's right to reproductive services. In the deluge of media attention the abortion issue has attracted since *Roe* v. *Wade,* many of us have lost sight of this core point," Dr. Romero said. "The clinic I run provides a full range of family planning services, from education and counseling to medical services and AIDS testing.

"Yes, we perform abortions.

"As we also provide a full range of birth control methods, prenatal care, Pap smears, STD testing, pregnancy planning . . ."

We were in the New York Room now, Dr. Romero on

the platform, leaning intently toward the microphone. Her speech was in front of her on the speaker's podium, but she was hardly referring to it, glancing down at the yellow legal sheets occasionally only for reference. She spoke clearly, committed to having her words heard and understood.

And again, I was on the platform, four feet back from her, off to the right, listening to Natalie's hot wash in my ear, letting my eyes scan the crowd. Of the five hundred seats that had been set up, all of them were filled, and again people stood at the back of the room and sat on the floor, away from the aisles. The metal cover to the light switches I'd noticed the day before had been replaced, and Rubin stood beside it at his post by the entrance.

This crowd had busy hands, though, many of the people taking notes. Rubin had noted four reporters, and, again, there were multiple photographers. Veronica Selby was in the audience, also, her chair parked on the outside of the second row on my right, the side nearest the entrance.

"Looks like the SOS protest is breaking up outside," Natalie said in my ear.

"Confirmed," I said.

"I'm working back to the second floor," she said. *"First floor clear."*

"Black coat, black tie, ninth row, near the aisle," Dale said. *"Reaching in bag . . ."*

I shifted my gaze, saw the man Dale meant. He was young, blond hair, but not big enough to be Grant and too big to be Barry.

"Photographer," Dale said. *"He's changing lenses on his camera."*

I looked away, letting my eyes sweep back to the right quadrant of the room, and then saw a face I knew.

"Mary Werthin is in the audience," I said softly. "Fourth row, fifth from left, blue floral print dress."

"Looking . . ." Rubin said. *"Hands are clear."*

"Confirm, hands are clear," Dale said. *"She has a purse."*

"Watch her," I said. "Dispatch, advise Detective Lozano that Mary Werthin is in the audience."

"Will do," the dispatcher said.

"Want me back?" Natalie asked.

"Negative. Continue float."

"Confirmed."

Mary Werthin was watching Romero, but it didn't seem that she was listening. Her hair was tied back, and she looked quite young. My immediate concern was more for Felice. As far as I could tell, she hadn't seen Werthin yet.

". . . cannot say it is simply an issue of family. It is an unstable word, treacherous and constantly changing," Dr. Romero was saying. "To maintain that the only family of merit is, by definition, one husband, one wife, and a minimum of one child is ludicrous in this day and age. More to the point, perhaps, it is impractical. The need for family planning services, then . . ."

"Lozano's here," Rubin said.

Sure enough, the detective was standing just inside the door, next to Rubin, who indicated Werthin's position.

"He wants to know if she should be removed."

"No need yet," I said.

I watched Rubin relay that to the detective, who nodded, made brief eye contact with me. He remained by the door.

I resumed scanning, trying to concentrate on the crowd, trying to keep tabs on Mary Werthin. She didn't move much, barely reacting to Romero's speech, even when the crowd applauded something. But she flinched every time Felice said the word "abortion."

Cute effect, I thought.

"Atticus," It was Natalie. *"Bridgett Logan is on her way up to the New York Room."*

"Confirmed."

"She says she needs to talk to you."

"It'll have to wait."

"Obviously."

A man seated on the floor by the front row moved suddenly, and I zeroed in on him. "Movement, floor left, front row," I said.

"Responding," Rubin said, and I saw him step forward in my periphery. The man reached for a pocket and I started calculating my takedown, then stopped when I saw he had removed a handkerchief from his pocket. He blew his nose quietly, checked the cloth, then folded it again and returned it to his coat.

"Hands clear," Rubin said.

"Confirmed."

"Logan's here," he said.

I glanced over at the door and saw Bridgett standing there, and we made eye contact and she grinned. She looked amazingly out of place, and a couple of heads turned and stared at her. After a moment, she started down the aisle to where Selby was parked.

I went back to scanning the crowd, listening to the traffic in my ear.

". . . will not change. This right of self-determination will not go away," Dr. Romero said. "It has existed for thousands of years. Abortion is only a small part of it. The battle over the right to one's own body will continue. Making any of these services illegal, restricting them through claims of immorality or decadence, will do nothing to remove the inherent right of freedom of choice."

She stopped speaking. For a moment she just looked over her audience. Then she said, "That's my talk. I want to thank you for coming, for listening with open minds. I've only one more thing to add.

"The last several weeks leading up to this conference I can say, honestly, have been the most difficult of my life. Certain organizations, certain individuals, were determined that I should not speak today.

"I do not know why I was singled out among all the

doctors and clinics in Manhattan. It's an arbitrariness that cost the life of my daughter, Katherine. It's an arbitrariness that has revealed all the worst about the human spirit to me. Frequently in the last few days, I reconsidered my decision to attend. There hardly seemed a point."

Dr. Romero stopped long enough to take a drink of water from the paper cup on the podium.

"When I resolved I would still attend today, I did so simply to spite those people who had worked so hard to keep me from coming," she said. "I did it as an act of defiance, which I told myself was for the memory of my daughter.

"Arriving here this morning, surrounded by policemen and bodyguards, I expected the worst.

"When I read the first card given to me this morning, I feared what it would say. The letters I've received in the past have been hardly kind.

"This card offered sympathy and condolences.

"The card was from an organization called Christian Mothers for Life. An antiabortion group, a pro-life group, call it what you will.

"It made me weep.

"I had forgotten, you see? I had forgotten exactly what this conference was about. My motive in attending had changed. I did not arrive this morning wanting peace. I wanted vindication. Victory.

"And this card made me see that I had become exactly the kind of person this conference was designed to reach out to," Felice said. "If I can be reached, after all that has happened, if I can see moderation and hope, then we all can.

"Thank you again."

"They're going to their feet," Rubin said in my ear.

He needn't have bothered with the transmission. They were up before he had finished speaking, applauding so loud that I almost lost what he was saying. I saw Veronica Selby beaming, her smile radiant, clapping with the rest of the crowd. Bridgett stood behind her, shaking her head slowly from side to side.

And I didn't see Mary Werthin.

"I've lost sight of Werthin," I said.

"Can't see her," Dale said. *"Too much traffic."*

People were starting to push forward in the aisles, and I saw more flowers being held up, more cards. The crowd was a mass of noise, still applauding, now cheering. Felice took a step to the edge of the platform, taking someone's offered pen and program, and she was blushing as she autographed it. I moved in closer to her, scanning like mad as too many people pushed toward us. Romero began handing me cards and bouquets, and I began dropping them in a pile behind me just as quickly.

"Natalie, get in here," I said.

"Confirmed."

". . . see her," Rubin came in. *"I see her, she's got something in her hands."*

"Repeat?" I said.

"Werthin's got something in her hands, it's not her purse. . . ."

"I can't see her," Dale said.

"What's in her hands?" I asked Rubin.

". . . something, looks like a book. . . ."

"Where?" I said.

"Just fantastic," a young black woman was saying to Dr. Romero. "God bless you, Doctor. . . ."

"She's in the crush, I've lost her, I can't see her," Rubin said.

I pulled Felice back a half step, further from the edge, but she went right back, taking another card and transfering it to me, thanking the couple that handed it to her. Then she stepped off the platform, taking another offered pen and program, scribbling her name. I dropped off after her, trying to stay tight.

"Pogo's off the platform," I said.

". . . her," Dale said. *"Ten feet up, center aisle."*

I couldn't see anything in the crowd. "Hands?"

"Can't see them. No purse."

"Rubin?"

"Nothing, boss, shit," he said.

"She's moving up," Dale said. *"No, damnit, I've got to move in."*

"Hold your position," I told him, taking another bunch of carnations and dropping them behind me.

"Confirmed."

A woman with silver hair held up a wicker basket for Romero to take, a shiny white bow on the handle. I flinched as Felice grabbed it, taking it from her as gently as I could and setting it on the platform beside me. Turning back around, I saw Mary Werthin at the front of the line, holding a pen and a hardcover book.

Abortuaries and the Death of America, by Jonathan Crowell.

Felice was leaning to take the book, but then she recognized Werthin and stopped long enough for me to move forward and intercept. "I'll give it to her," I said.

"I want her to sign it," Werthin said. "She has to sign it." She pushed the book forward, trying to get it around me.

I blocked her arm with my body, and she drew the book back. "I'll give it to her," I said once more. Under the edge of the cover, opposite the spine, a sliver of blue fabric jutted free. The edge looked rough and curly. I took the book with my right hand, Werthin still holding it.

It was too heavy.

She tried to jerk the book back, saying, "She has to sign it!"

Then the adrenaline dumped and I thought a lot at once. Velcro, I thought. Velcro keeping the book shut and the book's too heavy and it's not a gun inside this book, no, it's a bomb.

I keyed my transmitter, and as I did it I knew that the bomb wasn't radio-controlled, couldn't be with all the radio traffic in the hotel, or else it would've gone off as soon as Werthin arrived. Wasn't motion-sensitive, or else it would've gone off as she brought it through the crowd. Must be a timer, must be a timer or a switch. I swung my left foot around and behind Werthin's legs, jerking the book toward me with my right.

She's pregnant, I remembered.

Then I hit her in the middle of the sternum with the palm of my left hand, sending her back over my leg, into the crowd of people still milling there, looking shocked. She released the book when she fell.

And I said, "Bomb."

The adrenaline made it come out far louder than I would've liked.

People began backing away, and then someone screamed, and almost en masse, they turned and ran for the door.

"Dale, get over here," I yelled, and he was already halfway to me, climbing over the seats as I turned and pulled Felice back onto the platform, away from the people, out of the crowd. Most of the people were packed into the far side of the room already, pushing for the exit, and I heard Rubin try to transmit and then give up as he was washed out by the panic.

"Evac," I said. I said it three times, and tried to make it clear.

"En route," Natalie said.

Dr. Romero's eyes were wide and on mine and then she looked at my right hand and took a quick step back, her left shoe knocking the wicker basket over. A stuffed bear fell out onto the floor. The bear had a yellow hat and a blue jacket, and something was pinned to its coat.

I'm holding a bomb, I realized.

Bridgett shouted, "What do I do?"

"Hold her," I said, indicating Werthin with my head. Dale had made the platform and had already drawn his weapon, scanning for a secondary threat. I looked, too,

and saw Veronica Selby still seated in her wheelchair, eyes
on us. She was bone-white.

That was it. The crowd was still pushing out the door
with one mind.

Bridgett went down and grabbed Werthin, who was trying to slide away on her rump. Dale went down to help
her.

"You can't do this, you pushed me, you bastard,"
Werthin kept screaming.

"Natalie, where the fuck are you?" I asked.

"En route, goddamnit," she said.

"All units, repeat, we are evacuating, we are evacuating," I said. "Get Pogo the hell out of here, now."

I saw Natalie push through the doorway, running to us,
followed by Rubin and Lozano. As soon as Dale saw them,
he went to the side door. He opened it with a sharp push,
stepping back, then looked down the corridor, his gun
leading.

Bridgett was telling Werthin that she had the option to
stop moving voluntarily or to become permanently dis-
abled.

"Rubin, get Selby out of here," I shouted to him, and he
veered off from heading to us and went to her wheelchair.
Lozano made straight for Werthin. He reached her as Natalie finally made the platform, grabbing Felice with both
arms.

"Do exactly what I tell you," Natalie said to the doctor.

"But Veronica—"

"Rubin's handling it," I said. "Get out of here. Now!"

She started to say something more but Natalie lifted her
off the platform and then ran her to where Dale stood by
the exit. Rubin had Selby almost to the door, and they
were practically bowled over by three more men coming
in, one marshal, Fowler, and an NYPD uniform. The uniform took over on Selby's wheelchair and Rubin headed
back toward me.

"No," I yelled at him. "Not me. Go with Pogo, damnit."

He stopped, looked at me, then turned and followed in the direction Natalie and Dale had gone.

Lozano was cuffing Werthin, who screamed that he was trying to kill her baby.

"You're under arrest," he said, pulling her to her feet.

"What kind is it?" I asked her, showing her the book.

"Rot in hell, you bastard, you tried to—"

"What kind of bomb is it?" I asked her again.

Her mouth stayed open but she issued no sound, and all that was in her eyes before turned to panic. She tried to run for the door, but Lozano had a good grip, and the marshal helped him hold her. She said, "Oh my God, oh my God, that's why I wasn't supposed to open it, oh sweet Jesus—"

"Who gave this to you?"

"It's—oh God, I swear I didn't know," she said, turning her head from me to Bridgett to Fowler to the marshal, trying to convince all of us at once. "He gave it to me, I swear—"

"Who?" Bridgett asked her.

"Mr. Rich, he gave it to me, he told me to have the butcher sign it, oh my God."

"Get her out of here," Fowler said, pulling his radio. He keyed it and said, "All units, search the immediate area for Sean Rich. Consider him armed and extremely dangerous. He's wanted for questioning."

The marshal helped Lozano remove Werthin from the room. At this point it wasn't truly necessary; she had become almost docile.

"I didn't know, oh God, I swear I didn't know. . . ." she kept saying.

"The bomb squad should be here any moment," Fowler said to me. He said it very gently, as if he was talking to a child.

"Oh, good," I said.

"You want to put the book down now, Atticus?" he said.

I looked at the book in my right hand, watched a drop of sweat from my forehead hit the cover, heard it splat on the glossy surface. "Yeah, I'd like that, Scott," I said.

"Go ahead, then," he said.

I looked at the book. I looked at him. I looked at Bridgett. "Maybe you guys should leave the room," I said.

"Not without you," Bridgett said.

"See," I said. "I don't know what the mechanism is, and if it's a timer, it could go off any moment. So better that there's just me here, you see?"

"And you'll do what, exactly?"

"I'm going to put the book down," I said. "Then I'm going to lay the podium over the book, to tamp the blast. Then I'm going to run away. Very fast."

"Sounds like a plan," Fowler said softly.

"See you in a minute," I said.

Scott started to back out of the room. Bridgett didn't move.

"Go," I said.

She didn't move.

"Bridgett, please. Go away."

She held my eyes for a moment, then took three or four steps back. Then she stopped.

"Dinner's at eight, stud," she said.

Then she turned and ran with Fowler to the exit.

When they were out the door, I stepped back onto the platform. I figured the bomb was plastique, and it didn't feel more than six or seven pounds. More than enough to make finding all my pieces a true challenge were it to go off. At the center of the platform I knelt down, setting the book beside where the teddy bear had fallen from the basket.

The note pinned to the bear's coat read, "Please look after this bear."

It took some effort to get my fingers off the book. I held my breath when I let go, as if that would have made a damn bit of difference.

The book didn't do anything.

I stood, grabbed the podium, and pulled it toward the center of the platform. Romero's speech fluttered off the stand, and her cup of water fell over. My hands were sweating, and my grip slipped when the cup hit the ground, the noise scaring the hell out of me. I caught the podium before it fell, then lowered it over the book. It wouldn't do much, but it was something.

I scooped up the bear on the way out.

CHAPTER TWENTY-FOUR

I ran like hell.

The second floor had been evacuated, and I jumped the rope that had been strung over the end of the escalator and went down it faster than my hurt ankle would have liked, and still too slow for my taste. The metal detector shrieked at me when I ran through it, but I didn't stop, sprinting through the empty lobby and out onto Fifty-third Street, where the evacuees had gathered.

Evacuating an entire hotel into a Manhattan street on a summer's evening is truly a sight to behold. People were everywhere, most with dazed looks, some pissed at having their lives disrupted, some enjoying the confusion. I wondered how many of them knew exactly what was going on.

I moved off to the other side of the street, then keyed my radio. "Natalie?" I said. "Come in."

She came in faint, cut with static. *"Atticus? Are you all right?"*

"I'm fine. How's Pogo?"

"We've almost gotten her home."

"Confirmed. I'll be in touch," I said. Then I looked around, trying to find a face I recognized. There wasn't one. After a few minutes of looking, I saw a man in a Sentinel uniform and cornered him, asking to use his radio. He relinquished it reluctantly. I guess he didn't trust my teddy bear.

"This is Kodiak. Somebody come in," I said.

Trent came on. *"Atticus? Where are you?"*

"North side of the building."

"Come around to the west."

I told him I would and handed the radio back to the guard. He checked it carefully, making certain I hadn't hurt it.

The bomb squad was entering the building as I came around the corner onto Seventh Avenue. The fire department had already arrived, and was cordoning off the street. I worked through the crowd and found Trent in a cluster of people, with Selby, Madeline, and Bridgett.

"You're all right?" Selby asked when she saw me. "You're fine?"

I nodded. Selby touched my hand, and said, "And Felice, she's all right, too?"

"She's safe," I said.

Bridgett put her hand on my arm and brought her mouth to my free ear, saying, "NYPD found Rich."

"Where?"

"He was parked in the garage. When the evacuation started, he couldn't get out of the lot. Fowler and the rest took him and Werthin to Midtown North."

"Let's go," I said.

"I'm just waiting for you, stud."

In her Porsche, I examined the teddy bear carefully. It was the real thing, not stuffed with anything more dangerous than wadding.

"Cute," Bridgett said.

"I'll get you one."

"I'd die first."

I set the bear on the floor, then shut off my radio and began removing my wires.

"Did Fowler get an ID on the fellow we ran into yesterday?" she asked.

"His name is Paul Grant," I said. "No record. That's about all he got."

She pursed her lips for a moment, then reached into her jacket pocket and pulled out a sheaf of papers, folded in half. She handed them to me, saying, "This is what I got at the clinic. All the inactive files of the last year. I haven't had a chance to sort them yet."

I looked them over. It looked to be over one hundred names, and they were listed alphabetically. There was no Grant.

"Sorry," I said.

"Stab in the dark," Bridgett said. "You okay?"

"I'm waiting for my heart to start beating normally," I said.

"Patience."

One of the marshals who had worked the conference was at the Midtown North front desk, talking to a cop, when we arrived, and he escorted us to the room that had been commandeered for the combined agencies. Lozano was the only person inside I recognized.

"Hey, it's the hero," he said when he saw me. "Let me buy you a cup of caffeine. Have a seat."

Bridgett and I sat down and Lozano poured two cups of coffee from the urn on the stand in the corner, asking, "Either of you want it doctored?"

We both said no.

He brought us our coffee and sat down at the table, watching as we sipped.

"God almighty," Bridgett said, and set down her cup. "This is obscene."

Lozano chuckled and lit a cigarette. "They're making me sit it out," he said. "Not my precinct."

"Rich's in interrogation?" I asked.

"Yeah. Captain Harner and Fowler are running at him right now."

"Was it a bomb?" I asked.

He raised his eyebrows at me. "Be a bit anticlimactic if it wasn't, huh? Yeah, it was a bomb. They disarmed it about fifteen minutes ago, said it was a real simple device. They're running it over to forensics now, doing a rush job. We'll see what they get off it."

"I want to know how she got it into the conference," I said.

"Well, I don't know how it got past the detectors, all that," Lozano said. "But Werthin gave a full statement. Says she was protesting outside, and Rich showed up about noon. She saw him asking if anyone had seen Crowell. She says he left shortly after that, but came back around three. Rich called her over—he knew her from the paint incident, he was the one who told her to do it, she says—handed her the book, and said that Mr. Crowell wanted her to take it in and get it autographed by Romero. Says that Rich told her it would be a perfect reminder of exactly what a mockery Common Ground is, or words to that effect."

"And whatever you do, don't open it?" I said.

"Yeah. She didn't think it was odd, figured there was something inside, maybe some fish guts, she says. He told her to hide it in her dress, since she was pregnant and all."

"Christ, is that woman stupid," Bridgett said.

"She's committed," Lozano said. "That's not the same thing."

"In this case, Detective, it is."

He shrugged, put his cigarette out in his coffee, then stood. "I'll tell the captain you're here." He left without looking at Bridgett.

I loosened my tie, then got up and threw the rest of my coffee into the trash can.

"How's the pulse?" Bridgett asked.

"Better," I said. There was a phone in the room, and I used it to call the safe apartment. Rubin answered, and I asked him how things looked.

"We're fine here," he said. "Nobody followed us, and we've locked down. Felice is a bit shaky, but that's it."

"Good work," I said.

"Yeah? You're fucking nuts, you asshole," Rubin said, and there was true anger in his voice. "What were you going to do? Disarm it yourself?"

"I had to make sure it didn't go off while anybody else was there."

"I kept imagining what I'd tell your parents. 'Dear Mr. and Mrs. Kodiak, I'm sorry but your little boy Atticus got himself blown up.' That would have been quite a phone call," he said, still mad.

"Not one you need to make."

"For now. So, what's next?"

"I'm at Midtown North. They found Rich at the scene, and he's in interrogation. I'm going to stick here for a bit, see what's what."

Rubin said that sounded fine to him, and then I asked to talk to Natalie. I double-checked that Felice was all right, then told her I'd try to come back sometime that evening.

"Romero's writing the check," Natalie said.

"Guess that means we're out of a job," I said.

"Day after tomorrow, she says. Wants us until the funeral, I think."

"It's her choice."

"And the client is almost always right," Natalie said. "We did it. Got her in and out in one piece."

"I owe you a drink," I said. "You did good work today."

"Yeah, I did."

"Don't let it go to your head."

"We've got an all-points out for Crowell and Barry," Fowler told me. "He won't tell us where they are, says he doesn't know."

He gestured to the one-way mirror, and I looked in on Rich in the interrogation room. He was seated at the desk, a paper cup in front of him. He was wearing jeans, no holes, and a red button-up shirt. He had cowboy boots on, too, crocodile skin. He didn't look worried.

"Has he lawyered up?" Bridgett asked.

"Not yet," Fowler said.

"You serious?"

He nodded, eyes on Rich. "I don't understand it, either. He knows his Miranda, says he doesn't want a lawyer. Not even when Harner showed him a copy of the CSU prelim on the bomb. His prints were all over it."

"Tell me about the device," I said.

"Six pounds of Semtex tied to a variation of a mouse-trap switch," Fowler said. "Spaced the wires so the mass of the metal was diffused. The detector didn't pick it up."

"It would've if Carter hadn't lowered the setting," I said.

Scott shrugged. "Thing is, Semtex is a professional's explosive, like plastique. I mean, it's not that hard to get, relatively speaking. The IRA bought tons of it off the Czechs a few years back, then brought it into the country."

"In the spirit of capitalism," Bridgett said.

"Give the lady a cigar," Fowler said. "They sold it to anyone who had the cash. It's been popping up everywhere."

"Where'd he get it?" I asked.

"Won't say. Won't say if there's any more of it, either."

"Can we talk to him?"

Fowler looked back through the mirror, then nodded. "Hand over your weapons, first," he said.

We gave him our guns and he let us into the room.

When Rich saw me, he grinned. "Hey, boy," he said. "You're one lucky son of a bitch, aren't you?"

"Blessed," I said.

"Well, God works in mysterious ways," Rich said, and laughed.

I pulled a chair and sat down. Bridgett leaned against the wall.

"You're a pretty one," Rich told her. "Come sit on my lap."

She snorted and pulled a quarter from her pocket. "Here's twenty-five cents; buy yourself a new line." She tossed the coin over to him and Rich batted it out of the air, knocking it to the floor with a jingle.

"Cunt," he said.

"My, you're a regular Oscar Wilde," Bridgett said. "That was a shitty piece of work."

"What are you talking about?"

"Your bomb," she said. "It stank."

"Now, why do you go and say a thing like that, hon? There's no need to be mean."

"Just stating a fact, Sean," Bridgett said. "That was shoddy work. I mean, it didn't even go off, and your prints were all over it."

"Well, see, sweetheart, thing with a bomb is, when it goes off, you don't have a whole lot to look for prints on."

"But it didn't go off," I said.

He looked at me. "It would have, boy. It would have blown her to hell without breaking a sweat."

"And Mary Werthin, too," Bridgett said.

"She'd have gone to heaven, hon. She'd have gone to heaven."

"And Mary Werthin's baby?" I asked.

There was a pause. Rich kept his eyes on Bridgett.

"Would her unborn baby have gone to heaven?" I asked.

"You bet your ass."

I sighed. "She's right, Sean. That was sloppy work. You were so hard to kill Dr. Romero, you'd have killed a baby to do it."

"You don't know what the fuck you're talking about, boy."

"I'm talking about your firecracker," I said.

"Where's Crowell?" Bridgett asked.

"I don't know," Rich said.

"Did he know you made that bomb? That you were going to kill a baby to kill Dr. Romero?" I asked.

"Or is that just the way it works?" Bridgett asked. "Like killing Katie."

"That's probably it," I told her. "He builds bombs to kill babies with."

"I didn't have anything to do—" Rich said.

"You're a liar," Bridgett told him.

"About as good a liar as a demolitions man," I said.

"Well, I'm a damn good demolitions man," he said. "And I'm not lying."

"Then who killed Katie Romero?" Bridgett asked.

"Shut up, bitch."

She smiled. "Who's Paul Grant?"

"Never heard of him," Rich said.

There was a knock on the mirror, and then the door opened and Fowler said, "All right, that's enough."

"We were just getting started," Rich told him.

"Don't worry, Sean. You'll have more company soon."

"He was lying about Grant," Bridgett said. "He knows him."

Scott nodded.

"How do you know?" I asked.

"He was taking his time on everything else, except when

we were pressing him," she told me. "On that one, he had the time, and he rushed. Trust me."

"It may not matter," Fowler said. "We get Crowell in for questioning, I'm certain one of them will roll on the other."

"Nobody's brought him in yet?" I asked.

"We can't find him," Scott said.

"First Barry, then Crowell."

"They probably left town. If the bomb had gone off, they'd have been at the top of our suspect list."

"So they left in anticipation," Bridgett said.

He nodded. "Rich thinks he's buying them time. We'll give him a little while to stew on it, then hit him with Katie's murder, see what else breaks loose. He's already confessed to building the bomb, so he's got to know that his options are diminishing. He'll break, and when he does, we'll know who killed Katie."

We went to a bar near the precinct house. Bridgett had a pint of Guinness and I had a Scotch.

"He's wrong about Rich and Katie," Bridgett said. "There's no link there to Romero, no revenge motive."

"None that we've found," I said. "Does this mean you buy my theory?"

"At this point, yes. Look at the list. Is there a Rich anywhere on it?"

I pulled it out and flipped to the last page, looking. "Rafael, Rodriguez, Rossi, Ruez," I said. "No Rich."

"Sigh and double sigh," she said, and drank some of her Guinness.

I put the papers on the bar and sipped my Scotch, thinking. The names on the list were in small print, in four columns, starting with the last name, then the first, then a date, and then a number.

"The dates are for what?" I asked Bridgett.

"When the file went inactive," she told me. "Lynn explained it to me. If a patient misses three follow-ups, moves, has their records transferred, or dies, they close the file. The last number is the actual file code."

I finished my drink, looking at the dates on the first page. A couple of them were recent, in the last month. One of them only ten days ago. "Baechler, Melanie," I said.

"She on there?"

"Closed out about a week before Katie died. Melanie Baechler," I said, and then it hit me, and I read it again.

"What?"

"Katie," I said. "Oh, yes, that's it, that's got to be it. Katie knew her. Melanie B. Melanie Baechler. Katie knew her."

Bridgett turned on the stool and looked closely at me. "What are you talking about?"

"Why's she on the list?" I asked her. "It doesn't say."

"I don't know. I told you, she could have moved or missed a follow-up or—"

"She's dead," I said. "That's got to be it."

"Explain it to me," Bridgett demanded.

I ordered a cup of coffee and did just that. Then I asked the bartender if he would let me see his white pages. I found the address I wanted, and Bridgett and I paid and left.

CHAPTER TWENTY-FIVE

Melanie Baechler's apartment was up on West 124th off Claremont, directly north of the Columbia campus, one of the many buildings consisting entirely of apartments rented to students, and it showed. Clean, well-lit, and fairly secure, but not so nice as to buck the average rent in the area. The first floor of the building on the south side had been converted into a bodega, so access to the interior was limited from the west. Standard New York fare, the same two-door setup that allowed entrance into my apartment building in the Village. The building was prewar design, gray with orange and blue art deco tiles around the trim. The tiles looked original, faded and weathered, and had a pleasant sheen in the fading light of dusk.

I held the door of the building for Bridgett and we stepped into the foyer, searching the intercom listing. Next to the button for 4A were the names "Baechler & Scarrio."

"You or me?" Bridgett asked.

"You," I said. "Your melodic voice and gentle manner will immediately put whoever answers at ease."

She gave me the finger and a smile and pressed the button.

After a few seconds we got a garbled voice saying, "Yes?"

"My name is Bridgett Logan. I was wondering if I could speak with you about Melanie Baechler?"

"She, uh . . . I'm sorry, but she . . . she passed away about a week and a half ago." Even with the distortion of the intercom, you could hear that the wound was still fresh.

"This is in connection with her death," Bridgett said. "I'm wondering if you would answer a few questions."

There was a long moment, filled with just the sound of the traffic on the street, and I wondered if this wasn't a wild goose chase after all. Melanie B. wasn't a real person. Katie had probably been referring to a character from a television show.

There was another click and the voice said, "All right." The intercom clicked off and the door buzzed. I pushed it open and we walked into a large and brightly lit lobby. There was a fern in the corner by the elevator, and it looked real, but I get fooled by the plastic ones a lot. A flight of broad stairs started at the left of the plant. We took them up. From over the rail I could see that the next floor, and the stairs, too, were well-illuminated. Security-conscious management, I suppose. It would be hard to take anyone by surprise around here. Maybe the owners could talk to my building's management.

At the end of the fourth-floor hall, opposite 4F, was 4A. The door was metal and painted white with no other markings upon it but for the peephole. Bridgett pressed the buzzer. The door opened immediately and a woman, perhaps in her early twenties, stood there.

"Are you the police?" she asked, looking at each of us

suspiciously. We were quite the couple, I admit, with Bridgett in her leather jacket and nose rings and me in my Brooks Brothers suit.

"No." Bridgett reached into a coat pocket. She produced a business card and handed it to the woman. "Private."

The woman glanced at the card, then asked, "What can I do for you?"

"We have some questions about Melanie Baechler," I said.

"Did Melanie's family hire you?" she asked. "The police haven't found the guy yet. They probably never will."

Bridgett said, "This is in relation to something else. Miss—?"

"Scarrio, Francine Scarrio." Francine had curly black hair, glossy and wild, wrapping her head and shoulders. She was wearing either a perfume or hair spray that smelled like strawberries and made my nose itch. Tugging a curl, Francine looked us both over again, then moved out of the way to let us in. We stepped onto a throw rug with blue-and-black five-pointed stars stitched into the weave. Francine Scarrio closed the door behind us, then slipped past in the narrow hallway and said, "Why don't you have a seat in here?"

"Here" was a combination office/living room/dining room, with a short hallway leading to the left and a galley kitchen off to the right. The walls had posters of different musicians and bands mounted with green thumbtacks, ranging from Melissa Etheridge to Miles Davis, and I counted six separate shoes, each without an apparent mate, as we walked into the main room. A table was positioned flush against the wall, and on it were a pile of envelopes, a roll of stamps, and a stack of stationery. The envelopes and stationery matched, each with a drawing of unicorns in the lower left corner. Scarrio took a chair from under the table, saying, "I was writing letters." It sounded like a guilty pleasure. She gestured to a small brown love seat and companion chair, saying, "Please."

Bridgett took the chair while I took the love seat. Scarrio was looking at the business card again. I looked at her. She had on a tight navy blue top, short-sleeved and low-cut, just above the swell of her breasts, and she had on white shorts and no shoes. Her skin was tanned, and she projected that collegiate vitality I'd seen in Alison when we first met. I wondered if anyone had ever complained about Francine's perfume.

She looked up at me and said, "Who are you?"

"My name's Kodiak."

"Are you both private eyes?" She didn't wait for an answer, but said, "What's this about?"

"Have you heard of the Women's LifeCare Clinic on Amsterdam and One Thirty-fifth?" I asked her.

"I've even been over there a couple of times—NARAL and clinic defense stuff. You know, demonstrations."

"When was the last time you were there?"

"Couple weeks ago, I think. Why?"

"You know about Katie Romero's murder?" Bridgett asked.

"The retarded girl?" Francine nodded, and her curls bounced on her shoulders.

"Did you know Katie?" I asked.

"I spoke to her once or twice."

Bridgett rolled her shoulders and looked around the room. "Baechler was your roommate?"

"Yes. What does this have to do with the clinic?"

"What can you tell us about Melanie's death?"

Francine frowned. "Melanie got mugged. She was coming back from dinner and she was mugged, some guy stole her purse and stuff. The police told me they think it's some crackhead, but they haven't found the guy." She picked at her nails for a moment. "He beat her to death."

"When was this?" I asked.

"Wednesday before last," Francine said, softly. "She'd

gone out to the library and then went to dinner off campus, at Kowloon's, and she got mugged on her way back. The guy beat her to death," she said again. "I had to identify her." She had a broad face with heavy freckles, and the lines around her eyes suddenly became vivid with the memory. "She's from Cincinnati, see? And her parents couldn't arrive until the next day."

"Were you close friends?"

She nodded.

"I'm sorry."

"I don't even know why she went out. We had done all this shopping the day before," Francine said. "We had all this food and she wanted to make a shepherd's pie."

Bridgett asked, "Did she have any boyfriends? Anything like that? Anyone she might have been out to eat with?"

"Melanie had a lot of friends, some were guys, if that's what you mean, but, like, she wasn't sleeping around."

"Both of you used the clinic, right?"

"We'd both been there."

"But inside?" Bridgett asked.

"No."

"How'd you meet Katie?" I asked.

Scarrio blinked. "She was outside once or twice."

"She didn't normally go out."

"It was at a demonstration."

"Francine," Bridgett said. "We don't really care what you've done at Women's LifeCare. We're just trying to figure out what Melanie's relationship to the clinic was."

She bit her lip. "We went there for our checkups."

"Columbia has a health service."

"We couldn't get the doctor we wanted," she said. She looked directly at Bridgett. "It's stupid, but I don't like having a male OB/GYN, you know. And Melanie didn't either, so this one time we went to the clinic and got examined there."

"There must be a female OB/GYN connected with the school," Bridgett said. "Why didn't you use her?"

"Dr. Lucas, the one we normally use, she's not here during the summer session. I was embarrassed. We'd made the appointment, found out it was Dr. Ferrer, he's this old guy, really nice, but just, you know? And I got all embarrassed. So I told Melanie and we decided to go to the clinic. We only went inside that one time. We didn't have abortions, if that's what you're trying to find out." She kept her eyes on Bridgett.

"That's where you met Katie?"

"She was just wandering around the building with, like, this Walkman on and the cord had gotten all tangled. Melanie asked her if she could help and they started talking about music."

"Madonna?" I asked.

"No, Cyndi Lauper, I think. Yeah, that's it, because we all sang a couple verses of 'Girls Just Want to Have Fun.' She couldn't sing very well. She was sweet."

"Anything else happen?"

She shrugged. This was ancient history and it was already cold for her. "We had to wait for a couple of hours before they could see us; they were busy, because there were protesters outside that day. Not many, but it was distracting. We spent a lot of that time talking to Katie. She couldn't pronounce my last name really well, so I told her to just call me Fran and she said she should know my last name so we settled on S. Fran S. So she was Katie R. and I was Fran S."

And Melanie was Melanie B.

"Melanie had no boyfriends?" Bridgett asked again, a little more insistently.

"She'd just broken up with a guy. They'd been seeing each other for maybe a month at the most. No big thing."

"When'd that happen?"

"The breakup? End of the term, would've been last week of May, I think."

"Why'd she stop seeing him?" I asked.

"Dunno. Melanie said he was hard to talk to, real old-fashioned."

"And she didn't see him after that?"

"No. I mean, if she saw Paul again, she didn't tell me about it."

There is a God, I thought.

"Could you describe Paul Grant?" I asked.

She stared at me a second as if she hadn't truly noticed me before, then got up, saying, "There's a picture of them." She disappeared into the last door on the hall, returning quickly with a Polaroid. She handed it to me. "I took that at a Yankee game we went to. That was the beginning of May."

Melanie Baechler was wearing a navy-and-white Yankee cap, pale hair spilling out around a thin face. She wasn't a big girl. My memory of Grant put him at over my height, and Melanie came to above his elbow in the photograph. She was smiling for the camera.

There was no question that the man holding Melanie's hand was the same one I'd seen outside the clinic, the same one Bridgett and I had chased out of Romero's building the previous night.

I handed the picture to Bridgett, asking Francine, "May we keep this?"

She hesitated, then nodded. "Sure."

"Where's he live?" Bridgett asked.

"I don't know."

"Did he ever go to the clinic?"

"Paul? Why would he?" Francine asked. She was looking bewildered and now just a bit scared. Her fingers tugged at one of her curls. "Do you think he knows something about Melanie's death?"

I looked at Bridgett, and she looked at the picture, then back to me. Then she said to Francine, "There's a chance that he may have murdered Melanie, as well as Katie Romero."

"What? What are you saying?"

"Francine—did Melanie have an abortion?"

"No! She didn't sleep around, I keep telling you, and besides that she was on the pill. We both were. That's why we had to go to the clinic, we had to get our prescriptions filled."

Bridgett stood up and I followed her lead. "Thank you," she said. "Keep the card. Maybe you'll remember something and give me a call, all right?"

"Wait, what do you mean he killed her? Why would he do that?"

Bridgett said, "Because he saw her enter the clinic. We know Grant was attending SOS demonstrations there. He saw her go into the clinic to abort his baby."

Francine shook her head, saying, "No, that's not right. We went for a Pap smear. She never had an abortion."

Bridgett didn't say anything.

"It's not right," Francine said. "You're not making sense. It's not right. That's crazy."

Out on the street Bridgett popped another mint. It was dark now, and the sodium lamp over the bodega made her hair shine. "Poor kid," she said.

"Francine and Melanie both," I said. "What do you think happened?"

"I think Baechler and Grant slept together, and when he saw her going into the clinic, he jumped to the conclusion that she was there to abort their child."

"And he killed her for it."

"And he killed Katie believing that he was balancing the scales, I guess. Romero took his child, so Grant took hers," she said. "They both died because Melanie Baechler needed a Pap smear."

We were getting into the car when my pager went off. I got back out and used a pay phone by the bodega.

"We've found Barry," Fowler said. "He's at your place."

"My place?"

"Asshole's threatening to blow the building up."

CHAPTER TWENTY-SIX

"I was making a circuit of the building," the patrolman said. There were sweat stains under his armpits, and around his collar. "Came around through the alley on Sullivan into the courtyard here, saw this guy up on the fire escape on the sixth floor. For a moment I thought, I don't know, I thought it was just some fuck trying a little B and E. He was toting a duffel bag, big blue-and-green thing. So I called backup and we went around, left my partner at the bottom of the fire escape in case he tried to come down that way. We're halfway up the stairs when my partner calls us back. Says he'd been made, said the shithead swears he has a bomb and is going to blow the place up. I got up to the sixth floor and Barry—and it's him, he gave his name—said if anyone comes any closer he is going to start shooting. Says he has a gun and a bomb.

"Then the circus came to town." The patrolman waved

his arm around the courtyard, smiled apologetically at me, then asked Lozano if that was all.

"That's all," the detective told him.

Lozano, Bridgett, and I stood on the outer perimeter line, at least twenty-five uniforms between us and the inner perimeter, where the commanding officers were assembled. There was no radio traffic, that had been disallowed the moment it was suspected that Barry might have a bomb, but the racket was still considerable, mostly from the crowd that had gathered. The media was still arriving, camera crews and photographers and reporters, and then there were the spectators, a lot of them kids freed for summer, with nothing better to do it seemed than to take bets on whether my home would be going up in a ball of flame.

Floodlights were up and running, bathing the building in halogen light. The courtyard spread in a perfect square at the back of all four buildings, with my apartment on the east side, sixth floor. Barry had pulled the blinds in Rubin's bedroom, preventing prying eyes from seeing just what he was up to. Facing that window, from the opposite building's roof, was one ESU sniper, poised and set with his rifle sighted on the bedroom window. Snipers waited on other roofs, covering all the possible angles of attack. There were really only two shots they could take, the first through Rubin's bedroom window and the second across the alley, and the snipers would take the shot only if Barry started gunning for lives.

Or if Barry was really serious, if he was really going to burn the place down.

And the cop was right. It was a circus.

Bridgett and I had arrived only seconds after the Manhattan North Emergency Service Unit team. Manhattan South had already been there, in position, for five minutes. They used to be called SWAT teams, but the title was changed to something less provocative, I guess, and now there were roughly forty ESU personnel milling about outside and inside the buildings. Only eight of them were snipers, the rest devoted to other tasks I could only guess at.

The Sixth Precinct commander was already on scene when we arrived, but he was quickly replaced by some inspector from One Police Plaza; I don't know what he did, either, but everybody deferred to him until the Chief of Detectives arrived and started commiserating with SAIC Carter, who showed up at roughly the same time, that is, about three minutes after we got there. Fowler was already there, and joined Carter when he saw him. Scott and I hadn't had a chance to speak, and I knew we wouldn't get one. Not now.

Then there was the Bomb Squad supervisor and one of his technicians, and a TARU guy, though nobody seemed to know what exactly he was supposed to do, but he was working closely with the hostage negotiator and all the personnel under the HN's command. That was just the police, mind: I'm not even talking about the fire units or the EMS units or the press, or all the units that had been evacuating the building. Everybody inside the perimeter wore heavy ballistic vests, the kind that would stop a .44 bullet, and consequently everyone was sweating like pigs. The night had cooled things a bit, but the humidity was rough. At least the snipers were comfortable; they don't wear the vests—hinders their movement, don't you know.

The hostage negotiator was on the phone when we arrived, talking carefully, but I couldn't hear a damn thing he was saying. He was talking to Barry, though, I knew that, because the negotiator kept watching the windows as he spoke.

So that was the circus, all gathered to see a little man from the Appalachians try to blow up my home because I scared him enough to wet his pants.

Lozano had his badge out, hung off his belt, and he wandered around inside the outer perimeter, and then returned to tell Bridgett and me what was going on, tugging at his vest like it pinched him. They wouldn't let us through; civilians had no place here. Bridgett ate Life Savers and I stood beside her in a corner of the courtyard, in a patch of shade, my hands in my pockets. It was a beautiful night, the sky deep and dark, no clouds, nothing to cut the depth. Every so often Bridgett would lean in and whisper something in my ear.

"They've cut the power and the water to the apartment," she would say.

Or, "See that guy? He's taking high-res photos. They'll develop them here and see if they show anything going on inside."

Or, "Looks like Barry cut the phone, they're going to have to use bullhorns now."

Lozano came back, sweat beaded like glass pebbles across his brow. "He wants you to go up," he told me. "He's demanding you go up, and then he wants safe passage to La Guardia and a flight to fuck knows where. Or else he blasts the building. He says he's got fifteen pounds of Semtex and he's holding the detonator."

Bridgett said to Lozano, "He's not going up there." It took me a second to realize she meant me.

"Of course he isn't," Lozano said. "You think we're nuts?"

"You got a phone I can use?" I asked him.

He pulled a cellular out of his jacket. "He pulled the line to your apartment."

"Yeah," I said, and dialed the safe apartment.

Rubin answered on the first ring. "What's up?"

"How's it look there?" I asked him.

"Dale and the doctor are napping, Natalie and me are just hanging loose. Why?"

"You got the television on?"

"Not yet. Hold on. Any channel?"

"Pick one."

I waited while he turned on the TV, watching the crowd. There was activity inside the perimeter now, the ESU commander having a heated debate with the negotiator. Lozano lit a cigarette.

"Fuck me," Rubin said.

"Yeah. I'm outside right now."

"Barry is in there?"

"Yeah."

"Oh, fuck me. Atticus, all of our stuff . . ."

"It's just stuff," I said. It came out flat.

"The cocksucking motherfucking pimple-gnawing son of a bitch," Rubin said softly. "What does he want? The TV isn't saying what he wants."

"He wants me to go in there, I think."

Rubin didn't ask why. He didn't need to ask why. Instead he said, "How's it look?"

"Barry just killed the phone connection, they've evacuated the building and the neighboring ones, too, and I have no idea how this is going to jump. He's nuts. He's gone around the bend."

"I'm coming over."

"Come around on Sullivan. Bridgett and I are in the southwest corner of the courtyard." I handed the phone back to Lozano in time to see two women who lived across the alley from me get escorted firmly away from the perimeter line by a uniform. One of them saw me and said something to her friend and pointed and they both looked at me like I was Evil Incarnate.

Lozano was asking me what was in my apartment, if there were any weapons or things like that.

"Kitchen stuff, knives. No guns, but there's about one hundred rounds of nine-millimeter ammunition in the lockbox in my room," I told him. "There's a bottle of lighter fluid for my old Zippo, and Rubin's got some turpentine, paint thinner, you know. That's about it. Nothing much there."

He nodded, and tried to readjust his vest.

Up on the roof two ESU guys were setting rappelling lines to jump down onto the fire escape if it came to that.

"We sent a team up there with the fiber-optic camera," Lozano told us. "He's lying about the amount of Semtex, apparently, not more than one or two pounds. He's got some gasoline spilled around, too. He's pretty much trashed the place."

"What's the procedure?" Bridgett asked. She hadn't said anything in a while.

"We want him alive, if he's willing, but we're not too sold on that happening. When he saw the sniper across the alley Barry freaked, that's when he cut the phone connection."

"I don't believe this," I said, and sat down with my back to the wall, looking up at the window. "I just don't believe this. This just isn't fucking happening."

Lozano stepped on his cigarette, then headed back to the command post, and Bridgett knelt beside me. She put a hand on my shoulder, resting it there for only a moment, then withdrawing it.

She didn't have anything to say, I guess.

"Clarence, can you hear me?"

The bullhorn's sound echoed and reverberated off the buildings, and the negotiator's voice bounced around the courtyard like a Super Ball.

No movement at the window.

"Clarence, can you hear me?" the negotiator called again. "Clarence, we've been talking about what you want and we're working on it, but you've got to understand we can't send a civilian inside, you know that, don't you?"

Nothing.

"Clarence, I think maybe we should talk about this, try to work something out, okay?"

Just the echoes.

"Clarence? If you don't talk to me we can't—"

And from an open window, "Fuck you, you nigger, give me Kodiak, you cocksucking ape, give me Kodiak or I'll turn the whole block into rubble!"

The negotiator lowered his bullhorn, and even from where I was I could see him struggling for control, for the right words, the words that wouldn't act like a match to Barry's anger. He raised the bullhorn back to his lips and said, "We can't send him inside, Clarence. Why don't we talk about what we can do?"

All the snipers were motionless.

There was a slight breeze now, smelling of exhaust.

"I'm going to fucking do this place, damn you!"

Rubin showed, working his way through the crowd and then pushing over to me, looking wound up and a little ill. He had changed out of his suit, at least, now in jeans and a T-shirt, both black. He sat beside me on my right, Bridgett on my left. It was almost nine, and some of the crowd had dispersed, but other people had shown up, had heard about it on the news and commuted in from wherever they had been to watch the show.

"Sorry it took me so long," Rubin said.

"No problem."

"What's he said?"

"Nothing for about an hour. He wants me to go in there or he's going to set off the bomb."

"You're not thinking about doing it, are you?"

"What do you think?" I asked him.

"Stupid question, sorry."

We were quiet for a while, watching the cops, watching the crowd. Then Bridgett said, "I think he's realized he's not getting out of this free and clear. I think he's realized he's gonna die."

———

She was right. About twenty-five minutes later a new negotiator, this one white, tried one last dialogue with Barry via the bullhorn and that ended with Barry shouting that he either got me to kill or that was it, end of block, end of story.

Lozano came over shortly after that and was telling us that ESU was probably going to try to take him, break through the wall from the next-door apartment, when Barry stuck his hand out of Rubin's window and started firing.

It happened really quick.

He was using a .357 revolver and the reports were loud. His first or second shot hit one of the ESU personnel on the ground, punching hard into the vest and knocking the cop down. Barry kept firing, but that was the only person he hit, and he sent bullets whistling in ricochets off the brick and brownstone, and everybody dove for the ground with the exception of Rubin, Bridgett, and me, and maybe a couple of others who felt secure under their cover. Which is why most of the people missed what happened next.

Barry's first or second shot must have sparked the gasoline he had spilled. By the third shot, a blossom of fire already licked out the window. Barry's hand was visible for less than a second, but the snipers had been waiting with a green light, and that second was all they needed. They're professionals, they know their job, and from the angle of a hand they can estimate where the rest of the body is. The two working the west rooftops fired at the same time, high-velocity rounds that flew supersonic. Barry fell through the blinds face first, on fire, onto the fire escape landing. He screamed once as he fell to the metal grate, but that was it, and he was probably dead by the time he hit the landing. The gasoline must have gotten into his clothes, though, because he continued to burn outside while our apartment went up. The detonator fell with him, clattering on the metal, then falling until the wires running off it went taut. It swung in the air, maybe fifteen feet under the landing where Barry burned.

The Bomb Squad went in immediately and pulled the device out, disarming it, while the fire department got the blaze under control. There was no explosion, much to the crowd's disappointment. Worse, from the crowd's point of view, the fire didn't spread out of our apartment.

But the apartment and Barry, both were a total loss.

CHAPTER TWENTY-SEVEN

It was after eleven that evening before Rubin and I could get into the apartment, and even then we got only a quick look around. It was depressingly straightforward. Barry had soaked everything he could with the gasoline, and when it went, it went fast. Some things caught, like the futons, and kept going, others smoldered and died. The bathroom had survived relatively unscathed. My room was a distant second as it was furthest from Rubin's, where the fire had ignited. But Barry had ripped, shredded, and otherwise destroyed everything identifiable as mine. Some of my clothing was dry and had escaped the fire, and I thought maybe I'd have some changes of underwear, but they hadn't escaped Barry, either. Each shirt had been sliced up the back, and he had pissed and defecated on my underwear. Every book I owned he had stacked in the kitchen, along with every book Rubin had owned, including his six thousand comic books, and they were nothing more than wet ash. That made me feel it most, what he had done to our books, our things. I loved my books, many of them gifts, many of them prized possessions I had haunted used bookstores for or had picked up in library sales or when I was with the service.

All of Rubin's art supplies, all of his drawings, all of his paintings, were ash. As he moved through the wreckage, Rubin trailed his hands alongside him, lightly brushing each blackened object, tears shining in his eyes.

We were out about five minutes after going in, and none of our neighbors said anything to us, but their accusing stares dug at our spirits as much as our backs when we descended the steps.

Natalie was waiting for us outside, having come over when Rubin called her. Dale was with Dr. Romero, and for now it seemed that one-person coverage would be enough. Bridgett stood with her. When Natalie saw Rubin, she went to give him a hug, and I watched them as they held each other.

"It's so fucking stupid," Rubin said. "It's just . . . stuff . . . it's just stuff and it's nothing. . . ."

"It was your stuff," Natalie told him.

They held each other. Then Rubin pulled back and turned to me. "So, what now?"

The question surprised me a bit. "We think we know who killed Katie," I said. "Bridgett and I need to find Fowler, let him know what we've found."

"Is Felice still in danger?"

"Barry is dead, Rich is in custody, and Crowell has probably bugged out," I said. "With everybody looking for Grant, I think the threat's diminished considerably."

"I'll go back to post," Rubin said. "Natalie and I will go."

I looked at him, at the fatigue and grief in his eyes, and I knew he would be useless.

"No," I said. "Natalie, call your father, see if we can get some of his people to cover for us tonight. I'll call the marshals, let them assist. Then you both go home, get some food, something."

"She's expecting us to cover at the funeral," Natalie said. "I think she really wants us there."

"Monday morning, day after tomorrow, we'll resume coverage," I told them. "We'll meet at the apartment before the funeral."

They seemed okay with that, and Rubin and I talked about the insurance and stuff for a little bit, and we were covered, and that was good, and it could have been worse, it could have been one of us, and I said yeah, and he said yeah.

"Get some rest," I told him.

"Practice what you preach," he told me.

I called Fowler's cellular from a pay phone by the drugstore on the corner, asking him to get me in touch with Deputy Marshal Pascal. He gave me the number and I dropped another quarter while Bridgett went into a bodega for more Life Savers and some coffee. I was put on hold at the marshals' office, then told that Pascal was out, and did I want to leave a message?

"My name's Kodiak. I'm the guy who's been running Dr. Felice Romero's protection."

The woman I spoke to said she would transfer me. I waited, watching the street. Saturday night in the Village, and people had things to do. There was a newspaper machine holding a copy of *Newsday*, and I could see a tag line about a story on page two regarding Katie and the hunt for her murderer. A homeless woman reclined on a large piece of cardboard in front of a toy store down the block, singing Billie Holiday. Even over the traffic I could hear her voice, clear and clean. An invisible woman singing a dead lady's song.

Pascal came on, saying, "Kodiak? What is up?"

"My people are done in," I said. "We're bringing in

some guards from Sentinel for the night to take over. I was wondering if you wanted some of your folks there."

"Until the morning?"

"Tomorrow, too. We'll resume coverage for the funeral."

"When do you need them?"

"As soon as possible. I've only got one person covering her right now."

"I'll send two men over. Where's she at?"

I gave him the address of the safe apartment, then got off the phone. Bridgett was sitting on the front fender of her Porsche, watching me. I crossed Bleecker to where she was, taking the cup she held out for me.

"Black and sweet," she said.

"Thank you," I said. "Can you give me a lift to the safe house?"

"Sure."

As we drove, she asked, "Where are you sleeping tonight?"

"I thought I'd stay at the safe apartment."

She signaled a turn, sliding over a lane. "You're staying at my place, and if you offer one word of argument, I swear I'll kick your ass so hard you'll never walk right again."

"Yes, ma'am," I said. I took the teddy bear off the floor and put it in my lap.

The marshals and Sentinel had beaten us to the safe apartment. They were inside with Dale when we arrived.

"They say they're taking over," Dale said, eyeing one of the Sentinel bodyguards. "What's that mean, they're taking over?"

" 'Til Monday morning," I said. "Go home, get sleep, be back at seven Monday."

He looked at the marshals and the guards, weighing their worth, then said, "I'm out of here." Before he went to the door he put a big hand on my arm, saying, "I'm sorry about your place."

"See you."

The new crew settled in easily enough, and although I didn't have a whole lot of faith in the marshals as bodyguards, they paid attention to what I told them. It's not that I don't like the Federal Marshals Service; it's more that I just don't see how apprehending fugitives qualifies them as personal protection specialists.

Done with them, I went to look in on Felice. She was asleep. I debated for a moment by the side of the bed, then called her name. The third time I said it, she stirred, reaching for the light. It came on to reveal her disheveled, her hair stuck straight up on one side of her head. She found her glasses, put them on, then sat up, pulling the sheets around her.

"There are two federal marshals here," I told her. "And some people from Sentinel. They're going to stay with you tonight and tomorrow. We'll be back Monday, early."

"You're done?" she asked.

"Not until after Katie's funeral. We'll be there. But we all need rest. You'll be okay with the marshals until then."

She nodded, her hands moving to her hair, trying to smooth it. "I survived," Felice said.

I handed her the teddy bear. "I'll see you Monday, okay, Doctor?"

"The last day," she said.

CHAPTER TWENTY-EIGHT

Lozano was thrilled to see me. "What the hell are you doing back here?" he asked.

"I want to talk to him again," I said. "I want some answers from that son of a bitch."

"Go home, Kodiak," Lozano said, and then probably realized how impossible that was. He started to say something else, then changed his mind and scowled.

"Where's Fowler?" I asked.

"He's in the box with Rich."

I turned around and walked out of the room, heading back to the cubicle where earlier we had watched Rich in interrogation. Bridgett came with me. Lozano followed, grumbling.

"You can't just walk in there," he said.

"I know."

We passed a couple of uniforms, then went into the

observation room. Pascal was inside, watching the proceedings through the glass.

"I thought you were done for the night," Pascal said.

"He say anything more?" I asked.

He shook his head. "But he doesn't know about Barry yet. Fowler's still playing him." He reached over and clicked the switch on the speaker, so we could hear the conversation inside.

". . . got to know who this guy is, Scan. We know you know him," Fowler was saying.

"Maybe I do. Might have seen him before," Rich said. "We have a lot of members." He looked wilted now, tired. But the energy in his voice was still there.

Scott played with the stud in his ear, then shook his head. He looked better than Rich, but not much.

"I don't think you see your situation, here," Fowler said. "Let me explain it to you clearly. You're dead-to-rights on the bomb, and that's not only state, that's federal. I've got you for conspiracy, possession, harassment, three counts of attempted murder, and one successful straight-up—"

"I keep telling you, I didn't kill the retard."

"Maybe you didn't pull the trigger, but accessories are tried just the same as murderers, Sean. And now that New York has the death penalty, you might just want to think about how a plea could help you. . . ."

Pascal switched the speaker off. He sighed, rubbed his chin. "It's been like that since Fowler went in there. Real illuminating."

I shifted my weight off my sore ankle. "Can you get Scott out for a few minutes? We've got some information that may help."

"Like what?" Lozano said.

Bridgett said, "We can link Grant to Dr. Romero."

"How?"

"Call the Two-six," she said. "See what you can find on

the murder of Melanie Baechler. Paul Grant and she were going out." She spelled out "Baechler" for him.

"And?"

"Baechler was murdered ten days ago," I said. "Katie knew her."

We were in the box with Rich. On the table in front of him lay the photograph that Francine had taken of Grant and Baechler at the Yankee game. Beside it were photographs of Baechler's body at the crime scene, and a copy of the autopsy report. The photographs showed ugly bruises around her neck. The left rear portion of her skull was caved in.

Rich sniffed the air. "Now that smells like gasoline." He looked at each of us, then settled on me. "Have an accident, boy?"

I pictured what his eye would look like with a pencil through it and smiled.

"Look at the photographs, Sean," Fowler said.

He did, then asked, "Who's the bitch?"

"Melanie Baechler. She's dead," Fowler told him. "Grant beat her to death."

Rich shrugged.

"You know why he killed her?"

"Tell me," Rich said.

"He beat her to death because she aborted his baby," Scott said.

Rich looked at Bridgett. He smiled. "Sound like the gash got just what she deserved."

Bridgett cuffed him at the back of his head. Her eyes were like glacial ice. "Be polite, Sean," she said softly.

"Funny thing, though," Scott said. "Melanie wasn't even pregnant." He tapped the autopsy report. "See? Says so right there. Wasn't pregnant, no sign of an abortion."

Rich's smile stayed on his face. "Then the report's a lie,

but that isn't a surprise, now, is it? All them doctors are in it together, changing the facts and spreading lies."

"No lie, Sean," Bridgett said. "She never had an abortion."

"You say."

"Grant murdered her," Fowler said. "And he murdered Katie Romero, and he wants to murder Felice Romero. With your help."

"He still might," Rich said. His eyes were on me. "You don't have this guy, do you? Whoever he is?"

"He won't be able to do it," I said.

"He's not alone. The army still marches on."

"You mean Barry? Crowell?" Bridgett asked.

Rich kept looking at me. "Like that."

"Barry is dead," Fowler said. "Got himself shot at Mr. Kodiak's apartment."

Rich's smile flickered.

"He was about as good with demolitions as you are," I said. "Hope you didn't need that Semtex."

"It's easy to get."

"Not where you're going."

He sniffed the air again and I felt my anger start to rise. "Well, maybe Clarence didn't need the Semtex? Your apartment? What happened, boy, did he torch it? Is that why you smell like a truck stop?" He leaned forward in his chair. "Did he torch your little nest, boy? Did you lose again, like you lost when the retard got capped?"

I was over the table before Fowler or Bridgett could move, driving Rich out of his chair and back into the wall with both my hands on his neck. I was pulling back, preparing to start slamming his skull against the concrete, when Fowler caught my arm, and then Bridgett had her arms around me, pulling me back.

Rich was laughing.

The door to the box flew open and Lozano came in, grabbed me, and with Bridgett, got me out of the room.

The look Fowler gave me as I went through the door was one of disgust.

Rich kept laughing. I heard it all the way out into the hall. I heard it when Lozano told me to go home and get some rest. I heard it when Bridgett and I got our gear back, and again when she disarmed the alarm on the Porsche.

Sisters of Mercy screaming on her tape deck did little to shut it out.

CHAPTER TWENTY-NINE

We had stopped for groceries and to buy me clean underwear, and after wc unpacked, Bridgett told me to stay out of her way, she was going to make dinner. I sat on the old couch and tried to watch the television. A framed photograph hung over the bureau, a picture of a lighthouse with the mother of all waves crashing about from the far side. In the photograph you could see a person, either a man or a woman, it was impossible to tell, standing in the little doorway of the lighthouse. The wave threatened to swamp him or her, to wrap around the pillar of light and toss the little person off into the maelstrom. It was a beautiful picture, though sad, and I stared at it, trying to understand what I was feeling.

I thought about calling my parents or my brother or Alison, letting them know what had happened, but I didn't.

Bridgett brought two bowls of soup over to the coffee

table, and a bottle of beer for each of us. "Fresh from the can," she said. She sat in the chair by the couch, took her bowl into her lap and then put her feet up on the coffee table. Her shoes were off. She knocked over a stack of magazines, mostly periodicals but one or two literary journals, too, and I saw *Time, Harper's, The Advocate,* and *On Our Backs.*

We watched CNN and ate the soup. They ran a short piece about the fire, without identifying Barry as a member of SOS, then followed it with a seemingly unrelated piece about the bomb scare at Common Ground that afternoon. They ended with a reminder that no arrests had taken place in the search for Katie Romero's murderer, but that the FBI had someone who was "assisting in their inquiry."

"That Rich, he's so helpful," Bridgett said.

By the time they started talking sports, we'd finished our soup and beer. I took the dishes into the kitchen, washed the bowls, then washed the pot Bridgett had made the soup in.

"You don't have to do that," she said.

"I know."

"You want a drink? There's Scotch in the far cabinet. You drink Scotch, right?"

"Scotch is good."

"Pour me one, too."

She had a bottle of Glenlivet, so I poured two glasses, then returned to the couch. Bridgett flipped channels, and I looked around the apartment some more. On the wall by the bathroom door were two pictures, one of a young woman that I took to be Bridgett, her black hair cropped short. The other was of Bridgett looking much like she did now, her arm slung around the shoulder of a man in his fifties, and a woman of roughly the same age. All were smiling.

"Who's that?" I asked her.

She followed my finger and said, "That's my ma and da." She pointed at another framed photograph, this one by the door to her office, and said, "And that's my baby sister."

Her sister looked to be about Bridgett's height, maybe a little shorter, but there was no practical reference in the photograph to really give scale. She was very beautiful. She was wearing a heavy winter coat in the photograph and a stocking cap, and was looking out of the frame at something that made her laugh.

"What's her name?"

"Cashell. You have siblings?"

"A younger brother. Alex. He's in grad school."

I looked around for other photographs and didn't see any that looked to be of friends or relatives. She had an Ansel Adams shot of Half-Dome in a black frame, but that was about it. I looked back at the picture of her parents. "What does he do for a living?"

"He was a cop," she said. "A Good Irish Cop. He died two years ago. Lung cancer. And Ma was a Good Irish Cop's Wife."

She opened a tin of Altoids and sucked on one. She smiled to herself, one of those smiles that you know means whoever is doing it has gone inside and is amused by what they see there. She sipped her drink, then shook her head and said, "Two tastes that don't mix well at all." She swallowed the mint, then set her glass back on the table and looked at me. "How are you holding up?"

"I'm tired."

"That's not what I meant."

"I know," I said. "I wanted to rip his throat out with my hands, Bridgett." I emptied my glass, looked at it. "He went right for my buttons and I took off like a rocket. I don't know what's wrong with me, I don't know what's going on in my head. Since before Katie died . . . I've been having nightmares."

"About the shooting?"

"Maybe, I don't know. In one of them, I'm on a killing spree, I . . . it's the same feeling I had when I saw Crowell at the hospital, the same feeling as when I was holding Barry's gun. And now Rich, and he's nothing, he's fucking nothing, and I let him set me off like that."

"Some of it may be fatigue," she said softly.

"Yeah."

"You want a refill?"

I looked at the glass again, thought about nodding. She went and retrieved the bottle, refilled my glass, refreshed hers.

"I've got no home," I said. "I keep thinking about how I'm guilty, here, how I've done this to myself. I couldn't protect Katie. I pushed Barry too far and I didn't need to push him at all."

"Barry was waiting for an excuse," she said. "Don't flatter yourself."

I finished my drink and stared at the glass. Eventually she got to her feet and turned off the television.

"There's clean towels in the bathroom," she said. "I bought you a toothbrush. Go take a shower and I'll make up the bed."

She had a good shower, plenty of water pressure, and the head was high enough for me to stand under without stooping. There was a bar of oatmeal soap in the dish in the shower, and I used that and managed to get the smell of burning out of my nose and mouth. Her selection of shampoos was generous, and I sampled the organic one made in Australia. It made me smell like a mango, but that got the gasoline stench out of my hair.

The mirror was covered with condensation when I shut off the water, the clouds of steam hanging in the room, sticking to the plaster and tile. I turned on the overhead fan, realizing I should have done so before taking the shower, and dried myself off with one of the thick, clean, fresh towels. My ankle throbbed when I touched it.

I put on my glasses and looked at my face, and it

brought me down. Pale brown eyes and too-long hair and a shadow of stubble and lines starting to find permanent homes about my mouth, eyes, and forehead. The bruise on my cheek was turning yellow-green. And I thought, I'm twenty-eight years old, and I'm in the wrong line of work.

I opened the new toothbrush and cleaned my teeth, and then, with the towel wrapped around me, I left the bathroom, heading back to the couch where Bridgett had made a very passable bed. It was a long couch, and it would hold me. She came in from the kitchen and looked me over. Then she said, "Sit down," and went into the bathroom. I heard her rattling around and took the opportunity to put on a new pair of boxers.

She came back out with an Ace wrap and tape and told me to lean back on the sofa. She began to wrap my ankle. She sat on the couch to do it, her back to me, leaning forward to my legs. Each time she touched me I felt it, a little stroke, the caress of her hair, and it made me think about her, it made me very aware of her.

When she finished she said, "That better?" and I said, "Yes," and she nodded and moved into me, one hand lightly on my shoulder, the other slowly tracing its way up my neck, and I put my arms around her, lost my fingers in her hair, and we kissed.

She tasted of her mints and the Glenlivet, and her first kiss was kind. Her second was safe and reassuring, gliding into a rising passion at the third that I fell into gratefully. Her grip on me tightened, and she fit into me, her skin pleasantly hot, and we moved slightly. I brought my mouth from hers, and with her hands now in my hair, she guided me to her neck, and I tasted her skin at the hollow of her throat.

That was all I could do.

I stopped, and she held me against her, and I could feel her heart beating against my chest, feel my breath as it bounced back from her skin. We lay like that, neither of us moving, just my breathing and her heart, and then the sounds of traffic. She began to stroke the back of my neck.

"I can't," I said.

She kept her hands in my hair and on my neck, moving them gently. For a while my mind fumbled for more words but then just gave up, gave out, unable and unwilling to work to label emotions that wouldn't keep in line and that I couldn't properly articulate.

Bridgett slid her hands to my shoulders, and I brought my head back to face her. She brushed my lips with hers and then shifted off the sofa, standing, her hands still on me. "Lie down," she said. When I did, she covered me with the blanket and took my glasses off my face and set them on the coffee table. I watched her walk away, heard water running from the bathroom, the sounds of her brushing her teeth and washing her face. They were enduring noises, and they lulled me closer to sleep, and my eyes closed and shut out the light. I opened them when the water stopped, hearing her move from the bathroom to her bedroom, and I shut them again, thinking that was all.

But she came back, and I opened my eyes to see her looking at me lying on her sofa, and now she wore a man's nightshirt that fell to the middle of her calf and made her legs seem very long, blue-and-white pinstripes with an old-fashioned short collar, and the stripes blended into one shimmering smear. She pulled the blanket back and lay down against me, and somehow we fit on that little sofa, and that was how we slept, together, the first time.

Barry is a blackened corpse, with an insane grin from the contraction of his muscles during the fire that ate him alive. He's standing beside Rich, at attention, and both are wearing uniforms that look like a cross between something the Klan wears to rallies and desert fatigues. They have military insignia on their collars, and their left breasts are laden with medals, pips for meritorious service.

Each pip is a tiny enameled carving of a fetus.

Crowell is standing before them, and through a megaphone he says, "For service above and beyond the call of duty . . ." and he opens a wooden box, and resting on the pink satin inside is a large medallion on a black ribbon. Engraved on its surface is Melanie Baechler's head in profile, the side that collapsed when she was beaten. Crowell lifts the medallion and on the other side is carved Katie Romero, an artist's interpretation of how she looked when she fell.

The artist has made her look like a monkey.

Crowell offers the medal to me.

In my dream, I think that if I take it, I'll be close enough to kill him, and that'll end this whole damn thing once and for all. That's what I think.

But between Crowell and me stands Felice Romero. She's dressed all in mourning and she's holding a stuffed bear. I have to push past her to reach him. When I do, Felice falls down, shatters into pieces.

Barry and Rich applaud.

I start toward Crowell again, but now there's Bridgett. I try to push past her, but she won't be moved so easily. She pushes back, and is joined by Rubin, and Natalie, and finally Dale. All try to restrain me. In my frenzy to reach Crowell, I start struggling violently, thrashing against them. I kick Rubin in the leg, and he flails, loses me. I strike Natalie with the back of a hand and gouge at Dale's eyes. As Dale falls away from me, I grab his revolver, trying to train it on Crowell.

But of course, he's gone, and I shoot Bridgett instead.

CHAPTER THIRTY

When I opened my eyes, Bridgett was watching me. For a moment I thought I was still dreaming, and I started, almost falling off the couch. She put an arm out on me, guiding me back to safety. I was pulling deep breaths, and she settled back against me, resting her head on my shoulder. Her hair smelled of green apples.

"Relax, stud. You're okay."

"I shot you."

"No, you didn't," she said. "That was a dream." Her fingers went to my brow, then my hair, smoothing it. "You're okay, stud. Just you and me here. You're okay."

She made me think of Romero, the way she said it, made me think of how I had spoken to her when the toilet had overflowed. After a moment I nodded, felt myself relaxing against the cushions of the couch.

Bridgett pressed her mouth delicately to mine, let the tip

of her tongue stroke my lips lightly. Then she put her head back on my chest.

I fell back asleep.

When I woke I felt better. I shouldn't have, I suppose. Four hours on a lumpy couch and nightmares to boot, but the sunlight was reflecting off the photograph of the light-house, as if the keeper there had thrown the switch on. Storm warning, Atticus, he or she was saying from high in that slender tower. Fog's coming in. Here's a light, follow it; see what you can; go where you must.

Bridgett stirred against me as I reached for my glasses, and her weight was a pleasure, the way she was pressed between me and the back of the sofa, one strong leg wrapped around mine. I put the glasses on and tried to negotiate a way off the sofa, but it wasn't going to be possible without disturbing her. Then her eyes were open, looking at me, her face blank. She raised a hand and patted my head and then pushed herself off me so she was on her knees. She jerked the hem of the nightshirt down from where it had climbed to her waist, getting off the couch. She said, "Make coffee," and headed for the bathroom.

I found everything and made coffee. The clock by the stove said seven-fifteen. I rang the safe apartment and spoke to the marshal who answered the phone for a few minutes, getting a rundown on the previous night.

"Nothing happened," the marshal told me. His tone said he hadn't expected anything to.

"Just keep sharp," I said. "Crowell and Grant are still wandering around out there. When Romero gets up, ask her to call me with the funeral details." I gave him Bridgett's number and hung up.

The shower was running in the bathroom so I poured myself a mug. I turned on the television and listened to the mindless babble of some morning show about what a wonderful summer day it would be in New York City while I stripped the blankets and sheets from the couch and cleaned up. Bridgett came out of the bathroom in a robe, wet hair clinging to her face, her nightshirt bunched in her hand. She tossed the shirt through the open door into her bedroom, went into the kitchen and poured herself some coffee.

"Hot damn," she said after a sip. "This is passable, stud. Keep it up and I might even let you stick around."

"Don't make offers like that to a homeless man," I said, and went to use the bathroom.

She was dressed in black jeans and a black sleeveless T-shirt, her shoes in one hand and the telephone in the other, when I came out. When she saw me she said, "It's Fowler. He paged you."

I nodded and she went back to talking with Scott while I pulled on my pants from the previous day and a T-shirt we had bought the night before.

"That's none of your business," Bridgett said. "No, he isn't . . . Wait, wait . . ." She pressed the receiver against her shirt and said, "He wants to talk to you."

I took the phone. "Scott? What's up?"

"Have a nice night?"

"Delicious. What?"

"Nothing so far on Crowell or Grant. We searched Grant's rooms this morning, found a pair of gloves that tested positive for blood. Nothing else."

"Baechler's blood?"

"Probable match. NYPD is going over everything again."

"What about Crowell's place?"

"He's not there."

"No, I meant, what did you find?"

"We haven't looked." He said it patiently. "No warrant, no probable cause to search the location. We need to wait for him to turn up, or to be listed as missing, and we can't list him as a missing person until tonight. We've got somebody watching the building."

"You might want to ask Veronica Selby if she knows where he is," I said.

"Why? Since when did she become involved?"

"No, not like that, but she was engaged to Crowell at one point. She might have an idea where he'd go."

"I'll talk to Selby, then," Fowler said. "You know funeral details?"

"Not yet. Romero said that Katie'll be buried in Westchester."

"There going to be a Mass?"

"I imagine so. Don't know where yet, but I've got a call in to Felice and she'll let me know."

"And you will pass that information along like a good soldier, right?"

"You can't see it, Scott, but I'm saluting you as we speak."

He chuckled and I put the phone down. Bridgett was seated on the couch, pulling on her shoes. "What was that about Crowell's apartment?" she asked.

"He hasn't returned to it," I said. "They're watching the place."

"What did they find there?"

"They haven't gone in yet. No warrant."

She just looked at me, her blue eyes waiting. I knew what she was thinking.

"Somebody's watching the place," I told her.

"So? They're watching for Crowell, not us."

"You're talking about breaking and entering."

"Like you've never done anything illegal before, stud." I kept my mouth shut and she leaned back against the couch and grinned like she knew my darkest secrets. "You're not all Boy Scout, are you? You've got the naughty streak in there somewhere."

"You're a bad girl," I said.

"Thank you."

I went back to the kitchen and poured myself another cup of coffee. "I'm waiting for Felice to call," I said.

"Hey, we've got all day, right? Nothing else on the agenda?" Bridgett turned and found the remote control, snapped on the television, and started surfing channels. "I like the idea of breaking and entering for our first date," she said.

Around ten Felice called, told me that the Mass for Katie would be held at St. James at nine the next morning, followed by a drive to the cemetery in Westchester for the burial. I asked who she had invited.

"Not many people. Colleagues. Most of the clinic staff will be there, I expect."

"Your husband?"

She blew smoke into the receiver, and the sound rustled like newspaper in my ear. "Marcus can't make it." I listened to her inhale and exhale again. "I want you all to sit with me. You were Katie's closest friends when she died, and I want you to sit with me, please."

"Felice—" I started.

"Yes, my safety, yes, my protection, I know. That's not why I invited you, Atticus. You're coming because you knew Katie. There will be marshals and FBI and the National Guard, too, for all I know. Let them protect me. I want you to sit with me. Katie would have wanted it."

"I'll see you tomorrow morning," I told her.

"For the last time." Her voice was sealed with irony.

I watched the phone for a minute after hanging up. From down the hall I could hear the television, and then Bridgett's laugh over the dialogue from the set.

I called Alison. She was surprised to hear from me, I

think. "I wanted to know if you had thought about attending Katie Romero's funeral."

"No," she said.

"No you hadn't thought about it, or no you're not attending?"

"I don't think I could handle it, Atticus," Alison said. "I just don't think I can deal with another dead child."

"Interesting equation."

"Perhaps." I heard her moving over the line, pictured her in the kitchen, putting dishes away. Then she said, "I saw your apartment on the news last night. I thought about calling you and then realized I didn't even know where you were."

"You could have paged me."

"Yes, I could have, I suppose," Alison said. "But I . . . I wasn't sure you wanted to hear from me, you know? After what had happened."

I thought, after breaking up with me the same day that Katie was murdered, you mean. "I'm staying at a friend's," I told her. "You want the number?"

She said yes and I gave her the number. "That Dale's place?" Alison asked.

"No, Bridgett Logan's. You haven't met her."

"Bridgett Logan." She tried the name thoughtfully. "Cute name."

"Oh, believe me, she's not cute."

"No, I don't suppose she is."

"Look, Alison, I just called to see if you were going to the funeral. I'd like it if you were there, but if you're not going, fine, whatever. I'll talk to you soon."

"I'm not planning on going."

"So you've said. That's it, that's all I wanted to say. Have a good day, all right? Take care."

"You, too."

Just before I put the phone down, I heard her voice, shrunken over the wires. I think she said, "I'm sorry."

———

Bridgett drove the Porsche twice around the block, then parked up the street from Crowell's building. The same doorman from our first visit was on duty.

"He'll remember us," I said. "He got reamed for not stopping us the last time."

"No way," Bridgett said. "You think he even knew what Crowell was yelling at him about?"

"There was a time when all doormen knew the tenants in their building."

"There was a time when a gallon of gas cost a nickel, but I don't remember that either," she said. She reached around onto the backseat and found a short crowbar, which she stowed inside her jacket.

We got out and walked along the sidewalk, her arm around my waist. She slipped in front of me just before we reached the awning, turned, kissed me, then said, "Call me a name."

"Bitch," I said.

She slapped me hard and then turned and ran into the building, covering her face, calling me a bastard.

It took me a moment, but then I said, "Honey, wait!" and ran after her. She had already hit the elevator button, but it was on the third floor and descending. So she turned around and slapped me again.

"Bastard," she repeated.

I straightened my glasses and rubbed my jaw, watching the doorman's reflection on the marble. He was sneaking curious glances our way, but nothing more. Bridgett mouthed "sorry," then turned her back on me again just before the elevator arrived. I went in after her, blocking her body from the doorman's view as she turned to push fourteen.

When the doors had closed, I said, "You might've warned me."

"Method acting," Bridgett said. "You're very good."

"Thank you. Now I know what to do if this bodyguard-ing thing doesn't pan out."

The fourteenth floor was empty when we arrived, and we walked to Crowell's door and knocked loudly three times. Nothing happened. Bridgett handed me the crowbar and then got down on her hands and knees, pressing her nose to the space between the bottom of the door and the floor.

"Can't smell anything. Don't think there's a corpse."

"The air conditioner could be on."

"True." She took hold of my belt and pulled herself up so her nose was nearly touching mine. "I love this shit," she said, then turned to shield me from the elevator. "Go to it, stud."

I worked the crowbar into the jamb. It took some good muscling, and I tried to remember how many locks I'd seen when we'd been inside before. Most New York apart-ments are locked up so tight one needs a diamond-bit drill to crack them rather than a crowbar, and I didn't have much faith that this was going to be successful. Just as I thought that, though, the wood tore with a snap and the door flew open. We went inside, closed the door af-ter us.

The apartment looked exactly the same. Clean and still, devoid of any life. We took a few steps into the open room where Crowell had received us, looking around, listening hard. The air conditioner hummed, but that was the only sound.

Bridgett headed down the hall, and I went to the kitchen. I heard her opening doors as I checked the refrig-erator. It was nearly full, bottles of mineral water and fresh fruit, some hot dogs, eggs, cottage cheese. I closed the door and then put my palm on the stove. It was cool.

I looked back at the door. There were four locks mounted on the frame. None of them had been closed. I walked over and checked the knob, and saw that, in fact, the crowbar had been unnecessary; the door was unlocked.

"Atticus?" Bridgett called. "Come take a look at this."

She's just used my name, I thought. She must have found a corpse.

And, lo and behold, she had done exactly that.

CHAPTER THIRTY-ONE

Jonathan Crowell lay on the carpeted floor of his office, flat on his back, three holes in his chest. Black powder burns radiated from the wounds in his linen jacket. He looked like a discarded rag doll, limp and with the stuffing exposed; except for the holes in his chest, the image might have offered some comfort. His blood had soaked the carpet, turning it from gray to black.

"Can't say I'm broken up about this," Bridgett said, staring down at the body.

"Fowler is going to love us."

"It's just jealousy. It's because we're having all the fun."

"It's jealousy all right."

She shrugged, knelt down beside the body. "He's got a nasty scrape on his cheek, here, and some bruising. Looks like he took a punch or two."

"Grant," I said.

She craned her neck my way. "Well, possibly, yeah. But why?"

Now I shrugged. "Is there a reason one of us isn't using the phone?"

"I want to nose around some more first."

"You'll contaminate their crime scene."

"Fuck their crime scene." She got up and frowned at Crowell's body, then turned away and opened the closet. I counted seven briefcases inside, vinyl and fake leather, all roughly the same size and color. I grabbed one and opened it. It was empty.

All of them were empty.

"Who needs seven briefcases?" Bridgett asked.

"Seven attorneys for seven prenups for seven brothers?"

"That's very clever," she said approvingly.

On the floor of the closet was a yellow-and-green molded plastic tackle box. Inside we found three spools of wire, some tools, pieces of electric equipment, a radio speaker, stuff like that.

I went over to the desk. In a letter holder were two white business envelopes, stamped and sealed. I pulled them, saw they were both addressed to the clinic. I handed one to Bridgett, then tore open the other.

The letter inside was identical in format to the ones we figured were sent by Grant. It read:

DOCTORS OF DEATH—
MY BABY'S IN A BOX.
HER MOMMA'S IN A BOX.
ANOTHER CHILD IN A BOX.
HER MOTHER GOING TO THE BOX.
TIME TO FINISH WITH A BANG.
NO MORE BUTCHERS.
MY JUSTICE.

It was, as always, unsigned. "It's like the others," I said to Bridgett. "It's another veiled threat about Romero and—"

"Read this one, stud," she said.

We traded letters.

To Whom It May Concern,

This is my final letter. I have finished my work now, and now the world knows. No more tricks, no need for games. We are both dead, and I am now to be judged by the only Law that matters.

I did what I've done because Dr. Felice Romero murdered my child. Her punishment was something I am glad to give my life for. Common Ground has failed.

I did what my Lord wished. I have no regrets.

Paul J. Grant

"It's a suicide note," I said.

"An unmailed suicide note," Bridgett said. "Grant was supposed to carry the bomb to the conference. These should have been mailed yesterday, or even the day before."

"But he didn't show at the conference," I said. "And the letters are here."

Bridgett scowled at Crowell's body. "So Crowell knew what Grant was going to do. Rich made the bomb on Crowell's orders, and Grant was supposed to deliver it."

"But he didn't. For some reason he didn't."

"No. So Rich used Mary Werthin as a backup when neither Grant nor Crowell showed at the conference."

"Grant had killed Crowell," I said. "That's why Crowell didn't attend."

"Why, though? What's Grant's motive? Baechler, we've got that, but why kill Crowell?"

"Grant never wrote the letters Felice was getting," I said. "Crowell did. He was setting Grant up. Somehow Crowell or Rich or Barry, one of them, found out that

Grant murdered Baechler, and they decided to use that to get Grant to kill Felice."

"And they never knew he wanted to kill Katie, too?"

"I don't think so, no."

Bridgett opened her Altoids, dropped the remaining mints into her mouth. "One of us should call Scott."

"You can," I said. "He's got a crush on you."

"I know," she said, and went to find a phone.

Scott tore each of us a new asshole, threatened to have us arrested, and then, when he arrived, threw us out of the apartment.

"Go back to Logan's and stay there or I swear to God I'll shoot you both," he said when we were in the hallway.

"I like a man who shows his anger," Bridgett told him.

"Then you're falling in love with me," Scott said, and slammed the door on us.

"Whatever gets you through the night," she told the closed door, then hooked her arm through mine and led me to the elevator.

In the lobby, the doorman finally asked us if we lived here or not.

"Sure do," I told him. "We're the McKennas in fifteen-G."

"But I'm not his wife," Bridgett said, patting my hand. "I'm his mistress. Maybe you recognize me? I'm Kim Basinger."

The doorman politely asked us to leave.

We went out arm in arm.

Bridgett decided she was hungry and that we should stop for brunch before going back to her place. I had no objections to that, so we ended up at a diner off Tenth near a taxi depot, both sides of the street outside lined with yellow cabs in various states of health. I had a bowl of oatmeal with some brown sugar, and Bridgett had a plate of steak and eggs. She didn't clean her plate.

My punchiness wore off over the meal, and when we were back in the Porsche, heading to her place, she said, "All right, stud, spill it."

"Where's Grant?" I asked.

"Fuck if I know."

"My point exactly. He hasn't left town."

"You don't think so? He missed the conference, he's got three bodies to his name. He's got to know that the FBI, the NYPD, and the marshals are all looking for him."

"He hasn't finished the job," I said. "He wants Romero."

"Maybe, stud. But he's run out of opportunities."

"There's the funeral."

She pursed her lips for a moment. "Yeah, there is. But then again, that's what you're for, right? And he knows by this point that you're no slouch."

"I take the compliment as it comes."

"Take it however you find it."

Bridgett went out to rent a couple of videos, and while she was gone I called Dale and gave him a quick brief over the phone about the funeral. After that I called Natalie's place. Rubin picked up.

"Enjoying your time together?" I asked him.

"A night of rarefied bliss, my friend," Rubin said. "I can almost forget that my *Cerebus* issue-one went up in smoke."

"You lie."

"I do," he said. "I'll mourn that issue forever. But I'm trying."

"Crowell's dead," I told him, and then ran it down.

"So tomorrow we worry about Grant?"

"Most likely. I expect Fowler will call to confirm that one way or another. But the funeral will be well covered, let's face it. All of us, cops, Feds, what more could we ask for?"

"Close air support?"

I laughed.

"So, what's the deal with you and Logan?" he asked.

"She's like her car," I said. "A wild ride that pushes the envelope."

"That's an awfully sexual metaphor. Are you speaking from experience?"

"No," I said.

"But?"

"But what?"

"Remember who you're talking to, buddy-boy," he said.

"It's crossed my mind," I admitted. "We came close last night."

"What stopped you?"

"An inability to perform."

"You had that problem, too?"

"Oh, yeah."

"Thank God," he said. "I thought it might've been something I ate."

I heard the front door opening and said, "I'm going to go. See you at the safe apartment tomorrow, all right? Tell Natalie to get there by seven."

"Will do," Rubin said.

We were finishing the third of the four Jackie Chan movies Bridgett had rented when Fowler called. She answered, then handed off to me.

"Grant's prints were at the scene," Scott said.

"Did he shoot Crowell?"

"That's how it looks, but we're not certain yet. We found some interesting stuff in Crowell's files, though. Your address and a couple of photographs of you with a young woman, both going in and coming out of the clinic."

"That would be Alison."

"There were lots of other photos, too. I just bring this to your attention because I know you, you understand. Nice to know that you were under surveillance just for going to the clinic. There's something else, though . . ."

"The tackle box and the briefcases," I said. "I know."

"What do you want to do about it?"

"Who's going to be covering at the funeral?" I asked him.

"We'll have local NYPD and marshals at the church. Sheriffs and marshals in Westchester. We'll run dogs at both locations," Scott said. "Grant may have just taken it and run. He doesn't necessarily know where the Mass or the cemetery service are going to be held."

"Do you really think he can't find out?"

"No, but I don't know what more we can do, dude. We've got people checking hotels in Westchester in case he's already up there, but you and I both know they're not going to find jack-shit. We'll just have to keep a sharp eye and hope he's decided not to risk it."

We had pizza for dinner, and I told Bridgett about the bomb.

"It's a better one, not like that piece of crap that Rich threw together for the conference," I told her. "This one, the original bomb, is Rich's masterpiece. That's why he was so fucking smug. It's in a briefcase or something like that, and it's radio-controlled."

She folded her slice lengthwise and dripped grease onto the wax paper at the bottom of the pizza box. "You mean Grant can plant it tonight and then just sit back somewhere with the detonator?"

"Yes and no. Theoretically, he could do that, but he won't risk it going off too early. The longer the bomb stays armed, the greater the chance of some stray transmission detonating it by accident, and he probably knows that," I said. "He'll plant it tomorrow morning, most likely at the cemetery, and he'll wait."

"A trap."

I wiped my hands with a paper napkin and Bridgett closed the pizza box, took it to the refrigerator. She put it inside and came out with two bottles of Samuel Adams, which she opened. "Considering what you've just told me, you're remarkably calm," she said.

"The optimal way to deal with the threat would be to find Grant, and I don't even know where to look. Best to leave that to the Feds and the police. Tomorrow, both the church and the cemetery will be swept with electronics and dogs, and we'll have done everything short of forbidding Felice to attend. And that last is clearly not an option."

"And that'll be enough?"

I shook my head. "No. That'll be the best we can do."

She brought me my beer and sat down beside me on the floor. We were both leaning with our backs against the couch. "Can you get to St. James by yourself tomorrow?" she asked.

"You're not going?"

"I've got to go early for confession if I want to take communion."

"I pity the priest," I said.

She elbowed me. "You going to put an arm around me or what?"

I put my arm around her shoulders and she put her free hand on my thigh, leaning against me. We each drank some of our beers.

"It's going to take you and Rubin at least a week or two before you boys can find another apartment," Bridgett said. "I'm thinking that you're welcome to stay here until then."

"You sure? That's a hell of a nice offer and you strike me as someone who values her privacy."

"True. But you're a friend in need." She took another swig from her bottle. "Ready for the last flick?"

"Shoot."

She reached for the remote control and we watched the final installment in our Jackie Chan fest, my arm around her, her head against my shoulder. We killed another beer each before it ended, and when the film was done, she rewound the tape and helped me set up the sheets on the couch.

"You're going it alone on the couch tonight, stud," she said. "Think you can handle that?"

"I may roll off but I imagine I can survive the fall."

"Good thing, 'cause my back can only take so much of that action." She took the empty bottles and headed to the kitchen, dropping them in her recycling bin under the sink.

"Night, stud," she said, and headed for her room.

"Good night, Bridgett."

She stopped, pivoted on a toe, and came back. With no preamble she put her arms around my neck and kissed me, holding me to her mouth for the duration. She released me with a crooked smile.

"You can call me Bridie," she said, and then went back down the hall.

The photograph on the wall, the one of the lighthouse, bounced blue light from the street to where I lay on the couch, alone. I listened to Bridgett down the hall, where she was sleeping with her door open. She talked in her sleep, soft and incoherent, and I gained no insight trying to decipher her mumbled words, instead falling into visions of Grant lurking in the Westchester woods with Rich's bomb. The imagined images taunted me until sleep came.

No dreams.

CHAPTER THIRTY-TWO

It was the hole in the ground that I kept returning to, earth cleanly pared away to hold the white casket that had traveled from the city to the sloping and grassy hills of this cemetery, that turned me from observer into mourner. In the hot and humid air, I kept finding the smell of wet earth on the breeze, and my eyes went back to the grave again and again between sweeps of the area.

Felice sat between Natalie and me, slim and stoic in her black dress, hard as coal. Dale and Rubin sat in the chairs behind her, and the other mourners spread from there, familiar faces from the clinic staff and others I didn't recognize. Veronica Selby sat in her wheelchair with Madeline beside her, both their faces fixed in granite sorrow. Bridgett sat on my left, her hands in her lap, focusing on the coffin, her emotion unreadable. All of us on the gray metal folding chairs, listening to the breeze, or the birds, or the sobs, or the priest.

"We gather here to commend our sister Katherine Louisa Romero to God our Father . . ."

A radio crackled, its volume turned down low, and a sheriff's deputy turned away to answer it. Transmissions were being made with less care now that the sweep had been completed. No signs of a bomb or Grant, no signs of danger or distress. I watched the deputy listen to the transmission, radio a response, and take the ten steps to where Fowler stood at the end of our row. They put their heads together briefly, and then the deputy stepped away again, sent another transmission.

". . . says the Lord, inherit the kingdom prepared for you . . ."

The earth in the grave looked soft, and I imagined it sweet, perhaps comfortable. The casket had been open at the Mass. Inside it, Katie's face was still kind, the smile fixed and clearly not her own. I'd looked at her face and seen only the expression she had when shot, the tears pooling in her eyes and the turn of her mouth as she asked for her mother.

Now the casket was sealed, set on a platform beneath an evergreen. When the breeze moved a branch, sunlight would grace the coffin, the white metal impossibly smooth and shiny.

A marshal stood beside a sheriff's van in the distance, helping the deputies there load the dogs back inside. The dogs made no noise, wouldn't unless they caught the scent of an explosive.

"Grant that our sister may sleep here in peace until You awaken her to glory, for You are the resurrection and the life," the priest said. He was in his thirties, and his voice was full and strong enough to carry clearly. He spoke with sincerity and faith. He spoke the way Crowell pretended to speak. "Then she will see You face to face and in Your light will see light and know the splendor of God, for You live and reign forever and ever."

"Amen." I heard Bridgett say it clearly, but Felice

seemed to only mouth the word. She took off her glasses, set them in her lap. Somewhere behind us, I heard someone crying.

A woman stopped at a headstone some fifteen feet away, holding a fresh and simple bouquet. She unbuttoned her blazer before kneeling and then she offered the flowers to the deceased. Her head pitched forward with tears then, and I looked away.

The van pulled out, passing the line of parked cars that had been our procession out of the city. The road was one hundred yards from where we now sat, perhaps further. The marshal looked our way, wiping sweat from his forehead. He turned and walked back along the line of cars, stopping to check the Sentinel Ford that Dale had driven. The marshal dropped to his knees and looked under the vehicle, then rose and continued, passing a groundskeeper in brown coveralls who was pulling a black trash bag of cuttings beside the road. The lawn had been freshly cut this morning, and the smell of the grass was thick.

". . . when the love of Christ, which conquers all things, destroys even death itself," the priest said. He looked up from his book at us and added, "We will pray silently."

Heads bowed. At the far end of our row, in the last seat, Alison looked my way and offered me a smile. She was wearing a white blouse and a black skirt, and I moved my eyes back to the grave, wondering what the smile meant.

During the silence, Felice shuddered once and began to weep.

The priest moved to the coffin, sprinkling the glossy surface with holy water. Another radio crackled. The groundskeeper hoisted his bag and then dropped it, bending to clean the spilled cuttings. He adjusted his cap and looked around, embarrassed.

The priest began to read the Gospel, Matthew.

"Blessed are the poor in spirit . . ."

Alison had come after all, had changed her mind. I wondered why she had done it, what had happened to make the funeral become something she felt she could attend.

". . . for they will inherit the land. Blessed are they who hunger and thirst for righteousness . . ."

It was confusing that she had changed her mind. Had she come for me or herself? Or was this, for her, more about our aborted child?

The priest began the Song of Farewell, and again I heard Bridgett's voice clearly amongst all the others. She knew the words, and sang with the confidence of someone who's had voice lessons.

Natalie had put an arm around Felice's shoulders. Her eyes were on me, sympathetic for my loss.

Catalogue of losses, I thought. Home, child, and child again. Felice had said that no matter where you stood on the line, somebody always got hurt, and she had taken the worst of it. What could be worse than outliving your own child?

I looked at Alison again, and she was still looking at me, now only serious and concerned. She'd never been one to change her mind, and if she was playing games, if this was some guilt maneuver, I wanted no part of it.

The priest began the Prayer of Commendation as I turned away from her, seeing the groundskeeper get back to his feet, the spill cleaned up, on his way down the road and away from our car.

". . . console us and gently wipe every tear from our eyes: in the name of the Father, and of the Son, and of the Holy Spirit," the priest said.

"Amen." Chorused, and I imagined Alison adding her voice to the rest.

"Go in the peace of Christ."

"Thanks be to God," and that was the only time I heard Felice clearly. Then she was rising, taking my hand as I stood beside her. Dale, Rubin, and Natalie closed around her, too, and we stood with her as she accepted condolences, as if we were part of the same family. Bridgett waited, looking sculpted and immovable. She was wearing a white vest under a black double-breasted jacket and tuxedo pants, and she made them work, made them seem the most appropriate clothes possible for mourning Katie. I had arrived with her, and I would leave with her when the time was right.

Because the job was over, now.

Madeline guided Selby's chair to Felice, and waited while Veronica spoke softly to Dr. Romero, holding her hands as she had before the conference. Then Selby released them, wiped her eyes, and said to Madeline, "We should be going."

Madeline nodded once and began pushing the chair toward the road.

Lynn Delfleur gave Felice a hug. There were tears in her eyes.

"Katie was a princess," Lynn said. "Perfect."

Felice kissed her cheek, then pulled away, turning to the consolations of another mourner. Lynn stood still for a moment, looking at each of us, then touched Dale's arm before heading toward the road.

Fowler caught my eye, held his hands open in an empty gesture. Nothing. I nodded, and he moved to speak to one of the marshals. Most of the law enforcement types were heading to the cars. Already one of the sheriff's vehicles had pulled away.

Rubin asked, "How're you feeling?"

"I don't know."

He worked a thin smile up, then sighed. "Me, too. It's over, I guess, huh?"

"I guess."

"It wasn't our fault, was it? Katie?"

That seemed the most important question, suddenly, and I could say only what I had told him before. "We did everything we could, Rubin. It wasn't our fault."

"You don't believe it, though. You haven't forgiven yourself."

The woman with the blazer and the flowers rose from the headstone she had been tending, and I watched her walk away, wondering. "Have you?" I asked.

He shook his head. "But I'm trying to."

I focused on the grave again, heard Rubin move off a few steps.

When I brought my eyes back up, Bridgett had moved beside me and the mourners had withdrawn. Alison was taking Felice's hand.

"I'm so sorry for your loss," Alison said. "I wish I could say more."

Felice accepted the sentiment with a little nod. "And you, Miss Wallace? You're well?"

"I'm well."

"I'm glad." Felice was watching the casket now. "It's always a difficult choice to make."

Alison looked at me, at Bridgett, then withdrew a few steps near the evergreen, waiting. Only she was left now. Even the priest had withdrawn, leaving us, and a grounds-keeper to clean up.

"Why don't you guys take her back to the car," I said to Natalie. "I'll catch up."

"I'm having a reception at my apartment," Felice said. "Will you and Bridgett come?"

"We'll come," Bridgett told her.

They started toward the car, Rubin in front, Natalie in the primary position behind Felice, and Dale behind her.

"Alison," I said, "this is Bridgett. Bridgett, Alison."

"That's a nice outfit," Alison said.

"Thank you," Bridgett said. She patted my elbow. "I'll leave you two alone."

After Bridgett had left us, Alison asked, "How are you doing?"

"Reasonably well, I suppose."

She looked over her shoulder at Bridgett. "She doesn't seem your type."

"I don't know if she is," I said. "I'm surprised you came, you said you weren't going to attend."

"I hadn't planned to." She put a hand out on the casket, feeling the metal. "But we got off the phone and I felt guilty, and then that FBI agent called about the guest list and asked if I was coming. I told him no, and he said that you really wanted me here."

"Fowler said that?" I asked. Beyond the tree about fifty feet I saw Bridgett stop, turn back to watch us. Another forty yards or so down I could see Rubin leading the squad to the car.

"No, that wasn't his name, it was Burgess, I think. Did you really want—"

Grant must have taken the file on Alison from Crowell's office, I realized, and I was already stepping forward when I heard her suck quick air, saw the color leech from her face.

"Don't take another step. Just turn around. Turn around or I'll shoot."

Bridgett had her hands on her hips, waiting, but I knew we were too far apart, that she couldn't see my expression. My gun was at my hip, and even at my fastest I couldn't index it and fire in time.

I turned and Grant was only six feet away across Katie's grave, the same young face captured in the photograph, the same face I had seen in the crowd, looking just as much the groundskeeper now as when he had slipped the bomb under the car. He appeared almost serene, but that broke with the burn in his eyes. At his waist he held a service .45, pointed at my middle.

And in his left hand he held the small black plastic box Rich had made from radio components. The antenna was tiny, but more than enough to do the job. His thumb rested on the toggle switch.

"I'm going to finish this," Grant told me. "If you move, if you try to warn anyone, I'll shoot." He craned his neck to look past us, and I imagined the squad slowly making their way to the car. Maybe twenty yards left before Grant flipped the switch.

Alison swayed in my periphery, her right hand going to the casket for support.

"You're doing this for no reason, Paul," I told Grant. "Melanie never had an abortion—"

"She went to the clinic," he said.

"For a checkup, for a Pap smear. You killed her and she was innocent."

"Don't lie to me. Crowell lied to me. Barry lied to me. Now you're trying to lie to me," Grant said. He craned his neck again and I took the chance to move my hand to my belt, nearer my weapon, hoping Bridgett would see the movement, wonder why Alison and I were so suddenly enthralled by a rubbernecking groundskeeper.

Grant looked back at me. "I won't be used. I'm going to finish this." He saw my hand and cocked the pistol. I stopped moving. "You think I'm joking?" Grant asked.

"You fire and they'll know exactly what's up."

Perspiration had soaked onto the bill of his baseball cap. He exhaled sharply, then trained the gun on Alison, canting the barrel at an angle to put the bullet through her head. "You willing to sacrifice her? After all, she murdered your baby, too. Or don't you see it like that? This is all about choice, right? So you make a choice."

I pictured Felice walking with Natalie almost on top of her. Maybe ten yards from the car, maybe thirty feet. I wondered what the blast radius was. Alison was breathing rapidly, short breaths, close to hyperventilating, her eyes fixed on the gun. That was why Grant got her here, I realized. To hold her life in one hand, Felice's in the other. And the longer I took to decide, the less my decision would matter.

He tilted his head to look again and I made my choice, swung my left arm out and shoved Alison down hard as I sprang forward. Grant fired almost immediately on my movement, but I was across the grave, scrabbling at the dirt and grabbing at his arm and I couldn't tell if he had missed or not, if I had killed Alison or not. I got one hand on his gun, pushing it down, and was fumbling for the transmitter in his left hand when I heard the blast, felt the air shudder with the concussion.

Then Grant was on top of me, and we were falling into the grave, my head bumping against dirt all six feet down. He landed on me, flat, pushing my air out, still struggling to regain control of the gun. I punched him quick and hard twice in the face, tearing my knuckles on his mouth with the second blow, and he pulled back, but wouldn't let go of the gun. His left hand came down and I twisted, caught a piece of the blow on my jaw.

"Wrong choice," he was screaming at me, over and over.

I got a hand up and threw the edge of it at his throat and he turned his head, presenting neck instead. It was enough, and he went back against the opposite wall of the grave, releasing the gun. I felt for the handle of the .45, swinging it between us as he started for me again, when three shots punched Grant in the chest.

He slumped back, his legs digging furrows in the loose earth of the grave. His eyes opened wide with the shock and then pain, and his mouth moved once more, but only rattling air escaped.

I pulled myself to my feet, turned, and found Bridgett's left hand reaching into the grave for me, the Sig still in her right. She helped me up, and I saw Alison standing with her back against the tree, very much alive. Grant's bullet had torn bark three inches from her head.

Then I was running across the grass, Bridgett at my heels, pounding toward the circle of marshals and deputies and the blazing car. Fowler caught me outside the ring, tried to push me out, saying my name. I elbowed past him, past Selby in her chair and Madeline frozen at her side.

I saw the body then, Natalie standing over it, went down on my knees on the clean grass.

She didn't look at me.

In my mind I could see what had happened, see it so clear and clean that I thought I could feel the wound.

Grant fired his gun, and the squad, knowing only that the shot had come from behind them, not able to take the time and find the shooter, did an immediate takedown. Natalie knocked out Romero's knees with her own, pressing the doctor flat and then following with her own body. Dale had done the same, drawing as he fell, turning to find his shot.

Rubin, in the lead, had spun and drawn, and when the car exploded, he'd taken the force of the blast in his back.

Felice had rolled him face up to work on him, Rubin's life flowing out from beneath his torn body. There was too much trauma and now her hands were stained with blood that clung to the grass, shining in the sunlight.

I looked at my friend. His eyes were open and his mouth, and my first thought was that I would never hear his voice again. He still had his gun in his hand, fingers darkened with old ink frozen around the butt. Cut grass clung to his face. A single blade had stuck to his right cornea, a sliver of green cutting the brown into two mismatched halves.

Patrol cars were sliding onto the lawn, their doors swinging wide even before they stopped. Deputies ran in all directions, some reaching for fire extinguishers to fight the dying flames of the car. Alison still stood beside the grave where Grant had fallen, staring at me, still not moving, and some of the cops were making their way toward her now, too. The air tasted of charred upholstery, gasoline, and soot, and black smoke from the burning rubber spilled to the sky.

"Evac Pogo," I said.

I was afraid she would make me repeat the order, but Natalie nodded slowly once, her eyes still on Rubin. She holstered her weapon and stepped around to Felice, reaching a hand for Dr. Romero's shoulder. Dale moved after her, offering assistance, and I saw he was crying, silently. They helped the doctor stand, and she was staring at me even as each of them took an arm. Fowler guided them to a car, holding the door open and then slamming it shut once they were all inside. Felice never took her eyes off me, sharing our new bond.

When the car was out of sight, I sat down on the grass next to Rubin and waited for the rest.

About the Author

Born in San Francisco, GREG RUCKA was raised on the Monterey Peninsula. In his twenty-five years he has worked at a variety of jobs, from theatrical fight choreographer to emergency medical technician. He and his wife, Jennifer, reside in Eugene, Oregon. He is at work on his next Atticus Kodiak novel.

If you enjoyed Greg Rucka's first Atticus Kodiak
novel, **KEEPER,** you won't want to miss the second
novel from this talented young writer. Look for
FINDER at your favorite bookstore in June 1997.

And in the meantime, turn the page for an exciting
preview of **FINDER.**

FINDER

by

**Greg
Rucka**

An Atticus Kodiak Novel

She was lost.

I only saw her because I was doing my job, just looking for trouble, and I must have missed him when he came in, because I didn't see him enter. He was a white male in his early thirties, neat in his clothes and precise in his movement, and he clearly wasn't with the scene, the way he lurked in the corners of the club floor. The Strap had been built in an abandoned warehouse, the walls painted pit-black and the lights positioned to make shadows rather than eliminate them. For people who were serious about the scene, The Strap wasn't a club of choice, and if they showed at all, it wasn't until after midnight, when the wannabes had gone to greener pastures or to bed.

Bouncing is a people-watching job, a process

of regard and/or discard. You look for potential trouble; you isolate potential trouble; then you wait, because you can't react until you're certain what you've got really will be trouble.

I was waiting, watching him as he looked for her, as he weaved around the tops and bottoms playing their passion scenes. It was after two now, and the serious players had arrived, a detachment of leather- and PVC-clad types who took their playing very seriously indeed. Now and again, over the industrial thud of the music, the slap of a whip hitting skin, or a moan, or a laugh, would make it to my ears.

Trouble stopped to watch a chubby woman in her fifties get bound onto a St. Andrew's Cross, black rubber straps twisted around her wrists and ankles, making her skin fold and roll over the restraints. His hands stayed in his coat pockets, and I saw that he was sweating in the party lights.

Maybe cruising.

His manner was wrong, though, and when the woman's top offered him his cat-o'-nine-tails, Trouble fixed him with a level stare that was heavy with threat. The top shrugged a quick apology, then went back to work. Trouble cracked a smile, so fast it was almost a facial tic, then turned and headed for the bar.

It wasn't a nice smile.

Hard case, I thought.

I followed him with my eyes, then let him go

for a minute to watch two new entrants. As the newcomers came onto the floor a woman cut loose with a pathetic wail, loud enough to clear the music, and the younger of the two stopped and stared in her direction. Both men were dark brown, with skin that looked tar black where the calculated shadows hit them. The younger looked like a shorter, slighter version of the older, right down to their crewcuts. Both were dressed for watching, not for playing, and the younger couldn't have been much over twenty-one, just legal enough to get inside. His companion was older, in his forties. He shook his head at the younger man's reaction, said something I couldn't hear, and as they began moving off again, I looked back to the bar.

Trouble had ordered a soda from Jacob, the bartender. The Strap was a licensed club, and since there was nudity on the premises, it couldn't serve alcohol. Trouble paid with a wallet he pulled from inside his jacket, and when he put it back, the hem of his coat swung clear enough for me to see a plastic clip hooked over his left front pants pocket. The clip was blacked, the kind used to secure a pager, or perhaps a knife.

So maybe he's a dealer, I thought. Waiting to meet someone, ready to make a deal.

Or he really is trouble.

He sipped his soda, licked his lips, began scanning again with the same hard look. A man and a woman crawled past me on all fours, each wearing a dog collar, followed by a dominatrix clad in red PVC. She held their leashes in one hand, a riding crop in the other, and gave me a smile.

"Aren't they lovely?" she asked.

"Paper trained?"

"Soon," she said.

Trouble had turned, looking down at the other end of the bar, and I followed his gaze, and that's when I saw Erika.

She wore a black leather miniskirt, torn fishnet stockings, and shiny black boots with Fuck-Me heels. Her top was black lace, also torn, showing skin beneath. Her hair was long, a gold like unfinished oak. The club lights made it darker and almost hid the stiff leather collar she wore, almost obscured the glint from the D ring mounted at the collar's center.

She was brutally beautiful.

She was just like her mother.

She was only fifteen.

Trouble and I watched her light a cigarette, tap ash into her plastic soda cup while watching the scenes play around her. She looked carefully bored, meeting gazes easily as she found them, no change in her expression.

The pitch and yaw in my stomach settled, and I took a breath, wondered if it really was Erika, wondered what the hell I was supposed to do now.

Trouble finished his soda and moved, settling beside her, his lips parting in an opening line. She didn't react and didn't look away, and he spoke again, resting his left arm on the bar, his right in his lap.

Erika cocked her head at him, then turned away on her stool, tossing her hair so it slapped him in the face.

He responded by grabbing her with his left hand, taking hold of her shoulder and spinning her back to face him, and that's when I started moving.

Erika tried to shrug his hand off, but he didn't let go, and I was close enough now to hear her saying, "Fucking fuck off, asshole."

"We're going," he told her.

Jacob had turned behind the bar, figuring maybe to break them up, but Trouble's right went to his pocket, and it wasn't a pager he'd been carrying, but a knife. He thumbed the blade out and it left a trail of silver in the light, like water streaming in a horizontal arc, and he casually swiped at the bartender's eyes. Jacob snapped his head back, both hands coming up for defense. Trouble kept the point on him over the countertop, his other hand still on Erika, and I arrived to hear him saying, "Don't be a hero." He had an accent, British and broad.

His back was to me, but Erika saw me coming, her mouth falling open with surprise and recognition as I brought my left forearm down on Trouble's wrist, pinning it to the bar. The surprise of the blow made him lose the blade, and it skidded over the edge, landing in a sink full of ice. It was a nice-looking knife, with a chiseled tanto point, the blade about three and a half inches long, and Jacob went for it immediately as Trouble started swearing. I felt him shift to move, and I snapped my right elbow back as he was bringing his free hand around for my head. I hit first, catching him in the face, and I came off his pinned arm, turning, to see him staggering back. He had released Erika, and had one hand to his nose.

She said my name.

"Erika," I said, still looking at Trouble. If he had reacted with any pain or surprise, I'd missed it, because now his hand was down and he was smiling at me. He looked at Erika for an instant, then back to me, and I took the opportunity to check his stance.

He knew what he was doing. He knew how to fight.

Blood flowed over his upper lip, and the smile turned bigger, and I could see dark pink around his teeth.

"You want me to show you out?" I asked him.

Trouble shook his head, and the smile blossomed into a grin.

"You took my knife," he said. The lighting made the blood from his nose look black.

"That's a fucking precious knife, and you took it."

"You didn't have a knife. If you had a knife, you would have just committed a felony, and we'd have to call the police."

"Fuck that," Jacob said. "I *am* calling the cops." I heard the rattle of plastic on metal as he reached for the phone.

Trouble shifted his weight, settling and coiling, wanting the fight, and I took a step to the side, putting myself between him and Erika, figuring that if I was about to get beaten, at least he'd walk away without her. His hands were up and ready, and his breathing was under control.

If he was a serious martial artist, I was deep in the shit. Despite my chosen profession, I don't like pain, and at seven-fifty an hour, I'm not getting paid enough to change that fact.

"You've no idea the world of hurt you've bought," Trouble said, showing me his teeth. His eyes moved from me to see beyond my shoulder, and then everything changed. His glee vanished with the grin, face turning into a battle mask, and he spat blood onto the floor.

I wondered how much this was going to hurt.

His hips began to torque, and I thought he was starting with a kick, prepped myself to block it.

But the leg didn't launch.

Instead he turned, breaking for the fire door, pushing through the people who had stopped to watch this different scene being played, knocking over the PVC woman with the leashes. She went backward, falling onto her slaves, crying out, and he kept going.

I went after him, trying to be more polite about my pursuit, but the fire door had already swung shut by the time I reached it. I slammed the release bar down and pushed, stepped out into the alley, checking left and then right, spotting him as he reached Tenth Avenue, then turned the corner.

By the time I could make the avenue, he'd be gone.

I thought about going after him anyway, then decided I'd gotten off easily and had better not push my luck. My breath was condensing in the mid-November air, and it was cold out, and getting colder. There was a wind blowing, too, floating the smells of alcohol, urine, and exhaust down the alley.

I heard the rubber seal at the base of the fire door scraping the ground, saw Erika stepping out to look past me to the avenue. The door swung shut slowly, and I heard the latch click.

"You broke his fucking nose," she declared.

"Probably," I said. "What'd you do?"

"Me? I didn't do anything."

"Something scared him off," I said. "What did he want?"

"He wanted to top me."

"With a knife?"

She shrugged, faked a shiver, and said, "I'm going back inside."

"The hell you are."

Erika stopped, turned her head and tossed her hair much as she had done to Trouble. "What?"

"You're fifteen, Erika. Isn't that right?"

"Twenty-one," she said immediately.

"You got some proof of that?"

"Atticus. You know who I am."

"Exactly."

She waited for more, and then realized that was my whole argument.

"Fuck you," she said, finally, then spun on one of her too-high heels, making to go back inside. I let her, because she couldn't get far. It was a fire door, after all, and there was no handle on the outside. Great for exiting the building in a hurry, not so good for a return trip.

It took her a second to come to the same conclusion. "I'll go through the front. No problem. I've done it before." She brushed past me, heading down the alley.

"I'll make sure you're carded."

"I've got ID."

"I'll tell them it's fake," I said.

That stopped her once more. Without turning, she said, "I fucking hate you."

"Nice to see you, too."

"Go to hell," Erika snarled. She turned and

pointed a finger at me. "Where the fuck am I going to sleep tonight?"

"At home."

"You are so wrong." She threw her hands out as if to ward me off, then began shaking her head and muttering. The wind kicked up, gusted down the dark street, and I felt its teeth through my jacket. Erika had goose bumps on her skin, and the cheap lace of her top made her pale breasts stand out in contrast. I looked toward Tenth Avenue, feeling like a dirty old man.

She certainly wasn't dressing fifteen.

"Why the fuck are you doing this?" Erika demanded.

I took off my jacket and offered it to her.

She ignored it. "Where the hell do you get off telling me I can't go back in there? What's your fucking problem, huh?"

"You're underage, Erika," I said. "Will you put this on?"

"So fucking what?"

"So it's illegal that's so fucking what. How'd you get in there?"

"None of your business."

"Will you please put this on?"

"Why?"

"Because I can see your nipples and they're erect and I embarrass easily," I said.

Erika checked her front, then grabbed a breast in each hand and looked at me. "That's the point, asshole," she said, squeezing, her thumbs and forefingers pinching flesh.

"Put on the goddamn jacket, Erika."

She grabbed my coat and put it on.

"Thank you," I said.

"You're a fucking asshole," she said.

I began heading toward Tenth Avenue, walking slowly, hoping she'd join me. After five steps, she did, falling in on my left.

We were almost to the corner when Erika asked, "How you been?" She asked it like I'd seen her yesterday and we'd maybe just caught a movie, then done some window-shopping at Macy's.

"I've been better. Why aren't you at home? Why aren't you in D.C.?"

Erika laughed. "The Colonel retired, lives in Garrison now. I don't even live with him."

"So where do you live?"

"Wherever I find a bed, dipshit." She stopped, checked her tone, then continued, more patiently. "That's why I need to get back in there, Atticus. That's where I'm going to find my shelter for the night."

This time, I stopped. "You're tricking?"

"Sometimes, I guess. Sure."

"What the hell's happened? Why aren't you living at home?"

Erika took an impatient breath and looked off past my shoulder, shoving her hands into the pockets of my army jacket. The gesture revealed her age, the jacket much too big for her, the miniskirt almost entirely swallowed by its hem. The light on the street wasn't fantastic, but I could see her eyes clearly, and they looked fine, her pupils equal. She didn't seem to be on anything. I waited.

Erika said, "They got a divorce, you know that, right?"

"I heard a rumor."

She ran a knuckle over the bridge of her nose, wiping imaginary club grime away. "Yeah, well, the rumor is true. Maybe a year after you left, Mom took off. They've been fighting since then, over money, over me, you name it. It all went final about a year ago. I don't even know where she is these days, and frankly I don't fucking care. So, I live with the Colonel, just him and me . . . and he doesn't go out much anymore, you know?" She was still watching something beyond me, keeping her gaze distant. "He sort of sees me . . . he sort of sees me as in-home entertainment. So I don't like to be around the house that much."

In-home entertainment. I swallowed, felt a little sick as all of the implications of that phrase hit home.

An NYPD sector car turned off the avenue and headed down the street, passing us. Erika watched its progress, and when it stopped in front of the warehouse, she said, "Guess somebody called the cops, huh?"

"How long has it been going on, Erika?"

She shrugged, picking a spot on the pavement that interested her. "He retired a little before it went final, brought me home from school, I was going to boarding school in Vermont." She rubbed her hands against her upper arms, making friction for heat. "You going to take me home now? I'm fucking freezing my tits off."